Love's Secret Storm

Love's Secret Storm

LEONORA PRUNER

BETHANY HOUSE PUBLISHERS
Minneapolis, Minnesota 55438
A Division of Bethany Fellowship, Inc.

Published by Bethany Fellowship, Inc.
6820 Auto Club Road, Minneapolis, Minnesota 55438

Printed in the United States of America

Library of Congress Cataloging in Publication Data

Pruner, Leonora, 1931-
    Love's secret storm.

    I. Title.
PS3566.R83L6   813'.54   81-2459
ISBN 0-87123-347-9 (pbk.)   AACR2

Dedication

To Doris Mooney and the many other librarians whose interest and help made authenticity possible.

About the Author

LEONORA PRUNER was born in Dubuque, Iowa, and moved to California at the age of twelve. There she took degrees from John Muir College and Westmont College. She married Darryl Pruner in Pasadena in 1953 and has a son and a daughter. Her writings include articles for *World Vision Magazine* and *Presbyterian Life*, short stories, and radio commercials. This is her first published novel. She and her husband now live in Santa Barbara, California.

Love's Secret Storm

Chapter One

Behind our house, the frantic peals of St. Mary's bell called Oxford University to arms. Startled, I ran to peer anxiously between the heavy drawing-room drapes into uncertain twilight. The walls of Oriel's newly erected wing rose on the far side of the lane. The clatter of running feet on cobblestones grew as undergraduates from Corpus Christi, Oriel, and Merton raced to the Higher.

"Gown! Gown! Gown!" they shouted, their black robes billowing behind them.

Clapping my hands over my ears, I ran in terror to the far end of the room. The centuries-old antagonism between the town and University was about to burst into another riot. Again it would probably be a dispute between the townsmen loyal to the House of Hanover and Jacobite students supporting the Pretender's claims. Why must they continue their quarreling? George II was in fact England's king. It did no good to insult him and stand for the Pretender James. Surely after bloody Cullodon two years ago, even the most radical students must realize he would never sit on our throne!

The distant Carfax bell rang an answer, summoning the town to battle. How many rioters would be injured or die this night? Would my home be one of those broken into?

I hurried into the dim hall and glanced at the closed library door. Father probably heard nothing, engrossed in his eternal writings. Holding my gray petticoats high, I ran down the stairs. At the bottom, I nearly collided with Bessie coming from the back, her dark eyes wide, mob cap half off, and black hair in straggling disarray.

"Is the back door bolted?" I asked quickly.

"Yes, ma'am, and the shutters latched," she gasped out.

I secured the front door, hoping its solid oak panels would keep rioters from breaking in. It was but three weeks since Dr. King's home was ransacked. Bessie and I were fastening the front room shutters when the doorbell was pulled.

The loud clang sent shivers of fright through me. It rang a second time. Trying to hide my anxiety, I walked sedately into the entry hall, Bessie whimpering behind me. Now a fist pounded on the door.

My mouth dry, I demanded as forcefully as I could, "Who—who is it?"

"Gown! Charles! Let me in!"

With trembling fingers, I unlocked and opened the door.

Charles staggered against me, his black gown ripped and muddied, his suit scarcely better. Another gownsman, several years his senior, supported him.

"Forgive us for intruding, Miss Castleton," the tall stranger said, "but Mr. Heathton insisted on coming here. We cannot reach Christ Church before the curfew."

Father shouted from the upper hall, "Bessie, Meg, isn't anyone going to answer that infernal bell?" He appeared at the top of the stairs, his grizzle wig jammed on crooked, a quill in his ink-stained hand.

The stranger withdrew to the shadows as I answered, "I did, Father." Being nearsighted, he might not notice Charles' condition.

He pushed his glasses from the tip of his nose to their proper place. "Oh, it's you, Charles!" He descended a few steps. "Have you come to play chess, my boy?"

Charles made an unsteady bow. "Yes, sir, if you're not already engaged."

"I see." Absently he straightened his monstrous old periwig. "Well, I'm sorry, my boy, but I'm writing an answer to those Jacobite rabble-rousers. They are given to the folly of drunken rioting! Disgraceful! And if they're not stopped, they will one day bring the wrath of the Crown on our heads. Meg, entertain our friend properly. Bessie, bring up some refreshment. Be sure you're in by curfew, my boy."

"Without fail, sir."

Father laboriously mounted the stairs and vanished into the dark hall. Bessie darted back to the kitchen. Charles slumped to the steps and sat holding his head.

"What happened?" I whispered.

"Lord knows! I was in the Blue Boar when some town bullies jumped our men outside. Naturally I'd not turn a deaf ear to the cries of my mates being set upon by the town! We chased them towards the East Gate. Others were waiting near Logic Lane so they made a stand there. What a time we had! My head was knocked, but I knocked a few myself. We were by St. Mary's Hall and I was too unsteady to make it back to college, so we came here."

Big Tom began tolling its nightly one-hundred-one strokes.

"Come upstairs to the north room. You can't go back now," I said. "And your head wants mending," I added, as I peered at a red blob on his forehead below his wig.

He pushed his wig back and I gasped at the blood on his cropped black hair. "It aches like," he looked at me with a wry smile, "too much." Grasping the rail, he pulled himself to his feet and followed me, stumbling occasionally on the steps. "Send up Will Knight, would you?"

"Who?"

"Will Knight. He was with me."

"Oh." I looked down the staircase. "Where is he?"

"Gone with your girl to fetch up what he'll need, I 'spect." He managed a ghost of his usual gay smile and patted my shoulder. "Don't worry, little dove. A crack on the head ain't much, and Will has the magic to make me presentable for Father tomorrow. He'll never guess what fun I had tonight!"

In the north room, I lit two candles and the fire, then went to draw the plain red drapes. I wished for the thousandth time they were fringed. St. Mary's silent spire rose against the moonlit sky. A few lights burned at St. Mary's Hall on the corner where the lane met the High. Only dim shouts indicated all was not calm in Oxford.

Charles leaned against the bedpost, struggling out of his gown. I took it and helped him remove his coat and vest, keeping my dismay over their state to myself.

"How the Proctors'll roar and swing their clubs! Too bad that fellow bashed in my hat when he did! Damned inconsiderate!"

A thin line of blood crossed his fine, high forehead, hovering above his right eye. I daubed it with my handkerchief. Pain clouded his black eyes, normally snapping with humor, and etched fine lines around his full lips so quick to laugh. He was the handsomest and gayest of undergraduates.

"I'll be all right, Meg. Show Knight up, like a good girl."

"I should bathe that wound."

"He'll do that."

After leaving his clothes in my room for mending, I went to find his man.

This undernourished servitor met me at the foot of the stairs, his arms filled with cloths and bottles. A common string held his light hair in a queue, coarse, dirty stockings sagged over broken shoes, and his gown was patched upon patch. Despite his menial appearance, he was not servile. Rather, his manner was assured; quite improper for his station, I thought.

I drew myself up, imitating Amelia Forsythe's haughty bearing. Unfortunately, my short stature created a distinct disadvantage before his height.

"Please take me to Mr. Heathton." His voice was calm and deep.

"Yes, of course. He sent for you." I led the way, stiff with dignity, determined not to be intimidated by a bold inferior merely because he was overly tall.

Charles lay sprawled across the bed. When his man gently touched Charles' forehead, his eyes flew open and he smiled. "Ah, Will, my friend!"

"Is there anything I can do?" I asked, feeling like an outsider.

The stranger replied, "I would appreciate a cot. I regret we must impose upon you for the night. However, we'll be gone early to attend chapel."

"Lord Rockivale arrives tomorrow. Will Charles be in any condition to see his father?"

"Oh, yes. He'll carry it off very well."

Before going to my room, I instructed Bessie to take the cot from the box room to the north room. Alone, I began repairing Charles' coat.

While stitching and sponging Charles' clothes, I thought back to our childhood. Father, as Vicar of Rockivale, had tutored Lord Rockivale's sons, Arthur and Charles. The parsonage where we lived stood on the estate beside the old church built generations ago by a former lord for a penance.

Remembering Charles' grand home, I looked around my own dull room. How I longed to replace its worn rug with a thick Chinese one, to have the walls covered with bright paper, and fine furnishings placed in it! The only hint of the elegance I desired was the oval, gold-framed mirror owned by our landlord, Mr. Finchwythe. Mother's lovely pink-flowered pitcher and bowl stood on a marble-topped table. I kept the chip and ugly brown crack turned towards the wall, but I always knew they were there.

Charles and I had become good friends. Being two years my senior, he led me in conquering Rockivale's hills and holding them against the Danes or French. He taught me to ride like a boy with my skirts tucked up. On rainy days, we lay before the crackling fire in the manor library, reveling in the stories of King Arthur and Shakespeare. We memorized large portions of poetry, enjoying the rhythms of the words. Charles was my Sir Galahad, for whom I conceived a deathless passion. But he thought of me as only a friend, and pursued every other pretty bit of muslin coming his way. Though I no longer saw him as often as I had at Rockivale, I was determined that one day he would come to love me and that we would wed.

What of that strange servitor tonight? Charles called him "my friend" with real warmth. Usually he never thought of a servant save to give an order. And this one lacked the attitudes proper to his place.

When finished, I took Charles' things to his room, avoiding the squeaking boards in the middle of the hall. A line of light showed under the door. Softly I scratched the panel with my fingernails.

Charles' man opened it. The candle he carried cast eerie shadows on his face. "Yes?"

Stifling a desire to flee his sinister appearance, I held out the clothing. "I've done with these." I noticed the reflection of the flame in his eyes and found myself fascinated.

"Thank you," he answered, taking the clothes, his gaze bold and intense. "May I be of any service to you?"

"Ah, no. Is Charles all right?"

"He sleeps. Other than a sore head, he should have no ill effects. Thank you for your hospitality."

"Oh, I'd do *anything* for Charles! I mean, I. . . Good night."

I sped to my room, closed the door and leaned against it, trembling. What a senseless way to behave! He had done nothing of a threatening nature. Yet. . . I'd never looked into a mere servitor's eyes. He was a *man*!

On impulse, I locked my door.

The next evening, while sipping coffee in the drawing room, I listened to Lord Rockivale chuckling over Charles' amazing new studious endeavors. Tall, wiry, fashionably clad in a mulberry coat with shining buckles on his shoes, he was a sharp contrast to Father's portly frame covered with rumpled brown cloth.

"I don't think there's much chance of his becoming so bookish that he misses the rest of his education, the most important part. We never did, eh, did we? There were some rare times! Remember, Philip?"

Father nodded, looking to me from the corner of his eye. It was hard for me to imagine him as other than a dignified don or conscientious vicar.

"But 'tis refreshing to hear Charles taking his studies so seriously. It won't do for him to lack certain knowledge when he takes his Tour. That's the point of all this, isn't it? Truthfully, I feared he'd be sent down for some scrape. But he's reading Thucydides tonight! Imagine! You've had a good influence on him, Philip. I'm grateful you came here. You should accompany him on the Continent. What a time you'd have!"

Father shook his head, about to reject this suggestion, but Lord Rockivale continued with a wave of his hand.

"No, no, I understand, with Meg here and all. Wouldn't think of insisting." He sighed and lit his pipe. "I do miss your company. Truthfully, one of the few joys of being a lord was giving you the preferment. Most of my duties are dead bores, eh, you know how it is. It was a real sacrifice to arrange your appointment here when Charles came up to Oxford. After he takes his degree, assuming he keeps out of trouble, I shall arrange Pettigrew's move so you can come back home."

Father's black bushy brows raised and he studied his patron over the bowl of his churchwarden's pipe as he tamped his tobacco down. I knew he enjoyed the leisurely life here too much to leave.

Lord Rockivale blew a ring of smoke towards the ceiling. "Pettigrew's sermons put me to sleep every Sunday and I get a crick in my back. He's so eager to hunt, he'll soon shoot all my game, and that won't do. Won't do at all. And truthfully, Philip, he can't talk."

"M'lord, you are most generous." Tapping his pipe stem against his cheek, Father pursed his lips. "However, I should think what you need is a young man with new ideas."

"Humph! How would a young man put a brake on Charles? You've always been able to manage him, to guide him from too serious a folly. Thank God Arthur is a steady lad. If only he would marry and give me an heir!"

"Let Arthur be that influence."

"No, no. They move in different worlds. In truth, Charles is like me. He needs a good wife," he smiled at me, "and a friend to take him in hand. Fortunately, I had both. I hope he will too."

Lord Rockivale's smile lifted my spirits. He would not oppose my marrying Charles, and Father would not deny me whomever I wished. Drifting off to dreams of a happy life with my beloved, I heard no more of their conversation.

The cries of liveried outriders on high-stepping horses accompanying gilded coaches rumbling down the High announced the beginning of the exciting festivities surrounding the Act. There were glorious concerts in the Music Room, dances in the Assembly Rooms and, of course, the annual procession of dignitaries into the Sheldonian. Refreshed by occasional breezes, I stood outside with Amelia to watch the splendid parade.

Scarlet-robed doctors, noblemen in violet damask and gold lace mingled with the black silk and stuff of others' gowns. Flashes of sunlight danced from the ornate silver trappings of the Bedels as they passed through the crowd. The haughty Chancellor looked neither right nor left as he strutted along, two little pages bearing the weight of his lengthy train. One of them stumbled over an uneven cobblestone in front of us. Although his train tugged and dipped, the great man gave no sign anything was amiss.

Following him, the pompous Heads wore bright red ceremonials, a welcome change from everyday black. The Proctors brought up the rear, their furs inappropriate for the noon-time heat. A few late dons scurried along behind them, trying to slip in before the doors closed.

Last year I had been inside, pressed by the multitude against a pillar. The scandalous behavior of undergraduates in the horseshoe-shaped balcony was amusing, but the interminable Latin speeches had threatened to put me to sleep on my feet.

With the show over, the mass of people dispersed up the Broad, Cat Street, Holywell and towards Wadham. Amelia and I waited a bit, then made our way leisurely to her carriage and drove to her home.

Once a college, it had been extensively altered in the last 200 years. Amelia's father added a large wing finished in the latest style and furnished with every luxurious device. We relaxed in the shade of her garden, among the roses and trees where past dons meditated on the finer points of metaphysics.

For a while we gossipped about the current reigning Toast, Marietta Debonnet, speculating on how long she took to develop her lisping French accent. Very likely she came from the slums of London, Dover, or even Oxford. I envied her popularity with the gownsmen.

Then Amelia began chatting about her plans to visit relatives and watering places the next several weeks. "And this time, while I am with Aunt Amelia—she's Mama's favorite sister, the one I'm named for, you know—I shall actually go bathing in the sea!"

"You will?" I exclaimed, scandalized. "In—in *public*?"

Amelia laughed lightly. "Oh, Meg, dearest! How shocked you look! Aunt Amelia has written they now have covered carriages with a—a, well, they make it possible for a lady to go into the sea without being, shall we say, unduly exposed. *She* has done so and found it very exciting. And Aunt Amelia is an excessively proper lady. If she did so, it is quite within the bounds of propriety, let me assure you!

"And then we shall spend some time at Rose Hills. . ."

She chattered on enthusiastically, leaving me trying to imagine what new device could make it possible for a lady to bathe in the sea unseen. Indeed, why would one wish to step into the sea, which would undoubtedly be very cold? Perhaps someday I would see this marvelous thing during a visit to the shore with Charles. Perhaps, even *use* it.

At the end of this week, Charles would be leaving also, going to Rockivale for the long vacation. Then I should be destitute of the two friends I treasured most. The dismal prospect cast a depressing shade over the bright day.

At teatime we went up to Amelia's large room. Our discussion of the upcoming ball improved my spirits. She showed me an effective way to arrange my hair and insisted I try on her new yellow ball gown.

"There! I knew it would become you! When you are properly powdered and painted, you will be most striking. Every man present will notice, including your Charles."

"But I couldn't wear it!" I fingered the heavy, expensive satin longingly.

"Nonsense! Of course you can. You must! In fact, I shall be deeply hurt if you judge my taste so poor that you refuse!"

"Oh, Amelia! You're impossible!" I exclaimed, hugging her.

"You sound just like Papa," she giggled.

I attended the Assembly ball prepared to enjoy this last social event with all my heart. Charles danced a quadrille with me and complimented me on my appearance. Later he asked me to stand up with him for a country dance. However, my joy was not unmixed when I saw his chief attention was focused on the young sister of a friend, a mere child, hardly out of the schoolroom.

Charles called on Monday, shortly before noon, saying he was on his way home. He left me in front of the house holding a pink rose he brought from Christ Church's gardens, watching him trot down the lane to the High.

With great care, I pressed the precious blossom between the pages of Shakespeare's Sonnets. During the boring, hot months, I often sought to ease my loneliness by touching its petals and savoring a bit of its remembered perfume. This next year, his last in Oxford, I must become enchanting to hold his attention as no other woman had done.

On a glorious afternoon with just a hint of autumn chill, Bessie announced that Charles awaited me below. Nervously I smoothed my hair and tucked a fresh lace handkerchief around my neck and into the bodice of my blue mantua.

"He wouldn't come up to the drawing room, ma'am. He insisted on waiting before the door," Bessie explained.

Despite my pounding heart, I proceeded down to meet him at a dignified pace. I paused on the second floor at the head of the stairs, seeing him checking his reflection in the mirror by the door.

He glanced up and smiled when I was halfway down. "Well, little dove. . . " he began.

Suddenly I was running down the steps, throwing my arms around him and kissing his cheek.

He hugged me tightly, then held me off, laughing. "What a welcome, my dove! You've become quite an armful, and such an undignified lady!"

I blushed and he laughed the more.

"You will be going to Fairchild's ball Friday, won't you?" he asked, pushing aside his gown and searching the pockets of his mustard coat. "I brought something I thought would be suitable," he cleared his throat and patted his emerald vest, "for a *lady*."

"I shall be most demure," I promised, folding my hands and dropping my eyes.

"And I should not know you. Ah ha!" He reached in the great cuff of his coat and removed a carved ivory fan, presenting it with a flourishing bow.

"How lovely!" I spread it, admiring its delicate design.

Charles stepped back a few paces and examined me through his gold quizzing glass. "Yes, that is the right one. It came from China, half a world away, just for you. Is your learned sire in residence?"

"No. But you will take a dish of tea, won't you?"

"I must be off to mind my boxes. Please inform your father his favorite scholar has returned. Till Friday, sweet dove."

That fateful Friday night I curtsied before my mirror. I was at my very best, a lady from my hair, carefully powdered to cover its auburn color, to my new brocade shoes. My blue satin gown opened in front over a white, quilted petticoat. Silver scallops down the front and on the sleeves gave a touch of richness. Mother's diamond pendant sparkled above my extremely low, embroidered stomacher. At nineteen, my figure was amply mature, the envy of some, according to Amelia. Father would think I should wear a handkerchief for modesty, but I was determined to show Charles I was no longer a child! The new gown became me well. If it caused Charles to notice me with pleasure, it was well worth having had to give up our cook to afford it.

I studied my face. My nose lamentably turned up, and no amount of pulling would straighten it. My eyes were blue, like insipid innocence. Would that I possessed, like Amelia, violet eyes, perfectly molded features, a delicate complexion and golden hair. If only *I* were a great beauty too!

Spreading Charles' fan beneath my eyes, I slowly lowered the lids and tilted my head, watching my reflection. I sighed. I was no coquette. Haughtily I raised my chin, a fashionably bored woman. That image was even less impressive. Walking across the room, I practiced raising my hoop slightly to reveal my sinful white stockings. Would Charles notice? Some way I *must* captivate him tonight! Fate, as my lavender scent, hung about me.

Impatiently I looked for Charles in the ballroom thronged with gownsmen and elaborately dressed women. Suddenly he was standing before Father and me, tall and slender, his black silk gown falling aside from a splendid green brocade suit heavily laced with gold. Ruffles of lace frothed under his chin. He bowed his head, covered by a perfectly curled white bag-wig, and kissed my hand. "Meg, my dove, you are the fairest of all."

Delighted, I quoted my answer from "Alexander's Feast," our favorite poem. " 'None but the brave deserves the fair.' "

"Then I shall be very, very brave. Dr. Castleton, may I lead out your daughter for the next dance?"

"Of course, my boy." Father beamed broadly. "I shall be in the gaming room."

Charles and I strolled about under shimmering chandeliers, chatting with friends. A year ago I had attended my first ball, overawed. Now, being part, at least for the moment, of this world of beautiful clothes and glittering jewels, I loved it.

As the orchestra struck up a minuet, he confided, "I have a surprise for you tonight."

I smiled my sweetest. "Oh?" We parted in the dance. Another gift? An adventure for us, together?

When we touched hands, he said, "I'm going to introduce you to the finest man I know."

On the next turn I blinked back tears and bit my quivering lips. Unable to trust my voice, I gave no reply.

At the close of the dance, he left me on a small lacquered bench under a crystal scounce to seek his friend. I sadly visualized myself an old maid in Father's house, or governess to some wealthy family's horrid brats.

Amelia broke through my gloom with a swirl of crimson flounces and black lace. "Meg, you're divine! Surely he noticed!"

"I doubt it," I muttered. Looking up at her I exclaimed, "You're magnificent!" Her vibrant beauty made all other women plain.

"I hope so. I think I've caught Mr. Simpson's eye. Oliver Simpson. He's in that group to your right in the gold suit. Isn't he marvelous?"

Casually I glanced at the handsome man.

"His father is a peer and ever so wealthy. I met him at the end of the season in town."

"You will charm him," I assured her.

"I hope so! Where's Charles?"

"He went to find a special friend to entertain me."

"Again?" She touched my shoulder in sympathy, then gasped as she looked beyond me. "What on earth! He can't mean to fob *him* off on you!"

I looked around to see Charles accompanied by the strange man attending him the night of the riot! A master's gown flared open over his plain black coat, its skirts unfashionably limp. Neither buckles nor jewels brightened his appearance. Even his blonde hair was unpowdered. He moved with confident poise, indifferent to disapproving glares.

I spread my ivory fan to conceal my distress.

"How insulting!" Amelia fumed. "He's an inferior!"

"Hush! They'll hear you."

"I don't care! He should know his place!"

Charles bowed before us. "Miss Forsythe, Miss Castleton, may I present a dear friend, Mr. William Knight, a tutor at Hertford College."

Mr. Knight bowed gracefully.

A fellow, even of Dr. Newton's poor college, was not an inferior. Amelia nodded coolly.

"Miss Castleton, will you grant me the pleasure of this dance?" Mr. Knight asked, his voice deep and resonant.

With an angry Amelia at my side, I was tempted to refuse, but I knew Charles would be displeased. "Delighted," I answered, extending my right hand.

When he helped me rise, a startling tingle raced up my arm. If his grasp had not been so firm, I should have withdrawn from his touch. The unexpected shock threw me into confusion.

As we danced, dynamic energy flowed from him, spreading throughout my body. My pulses pounded. My cheeks grew hot. So perfectly did he execute the required steps that I could do nothing wrong. Couples dipped and whirled and laughed about us, but my silent partner and I seemed totally apart.

After the final chords, Mr. Knight led me through a near doorway and across the hall to a recessed windowseat. Below lay a large garden strung with bright lanterns.

"How beautiful!" I exclaimed. "Spring Gardens in London must look like that!"

"It does, a little."

"You've been there? Is it as marvelous as they say?"

"It has an air of unreality, of pretense."

I glanced up at him. The intense gaze of his hazel eyes held mine. A depth of character beyond his years marked his firm jaw, slightly humped nose and smooth brow. Not nearly as handsome as Charles, yet he was distinctive. An air of determined purpose set him apart from all others I knew.

"You are very lovely, Miss Castleton."

"Thank you. You are very kind, Mr. Knight."

"Merely honest."

The excitement he aroused with touch and look alarmed me, somehow threatened me. "Ch-Charles has a high opinion of you. How did you know him?"

"I was his servitor," he answered with dignity.

Well I recalled his tattered appearance the night of the riot. "And now you are a tutor at Hertford. How—how many undergraduates do you have?"

"Nine. All gentlemen commoners."

"Is Dr. Newton such a strange fanatic as they say?" I chattered nervously. "I've heard he's set down regulations so severe the college cannot possibly last."

"He requires scholars to attend classes and us to teach them. You see, he believes a young man should be educated while here, not simply fritter away his time in meaningless activities."

"I've heard it said some are urging his appointment as Dean of Christ Church. That even the Duke of Newcastle and his brother are urging the king to do this. Could they succeed?"

"The college would benefit from the serious discipline he would bring."

"Surely there would be no college at all. They would all leave."

One of Charles' fine friends interrupted us, requesting a dance. He was an energetic person with no sense of rhythm. At the end of this romp, I was claimed by another gownsman. To my surprise I saw Amelia dancing with Mr. Knight! Later, while I tried to engage a shy partner in conversation, Mr. Knight appeared, presenting me with a glass of ratafie. Skillfully he detached me and led me to an alcove. Two chairs with rose tapestry seats faced a cheery fire. I sat, glad to rest my pinched feet.

Politely Mr. Knight inquired about my schooling. While I described the dull classes at Mrs. Spinets' Seminary for Young Ladies and her puckered face, his features so rightly assumed her expressions that I burst into laughter. With my handkerchief, I dabbed at the tears threatening to smear my white paint.

When he asked about my life before school, I told him of living in the vicarage at Rockivale until Mother died when I was fourteen. Lord Rockivale had arranged both my schooling and Father's later appointment as a Canon at Christ Church.

"I have seen you often about Oxford."

"You have?" I could not recall seeing him other than the night of the riot.

"It is not expected you would notice a servitor on the streets. I learned you were Dr. Castleton's daughter and a friend of Mr. Heathton's. I asked him to introduce me to you tonight."

"Not last July? We met then, I recall."

"I regretted that meeting, but there was no help for it. First impressions are strong."

"And there is a great difference between a servitor and a don."

"Precisely."

"So you begged an introduction tonight." I spread my fan and lowered my eyelids. "I hope you are not disappointed."

"Not at all. I asked your father about you long ago."

"Oh?" I was piqued at being discussed. "Did he warn you I am flighty and irresponsible?"

"He said you were kind, honest, and loyal."

"Oh!" Could he see me flush through my heavy paint? Turning to the fire I asked, "Where did you come from?"

"North."

"Very far? Scotland?"

"Where the chill never leaves the air." He rose. "We should return to the others, or tongues will start wagging."

As we came into the ballroom, we passed Mr. Simpson. He bowed and asked me to dance. Older even than Mr. Knight, he had an air of assurance and experience I found most attractive. His voice was pleasant and his manner condescendingly aristocratic. I wondered at his selecting me. By the final cadence, I had decided he would do very well for Amelia.

To my surprise, I discovered we were standing beside Amelia and a plump youth. Quickly I introduced them to Mr. Simpson, adding, "Miss Forsythe was in London last season. Perhaps you have already met?"

They became engrossed in the people and places they knew. As things were going well, I edged away with her former partner, forcing him to lead me out on the next dance. It proved to be a physical struggle, devoid of rhythm or grace. My sole enjoyment came from seeing Amelia with Mr. Simpson, her face radiant.

Unfortunately supper followed and I had to endure the overweight boy's attempts to play the part of a worldly-wise gentleman.

Finally, one of Charles' countless friends rescued me from stifling boredom.

I danced each succeeding dance until, feeling a trifle faint, I excused myself and escaped to the hall and an open window. Leaning out, I gulped air as deeply as my tight stays would permit. Such a disappointing evening! Charles approved of my appearance but his interest lay elsewhere. I should have known fate would not be with me.

There was a step behind me, then Mr. Knight's familiar deep voice. "I brought you a cup of ratafie."

I spun around to face him.

"You look tired. Would you like to sit down?" he gestured down the hall.

Smiling, I took the cup and shook my head. "It must be quite late. Father will be anxious to leave." I drank thirstily. Again my eyes encountered his intense gaze and I was charmed, even bewitched. No other man had so regarded me.

"Please allow me to escort you to him."

We found Father on the tottering edge of intoxication, talking loudly with friends.

"Dr. Castleton, I return your charming daughter to your keeping with regret," Mr. Knight said.

"Thank you, Knight. I should think you might be tired, my dear."

"Oh, no! It's been a delightful ball!"

Father bowed to Mr. Knight, nearly losing his balance. "I fear this night of revelry may dull an uncommonly brilliant mind."

Mr. Knight's right eyebrow flickered. "Stimulate, not dull, sir."

In our hired carriage, Father settled back in a corner to doze while we jolted homeward over the cobblestones. I pulled my cardinal about me, thinking of Charles' friend.

My strong response to this poor Hertford tutor worried me. He was the wrong man. Charles was the one I adored. If I didn't guard my emotions carefully. . . I drew back hastily from further speculation, forcing myself to think of Charles in his elegant blue suit—or was it green?

Chapter Two

I awoke around noon still troubled by the Hertford don. As I often did, I took my problem to Father, finding him in the library.

The scents of old tobacco and yesterday's ashes mingled with the smell of aging leather. Battered oak and mahogany bookcases crammed with books stood against the walls. Various volumes lay about on the tables and chairs, some open, others with ragged bits of paper or cloth sticking from between their pages.

Father sat at his scarred desk. His quill did not miss a scratchy stroke while we exchanged civilities. However, when I asked him about Charles' friend, he laid it aside. "Ah yes, the Black Knight. That's what they call him, you know." He brushed the tassle of his nightcap to the back, placed his spectacles carefully beside his paper and rubbed his eyes. "What do you think of him?"

I shrugged carefully. "Very different." Pulling out the worn copy of Shakespeare's sonnets, I leafed casually through its crackly pages. When I came to Charles' rose, I touched its dry petals gently, as a love talisman.

"Um." Father arranged the folds of his faded burgundy morning gown about his knees, picked up his pipe and lit it with deliberation, hunching over it. He leaned back in his chair, puffing silently, his sharp blue eyes peering at me. I felt he read my thoughts as easily as the *London Evening Post*.

"I—I don't know what to think of him. He's too serious. Didn't smile, even once. But he did make me laugh," I added, recalling his imitation of Mrs. Spinet. "Well—he's just different. And," I replaced the book and moved aimlessly about the room, "and I was drawn to him, though he's not at all handsome. Why is this, Father?"

"I should think it's because he is different—honest, sincere."

"Tell me what you know of him."

"William Knight was the most promising undergraduate at Christ Church. His master's examination was quite remarkable. He'll make an exceptional tutor."

"You *approve* of him? He was a servitor only last year."

"As have been other good men, including Bishop Potter. After Knight took his master's, he was offered a Fellowship at Merton. Abruptly the offer was withdrawn. Someone important must have pressured against him. So he continued at Christ Church as a servitor, studying for his doctorate.

"He'll be safe at Hertford. Newton won't give up a good Fellow, not with the Pelham brothers for support. I should think Knight'll rise as high as he chooses. Only his deliberate indifference to political realities may prevent his wearing lawn sleeves one day."

Holding his pipe with his right hand, Father removed his red nightcap with his left, and scratched his shaved head. "He's very poor. His position rankles him. Perhaps this comes from his origins. He's unusually adept at managing people. Perhaps too adept. But," he pointed his pipe at me, "he doesn't use them for his amusement. He's sensitive to the feelings of others."

He puffed a cloud, then added, "A very gentle man, strong, determined. There's more to him than any of those empty-headed smarts you call friends. They haven't learned there's more to life than fine clothes or sport."

Timidly I asked, "More than Charles?"

Father sighed. "Child, you know I love Charles as a son. I should think he, too, could go far if he chose, but he doesn't choose. Lord Rockivale has spoiled him disgracefully. Every day he becomes more of a foppish dandy. They did much better with Arthur, who has less ability. Arthur looks forward to running the estate. And Charles? Certainly a scholarly life is not for him, nor taking orders. He might do well in trade, perhaps."

"Mr. Knight said he talked to you of me."

Father closed his eyes and sent several gray puffs to the ceiling. "Yes, yes, he asked about my daughter one day." He looked at me with a twinkle. "I knew he'd arrange to meet you."

"He said he came from the north. Do you know anything about his family?"

"No one does. When he wants you to know, I should think he'll tell you." He knocked the ashes from his pipe, put on his spectacles and adjusted them on his nose. "Margaret, my dear, the only mistake you'll make with Mr. Knight is not being honest. If you don't like him, don't encourage him, even to be kind." He scrutinized my face. "I suspect you like him."

I colored under his gaze, dropping my eyes to the threadbare carpet.

"At some time he was deeply hurt. Occasionally I've seen the scars. Vivid ones. Add naught to them." He picked up his quill. "What will you be doing today?"

"Amelia asked me to visit this afternoon. She's sending her chair for me."

"Fine, I shall be dining with that country squire from Sussex, Addleby, I believe. He's here on his annual pilgrimage to Christ Church, and it falls to me to entertain him with my wit and profundity. Deadly bores, these country men. Still, one never knows when he might be useful. For all his stupidity, he's a loyal supporter of the crown and a sensible dispenser of justice. And, none other than the Duke of Newcastle is his lord lieutenant and is reputed to like him. It is worthwhile to cultivate the friends of the mighty."

Amelia and I lounged by a window in her room overlooking her garden. A plate of dainty biscuits sat on a tiny table between us. We nibbled on them and sipped bohea tea from fragile china cups covered with pink rosebuds.

"Mr. Simpson is going to call, I know he is!" she said, her violet eyes glowing. "He's the most divine dancer! Didn't you think so? I'm certain he noticed you and me together and selected you as a partner to secure an introduction to me." She giggled. "He said he wanted to touch me to see if I was real!"

"And?"

"And just as the music ended, he said, very softly in my ear, 'This must not be our last time together.' I tell you, Meg dearest, the shivers ran up and down my spine!"

"When do you suppose he'll call?"

"Soon, I hope. He came down to settle his younger brother at Oriel. He'll have to go home to Berkshire shortly. Of course, Mother will be most pleased. He's quite the finest catch in all of England!"

As I nodded agreement, my eyes strayed about her pink and white room, prettied with fringed drapes and a luxurious lace canopy over her bed. A large collection of expensive bottles and jars stood on her dressing table.

Amelia's grandfather was said to have made a great fortune in the South Seas Bubble, and her father added to it in trade. Being an only child, she was heiress to thousands of pounds. I longed for the day I would have a beautiful room in a huge house with servants—and an adoring Charles. I turned from my dreams to Amelia.

In her pale pink velvet negligee with lace at the wrists and neck, she was adorable. Her golden hair shone like a halo about her sweet face. Desperately lonely at Mrs. Spinet's, I had sought her out to ask about Oxford, her town, where my Father had moved. In her gracious way, she took me as her friend. If she wanted Mr. Simpson, I would do anything to help her.

"How did you like Mr. Knight?" I asked. "I was surprised to see you dance with him."

"I could not refuse without being excessively rude." She frowned. "He is no dullard. He was a servitor, you know, yet has the airs of a lord. He must have high ambitions."

"I hadn't thought of him as being ambitious. He's a gentleman, truly."

"Yes. If he'd wear proper clothes, he could pass for a peer. Instead. . . He puzzles me."

"He is kind and attentive."

"You like him!"

My face grew annoyingly hot as I said, "He's interesting. Quite different from appearances. As you said, a puzzle."

Amelia laughed in her light, gay manner. "Wonderful! If Charles thinks he has you in his pocket, he'd better think again!"

"What do you mean?"

"Just that. He always expects you to be there when he wishes. Now another man interests you."

"Amelia, really!"

"He does! I can see it in your face! When Charles realizes this, it may snap him around. If you let him know his friend appeals to you, he will see you as you are, and he can't fail to fall in love with you."

"Do you truly think so?"

"Of course. That's the way men are. It never does to let them think they have you safe in their pocket. The next time you're with him, let him know Mr. Knight fascinates you."

"He asked Charles to introduce us."

"But that's even better! If Charles knows you're attractive to another man, he'll wonder why, and then. . . Oh Meg, I'm so excited! This is just what you've needed!"

Sunday afternoon Charles drove up in his fancy red and gold cabriolet, quite the most sporting vehicle in town. His pair of bays were harnessed in tandem fashion.

"Meg, it's a glorious day for a drive! Come with me."

Father readily granted us his absent-minded permission. No doubt he was grateful not to interrupt his study of Locke (actually napping) in the library for a game of chess.

As I was about to go up for my cloak, Charles said softly, "Put on your riding dress," and gave me a wink.

I ran up to do his bidding. It had been months since I rode a horse. In my excitement, my fingers fumbled with the brass buttons on my brown double-breasted riding coat. After a brief, unsuccessful bout with my cravat, I stuffed it inside my coat, snatched up my brown three-cornered hat and perched it on my head. Catching up my petticoats, I hurried down to Charles, and we escaped outside unnoticed.

Tiny, his groom, was walking the horses up the street. He led them to us, holding them while Charles handed me into the cabriolet and sat at my side. When Charles picked up the reins, Tiny released the horses and leapt up behind like an agile monkey.

We sped down the lane to the High, turned right to sweep out the East Gate and over the old arches of Petty Pont. Charles flicked the whip above the horses' heads and we raced past St. Clement's in fine style.

I thrilled to the wind in my face, the sight of the running blooded stallions and Charles at my side. Overhead, the clouds seemed mounds of silver hanging from a sapphire sky.

"Cecil Wilber saw my pair yesterday and made me a bet."

"He did?"

"He claimed his chestnut was better than either of mine."

"Oh? He's certain to lose."

Charles chewed his lower lip a few moments, an unusual show of doubt. "Last Easter term you made me promise to take you the next time I raced. I shouldn't have done it."

"I remember. You swore a solemn oath."

"Well, I'm keeping it! But it ain't fitting!"

"Oh, Charles! I'll only watch."

"It ain't fitting for ladies to watch alone."

"I'm not alone. I'm with you."

"Don't be silly! You know what I mean, without another female present."

"That's the foolish notion of old gossips."

"The more I think. . . I ought to take you home."

"Nonsense! I think it's wonderful!"

"I see you've gained no sense at all over the summer."

I laughed at his grouchy tone. "I'd heard all these matters were settled over at Campsfield towards Wolvercote. Why are we going this way?"

"They usually are. I told Wilber if we ran, it must be done near Shotover, so your silly gossips won't be the wiser."

"You're a dear." I patted his knee and he glanced at me half-annoyed. "Oh, come," I coaxed; "it won't be as serious as you think."

He slowed the pair to a halt. "Tiny, hold 'em," he ordered, tying the reins. "Be that as it may, I'll not have you show up looking like the hoyden you are!"

He pulled the ends of my cravat from my coat and tied them. Even for him they would not fall right. "Turn about," he commanded. Reaching around my neck and peeping over my shoulder, he tied the stubborn cloth.

I hoped he would find it a lengthy task. However, he was pleased after the third attempt, and we proceeded on our way.

We met Mr. Wilber and a friend Charles introduced as Philip Cavenaugh near the base of Shotover. The men bowed to me, but their manner seemed rather too familiar.

Charles handed me down and Tiny unharnessed Kahn and Sultan while the men set the terms of the wager and race. I walked to the lead, Sultan, my favorite, to stroke his silky mane and pet his neck.

Kahn, the more spirited, was chosen by Charles to defend his bet. Tiny saddled him quickly while I held Sultan, who was becoming very restless.

"You appear quite at ease with that fine stallion."

I turned to the speaker who came to my side unnoticed. "Why, yes. I've known this pair since they were colts at Rockivale. Charles and I used to race on them."

Mr. Cavenaugh's eyelids drooped over his brown eyes as he looked down on me speculatively. When I flushed under his gaze, his lips formed an impudent grin. Chucking me under my chin, he said, "I'll wager you were a demon to catch."

Offended by his familiarity, I jerked from his touch.

Surprised, he commented, "A proud piece of baggage!"

"I am not a piece of baggage! My father is Dr. Castleton of Christ Church! I'll thank you to keep your hands off me!"

Laughing, he swept me a bow as insulting as his previous gesture. "I beg pardon, your ladyship!"

Deliberately turning my back to this offensive young man, I led Sultan a few yards away.

The course of the race was laid in the direction of Wheatley, partly cross country, partly on a lightly traveled lane. Charles asked me to keep Sultan, as Tiny could not control him as well. I took a position on a rise, the better to watch this race over the hilly course.

Despite the pride I felt in Charles' trust to leave me with his nervous pet and the excitement in this clandestine affair, Mr. Cavenaugh's attitude had impaired the glory of the day. Was my presence truly improper? Uneasily I shoved that thought aside as I cheered for Charles and Kahn.

They won easily.

Sultan did not like seeing his teammate run without him. I had all I could do to keep him from plunging down to the cabriolet and dragging me behind him. As it was, my hat fell off. I dared not stoop to retrieve it before joining the three arguing men.

"No! It's not to be thought!" Charles was exclaiming angrily.

"Very likely she would be afraid," Mr. Cavenaugh said with a sneer.

"Of what would I be afraid?" I demanded.

"Nothing, Meg," Charles answered quickly.

Mr. Cavenaugh explained, "I offered to double the bet Heathton just won if you would race that bay against me."

"I will not permit it!" Charles said flatly. "Tiny, harness 'em up." The groom set about his work immediately.

"What do you mean, 'permit'?" I asked. "You know I'd be only too eager to let Mr. Cavenaugh taste Sultan's dust!"

"Sultan's not been quite up to snuff this week and I'll *not* have him raced!"

So absorbed were we in our heated debate that a horseman nearly passed unnoticed on the lane a few yards away. Charles recognized him and hailed him, probably as a diversion from the proposed race.

The rider turned off to join us, jogging on an old white cob. A fine layer of dust lay on Mr. Knight from his wide-brimmed black hat to his worn black boots.

"My Kahn just beat Wilber's Lightning," Charles boasted, flashing a handful of gold winnings.

"Miss Castleton, gentlemen," Mr. Knight nodded politely to each of us. "Did you win by any great distance?"

"Yes!" Charles replied promptly.

"Not when you consider the length!" countered Mr. Wilber.

This led to a detailed discussion of the course, the hills, woods, streams, and road involved. By the time Charles agreed the win was conclusive, not a complete trouncing, Tiny had both horses harnessed, making Mr. Cavenaugh's proposed race impossible.

Nettled at not being able to show him up, I curtly ordered Tiny to bring my tricorn lying some distance away.

"Allow me," Mr. Knight said, and nudged his old horse to a trot. He brought my hat, dusting it carefully with his hands, and dismounted to present it. Although he was as courteous as if we were in a crowded salon, I sensed his disapproval.

Thinking of Amelia's advice, I smiled, thanked him and inquired after his health. He exchanged pleasantries readily enough, without unbending in the slightest.

As I replaced my hat, I felt my wind-tossled hair and realized how disheveled I must appear. Charles had called me a "hoyden" with good reason. I grew hot with embarrassment.

Mr. Knight bade me farewell, mounted, and with a wave to Charles, trotted off towards Oxford. Mr. Wilber and Mr. Cavenaugh, also preparing to leave, saluted me.

"You ran a good race, Mr. Wilber," I said. "Better luck next time." With neither look nor word did I admit to Mr. Cavenaugh's existence.

As they rode off I heard Mr. Wilber laughing. His words drifted back on a gust of air. "By Jove, Phil, that's one petticoat you couldn't bring round your thumb. I'll wager you. . . ."

Triumphantly Charles handed me into the cabriolet. "Little dove, you brought me luck today. But," he scowled severely, "never again! 'Pon my honor, it ain't the thing."

"Charles, you're as bad as a Granny!" I responded. To myself, I had to admit he was right.

"Are you going to the Williamson's ball next week?" I asked as we drove down towards Oxford's shining spires.

"Yes. They're such bores, but I've nothing better to do. You will be there, won't you?"

"Yes. Father and Mr. Williamson are great friends."

"I'll get Kate to invite Will too. Would you like that?"

I shrugged. "After today, he may not care to associate with me."

"Nonsense!"

"He disapproved of my behavior."

"Of course. I told you it wasn't fitting to be there. Well, never mind. I'll explain how it really was."

His tone caused me to wonder if he was encouraging my friendship with Mr. Knight. If so, it might prove more difficult to make him aware of me as a woman than Amelia anticipated.

Chapter Three

I wore a green silk gown to Kate Williamson's, my second best. It was woefully plain for a party, but I had to reserve my blue satin for special occasions. Wide ecru lace trimmed the neckline and hung around my elbows. Tiers of it flounced down the front of my petticoat, adding a touch of grace. The lovely emeralds Charles gave me upon finishing Mrs. Spinet's would provide some needed elegance. The brooch with several beautiful stones in a new baroque gold setting sparkled from the lace on the front of my bodice. Long matching drops dangled from my ears and a wide bracelet circled my wrist. The most valuable I possessed, I treasured these jewels both for their beauty and the sentiment.

Spreading my ivory fan, also treasured because of the giver, I peered over it at my reflection. Picking up the color of my gown, my eyes now appeared green. I fluttered my eyelids. The effect did not seem as pleasing as when Amelia did so.

Bessie rapped on my door and entered. "Dr. Castleton is suffering from one of his headaches," she said shortly.

Anxiously I brushed past her, dashing to his room. Father was sitting in a chair, massaging his forehead. "O Father! Is it very bad?"

"My head feels stuffed and over large. It's this infernal dampness! If only it would rain!"

"But you can go, can't you? Mr. Williamson will be expecting you."

He said nothing.

"Please," I begged. "There's no one else to take me."

"Is it so important, Margaret?"

"Charles will be there."

"I see." With a heavy sigh, he rose and made his way to his dresser. After donning his white bag-wig, he asked, "Are you ready?"

"Yes, yes." I rushed back to my room for my reticule and cardinal before he could change his mind.

The Williamsons' home was not so large as the Fairchilds', and the gathering more select. These were mostly people I'd come to know the previous year.

Charles met us in the grand salon. Promptly Father withdrew to his friends in the gaming rooms. Perhaps there he would forget the pain in his head.

As always, Charles was dressed in high style. His lavender coat, elaborately decorated with silver, was undoubtedly the latest London cut. Diamond buckles flashed on his shoes. As he led me out to dance, was it my imagination, or did he eye me more appreciatively than usual?

My hopes soared and I whirled around on a rainbow cloud.

"I'm pleased to see you wear my jewels so well," he said with a smile at the close of the dance.

"They are so beautiful! I love them!"

We had barely caught our breath when Mr. Knight appeared, garbed again in dull black under his master's gown. He made a magnificent leg. Charles entrusted me to his care and vanished among the bright silks and satins, taking my joy with him.

"Green becomes you well, Miss Castleton," Mr. Knight said, jerking my thoughts away from Charles. "You should wear it always."

"Thank you, sir," I answered primly. "I am amazed you care to talk with me after my disgraceful escapade last Sunday."

Suprisingly, his eyes seemed to dance in his sober face. "You were a disgrace, windblown and dusty. I was concerned for your reputation. You should value it more highly than the gems you wear and guard it even more carefully."

Music interrupted him. As we danced, I felt enveloped with a tingling, enchanting warmth. Afterwards we rested on a settee and I eased my feet free from my shoes. Why did every pretty pair have to pinch?

Amelia and Mr. Simpson swirled past, her pale pink petticoats rippling and swaying. I wondered if it was Mr. Simpson's brother or Amelia bringing him again to Oxford.

"She's a good friend of yours, isn't she?" Mr. Knight asked.

"Oh, yes! Isn't she beautiful? And so rich! Imagine, a dowry of ninety thousand pounds! She can have anything, anyone she wants."

"You think so?"

"I wish—I hope I can marry someone quite rich." Considering my circumstances, I must have sounded very forlorn, and I blushed.

"Do you think money is the most important thing?"

"Not having it, I do. Don't you?"

"No. Actually, it gives very little."

"How can you say that?" I rushed on. "If I were rich, I'd have a magnificent home, like this, with crystal chandeliers and fine china plate and silver, and a coach and four of my own and horses to ride, and a satin-padded chair to be carried in instead of sloshing around in the muddy streets, and clothes—many, many beautiful gowns."

"But would you be happier than you are now?"

"If I could have a new dress for every ball? Yes!"

"You look lovely in any gown."

His unexpected compliment startled me. "You're very kind to say so, Mr. Knight." I fluttered my ivory fan to cool my face. "There are so many things I want! Isn't that what life's all about? Getting wealth and enjoying the luxuries it provides?"

His brows arched. "There's far more to life than the possession of things and people." He spoke earnestly. "I've lived with the wealthy. They're not so happy as you think. Wealth of itself doesn't create happiness. That lies here." He placed his open hand over his heart.

"Very nicely said. *I* would like an opportunity to be unhappy in luxury." I cocked my head. "And you, Mr. Knight, what do you seek, if it isn't money?"

"Service and . . . " he hesitated, "love. Significant service gives one's life value. And, with love given and returned, one may be happy in any circumstance of life."

"Love is very nice, to be sure, but you can't eat it or wear it."

"You would give up love for wealth?"

Charles and a beautiful partner came into my view. "I would prefer both," I replied softly.

"Ideal, to be sure. And if they came separately?"

I looked into his warm hazel eyes. "I would choose wealth," I said firmly.

"And then, when you had all you desired, you would be bored."

"Bored? I should not be bored!"

"Look at the others. They're bored. They aren't really enjoying themselves or each other."

I flicked my eyes over the faces of the dancers. It was true. Even Kate looked bored with her own party. "That doesn't signify!" I exclaimed, determined not to be beaten. "It is the fashion to be bored. One shouldn't display one's pleasure over what is happening."

"You do."

I bit my lip, frowning. "I know. I've tried not to, but I cannot maintain an inscrutable look. Father says I'm as easily read as a book printed in large type. It's humiliating to realize anyone who looks at you knows how you feel or what you are thinking."

"And refreshing. Your spontaneity strikes me as a cool drink on a hot, dusty day. Which reminds me, would you like a cup of scrub?"

"Yes. I'll come with you and have two." I placed my fingertips on his arm as we strolled together. Mr. Knight's sober dignity and height encouraged me to walk as tall as I could with the smooth glide Mrs. Spinet taught.

As we sipped the tingling punch (I suspected Kate had a rather large portion of rum added), we stood to one side of the room. Opposite us was the long table holding a large crystal punch bowl and a huge arrangement of yellow flowers. Two footmen in bright green livery presided over it.

Ezekiel Walton swaggered through the door and surveyed us through his quizzing glass. A hand on his hip held back his gown, revealing a peach satin coat carelessly miss-buttoned. I thought he must be the despair of his valet to wear a beautifully embroidered coat so poorly. Charles would do it far more justice. Even Mr. Knight would.

Taking a position a few feet before us, he sneered, "So Knight, you are consorting with your betters again!"

Shock hit me as a blow in my stomach. How could anyone speak in such an unforgivable manner! His stance seemed too steady for him to be drunk. Philip Cavenaugh crowded behind him. Was he using Mr. Walton to gain revenge for my snub? Impossible! My hands began to shake so that I had to clasp my half-full cup with both hands to keep it from spilling.

Mr. Knight returned Mr. Walton's gaze calmly, drinking the last of his punch.

"Well," Mr. Walton demanded, "have you forgotten your place, you miserable servitor?"

Shame ran searing through my veins.

In icy tones, Mr. Knight replied, "I am here by invitation."

"Really? I thought better of Kate."

My companion grasped my elbow firmly and guided me into the next salon. At the moment it was deserted.

The terrifying men trailed us, snickering at our ignominious retreat. Mr. Walton rudely brushed past my petticoats, commenting, "At least he knows better than to force his presence on a person of quality. He keeps to his own kind."

Furious, I dashed the remains of my punch in his face. To my satisfaction, I saw a wet stain forming down his costly coat.

Glaring at me, then his clothes, he cried, "My coat! You've ruined my coat!" He dabbed at it and his face with a lace handkerchief.

"You dared insult me!" I stated coldly.

"How can I demand satisfaction from a *woman*?" he inquired of Mr. Cavenaugh.

"I will gladly represent the *lady*," Mr. Knight said, "any time, any place, any weapons."

From Mr. Walton's and Mr. Cavenaugh's pleased expressions, I quickly realized I had served their ends in provoking this quarrel. With the penalty for dueling being expulsion from the University, my thoughtless action might bring about Mr. Knight's ruin.

"Now! Here! With swords!" was Mr. Walton's quick reply.

I gasped at the irregular demand.

"And after I gain my satisfaction, you are not to spoil our festivities with your presence again! Ever! Is *anyone* willing to act as *your* second?" he asked with a doubtful sneer.

Charles appeared suddenly at our side. "I shall be honored to serve Mr. Knight in that capacity." He nodded to another friend to guard the door against intruders.

A pair of dueling swords materialized with astonishing speed, as if held in readiness. Charles and Mr. Cavenaugh inspected them. Mr. Walton struggled out of his gown and tight coat then removed his shoes. Mr. Knight slipped out of his gown, frock coat and shoes, leaving them with Charles. His left big toe protruded from his stocking. Mr. Walton tucked up the lace at his wrists and gestured haughtily for his opponent to take his choice of weapons. Mr. Knight selected one and gave it a flourish.

In that moment I saw him as my champion, about to do battle for my honor. Quickly I went to him and tucked my handkerchief into his collar. "I wish you well, sir. Beat him soundly," I whispered.

"As you wish, ma'am."

Impulsively I grasped his left hand in both of mine. "Do take care."

He bent to kiss my fingertips.

"Meg, do wait outside," Charles urged.

"No. I wish to stay."

"It ain't proper, you know."

"But he's my champion!"

Charles shook his head at my stubborn attitude and returned to his duties as second.

There was small hope for Mr. Knight. Mr. Walton was rumored to be undefeated, a victor delighting in doing severe injury. I bit my lips with regret.

Mr. Walton took his sword and faced Mr. Knight with a contemptuous salute. Those of us in the room leaned against the dark paneled walls to give the combatants space.

A smartly dressed young man next to me muttered to his companion, "I never thought Walton had such poor taste to do it here, did you, Dillworth?"

The swords touched with a soft metallic click. Mr. Walton's blade slithered like a flash towards my champion's heart. I gasped, visualizing Mr. Knight's blood staining the lovely carpet. The thrust was skillfully parried and he stepped aside.

"You impudent bastard! I'll teach you your place!" Mr. Walton exclaimed in a low voice as he pressed Mr. Knight back.

Although the back of Mr. Knight's neck turned pink, he said nothing. Bit by bit he yielded, his toes curling to grip the thick pile. He leapt agilely from several lunges, bringing low exclamations from the observers.

They had compassed the room to their original place when suddenly Mr. Walton's sword flipped from his hand, landing some distance away. Mr. Knight sidled to it, keeping his opponent at bay with his point, picked up the weapon and tossed it to his opponent. Mr. Walton caught it and lunged immediately. The blade tore Mr. Knight's left sleeve. A murmur of disapproval rippled around the room, shifting sentiment towards Mr. Knight.

Again he retreated part way around the room. Mr. Walton's drive seemed to lose its vigor. For a moment my champion faced me. Passion flamed in his eyes; sweat glistened on his flushed face. Abruptly he began forcing his adversary back.

Mr. Walton's haughty sneer faded. His sword flew from his grasp a second time, and a thin red streak formed on his right hand. With Mr. Knight's sword pointed at his throat, Mr. Walton backed against the wall. He slid to the floor, his eyes wide with terror.

"Crawl to Miss Castleton and beg her forgiveness," Mr. Knight commanded tensely.

As the cowed dandy crept to my feet, I heard a whisper, "A pound she refuses 'til he bleeds."

"Done," came the answer.

I looked down into Mr. Walton's twitching face.

"P-please forgive me, Miss Castleton."

"Tell her you truly respect her," prompted Mr. Knight.

"I truly respect you," the despicable man echoed.

I glanced at Mr. Knight, amazed by his intensity. He seemed to be having difficulty restraining himself from running through the craven creature on the floor. "You are forgiven, Mr. Walton," I said coldly.

A communal sigh followed my words.

Mr. Cavenaugh pulled Mr. Walton to his feet, tossed him his

coat and vanished with the swords, scowling. Left alone, Mr. Walton tended to his wounded hand. Charles assisted Mr. Knight into his coat and steadied him as he slipped on his shoes. Suddenly everyone began talking, punctuating the babble with high, nervous laughter. Badly shaken by the duel I caused, I stood as rooted to my place.

There was a commotion at the door and Dean Conybeare strode to the center of the room. His stern look silenced the room. "You look like cats with cream on their whiskers. Sims," he snapped to the man beside me, "be so good as to explain."

"Ah, well, sir, I, er, you see, sir, it was—it was a bet."

"Yes, yes?"

"I, uh, I bet Dillworth here a pound that, uh, that this lady, er, Miss Castleton, would, uh, would reject Walton's, er, pleas to stand up with him at—at the next dance."

"And?"

"I, well, you see, sir, I lost."

"I see." The Dean stared a moment longer at Mr. Sim's red countenance, then glanced at Mr. Walton's stained coat. "Well, well, a profitable evening for you, Dillworth. You rarely win. Your luck, too, may change one day, Sims. Enjoy yourselves, Miss Castleton, gentlemen." He wheeled about and marched out.

Mr. Walton was about to follow when Mr. Sims caught his arm saying, "Oh, no, Walton, you must have this dance with her or the Dean'll know something's amiss."

"He knows it already, idiot! You dance with her!"

"But he don't have to admit it. If he does, we'll all be in for discipline. What would your father say if you was sent down now? And for dueling?"

Mr. Walton stared at him, growing crimson. He snatched up my hand, knocking my empty punch cup from my grasp to bounce on the rug at our feet. With a kick he smashed it against the wall. Imperiously he commanded those present, "Get someone to clean that up!"

In the grand salon, we danced for Dean Conybeare's benefit. Never had music seemed so interminable! At its welcome conclusion, Charles presented his arm and took me aside.

"Why did that horrid Mr. Sims have to say what he did?" I fumed. "Making me suffer through that hateful dance with that creature!"

Charles patted my hand soothingly. "He said the best possible thing. I'm surprised at his unusual presence of mind."

"The best! I rather think it the worst!"

"It allowed the Dean to ignore what happened."

"But why the bet? Why include me?"

"Why not? Remember, my dove, you *would* stay. And the way Sims bets, it was quite credible."

"I still think it was horrid of him to force me to dance with that odious Mr. Walton!" I looked around. "Where is Mr. Knight? I must thank him." And, I thought, retrieve my handkerchief.

"Gone. He asked me to express his profound regret for involving you in this distasteful event."

"But he defended my honor!"

"True. However, he takes University regulations *very* seriously."

Father joined us. "Are you tired, my dear?"

"I—I have a headache, Father."

"Mine is worse too. Let us pay our respects to our gracious hostess and leave. It's unfortunate Mr. Walton had to create such an unpleasant scene. That brash young man is headed for disaster one day. Pity, he comes from a fine old family."

I stared at him. Did all the world know?

Chapter Four

When I called on Amelia the next afternoon, she hurried me to her room and, after closing her door, demanded to know what happened in the small salon. "They say Ezekiel Walton went on his knees to you, begging for a dance. I don't believe it!"

I swore her to secrecy and told her the whole.

She listened, her eyes wide, lips parted, shaking her head at the shocking events. "Charles was right. You shouldn't have remained. But *I* would have done as you. Meg, dearest, *you* have been the cause of a duel!"

I shuddered. "Those lunges! Several times I thought to see blood spilled before my eyes! I think Mr. Walton intended doing Mr. Knight serious injury. There was more involved than just me."

"Perhaps. I know! Your Mr. Knight must be a nobleman in disguise. How else could he fight so expertly? Mr. Walton's quite good, you know. And he was *twice* disarmed! I don't believe he's ever been defeated. Common people have no knowledge of such skill. Yes, he must be the younger son of an impoverished nobleman."

Distressed by her assigning Mr. Knight as "mine," I quickly asked her if Mr. Simpson was attentive.

"Oh, my dear! Look!" She pointed to a large bouquet of pink roses in a blue chinese vase. "You must read the card for yourself." She brought it from her jewel case.

The card was of heavy, costly paper. Large, carefully formed letters read, "Blossoms of such delicate color and sweet fragrance can only belong to you."

"There's no signature!"

"I know," Amelia said putting away her precious note. "Who else would have sent it? His hand is bold, don't you think? And, Meg, he is indeed a gentleman of the first stare! Mama is *so* pleased! He has a way with old women that charms them. Utterly charms them!" She settled on a chair beside me and arranged her violet-flowered mantua thoughtfully. "I believe if he offered for me today, she would prevail upon Papa to allow us to marry immediately!"

"Marry! You want to *marry* him? Soon?"

"Oh, yes!" she answered, her face glowing.

"But—but you rejected the many offers made in London. You said you did not wish to tie yourself to one man."

She dismissed those gentlemen with an airy wave. "They were all old men needing my money to repair their fortunes or else silly young bucks. *None* were like Mr. Simpson!"

"You are *seriously* thinking of marrying him?"

"*Very* seriously. Oh, Meg, he is in my dreams and thoughts constantly, endlessly! And we do make a handsome pair, don't you think? I'm so short and fair, and he's so tall and dark. Delightfully mysterious, rather like a rake, don't you think? He *will* declare for me, I'm certain he will!"

"And take you away. To London. Or his family seat in, in Berkshire, is it?"

She touched my arm reassuringly. "That is not like Newcastle. I should come for visits often. And you may come to see me. We will have such fun in London!"

But I knew, with Amelia having a husband, it would be different, very different. "He can't help but love you; you're so pretty."

"And he's so rich; there can't be any question of his seeking my dowry. It will be me, only *me*! Everything is so wonderful!"

Oh, that I could contemplate my future so confidently as she! However, Charles was only friendly—worse, brotherly. I decided to try her suggestion again, and pretend an interest in Mr. Knight.

Our drawing room was plainly furnished with tired things, an appropriate setting for a dull don. Raindrops made wiggily trails down the windows.

Charles sprawled in a deep chair, his head tilted to drain the last drop of Father's best French wine from his glass. I refilled it from the decanter.

Taking my seat on the faded maroon settee, I said, "Mr. Knight is so odd. How could he be ashamed of winning the other night? I'm sure his skill impressed everyone." I spread my gray petticoats to cover the threadbare seat and picked up my embroidery.

"Oh, it did. It did. He's a nine days' wonder."

"Yet he seemed to think he shouldn't have fought."

"He's ordained, you know. May have felt he broke his vows. He takes them more to heart than most men in orders."

"Ordained? I didn't know."

"You are a featherhead! How else might he be a fellow at Hertford? When he came on us racing, he was returning from Corbet's

Wood where he'd been preaching for a sick curate. Does it without pay, I imagine. He lacks practical sense."

"Take me to Corbet's Wood," I said impulsively. "I'd like to hear how this sober swordsman preaches."

"As you wish, my dove. Who would go with us?"

"Go with us?"

"Your reputation, little dove. What of your reputation?"

"What of it?"

"You are too careless of it, my dove."

"Nonsense! Your escort is quite enough. Why, all the world knows you are like a—a brother to me."

"I thought so too, but Knight convinced me that is not so. The world thinks quite differently."

"What do I care what he thinks! You and I know we are very proper."

"Nonetheless, he is right," Charles insisted. "Will your Bessie go with us? I doubt Dr. Castleton would."

"No. I wouldn't want him along. Nor Bessie either. That doesn't matter a fig. Father doesn't care as long as I'm with you."

"Perhaps not. However, we must be careful, else you might be prevented from contracting a respectable marriage. Would Amelia go, do you think? We'd have to leave by ten o'clock."

"So early?"

"Definitely," he said firmly. "It will take us nearly an hour."

"I'll ask her. This Sunday?"

"If your father agrees."

"Oh, he will," I assured him. "He never refuses me anything, you know."

We were crossing the Cherwell as Oxford's bells chimed ten in many voices. Tiny drove us in an open carriage pulled by a pair of docile hired hacks. The world sparkled with warm sunshine, fresh and clean from the rain of the past several days. Half-naked trees retained only rags of their autumn splendor.

A few minutes before the service began, we drew up in the yard of an ancient Norman church with a squat, crumbling battlemented tower. Amelia preceded us inside, splendid in wine velvet with the plume from her hat curling down around her right ear. I wore a lace palatine over my shoulders to make my best blue muslin more elegant. Charles came behind, drawing twittering admiration from the ladies for his handsome appearance in a fine brown cloth coat richly laced with gold under his flowing academics. We found seats on hard benches near the front.

Large brown seepage circles stained the peeling plaster on the vaulted ceiling. The altar candles were burning down near the plain brass candlesticks. Above them hung a grotesque portrait of the risen Christ with staring eyes and palid face, executed by an artist of little talent.

Mr. Knight, garbed in a plain black cassock and white surplice in keeping with his humble surroundings, rose to lead the service. A terrible old periwig covered his head, neatly curled. Without a trace of self-consciousness, he read the service. His deep voice gave overtones of earnest sincerity to the oft-repeated words.

When he began preaching, I realized he was not reading someone else's sermon, but had composed one of his own. It dealt with what some ancient prophet said about the Lord requiring one to do justly, love mercy and walk humbly. Most appropriate for these people. He so intrigued me, I became lost in speculating on his background and complex personality. Only an occasional word or phrase penetrated my mind as he exhorted his listeners. Amelia sat quietly beside me, appearing very attentive. Charles, on my other side, also seemed absorbed with Mr. Knight's rhetoric.

Following the benediction, we filed from the gloomy chapel and were nearly blinded by the sunshine. Charles insisted Mr. Knight ride back with us. After speaking with various of the parishioners and changing from his vestment and wig, Mr. Knight tied his bony mount to the back of the carriage and we departed.

A lovely meadow provided the site for a delightful picnic which Bessie had packed. We left generous scraps for Tiny, who fell on them ravenously.

Amelia was delighted with the drive, exclaiming over all the country's beauties. She flirted outrageously with Charles as if Mr. Simpson never existed. Charles played up to her with flattering words, kisses on her hands, and ardent looks. I stifled jealous twinges by reminding myself that neither meant what they were doing. Mr. Knight sat at my side saying little.

A brainless hare bounded across the road, spooking the horses. While Tiny was getting them under control, one wheel slipped into a muddy rut and we were suddenly tilted, nearly being thrown out. Amelia and I screamed with fright. Mr. Knight promptly jumped down to survey the damage while Charles helped us to the ground.

The wheel was firmly stuck. I was asked to stand at the horses' heads to keep them quiet and urge them forward at the proper time. Amelia took the men's gowns and coats and perched gracefully on a huge boulder to watch.

The three men strained and I coaxed the horses to pull. Finally, with a sucking noise, the mud gave up our wheel. An anxious examination revealed no breaks or cracks. Charles leaned against Amelia's boulder to rest from his exertions. A small scratch on his hand caused her to go into fluttering concern. Tiny relieved me and I went to join them, thinking her foolish to make a great fuss over the merest wound. Mr. Knight, his back to me, was intent on his left arm. I turned aside to see what was engaging his attention. A bright red stain spread over his sleeve. I gasped when I saw it.

"It's nothing," he said, looking up as I drew near.

Despite his protests, I pulled up the sleeve carefully, exposing a long gash on his forearm, bleeding freely. "But it *is* something!"

I insisted on helping him clean it in a stream a few feet from the road. No linen was available other than his shirt and my petticoats. I tore a ruffle from the latter to bind his arm, assuring him Bessie would replace it at home.

During the rest of our journey to Oxford, Mr. Knight sat quietly. Only his pale cheeks and the lines around his mouth indicated the pain he must have felt.

At Amelia's gate in New Inn Hall Lane stood a fiery red cabriolet drawn by a shining black horse. A groom in glittering silver and sky blue livery held the reins.

"Am I too windblown?" Amelia asked me anxiously.

I beckoned for her to bend within my reach. "Is that Mr. Simpson's?" I asked, tucking a couple curls under her hat.

"I hope so. No one in Oxford owns such a daring rig."

She made a lovely picture as she strolled up her walk on Charles' arm. Inside, I imagined her delighted surprise at finding Mr. Simpson. They would talk and drink tea under her mother's watchful eye, and he would be charmed.

As we drove on to Magpie Lane, I vainly wished Charles would show me the attention he gave freely to Amelia. When he took me to my door, I begged him to see that Mr. Knight's arm was properly cared for, exaggerating my concern.

Charles patted my shoulder. "I am pleased you take his welfare seriously, my dove. He risked life and position defending your honor. I will take him to an apothecary forthwith."

I went to my room, troubled that Amelia's advice was not producing the desired results.

A week or so after the excursion to Corbet's Wood, Bessie showed Charles and Mr. Knight into our drawing room.

With a mischievous glance, Charles bowed. "Little dove, you bade me take care of Knight. I have brought him to prove the good state of his health."

My cheeks burned as I made them welcome and sent Bessie for Father and refreshments.

A pleasant hour passed. We discussed Mr. Knight's fever and recovery, the congregation in Corbet's Wood, and the latest news from Rockivale, which included the possibility of Lord Rockivale's having found a bride for Arthur.

To my surprise, when our visitors left, Father suggested Mr. Knight drop in some evening for a game of chess!

The moment the door closed behind them, I burst out indignantly, "It was outrageous of you to invite Mr. Knight here like that! No doubt he thinks you are encouraging him to court me!"

Father drew himself up sternly. "Nonsense, my child. The world does not revolve around you. I've suggested this times out of mind and he hasn't come. I doubt he will now. In the event he does, you will not be required to sit with us." Warming to his subject, he continued, "I should think things have come to a pretty pass if I can't have whom I will for a game! I should move back to college!"

The next several days I felt a nervous flutter whenever the knocker thudded against the door or the bell was pulled. Mr. Knight did not come. Then I became angry that he did not accept Father's kind invitation. Evidently he did not realize how honored he was that a canon of Christ Church would interest himself in a tutor from Hertford.

Being preoccupied with an accident at Christ Church, Father probably did not give the game another thought. Some servitor had fallen downstairs and broken his neck. Father was certain it was foul murder committed by the villanous Jacobites.

After tea one day, he gave vent to his feelings. "I tell you, Margaret, they are traitors! Nothing less! They would force a Catholic king on us and undo all the good of our glorious Revolution! They would plunge us into a bloody revolt, for the people would not stand for such an atrocity!"

"Surely it can't be that serious!"

"It is! Look at their madness in '45!"

"But, Father, what could a mere servitor have to do with all this?"

"The truth may never come to light," he returned darkly. "But, mark me, there are Jacobites behind this. Perhaps he heard them plotting. Perhaps he saw something."

"More likely he simply stumbled and fell. Haven't they said he was reeking of gin and likely dead drunk?"

"It was murder! I should think friends of that blasphemer are behind it. Now *there* was a Jacobite of an excessively evil cast."

This was the way Father characterized a gownsman dismissed some two years previously on a charge of buying wine from an unlicensed seller. Actually the reason was a scandalous enactment of the Last Supper, with himself playing the part of Our Lord in a most unholy manner. I heard gossip about it while in Mrs. Spinet's.

"Wait until the assizes," I urged, "and we know the truth of the matter."

"Oh, I'll wait, with pen in hand. They'll not pass over this lightly! A life has been taken!"

"But he was only a servitor."

"They are counting on that. But *I* will not permit their treasonous activities to be glossed over. It must be plain to all that the University stands loyally behind the king! Margaret, our very existence is at stake!"

I was in my room repairing a dress seam one evening when the bell was pulled. Listening at my door, I heard Father welcome Mr. Knight on the floor below. Quickly I smoothed my hair and brown petticoats and gave a tug to straighten the scarf tied at my neck. An inspired thought took me to my chest to take out my lace-trimmed scarf normally reserved for Sundays. I secured the fresh one on my bosom with Charles' emerald brooch.

Casually I descended the stairs, feigning surprise at seeing Mr. Knight as he and Father were entering the library. Each held a glass of wine. Mr. Knight bowed with his customary grace.

"We'll only be playing a game of chess, my dear," Father said, plainly dismissing me.

Perversely I smiled and asked to watch. Permission granted, I brought my rose needlepoint and waited while Mr. Knight cleared some books from a chair and placed it for me beside a table. Father brought out his treasured board and men. Together the players sorted them out and set them up.

Briskly, with an air of single-mindedness, they took their places and each quickly moved his king's pawn forward. As the game progressed, more and more thought was given each move, their eyes rarely leaving the board. Both were oblivious to me tugging my wool through the canvas.

Father made little grunts and shifted about to ease his stiff joints. Mr. Knight remained silent, his face expressionless, moving only to pick up a man.

I fully expected to see Father soundly defeat this man, as he did all his challengers, but instead *he* was checkmated! While they reversed the board and set up the pieces, I brought Father's favorite brandy to fill their glasses. They drank appreciatively and set about another game.

This went to Father. Again I filled their glasses and the board was changed. Piece after piece was taken until each was reduced to two pawns and a bishop.

Father extended his hand across the board. "I believe we have played to a draw. Well done."

Mr. Knight took Father's hand and said, "I've enjoyed these games, sir."

Leaning back with a satisfied sigh, Father lit his pipe. "This was a good night." He nodded to me through his puffs, and I went down to the kitchen for punch and biscuits. Never did I think to see anyone defeat him. Where would this unusual man's talents end?

Chapter Five

A masked ball, one of the most exciting parties of the season, was held in late November, despite faculty protests that it was indecent. Charles decided to attend as a crusader knight and asked me to dress as his lady. Determined as we were to be authentic, he arranged for both our costumes. I fervently hoped my fancy dress would inspire him to think of me as his lady love.

After Bessie dropped my cream satin gown over my head and saw how it clung to my limbs, she shook her head. "It's not fitting for you!"

I laughed. "Because I'm not wearing hoops? All women dressed like this in time past."

She shook her head stubbornly.

"There's more to cover me properly." I slipped the deep blue surcoat of rich velvet over the tunic, its folds concealing what the other revealed. I wondered what Charles would think if he saw me without the surcoat. Or Mr. Knight? Perhaps he would not be there, and I would have Charles more frequently as a partner.

Bessie gave grudging approval.

The surcoat ended in a narrow, pointed train. On my left side it was caught up with a diamond clasp to show the hem of the tunic. Soft, flat leather shoes of dark blue covered my feet up to my ankles and extended before me in long pointed toes. Being used to high heels, at first I felt as if I were walking up a hill, and my leg muscles pulled uncomfortably.

Bessie adjusted a wig of long golden hair on my head. I was vaguely uneasy that Charles had selected a color other than my own, but had to admit it did alter my appearance considerably. For the finishing touch, I placed a beautiful pearl and diamond circlet on my brow and a silver mask over my eyes.

At the ball, Father withdrew to the card room as my crusader approached us in the ante room. A suit of chain mail encased him and a helmet, with the visor closed, covered his head. His metal glove felt cold and rough to my hand when he held it and bowed with Charles' typical grand flourish.

In a muffled voice he quoted John Dryden.

" 'The lovely Thais, by his side,
Sate like a blooming Eastern bride
In flower of youth and beauty's pride.
Happy, happy, happy pair!' "

"None but the brave," I answered, "none but the brave. . . ."
We finished together, " 'None but the brave deserves the fair.' "
I laughed. "We seem to be living our childhood fancies. Remember how we used to play that you were one of King Arthur's valiant knights, or read the 'Faerie Queene'?"

" 'A gentle Knigyt was pricking on the plaine,
Ycladd in mightie armes and silver shielde. . . . ' "

I touched the great red cross on his white surcoat,

" 'And on his brest a bloddie crosse he bore,
The deare remembrance of his dying Lord
For whose sweete sake that glorious badge he wore. . . .
Right faithful true he was in deede and word. . . . '

You look like him. Please, open your visor. I could hardly hear you quote the lovely Thais."

He obliged me, but shadows hid his features. "And you are like the gentle knight's lovely lady."

Those words set my heart to racing. Had my hopes at last been realized? I was giddy with anticipation as my gallant knight led me through the first dance. This was the night of my dreams!

The grand salon was crowded with our friends sporting bright apparel borrowed from the past or foreign lands. Near a group of Chinese, I recognized Amelia as dazzling Catherine de Medici. Her dark green gown sparkled with gold and jewels embroidered on the petticoat. Thin gold chains looped across her bosom, caught in a diamond brooch. Wide cuffs of ermine fell a foot or more from her sleeves. Her hair was covered with a cap of jeweled mesh.

Dancing with her was a large man in red and gold doublet and puffed breeches. A short, fur-lined cape swung from his shoulders. A pompous, plump sultan in magnificent purple robes turned past us. A heavy gold chain set with flashing gems hung down his broad chest and a soft white cloth fluttered about his head secured with gold cords. His partner, a lovely harem girl, indecently clad in shear draperies, smiled up at him provocatively. A gray-robed monk entered, his cowl pulled over his head. King Arthur and his queen, and Sir Walter Raleigh and Queen Elizabeth mingled happily with

Henry VIII, Cleopatra and even Socrates. Each contributed to the magic of the evening.

King Arthur became my partner and defied my attempts to pierce his disguise. Feeling awkward and far too short without my heels, I began dancing on my tiptoes. The man in the red and gold doublet whirled me around the room. I coaxed a laugh from him and knew him for Mr. Simpson.

My iron-clad partner reclaimed me and whispered bits of poetry, sending a delighted shiver through me. Perhaps Amelia was right and Mr. Knight stimulated Charles' interest. Whatever the cause, I thrilled to his words and even his metalic touch.

The tall hooded monk in his flapping robes turned past us, his partner, a pretty shepherdess, blushing from something he had said. He must be Mr. Knight. As many times as we had danced at previous balls, he never talked to me. Why did he to her? Maybe she was more entrancing. It stung my vanity that he had not yet chosen to dance with me.

" 'Shall I compare thee to a summer's day?
Thou art more lovely and more temperate,' "

my crusader murmured in my ear.

Shakespeare's words brought my attention from the monk to the bliss of the moment. If only Charles meant what he was saying. He must. He had no reason to hoax me so cruelly. As the evening progressed, I became increasingly intoxicated with the wooing of my poetic knight.

Just prior to midnight, the rotund sultan and Catherine de Medici were crowned as King and Queen of Revels. Delighted for Amelia, I joined in the general cheers as they were enthroned on gilded chairs with mock crowns and scepters.

During the next dance, with my knight's mailed arms about me, I cast aside all restraint and, using Robert Herrick's beautiful words, said softly,

" 'Thou art my life, my love, my heart,
The very eyes of me,
And hast command of every part
To live and die for Thee.' "

He made no answer. I could detect no response through his metal costume.

Suddenly the ensemble stopped playing and the midnight bells rang across the room. An expectant hush settled over us as all turned to the dias to watch the royal couple unmask.

Gallantly the sultan untied Amelia's mask. She beamed graciously as we applauded. Then she undid his mask. Everyone cheered. There, resplendent in flowing robes, stood Charles!

I gaped at him, then whirled to face my knight. The room began to spin and black closed in from the sides. Metalic hands gripped my arms, steadying me. The black receded and the room righted. Surprise, delight, and laughter bubbled about us as others shed their disguises.

My partner led me to a small deserted room. Strains of a precise gavotte trailed us, dimming around the corners.

"Who are you?" I demanded, my voice quavering.

He dropped his heavy gauntlets onto a small chair and tugged at his helmet, working it over his head.

I untied my mask while watching him labor. "Mr. Knight!"

He placed the helmet beside the gloves. Perspiration stood out on his forehead and red marks showed where metal had pressed against his pale skin. His hazel eyes met mine as he said, "I'm sorry to disappoint you."

Ashamed at having bared my heart to *this* man, I groped for words. "I—I thought you were Charles," I said lamely.

He nodded, his face devoid of expression. "He wanted what he termed a double masquerade."

Desperately trying to cover my humiliation, I argued, "But—but you quoted the lovely Thais!"

"He said it would keep you from sensing I was different."

"Oh, it blinded me completely!" I said bitterly.

"He said you enjoyed poetry, so I—"

"You did very well," I burst in. "You should tread the boards in Drury Lane! At least in the Sheldonian! You spoke your lines with *great* conviction!"

At that moment the sultan entered and enveloped me in a brotherly hug. "It took all the pillows we could find to make me so plump!" He patted his soft front. "Clever, weren't we? A disguise within a disguise. We did fool you, didn't we, Meg?"

I nodded, tears flooding my eyes. Although I tried to look away, he turned me towards him.

"What's this? Tears, little dove? I don't understand. It was only a joke, a bit of fun to relieve the tedium of another ball." His puzzled expression altered to one of anger. "Knight, what did you do to upset her?"

"I became carried away with my part."

"If you offended her in *any* way—"

"No, Charles," I interrupted. "Mr. Knight did nothing to offend me."

"It was something he said. What was it?"

"Nothing. Nothing at all. He was kind and attentive, and—and . . . I hoped . . . I thought—I thought he was you," I stammered.

"And you were disappointed, my dove?" He touched my cheek tenderly. "I'm flattered. You must have played your part to perfection, Knight."

I sank on a chair opposite the helmet.

Charles looked down at me, raised, then dropped, his hands. "Please, Meg, don't take it so. It was only a prank. A foolish one."

I bit my lip to still its trembling.

"Now I understand why they frowned on this cursed party!" Charles seemed about to say more. Instead he left abruptly.

I stared at my pointed shoes.

Mr. Knight stood before me a moment, then moved away, his sword rasping against his armor.

A log snapped loudly.

Covertly I looked at Mr. Knight's bent figure. His forearm laid along the carved mantle. With his forehead resting on his wrist, he gazed at the flickering fire. If, as I suspected, his interest in me was more than passing, he, too, must be greatly distressed. No wonder he gave no reply to my poem of love, knowing it was meant for Charles.

"Would you like a plate of supper?" he asked finally.

"Yes, please. In here. I'm too . . . tired to mix with the crowd."

I picked at the food he brought. Mr. Knight showed little interest in eating either. Gradually I brought my emotions under control and we returned to the others.

The ballroom was now filled with familiar faces. We mingled with them easily, expressing amazement and pleasure over their elaborate costumes.

Amelia came to me and whispered behind her fan, "Meg, must you always disappear with your Mr. Knight? It doesn't look good. People will talk, if they haven't started already."

"Mr. Knight means *nothing* to me! He took me out to regain my—myself. I was—I was upset with Charles."

"You were upset with *Charles*! You didn't know! You thought the crusader was. . . You didn't *say* anything, did you?"

I nodded.

"How awful! How unfair! That man is *cruelly* insensitive!"

Father stepped up beside us, obviously in good humor. "What an assortment of ages, fact and fancy! I think Conybeare was unduly apprehensive about this." He made a courtly bow to Amelia. "Your Highness, you are a rare vision of loveliness. Will you grant an old admirer this dance?"

She blushed prettily and gave him her hand.

One of Charles' friends led me out. Nowhere among the dancers did I see a man in a coat of mail.

As I snuggled under the covers with my feet against a hot brick, my tears dampened my pillow. Again I seemed to hear that voice I thought was Charles'.

" 'You frame my thoughts, and fashion me within,
   You stop my toung, and teach my hart to speake,
   You calme the storme that passion did begin . . . . ' "

The sincerity, even tenderness, of Spenser's words soothed my pained heart. He had not been speaking for Charles or acting a part. The knight far surpassed Charles' lighthearted gallantries. Powerful feelings lay beneath Mr. Knight's exceptionally calm exterior, feelings that escaped his guard during the duel and again tonight.

Drifting to sleep, I beheld a crusader knight against a purple sky. I ran to him. But the way was so long, I did not reach him before Bessie woke me, pulling back my curtains.

"He's really a man of mystery, so plain in his dress and so accomplished in all the social graces—even sword's play!" It was Amelia's voice.

"I haven't danced with him—yet, but I've heard it said by those who have that there's none better."

I sat sipping tea in Amelia's drawing room, my back to the speakers. Fastening my attention on five candles in a baroque golden candelabra beneath an aged oil painting, I strained to hear more.

Amelia answered, "I *have* danced with him, and, aside from Mr. Simpson, he's the most elegant in Oxford. And I heard he won a *duel* against a skilled swordsman!"

"I heard that too. Do you know what really happened? It was supposed to have been at Kate's."

With bated breath I awaited her answer.

"So they say," she responded lightly. "There's a mystery about him. I suspect," the girls twittered eagerly as she paused, "I suspect that he is *not* as he appears. Only think, where else can a man learn these things save in a house of wealth and position?"

"I heard," the voice dropped to barely audible tones, "that he was beset by *footpads* only the other night!"

"True," Amelia responded. "He beat off *three* of them. Charles Heathton happened along and helped put them to flight."

"Three!" the others gasped.

"Mr. Heathton was *convinced*, so I was told, that they were not ordinary footpads; for, you know, *they* would not go for one as poorly dressed as Mr. Knight."

"Might he be *P'wince Cha'wles* in disguise?" lisped a high voice, "and the footpads the *king's* men?"

"No, no. Mr. Knight has been here these *many* years. He used to be a servitor at Christ Church, you know."

The girls moved away. I was piqued that Amelia had not told me of the attack. Even Charles had not mentioned it. Since that horrible masked ball, I had not seen Mr. Knight. Indeed, I should be profoundly embarrassed if we met, yet I missed his attention. And I did owe to him the defense of my name.

After the others departed, I gradually brought our conversation around to the attack and asked Amelia why she had not told me of it.

She shrugged. "I really didn't think you would be interested. You said he meant *nothing* to you."

"Not *interested*, Amelia, merely *curious*. It is an exciting bit of gossip, and I *do* know him." Immediately I began discussing the pre-Christmas ball and Amelia showed me her new gown for it.

A dusting of snow on the ground, a crisp tinge to the air, made a perfect setting for the event. Every room in the host's house was festooned with holly, ivy, and evergreen boughs.

Charles led me through the first dance, the silver embroidery on his blue velvet suit flashing in the lights. At its completion, he suggested we go into a salon. As we passed through the door, he paused, grasped my upper arms and kissed me!

Startled, I stood as a statue.

He chuckled, reached up to the bunch of mistletoe above me and plucked a white waxen berry. "My first of the evening," he said, dropping it into his pocket.

I laughed shakily. "No doubt your pockets will be overflowing by the time you leave."

"Believe me, my dove, I shall make every effort to prove you right!"

A gownsman claimed my hand and I returned to the ballroom. Charles had kissed me. Perhaps it was because he caught me unawares in a public place that it was not as in my dreams.

What would it be like to have Mr. Knight walk me under the mistletoe? Such levity was alien to him. Before I could pull my thoughts from that gentleman, my eyes skipped lightly over the other dancers and saw him not.

As the evening dragged on, several berries were plucked at my expense. One was collected even by Mr. Simpson, virtually a resident of Oxford these days. Oddly, I found it all tiresome. For the first time I could comprehend Charles' complaint of boredom.

On a brisk afternoon, Charles took me for a short drive in his cabriolet. Winter snow gave Oxford a beautiful icing.

In fine style, rolling down Long Street before Merton, we slid excitingly around the corner into the High. We swept along the curve between the stern walls of University, topped with a whitened battlemented tower, and the new Queens on our right. Its dome over the entrance wore a collar of snow above the pillars surrounding Queen Caroline's statue. Indifferent to the oaths of those we splashed in the slushy street, Charles urged the horses to a smart pace, weaving around slower carriages and wagons.

I was admiring St. Mary's old spire rising from a nest of snow-crested pinnacles against the heavy gray clouds when he caught my attention with, "Father has commissioned me to request that you and Dr. Castleton visit Rockivale between terms."

My heart leapt at the opportunity, then sank. Father would refuse to leave his fire for a tortuous winter journey of even one day's length. "Thank you, Charles. I wish we might, but Father's joints have been hurting since the cold settled. I doubt he'd go."

Charles nodded in understanding. We rounded the conduit and turned up Fish Street as the effigies swung their hammers to strike the quarter hour. "I will explain," he said. "He'll be disappointed. The old man is lonely for your father's companionship."

Ahead, I saw Mr. Knight passing under Big Tom. I brushed a few flakes from my cheeks and asked, "Isn't that your friend, Mr. Knight?"

"Yes, it certainly is."

"I heard you saved him from some misadventure with footpads."

"What? Oh, that was *ages* ago."

"Do you think it had anything to do with that odious Mr. Walton?"

"Very likely. Walton took offense at some remark. Knight's very plain-spoken, you know. Last week Walton got into another scrape and was sent down. I think Knight's safe from his vengeance now."

"I haven't seen Mr. Knight around town," my voice matter-of-fact.

"He seems to have lost interest in social doings. Last October he was so set on attending them all. Since that duel, of course, he's been invited to everything."

Charles guided the horses into the narrow lane past Pembroke and along the aging city wall. The section rebuilt with Pembroke's new chapel made a raw patch on the mellowed old fabric.

"It's strange," Charles went on, "after the masquerade, he don't seem to care. I expect he's discovered how deadly boring they are, always seeing the same people doing the same things. Like enough he's decided they aren't worth his time."

"I see."

"It was a rather abrupt change, don't you think?" Charles turned to gaze directly in my face. I snuggled down among the furs he had tucked about me and stared ahead towards St. Peter's in the Bayly through gently falling snow. "I suppose so." We made another corner.

"Meg."

I looked up to meet Charles' serious eyes.

"Have you missed him?"

My cheeks grew hot and I glanced away quickly. "Of course. Hasn't everyone? He—he was so different."

"I think poor Knight believes you harbor a strong dislike for him."

"That's silly. Why should I? Of course I don't."

"May I tell him? It would raise the poor fellow's spirits."

"Charles, you couldn't be so tactless!"

"He's been very low."

"I am confident what I think doesn't signify to Mr. Knight in any way."

"I thought you liked him—a little, at least."

Amelia's advice came to mind. "A little," I admitted. "He is amusing. Different." I stole a look at Charles' intent on threading through market traffic, then heaved an exaggerated sigh. "Can I have no secrets? Yes, I miss him." My studied pretense shocked me with the feel of truth!

Charles chuckled. "Ah, I was right! May I tell him?"

"No! No, you may not!" I answered sharply. Mr. Knight was too insignificant. He must not matter to me. I would not let him.

Charles shook his head. "You females are always so devious!"

"M-men would not be intrigued if they understood us completely!"

At home, Tiny sprang down to hold Sultan and Kahn while Charles helped me out of the cabriolet.

"I'll invite Dr. Castleton to Rockivale myself," Charles said. "Perhaps he feels better than you think. It'd be great fun to have you there for the holidays. Walk them, Tiny. I may be gone some minutes."

By now the flakes were coming heavily and I was glad to enter the warm shelter of the house. While shedding my wraps, I offered a hurried prayer that Father would indeed undertake the trip to Rockivale.

We were drinking sherry before the blazing fire in the drawing room when Charles asked Father to visit his home.

Father looked at me over the rim of his glass as he took a leisurely sip. "Lord Rockivale is most kind. I well remember the holiday gaiety. However, my joints are uncommonly sore this year. Even that short journey in this uncertain weather is more than I care to contemplate."

"If you do not feel up to it, sir, would you permit Meg to come? With an early start, we could be there for tea. I would take her up and back most carefully, in a closed carriage."

I held my breath. At last Amelia's advice was working!

Father pursed his lips. "Um." Slowly he drained his glass and held it out. "Please, Margaret."

I rose to fill his glass and then Charles', knowing Father was delaying his answer to think.

"Do you wish to go, child?"

"I do love Rockivale, but I've no wish to leave you alone."

"Humph. Well, I should think I could get some work done. I've another pamphlet about finished. It's vital these Jacobites not be permitted to continue in their treasonous pursuits uncensored. Neither the Pretender nor his son, heretics that they are, will be welcomed in London. Their followers had best realize that and cease their trouble-making. That poor boy, what was his name? The one whose neck was broken?"

"Burke, sir?" murmured Charles, giving me a wink.

"Yes, yes. Burke. Murdered. Only a servitor, but murdered nonetheless. If they think they can get away with that, what will they try next? There is power in the pen to thwart them, to show them up for what they are."

He gazed into his half-empty glass with a faint smile. "You've no need to concern yourself about me, my dear. We have a merry time in the Common Room. A very merry time. Yes, I will stay here at my appointed task. Margaret, my dear, you may go to Rockivale without me."

Chapter Six

I paused at the foot of the grand stair in Rockivale's dark hall. In my misery, where could I go? From the morning room I heard Arthur's tenor voice interrupted with the warm alto and tinkling soprano of Martha Exley and her comely little sister, Beatrice. Then Charles laughed. They were a gay quartet, complete without me.

The journey here had promised so much! Charles had ridden Kahn beside the carriage, occasionally joining me inside when it came on to rain heavily, behaving most attentively. Lady Edith had welcomed us warmly, fussing over my comfort. I felt truly at home, even though the dear familiar rooms bore a strange appearance from new drapery and rearranged, freshly upholstered furniture.

That evening was like a beautiful dream. Lady Edith poured coffee in the drawing room. Charles favored me with his full attention, delightfully teasing and flirting. Lord Rockivale watched us with an approving attitude and Arthur ignored us in his usual withdrawn fashion, reading a book.

Then Lord Rockivale had announced that Martha Exley, Arthur's betrothed, would arrive on the morrow. She would remain over Christmas for a ball in early January to introduce her to their friends. Refurbishing the house was part of the marriage preparations.

Miss Exley's arrival shattered my happiness. For company, she brought her sister, a pretty child hardly out of the schoolroom. She captivated Charles with her blushing response to his every sally.

Oh, to escape this nightmare! Outside, the snow precluded a good long ride over the hills to clear my mind and lift my spirits. Another burst of laughter pushed me away from the morning room. I fled to my old rainy-day haven, the library.

The fire cast a warm glow over the dark old furnishings and a score of glass cabinets crowded with volumes. Even here was evidence of Lady Edith's efforts at renewal. The worn carpet was replaced with a chinese one in brilliant red with black, cream and blue oriental designs. Red-fringed drapes framed the windows.

Trying to ignore these foreign intrusions, I walked across the deep, soft pile to one of the tall windows looking onto the side terrace. I stared at glistening white mounds covering the balustrade, a hard lump in my throat.

Here at Rockivale I had never before known other than happiness. Here I had hoped to come one day as Charles' beloved wife. And here, I finally realized, my dreams could never be. That empty-headed child with shining black curls and cherry pouting lips held Charles' entire attention. To be sure, when he was again in Oxford he would not recall either her name or the color of her hair.

If I could not hold his attention from one silly child, I could never hope to hold it long enough to gain his marriage proposal. Or, if that, to hold it afterwards. As I possessed neither wealth nor great beauty, I must reconcile myself to a loveless marriage or a genteel position. With a sigh of bitter resignation, I turned from the dazzling sunlight.

A litter of papers lay on the long library table before the blazing hearth. A triple branch of lighted candles stood beside an inkstand holding a quill. I moved idly over to see what sort of work was being done.

As I approached the table, I noticed a tall male shadow against the light at a far window. "I beg pardon," I murmured. "I hope I haven't disturbed you."

He whirled around and I gasped.

As he faced me, his pale countenance reddened. Mr. Knight bowed. "Your servant, ma'am."

"I didn't know! I—Charles didn't tell me."

"Mr. Heathton pressed me to pursue my studies here between terms."

"He—he did?"

"Yes. He said I might work with fewer interruptions than in the Bodlean. You see, several of my students remain in Oxford and, for lack of anything to do, amuse themselves discussing life's imponderables with me."

"Oh?"

"Such questions as 'What is the place of fate in a universe created by God?' or 'Can the almighty Creator make something so big He could not lift it?' "

I stared at him, failing to grasp his words.

"Questions they have no real interest in answering. They merely serve as tools in an attempt to prove themselves more brilliant than their tutor."

"I see. Did they succeed?"

"Not yet."

"Did you know that I—did you know who were to be Charles' guests?"

"Only that several would be here. If I chose, he said I might stay in the library and work."

"When did he suggest you come?"

"A few hours before he left. I arrived last evening, after the household retired."

"Your horse did not appear hardy enough to travel this distance."

"Heathton insisted I ride his Sultan as the roads are bad."

"He did!" Never had I known him to trust Sultan with anyone but me, and then only when he was present. "I—fail to understand why he did not mention that you were expected."

Mr. Knight stepped to the table and picked up a sheet of paper, saying drily, "Perhaps he thought it would not be a matter of interest."

"Of course it is!" I exclaimed. "We are friends!"

He looked up quickly, "I had hoped we might be."

I blushed and said nervously, "Of course. Why not?"

His gaze remained steady; his right eyebrow twitched.

"Because of that stupid masquerade?" I plucked at the white bow on my bodice. "Naturally I was angry about the—about the impersonation. That, however, would not, could never affect a *friendship*!"

"I am glad to know it would not."

From his reserved manner, I felt he was eager to be back at his studies. I moved towards the door, asking, "Will you be dining here or with the family?"

He hesitated. "I have not yet decided."

"Oh. Until later, Mr. Knight—whenever that might be."

On my way to the morning room, I mused on the fact of Mr. Knight's presence at Charles' insistence. Whatever his purpose in having Mr. Knight here, I might use him after all to show Charles I was a person more worthy of his attention than that child.

At teatime, Mr. Knight did join us in the green and ivory drawing room. His plain black garb and sober countenance sparked no interest for the lively Exley sisters. Lord and Lady Rockivale were mystified by this eminently unsuitable person.

Charles brought me a buttered scone with a cup of tea and murmured, "Please give old Knight your company. I'm afraid neither of these girls would be up to him."

I smiled and agreed. After complimenting Lady Rockivale on her cinnamon gown, I drifted over to Lord Rockivale who was attempting to describe to Mr. Knight the joys of hunting on the estate.

Our host was relieved that my arrival permitted his escape.

Knowing interest in a scholar's project can draw out the quietest don, I inquired about the nature of Mr. Knight's papers in the library.

"They comprise my thesis."

"For your doctorate, I presume."

"Yes. I'm in the final stage of assembling it. Next comes the writing, then my examination."

"A very demanding task. What is your subject?"

"Forgiveness."

"Forgiveness!"

"Yes. I'm comparing the Old Testament doctrines with the New Testament."

"And have you arrived at any conclusions? Are they the same or quite different?"

"Less different than might be expected."

"Really!"

"It's all a matter of grace, you see, unmerited favor. Take David. He's a favorite of mine. We may find great comfort in the account of his life."

"How so?"

"As a man, he was far from perfect. He committed grave sins, even including adultery and murder. Yet God spoke of him as a man after His own heart."

Deliberately misunderstanding, I asked, "Do you mean God does not take grave sins seriously, or does that apply only to a king's sins?"

"Neither. He dealt most severely with David. The comfort lies in seeing that even when we sin most grievously, God is ready to forgive whenever we truly repent." He paused. "Please forgive me for being ponderous."

I laughed and was pleased to see Charles glance my way. "You are forgiven, of course. I asked the question. Remember, Mr. Knight, being raised in a parsonage, all my life I have heard bits of sermons and theological debates, some very ponderous indeed. However, never has David's dealings with Bathsheba been presented as a source of comfort to me."

"I did not mean it quite that way."

"Why did you select this subject? I would think it might be something more—more, uh, technical."

"This has been of interest to me for many years."

"Have you done something for which you seek forgiveness?" I asked lightly.

"Haven't we all, Miss Castleton? There is a universal need for forgiveness. I chose to study it because I've seen the transformation it can make in a person's life."

"I see. And you wish to understand this phenomenon?"

"In order to make it available to those needing it. Forgiveness is like a soothing, healing salve to an inflamed wound."

"At the moment I have no such wound. But, should one develop, I'll ask you about this salve. How was your ride here yesterday?"

"Very pleasant. Sultan is a fine mount."

"My favorite. Kahn is too unpredictable. You must have left after the service at Corbet's Wood."

"No. Rev. Ayres is fully recovered and no longer needs me. I am surprised you remember the little church."

"Oh, it made a deep impression on me that one who handled a dueling sword with such great skill could also preach eloquently."

Mr. Knight fixed his attention on something behind me and frowned.

Perversely, I continued, "You showed great ferocity in handling your blade. Tell me, Mr. Knight, have you ever killed a man in a duel?"

"No, Miss Castleton. It has not been necessary. I pray God I may never do so."

"Oh?"

"Life is a gift from God. It is for Him to take when He is ready, not for man to do so."

"Even when you are defending yourself? Or perhaps defending another? Surely killing a person who is attacking another is not to be frowned at!"

"I sincerely hope I am never forced to make that decision."

Charles joined us with Beatrice on his arm. "Meg," he chided, "I desired you to *entertain* Knight, not make him scowl. He does that very well without anyone's help."

"It was but for a moment. Do bear me out, sir," I protested.

"She has obeyed your instructions, Heathton. I failed to be cooperative."

After dinner, Martha Exley settled to playing the harpsichord with Arthur turning pages for her. Charles suggested that Beatrice, Mr. Knight and I join him in several hands of whist. Perhaps it was because Charles had to devote much of his time explaining the game to Beatrice that Mr. Knight and I ended far ahead. I had to admit that the invincible Mr. Knight made a more desirable partner than Charles in games of chance or skill.

When I entered the small yellow dining room the next morning, Charles was alone at breakfast. He seated me with a pleasing display of gallantry, asking, "Did I surprise you?"

"You always do. I thought you unable to rise this early."

"That's only at college. I mean about having Knight come up!"

"Oh. Of course I was surprised. You failed to tell me."

"Little dove, if I told you, it would have ruined my surprise! I must confess, I did think you would show it more at teatime."

"I met him in the library, in the morning."

He laughed. "My careful plans foiled in the library! And I hoped to witness great shock on your face!"

"Oh, I was shocked. We both were!"

"Would I had been there!"

"I trust Mr. Knight is not overly displeased with our interference in his studies."

"Displeased! He's the happiest he's ever been! I'll warrant he'll not be able to concentrate like he expected, but he won't mind it a bit. Not in the least. Anyway, it's not healthy to spend so much time with books. Your father has oft assured me of that. Tell me, little dove, are *you* pleased?"

I was saved from answering by the Exley sisters' bubbling entrance, followed by Arthur. He announced that we five were commissioned to deck the halls and trim the tree. The latter was an annual custom Lord Rockivale brought back from his tour of the continent in his youth.

These projects consumed several days. As we worked, I came to view Beatrice's flirting with Charles as amusing. Of greater interest were Mr. Knight's unexpected appearances to partake in our activities.

To my astonishment, while we were trimming the tree, it was necessary for me to demonstrate to him how to fasten the candles at the ends of the branches. I asked if he'd ever done this before.

"No. This is the first such tree I've seen."

His words gave me a sense of triumph. At last his record of superior achievements was broken.

He surveyed the partially trimmed tree, then looked steadily into my eyes. "You are very skillful. I am confident it will make a beautiful sight."

Unaccountably, a tremor ran through me as I thanked him for his compliment and hastily began afixing another taper to a limb.

The night of the grand ball honoring Arthur and his affianced wife, I wore my blue satin gown. While I watched the mirror over my shoulder as the maid arranged the folds in back over my hoop, I thought again of dressing for Fate. With whom lay my fate?

The delightful days of merrymaking had thrown me into confusion. Amelia's advice seemed to be working. Several times I saw Charles watching me with Mr. Knight. If I could catch his eye in the presence of pretty Beatrice, I would win him in Oxford.

Yet, when I donned my gown, my first thought was of Mr. Knight's reaction to my appearance. In fact, now that I reflected on the matter, the spice of these days was in anticipating his unannounced presence, seeing a light in his eyes, a lift to his eyebrow. Even when Charles was not with us, I sought his reserved attention. My plan to use Mr. Knight had gone awry. Suppressing these traitorous ideas, I resolved to keep a tight check on my emotions.

To me, the assembly of guests looked very gawdy without a single black gown to be seen. Mr. Knight was not visible. I saw Charles talking to the Exley sisters. Breaking off his conversation, he came to me, splendid in gold brocade, lace, shining buckles and a sprinkling of rubies. He was the handsomest in the room. A beguiling scent passed my nose as he bent over my hand.

"My dove, never have I seen you so ravishing!"

I spread my fan to cover my face and dropped my gaze. "Thank you, kind sir. In all the world, no woman could have a handsomer man attend her."

"You blush most becomingly, my dove. Unfortunately duty requires me the first two dances, but you must save the third for me. Promise?"

After attending the ladies of social rank, Charles led me out. He missed a step, something Mr. Knight never did. But promptly I shoved aside the disloyal thought.

"After much argument, I prevailed upon Knight to join us," Charles said. "He thought he did not belong here. Do be kind to him, so he won't regret coming."

"Where is he?"

"To your right, against the wall."

Mr. Knight stood alone, watching the dancers.

"Since you are such good friends, surely you could lend him some suitable clothes, other than a suit of armor."

"Touché. I've tried. He refuses to look like someone he ain't. You *have* forgiven him for our joke, haven't you?"

"Of course I have."

I met several people I remembered vaguely from my years in the vicarage before a young man down from Cambridge asked me to stand up with him. Over his shoulder I saw Mr. Knight with Beatrice. What must she think finding the man she snubbed these past days a most accomplished dancing partner?

Later, being thirsty, I slipped into the parlor to the wassail bowl. The footman, in green and cream livery with new silver tassels hanging from his sleeves, gave me a cup. I barely finished drinking it when a black coat and white bands came before me. Startled, I looked up into Mr. Knight's face.

He bowed formally. "Miss Castleton, will you honor me with the next dance, or are you promised to another?"

"Oh, no! I—my pleasure," I answered, annoyed at the rush of heat in my cheeks.

Moving precisely through the conventional dance figures, I wondered that he could charm me completely without a word of flattery.

Suddenly my ankle turned and I lost my high-heeled slipper. Mr. Knight scooped it up and whisked me out of the room so rapidly, I'm sure no others were aware of my embarrassment.

He knelt before me. I steadied myself holding his shoulder while he replaced my slipper and felt my ankle. "Did you hurt yourself?"

"No. I merely stumbled. So silly." I laughed shakily. "Thank you for rescuing me."

Taking my arm, he led me to a secluded nook with a blazing fire and a rose settee. "Perhaps you need to rest. You've been dancing constantly."

I sat down, the wide hoops of my voluminous gown spreading over the settee.

Mr. Knight leaned against the marble mantle, fixed his gaze on the sconce above me and commented the next snow should hold off until we were returned to Oxford.

Determined to break through his reserve, I pulled my petticoats to me and patted the seat. "Please, sit down. You must be as tired as I."

"I'm spared from wearing such shoes as yours."

"Consider yourself fortunate. Come, sit beside me."

He came as if testing each step for danger and perched on the edge of the settee.

Impulsively I said, "You know a great deal about me. I know little of you. Tell me about your family. You've never mentioned them."

His posture stiffened. Silently he stared at the orange flames flicking upward and falling back upon the log. So long a time passed, I feared I had placed a barrier between us. Then he faced me, his expression guarded. Spacing his words carefully, he said, "My mother died before I came to Oxford. She was a prostitute."

I stared at him, shocked. Amelia and I had discussed those sinful women in whispers one dark night at Mrs. Spinet's. It could not be that Mr. Knight was the son of one of them!

His penetrating gaze seemed to plumb my thoughts.

Finding my tongue, I blurted out, "You loved her very much, didn't you?"

His right eyebrow flickered. He turned away, but not before I saw a film of moisture in his eyes. Instinctively, I touched his arm. He covered my hand with his.

In a steady, impersonal tone, he began speaking. "I was raised in my father's house. He was the earl of—well, an earl. My mother was very beautiful, her hair of a honey color, her eyes like bluebelles. And she was sweet. She had a lively, independent spirit, much like yours. They loved each other deeply. However, Father was tied to a marriage designed to unite two great families and estates. He and his wife detested each other. Mother agreed to remain in his household as a seamstress if I was raised as his other children, a younger boy and girl.

"Always I was an object of scorn to everyone, including the servants. I learned to maintain my self-respect by excelling in everything, becoming a better student, dancer, horseman, swordsman, fighter and runner. The children gained revenge destroying anything that gave me pleasure and forcing upon me whatever I disliked. So I hid my feelings."

"Did you see much of your father?"

"More than the others, I think." He shifted his position to face me fully, his eyes alive and warm. "He took me riding about the estate, explaining its management. Improving the land through better methods of agriculture was his prime interest. As I grew older, he discussed some problems with me. When his mother died, I think he intended to adopt me. But he died first, late one night, with Mother holding his hand. Within the hour we were removed from the house in the family coach.

"After a day and night of travel we were left in a street before a cheap London tavern." His mouth formed a hard, straight line. "Being a poor seamstress and unskilled at any other occupation, Mother turned to prostitution. My education as a gentleman did not prepare me for London's streets. Since I was sixteen and strong, I worked at every job I could find. Together we managed to survive.

"Mother hoarded the jewels Father had given her against my attending Oxford. Obsessed with my rising socially, she taught me all she knew of the ways of wealthy people. And always, I must go to the University. . ." He was quiet for a moment.

"She took sick with a wasting disease. For weeks our only visitor was a doctor who attempted to make her more comfortable. Then a poor vicar found us. Often he climbed to our shabby room, bringing his Bible and occasionally a small parcel of food. I envied his inner serenity. Through his visits, he brought Mother the greatest gifts of all, a knowledge of forgiveness and of peace with God."

"Your thesis!"

He nodded. "Her face actually shone with happiness the days before she died. Under this parson's ministry I gave myself into God's service, hoping He would use me to bring His joy and peace to others needing it as desperately as she and I."

I pressed his arm in sympathy.

"My academic goal is nearly in hand. Now I need—I crave—a sign of approval, an indication for me to remain a tutor at Hertford or to seek a position as a curé of souls."

Hastily I brushed a tear from my lashes. Gently he dried my cheeks with his handkerchief, taking care not to damage my paint. For a beautiful, fragile moment we gazed into each other's eyes.

Faint music floated in from the ballroom.

"Do you waltz?" he asked.

I nodded.

He assisted me to my feet. To my surprise, instead of joining the others, we waltzed alone in the alcove. Gradually his hand moved from my left side across my back to my right side, until he held me in a tight embrace, his face pressed against the curve of my neck. The music ceased. We remained thus, his heart's rapid pace matching mine.

He loves me, I thought, and quivered in delight. I longed for him to kiss me. I blushed at my unchaste thought.

At length he released me, bowed over my hand, and pressed a burning kiss in the center of my palm. As if ashamed at revealing his emotions, he resumed his reserved, correct manner and we returned to the ball. Not once did he permit me to catch his eye during the sumptuous buffet.

Martha Exley's older brother soon claimed me as a partner. Anxious to repeat my exciting experience, I tried to observe Mr. Knight's direction. Suddenly he vanished, taking with him the heady magic of the evening.

In my nightdress, I leaned out my window and looked up at the bright moon. I pressed the kiss left in my palm to my lips. If he came to my window as Romeo, I would welcome him. If he came to my door with a light tap. . . I spun around and stared at it. What would I do?

I pulled the curtains about my bed, climbed in and imagined rash elopements. Oh, to feel his arms about me again! Hugging my pillow to my breast, I dreamed of flitting over the hills into Oxford, graceful grecian folds swirling about me. I sought my lover and found him, an arrow piercing his heart and great red blotches on his black coat.

Propped up on pillows, I sipped the hot chocolate a maid brought. What luxury to lie beneath fringed hangings in a room warmed by a fire lit before I awoke! Dreamily I relived that ecstatic moment in Mr. Knight's arms. Today I would find him alone, and. . .

Madness! Utter madness! He was *not* my heart's desire! It was being *loved* that excited me.

Agitated, I left the soft bed. Green. He said I should always wear green. Carefully I dressed in my most becoming calico and fastened a green bow in my hair. In the mirror, my reflection showed sparkling eyes and a smiling mouth surrounded with a complexion of unusually high color. If one is loved, I decided, she should make the most of it.

Humming gaily, I sped downstairs and went to the library, thinking to surprise Mr. Knight. Not a paper lay on the polished table! Nothing of his was in the room. I hurried to the dining room. Everyone was there, save Mr. Knight.

To hide my concern, I joined in the discussion of the Exley sisters' departure that afternoon. Charles evidenced more regret over Beatrice's leaving than Arthur did over Martha's. But then, Charles was always more demonstrative than his brother.

When we rose from the table, I plucked Charles' sleeve. "Charles, I have a question."

"Yes? You're very glowing this morning, my dove."

Beatrice, hovering at his side, looked at me expectantly.

"Thank you. I—I wish to speak to you in the library for a few minutes."

He sent Beatrice away and followed me to the large, empty room. There was laughter in his eyes and his lips were twitching as he waited for me to speak.

"Where is Mr. Knight?"

Charles looked around as if expecting to see him. "Do you think I misplaced him?"

"No! Charles, please!"

He threw his arm about my shoulder and drew me to a window. Pointing over the snowy hills, he said, "In Oxford, or nearly, I imagine."

"Oxford!"

"He don't sleep as late as you, little dove. He was on his way frightfully early, so the groom tells me."

"But why?"

"He left a note stating he felt he must prepare for Hilary term and thanking me for my hospitality." Charles put a finger under my chin and asked sternly, "Did you scold him and send him away? Did you reject him?"

"No! I. . ." I recognized his teasing. "Charles Heathton, you are abominable!"

Chapter Seven

Not long after we returned to Oxford, I concluded Mr. Knight was also abominable. Never before had I known the intoxication of having a man adore me. I could hardly wait until we met again. However, he did not call. Two weeks passed before I encountered him at a rout.

I noticed him across the room. Without once glancing at me, he made his way through the crowd in my direction. What would he say? With spasmodic flutters, I fanned my hot face. If only I could conceal my agitation!

He spoke politely about my appearance, the bitter cold weather, and asked about my father's health. There was not the least hint of that wonderful passion I experienced at Rockivale!

So it continued throughout a dreary January. I became blue-deviled, snapping at Bessie, pouting towards Father, and even moody with Charles. Resenting his poor treatment of me, I decided to ignore Mr. Knight completely.

St. Scholastica's Day passed, leaving Father smugly pleased at the University's receiving with due ceremony the penance of the town. In defiance of the ancient observation, Amelia gave a ball, including both town and gown. Usually any event she presided over was exceptionally exciting. I found this one commonplace despite the presence of both Vice-Chancellor and the Mayor.

Suddenly I saw Mr. Knight but a short distance from me. Our eyes met. I walked away quickly, stopping to chat with Kate Williamson. Repeatedly I denied my impulses to speak with him. By the time the musicians struck up the final dance, the strain of avoiding Mr. Knight had produced a monstrous headache and I was near tears.

Needing to deal privately with my unruly emotions, I slipped off to a small, empty room. I paced across it, touching my handkerchief to my brimming eyes. That man was *so* provoking! My rigid corset prevented me from gasping in air and I resorted to panting to keep from sobbing. Dizziness attacked me, like a case of the vapors. Clenching my hands, I refused to faint.

Then a man's ominous footsteps came down the hall. Not wishing to see anyone, I kept my back to the door, pretending to study a small oil painting. The steps paused at the door, then whispered across the rug to halt behind me.

Earlier I had seen a strange man of forbidding countenance. What if he found me alone! My screams would not be heard above the music in the other room!

"Miss Castleton, are you all right?"

Mr. Knight! My cheeks burned. Common courtesy demanded I face him. "Yes." I turned slowly, opening my ivory fan and flipping it briskly. "Why, Mr. Knight! How came you here? I thought you were dancing." Not daring to meet his eyes, I concentrated on the square tabs of his cravat.

"I wished to speak with you."

"La, sir, we've been in the same rooms for hours! But then, you've been the constant center of attention." I waved my fan more violently, annoyed with my wayward tongue.

Calmly ignoring my words, he said, "Miss Castleton, may I call on you?"

I took a quick breath and involuntarily met his intense gaze. My fan fell with a soft thud on the rug. He bent to retrieve it. With determination, I directed my attention to his plain black shoes. It was impossible to carry on a lighthearted flirtation with this man. "You wish to call on me?" I whispered.

"Yes."

"I—I don't know." I could hardly banish him from my thoughts now. If I permitted him to call, if I saw him frequently, I should be lost. Mr. Knight was a sober, poor don, far too cool and reserved for me. I wanted a gay, wealthy, passionate lover. Yet, at Rockivale. . . Time. I must have time. "My father—you must speak to Father, you know."

"I have, some time past. He said I might ask you."

"Oh." I would refuse him. Anxiously I sought how to hurt him least.

"Miss Castleton."

In response to his voice, my eyes raised from his shoes to the skirt of his coat and up the long row of black buttons. I paused at his chest, then warily met his eyes. The passionate desire I saw sent a shocking tingle to my toes.

With a slight tremor in his voice, he repeated, "Miss Castleton, may I call?"

As in a dream, I answered, "I should be pleased to receive you, Mr. Knight—at any time," and extended my hand.

He lifted it and pressed his lips against my palm. When he looked down on me again, there was a light of triumphant pleasure in his solemn face and even the barest hint of a smile.

That very week Mr. Knight called, and as often afterwards as his duties permitted. Usually he and Father played a game of chess before Father excused himself to read or write. These games were the long, concentrated efforts of masters, with Mr. Knight often winning. After Father left us, he would patiently teach me to play. Gradually I became skilled enough to give fair competition. Much as I wished it, I never beat him.

At times Charles accompanied Mr. Knight. It was unsettling to see them together. Charles' manners and speech were increasingly affected, making Mr. Knight's reserve more appealing.

One afternoon, after I served them tea, Charles held up his wrist and pointed to the lace about it. "What think you? Is it decent or shoddy?"

I examined it. "Fine enough, I think."

"Enough? Enough for what? Now, compare *this*!" He gave me his handkerchief with a wide lace border. "Finer, isn't it? Of course it is. French. Duty-free lace is the *only* suitable lace. Blast, I don't see why those illiterate smugglers should have better taste than merchants! Perhaps one needs romance in the soul to be truly discriminating! I might make a good smuggler. What say you, Knight? With your brains and my dash, we would make a fortune!"

Mr. Knight shook his head. "I've too much interest in living to risk death merely for adventure or money."

"Pity your feet are so mired in the clay of the ordinary. You're far and the best swordsman in Oxford. We should be invincible! Ah well, what's to do? In a few months' time I will take my round of the continent. Knight, you should come as my tutor-companion. We could do such delightful things!"

Again my sober caller shook his head. "I must remain here throughout the summer."

"Your doctorate. Was there ever anyone so faithful to duty? I expect you plan spending all the time in the Bodlian! Are you bound to stay at Hertford 'til you die?"

Mr. Knight frowned. "I think not. Dr. Newton's ideals are worthy, but my Fellow Commoners leave me dissatisfied. They are pledged to enter the ministry, yet I cannot interest them in *reading* Law's *A Common Call*, let alone *practicing* it."

"A stodgy work at best."

"A challenging work. An attempt to put one's faith seriously into daily practice."

"La, Will, I've enough to do trying to put it into practice on an occasional Sunday. Why burden me more?" Charles sighed deeply. "I was thinking of going over to Bagley Wood and hunt some boar. Must remember to bring a copy of Artistotle. I've always admired that brave fellow who killed one by stuffing old Aristotle down his throat. 'Graecum est!' he cried!" Charles acted out the deed with a flourish. "Always wanted to do that, but never could remember the Aristotle."

"It may be just as well. If your boar was not as cooperative as the other, you might be in serious trouble. They can be ferocious."

"Oh, I know. But it would break the cursed boredom we have surrounding us."

To my concern, the energetic sparkle I found so delightful in Charles seemed dulled.

"Come, Knight, do one for us," Charles said, sitting up in his chair, ready to be amused.

Mr. Knight rose, puffed out his cheeks, fastened his gown over a pillow and went to Charles, peering down at him. With much ado he pulled out his watch, holding it at arm's length to read, then looked down at Charles who had begun to chuckle. In a tenor voice Mr. Knight said, "Aren't you late for the hunt, boy? Bad for health, sitting in these stuffy rooms."

Charles roared with laughter, bent double, slapping his knees. "Old Cragey to the life! Marvelous!"

Mr. Knight bowed. He unfastened his gown, tossed the pillow on the settee and donned his cap so the tassle danced near the tip of his nose. With his thumbs hooked into his waistband, he thrust his head far forward, squinted his eyes and rocked from heel to toe. "Don't think—hic—the Dean'd mind, d'ye?"

Again Charles howled his delight. "Bunnybear, exactly! Another!"

This time Mr. Knight began at the far end of the narrow room, walking towards us with the mincing gait of one wearing high-heeled shoes. He turned with a languid air, tapped an invisible walking stick on the ground, twirled an imaginary quizzing glass, then raised it to his eyes and surveyed Charles quite down his nose.

Charles stared at him baffled. "Some smart. Dashed if I know him."

I could barely suppress my giggles.

Dropping the quizzing glass, Mr. Knight flicked a speck from his cuff, then fell to examining the plain wrist of his shirt with great distaste.

I began to laugh.

Charles asked, "Do you know who he is doing? Is he some friend of yours?"

I nodded.

Mr. Knight came to me, and made a flourishing bow over my hand.

"*None* of my friends behave in such a silly manner!" Charles protested. "Who is it?"

"Charles Heathton!" I answered, gasping for breath.

"Me! No! You're hoaxing me! I *cannot* behave in such a way!"

" 'Tis you to the life," I assured him.

"My two best friends, and they think this of me!"

"One rarely sees himself as he is," Mr. Knight said. "I expect I should not recognize myself if you presented me most faithfully."

"That would be easy," Charles retorted. "I should merely pull a long face and prop a book in front of my nose! I cannot recall your smiling *once* in all the time I've known you!"

"I gather that is so," Mr. Knight agreed.

"And if you laughed, I think your face would crack in two!" Charles added sourly.

Mr. Knight's right eyebrow flickered as he answered, "I hope not. However, I shall remember that in the event I am tempted."

"O Will! Meg, was there ever such a complete hand?"

Certainly not one so baffling. Since he began calling, I found him considerate company, totally lacking in the fervor I twice glimpsed and now craved.

Father seemed preoccupied during his chess game with Mr. Knight. Several times he had to be reminded of his turn to move. Finally he leaned back in his chair, pushed up his glasses and tugged on his lower lip. "Sorry, Knight, I cannot keep my mind on the game. I concede to you."

"I've noticed you were not playing with your usual skill."

"I must speak to you about something that plagues me."

"What is that, sir?"

I rose to give them privacy, but Father motioned me to stay.

"What I've to say to Knight is also good for you. You know what I think about the Jacobites. Virtual traitors they are. And *dangerous* troublemakers.

"Look at those fools Dawes and Whitmore! Saying 'God damn King George and all his assistants. God bless King James the Third of England!' Of course young men will do foolish pranks. It's to be expected that wild oats be sown. But this! It's beyond reason! And now the Vice-Chancellor has been summoned to London and the whole University will fall into disrepute! No telling where this will end! And all for a lost cause! George II is the king. Prince Frederick will succeed him. No one can alter that. They only make trouble!" Father pounded the table, then continued, "What concerns me to-night is a more serious threat."

Mr. Knight and I exchanged puzzled looks.

"There is a sect, with roots here in Oxford, I am ashamed to say, which is gaining a disturbing number of adherents in our fair country. I feel obliged to warn you against it. Actually, not it so much as the error its leaders fell into." Father picked up his pipe and went through the ritual of lighting it and sending aloft the first puff.

"Enthusiasm. There is no place for enthusiasm in the pulpit or in the practice of religion. It is a disgrace to men and meaningless in the eyes of God. The emotional upheavals created by these Methodists are unbelievable and bring shame to our faith. And they do it in the name of Christ, which is really unforgivable."

Two puffs of smoke floated upwards while I tried vainly to recall hearing of this sect.

"Unfortunately, its leaders were once students here. Yes, John Wesley himself was a student at our own Christ Church. Further-more, he was a serious, outstanding student, such as yourself, Knight. So much so that the Rector of Lincoln had the poor judg-ment to ask him to become a fellow there. He still is, although not in residence, I am glad to say. Take this as a warning. If *he* could fall into serious error, so may you. So indeed may anyone."

Father tapped the stem of his pipe against his forehead. "It is the dedication of a fine mind that pleases God and brings Him glory, not the tears of a person foaming at the mouth and rolling on the ground in an uncontrollable fit of emotion.

"This afternoon we heard a report from one who has attended these meetings. I tell you, it breaks my heart to hear of the uproar they are creating about this land with their noisy preaching! Even *out-of-doors*! And to ignorant miners at Bristol! Little better than animals they are and black as niggers. Without doubt it is a work of the devil and in time will come to naught.

"Did you hear that man Wesley three years ago at St. Mary's?"

Mr. Knight nodded. "The church was full."

"Oh, yes. We all went there from our ancient halls of learning to hear him tell us we were nothing but a generation of triflers! Such ef-frontery!"

"But he was right, sir."

Father blinked at Mr. Knight. He pushed up his glasses slowly. "I should think it strange to hear you say that, one of the most serious scholars I have known."

"Sir, I came to Oxford to learn all I could. How many others do you know with that desire? Including the Canons at Christ Church?"

"Why, why there are many. You are not the only one in Oxford, you know. Why, I should think there are hundreds!"

"Then why has Dr. Newton such a difficult time enforcing sensible regulations to encourage study? Why does he face opposition on all sides?"

"He errs in restricting academic freedom. You cannot regulate the intellect, you know."

"In truth, these dedicated scholars engage in their intellectual pursuits at the Greyhound, the Ark, the Blue Boar, the Seven Deadly Sins, *any* tavern. They shun the lecture halls. Most prefer a morning hunt to a morning lecture. I think there is more dedication to the pursuit of pleasure than knowledge. In this, Mr. Wesley was correct in saying we are a generation of triflers."

"No! That man is *totally* in error!" Father shifted in his chair, gave Mr. Knight a long look, and cleared his throat. "Just because good port is served in a tavern is no reason to think that that place is bereft of knowledge. Why, with all the dons there, in a relaxed atmosphere of fellowship, ideas are freely exchanged. Gems of knowledge float around, easily picked up by inquiring minds. I should think it much after Socrates' way."

After a pause, Mr. Knight said, "I'll remember your warning against excessive enthusiasm, sir."

"Yes, well, I hope you do. This wild movement is wrecking our beloved church, cutting away the basis of our society, endangering our tranquillity of life. I should think it can only lead to the mire of iniquity! Now, Margaret, kindly take Mr. Knight into the drawing room for some refreshment while I get to my writing."

As we crossed the hall, I asked, "Do you think he has a new obsession? It would be a relief. I am sick to death of hearing about the Jacobites!"

"Possibly. This does seem to be a movement on the rise."

"Are they really so dangerous?"

"Without doubt, in some places they are shaking up the church. I do think it needs a shaking. It has become cold and dull, concerned primarily with the outward forms of worship. People need more. But fanaticism is not the way. I think William Law has the right approach in personal piety. Are you familiar with his *A Common Call* ?"

"No. I own I've read little lately."

"Perhaps sometime I may introduce you to it. It's not as dull as you might expect."

"Mr. Law. William Law. Father says he is a papist, wanting to undo the glorious Revolution and put a Catholic king on the throne."

"A non-juror, not a papist. It is his conviction we were wrong to place the Elector of Hanover on our throne. Therefore he refused to take the oath of allegiance to George I. For that failure, he may not be a curé of souls. But his political ideas do not enter into his great work on personal piety. The influence of that volume will continue long after we are all dead."

Would Mr. Knight could address himself to me as enthusiastically! His correct friendship was almost more than I could bear! Was my lot in life to be an eternal friend? Was there not one man, however unsuitable, who could form a *passion* for me?

Before retiring, I examined my reflection. Mr. Knight once said I was very lovely. He sounded sincere. There was nothing of loveliness I could see. A very ordinary face, and that marred by my turned-up nose. No wonder Charles and Mr. Knight treated me as a friend. If only I were a great beauty like Amelia!

I shared my frustration with her over a dish of tea.

"Meg, my dear, what does it matter? Mr. Knight is only a means to gain *Charles'* attention. After a few weeks, tell him you no longer wish him to call and Charles will step in. By then he will regret letting his friend take the position *he* should have with you."

"Do you really think so? At times I feel he is actually encouraging my relationship with Mr. Knight."

"Do you? No matter. Remember, a woman is *ever* so much more desirable to a man when *another* pays her court."

"Pays court! It is so mild a relationship, I'd hardly say that!"

"Nonetheless! Let me tell you about Mr. Simpson's family. Mother was *enchanted* with them last week. Even Father was impressed. He's always feared a fortune hunter grabbing my money, you know. No need for him to fear where Mr. Simpson is concerned. They are *immensely* wealthy!

"Why, their manor is nearly as grand as Bleinheim! Not as large, of course. The park is very nice in an old-fashioned, formal way. Oliver, Mr. Simpson, has marvelous ideas about modernizing it by adding a lake, with a stream of course to fill it, and a dear little house beside it, all pillars like in Greece."

I envied her confidence. Having achieved a degree of intimacy with the family in Berkshire, she could be certain Mr. Simpson would offer for her soon. Regardless what Amelia said, I did not feel my position with either Charles or Mr. Knight to be the least satisfactory.

Chapter Eight

One spring afternoon, Charles arrived while Father was out. He sprawled in a chair in the drawing room with the air of one who has drunk at the fountains of pleasure and found himself still thirsty.

"Meg, sweet dove, it's all such a blasted bore! So pointless," he drawled.

Having heard this before, I ignored it. "Charles, tell me of Mr. Knight."

"What do you want to know? He's the best man alive."

"In what way?"

"In every way! Why, before he went to Hertford, he was more useful than my man Tutley. He knows more about setting a wig, polishing boots, or ways to turn me out perfectly than most valets. I feel my appearance has definitely gone down-hill since he was elevated to being a Don, but there's no help for it. I must resign myself."

"Is that all?"

"Lud no! Nights I was down, he'd cheer me up. Whenever the Proctors assigned me lines of Virgil, he helped me. He was a better servitor than the others and complained less. In fact, I can't recollect him complaining ever. Between you and me, I was dashed relieved when he became a Don, even though it left me in Tutley's hands. One can't be seen with a servitor, you know; but there's no shame attached to being in the company of a Don, even if he is only at Hertford."

"Charles, you know how important clothes are. If you regard him so highly, why don't you get him to dress, at least for a ball? Couldn't you lend him one of your suits? I think you look to be of a size."

Charles laughed. "We are. Times out of mind I've scolded him and offered the choice of my not inconsiderable wardrobe. He's refused, saying he don't want to appear to be what he ain't."

"Except when he posed as a knight."

"Ah, that still chafes you sore, don't it? But you *said* you'd forgiven us our little joke." He twirled his quizzing glass on its ribbon. "Remember the ball at Rockivale?"

I nodded.

"I offered him my blue and silver suit. I even got him to try it on to prove it fit. You should have seen him! It suited him more than me. Actually, I'm glad he didn't wear it. Would have put me completely in the shade."

"I doubt that. Beatrice Exley found you fascinating."

"Beatrice Exley? Exley. No, she's Arthur's fiancée."

"That's Martha. Beatrice is her sister."

"Ah, yes, the child with bouncing yellow curls." He dismissed her with a wave of the hand. "I told Knight it was a crime for him not to wear it. A positive crime! He raised his chin in that proud way of his and he could've passed for royalty! I swear he could! He asked if you'd like him better that way. I said good clothes wouldn't hurt, that he'd quite turn your head looking like that. He said, 'Clothes do not make a man. She must like me as I am or not at all,' and took it off. Incomprehensible!"

"Does he ever speak of me?"

"Of course. He asked me to introduce you, didn't he? He's forever talking about having been here. I wonder he has time for his infernal studying. Tells me he even *walks* here! Frightful thing, walking. I don't know how I'd manage without my hack."

"Oh, Charles, don't! Please, tell me, you know, does he—does he like me?"

Charles flicked his lace handkerchief at me. "La, Meg, you're too serious. If Fate has willed you together, together you will be. If not, nothing you can do will bring you together. Enjoy life. Take what you can get. The laws of Fate are inexorable."

"Charles, please! Please *talk* with me."

"I am, my dove. You speak, I speak, we are conversing."

"No, you are playing. Tell me truly, does he, well, like me? At times I think he doesn't. Not really."

The ennui slipped from Charles as an unneeded cloak. "Love. Don't you mean, 'Does he *love* me?' "

"No, no," I protested.

"Nonsense, of course you do, and I approve. He finds you very attractive. He admires your spirit—your unconventional independence that's always gotten us into trouble. And, above all, being your father's daughter, you can talk with him. I don't know of any other female who can. You're confused because he tells you nothing. Do you remember that old poem of Sidney's beginning, 'Because I breathe not love to everyone'? It ends,

'But you, fair maids, at length this true shall find,
   That his right badge is but worn in the heart;

Dumb swans, not chattering pies, do lovers prove:
They love indeed who quake to say they love.'

Such is Knight. He loves and quakes to say he loves."

"Are you sure?" My heart was beating far too fast.

"As sure as I can be about another. Meg, I've said 'I love you' to many pretty girls. And each time I meant it. Yes, I *swear* I did. Yet, I've never known that love of poets, what Shakespeare called 'the star to every wandering bark.' " He sighed. "I'm a wandering bark without a star."

Once I longed to be that star! Now I enjoyed Mr. Knight's company more than Charles', even preferred it. Was I a fickle woman with emotions like a flighty bird unable to find a resting place?

The scandal created by Dawes and Whitmore hung like a funeral pall over Oxford. Social life vanished as dons were urged to insist their pupils dine in hall and to keep the coffeehouses under constant observation. Even private parties were proscribed. There was little to do unless one wanted to risk being sent down for attending some clandestine affair.

"If I were a man," I said to Father, "I would wager Dr. Purnell wishes he were only Warden of New College and not serving his turn as Vice-Chancellor this year."

We were at dinner after Father spent the morning working on a pamphlet defending the University.

"Humph! Not even Sims or Dillworth would take that wager! Dawes and Whitmore were drunk, and like the irresponsible boys they are, uttered treasonable words and started a fight. It should have remained at that and appropriate disciplinary measures would have been taken. This business of Blacow's taking deputations privately and refusing to be examined about them appears most peculiar for a Fellow with the interests of the University at heart."

"Why didn't Dr. Purnell receive them and not make such a fuss?"

"He couldn't. After three days, he couldn't accept those deputations. And that is another strange thing. Blacow *knew* they were late. I should almost think he wanted a visitation brought down on our heads! More fool he! With matters before the King's Bench, there's no telling where they will end."

"He's an ardent Whig, I've heard. Perhaps he seeks royal favor by exposing treason."

"We're *all* Whigs. Most of us, the ones that matter. Brasenose should cast him out. He has created a troublesome cloud about us we'll be hard put to dispell. You may be certain there is much rejoicing over this in the halls of that upstart, Cambridge. They toady up to the king in a disgraceful manner."

When the rains paused enough for the muddy streets to dry, Mr. Knight escorted me to the High, through the old East gate, past Magdalen's new buildings, beyond the majestic Founder's Oak to the lovely water walks. This being the sole amusement left to Oxford, everyone was there. I saw Amelia with Oliver, a glowing couple, engaged to be married early in June. All I could do was wave to them, the press was so great.

Leaving the water walks, we went to the less-crowded physic gardens. As we wandered about the paths, we encountered two of Mr. Knight's undergraduates.

One, a boy with pox-marked cheeks and soft brown eyes, stammered through a string of conventional comments. The other, tall, dark and with a haughty air, stood silently at his side, offering nothing beyond a greeting.

When we were about to part, the former said, "Miss—Miss Castleton, we have had the, er, the privilege of—of reading your father's works. I, we, Mr. Hammarsley and I, would like to—to meet him. Might, er, might we call on him sometime, that is, of course, if he is not otherwise engaged?"

"I'm confident he would be pleased to meet you. Perhaps Mr. Knight may bring you one Thursday and introduce you."

They hoped Mr. Knight would be able to bring them soon, bowed and left.

My escort stared at the path, then said thoughtfully, "Mr. Fuddleston has never had a speech impairment before, neither has Mr. Hammarsley been so reluctant to speak. You made quite an impression."

I laughed with delight. "Did I? How flattering!"

He regarded me with a puzzled frown. "I suppose it is. Mr. Fuddleston's family is of Bristol. They have made a great fortune in shipping, primarily slaving. He is the third son. Mr. Hammarsley is the second son of a baronet who owns a large estate near Lincoln."

"Why did you tell me that?"

"You should know they are proper young men with good prospects. Of course, being at Hertford, they are to enter the clergy, but I am certain their families will see that they have good places."

"You are very thoughtful," I answered tartly, nettled by his attitude.

He fingered a leaf. "Plants are so simple. They grow, produce flowers, berries, whatever, finally seeds and die. Even animals have little choice in their lives. But men. We must select from many possibilities. The right one is not always clearly evident."

"Does it matter? As long as one does his best, I mean?"

He looked at me thoughtfully. "Yes, it matters. God has a place for each of us. The best place."

"And being a don is yours."

"I don't think so. I need a sign."

"A sign? What sign?"

"I don't know. Something to assure me wherein lies God's place for me."

As I prepared for bed, I thought of Mr. Knight's wish for a sign. He took everything far too seriously. Perhaps he was dissatisfied with Hertford. Small wonder. It had no prestige. But then, if wealth was not his aim, as he claimed, what difference did prestige make? Could he be thinking of leaving the University? I'd heard adventurous students talk about going to the colonies, even as far as India. But Mr. Knight was not an adventurous young man. The very idea of his leaving Oxford made me excessively restless.

To calm myself, I turned my mind to the two young men. Too young, barely over twenty, I guessed. However, they came from families of wealth and position. There were worse places to live in than a parsonage in Bristol or Lincoln.

Why did Mr. Knight make a point of telling me of their prospects? Surely if he indeed loved me, as Charles said, he would want to keep me for himself and discourage all others.

I brushed my hair with angry jerks. Why was Mr. Knight so difficult to understand!

On Thursday next, Mr. Knight brought Mr. Fuddleston and Mr. Hammarsley to call on Father. After a short time in the library, they came into the drawing room where I was reading, and Father rang for Bessie to bring up the tea. Mr. Knight claimed urgent business at the college and left early.

The two young men, beautifully dressed and powdered, sat stiffly across from me, stumbling over the few words they spoke. While they praised Father's work, they watched me constantly. They sipped their tea and ate their cake as self-consciously as if attending their first formal tea. When they left, I burst into giggles.

"A severe case of calf love," Father announced solemnly, his eyes twinkling. "I should think they both suffer sorely."

"Are they likely to return?"

"Without a doubt. One who is ill must needs seek out his physician. In this case, you have the curative powers."

"Oh, Father, really! They are children!"

"True. However, I should think either would make a good catch. They possess all your heart desires—wealth and position."

Stung by his words, I withdrew. True, they had what I wanted, but they were not what I wanted. And what was that? I could no longer define it confidently or clearly, even to myself.

Sunday was warm and bright with a light, freshening breeze. Mr. Knight called in the afternoon and suggested we walk a short distance about Oxford. We strolled down the lane, my plattens slipping and clattering on the cobblestones. As we crossed the High, Mr. Knight steadied me while I lifted my petticoats and stepped over the kennel of refuse down its middle.

As we entered Cat Street, he commented, "There is an inescapable haunting of the past in Oxford."

"What do you mean?"

"St. Mary's beautiful spire has been pointing to the heavens for four hundred years or more, so they say. Wycliffe preached there, no doubt contributing to his martyrdom. There Cranmer found the courage to deny the document he signed recanting his faith." He nodded to the stern walls of All Souls College. "They still pray for the souls of Henry V and those who fell in the French wars. And over at Brasenose, everyone taking a degree must swear never to give lectures at Stamford or to attend them."

"Why not?"

"They say ages ago some students stole the knocker whence came its name, taking it up there to start another college. I suppose they even think they may get it back some day."

"There's the new too," I countered. "Nearly every college has something of recent date, some quite beautiful, as those." I pointed to the tops of All Souls twin towers appearing above its walls. "And that thing too," I indicated the round Radcliffe building opposite us. "That is, if they ever finish it. Imagine a building so large for just one room! No wonder they call it the 'Mausolaeum.' Father thinks Mr. Gibbs lost his mind to design a structure that doesn't fit with anything else in all Oxford."

"The Sheldonian doesn't fit in either."

"I know, but Wren was a genius. Father is not at all convinced that Gibbs is. In a city all towers and spires, he thinks that dome is out of place."

"They've been working on it since before I arrived. Now they're talking about dedicating it come the fall. Would you like to see the view from above? The stairway is open."

"Oh, yes!"

Climbing the winding staircase made my legs ache. My petticoats weighed more the higher we went. Finally we emerged through a little turret onto the gallery. I waited there leaning on Mr. Knight's arm, my heart pounding, my face hot. He steadied me as we cautiously crossed the slatted flooring to lean on the balustrade facing All Souls.

How magnificent were the towers, rising from their oval quad! The forebidding walls of New College rose behind them and farther away sparkled glints of the Cherwell and soft bluish hills against the sky. In every direction were slanted roofs, treetops and chimney pots. It was thrilling to be among the spires and pinnacles I'd looked up to these many months!

I leaned over the parapet to see two small gownsmen with fluttering black wings on the street below. Suddenly the height overcame me and my stomach became my sole concern, threatening to turn inside out.

Some way Mr. Knight brought me down the stairs onto solid ground. Without commenting on my embarrassing reaction, he waited patiently for me to regain my composure before we resumed our walk. Silently I vowed never again to subject myself to a fearful height.

In an effort to pretend nothing extraordinary had occurred, I pointed at Hertford beside us, shabby in comparison to its surroundings. "Do you think it will become a great college some day?"

"Not like Christ Church. Perhaps like Corpus. Hertford provides a place for a serious student to learn. There may not be enough serious students for it to continue. I don't know. We've only been in existence a little over seven years."

"I wish you were in another college."

He guided me up Broad Street. "Oh? Where would you prefer?"

"Christ Church, Magdalen, University. University was founded by King Alfred himself. Why not one of those with a great tradition or prestige? From there you could gain a substantial preferment, become a person of importance. Even wear lawn sleeves some day."

"And wealth?"

"What have you against wealth? I think much is right with it."

"It doesn't necessarily bring happiness."

"Perhaps not, but it makes life more comfortable. And look at the good you can do. Dr. Radcliffe must have been tremendously rich to leave money for a huge building like the 'Mausolaeum.' And there's the Clarendon and the Sheldonian over there. Nearly every important building in Oxford's come as a result of someone's great wealth."

"It does good or ill, depending on a person's degree of selfishness. The wealth I've seen has bred arrogance and cruelty."

We passed Trinity's wrought iron gates and paused at the eroded walls of Baliol. "Out there, across from Baliol's gates," he said, "three great men were burned to death. Their convictions clashed with the established wealth and power. I wonder if the Master watched from His windows. He would not forget that sight quickly. The full cost of a man's faith is his life."

I shuddered at the thought of men being burned alive. "Not everyone dies for his faith."

"Then he must live it, far more demanding than dying."

I tugged on his arm. "Please, let's go back. The Borcado's up there. It gives me the shivers thinking of those criminals."

We retraced our steps, leaving the miseries of present and past.

"I sometimes think we are never free of what has gone before," Mr. Knight mused.

"We *must* be! I don't want to continue respectable and poor!"

"You would rather be disreputable and rich?"

"No, of course not! Isn't it possible to be respectable and rich?"

"Yes. It is possible."

"You say that like—like you don't believe it."

"Do you remember what I told you about my . . . family?"

"Yes, I remember." I pressed his arm at the tender memory.

"I spoke of a boy, my half-brother."

"Yes."

"He came to Christ Church while I was there."

"Really! Did he know you?"

"No. He said I reminded him of someone he knew, but he could not recall whom. I recognized his name, of course. He was one of the students I was to call of a morning."

"You were his servitor?"

"Yes. He studied little, drank much, and chased petticoats without caution. Once I lent him money to get out of a scrape."

"You did! You're impossible!"

He looked at me with mild surprise. "What do you mean?"

"Why help *him*?"

Mr. Knight frowned. "At first I thought it was no affair of mine. But he bears a strong resemblance to our father. And I was reminded I once promised him to look after the younger ones. This was my first opportunity. We almost became friends. There was a fight that grew into a riot and he was sent down in disgrace. He never returned to take his degree."

"I suppose you bowed and scraped to him and called him 'M'lord.' "

"As a servitor I neither bowed nor scraped to anyone, but, yes, I called him 'M'lord.' He does have the title. And he is very wealthy. He pursued happiness and caught frustration.

"Soon after Father's death, the boy's mother remarried," Mr. Knight continued. "His stepfather was very partial to his sister. My mother thought the girl was not Father's child, but a neighbor's who called often. Perhaps she was right. My grandmother made many people unhappy through her insistence that my father marry the boy's mother."

"If I had wealth, I should let my children marry whom they would!"

"Even someone beneath their station? Someone you thought was using them to better themselves?"

"I wouldn't want them to be used, of course. But I would not oppose a marriage if their affections were engaged."

"And what of yourself? Will you marry only if your affections are engaged?"

I thought of Charles. "No." I sighed and answered glumly, "A man will offer for me. Father will approve. I will marry him and—and I hope we shall be agreeable."

"You do not think you could become fond of such a man? Dr. Castleton has your interests close to his heart."

I blushed, recalling my foolish words at the masquerade.

"Do not look so downcast, Miss Castleton. It is quite possible for your affections to become engaged . . . again."

Thank heavens we were at my door and I was saved from the necessity of replying!

During May, Father became very active in the defense of the Vice-Chancellor who was to face prosecution in London for mishandling the Dawes-Whitmore affair. Most of my time was spent with Amelia, helping her prepare for her wedding. She particularly wanted me to do much of the embroidery on her new clothes, both because she admired my work and because it would be a tangible reminder of our love for each other.

She came upon me in her garden bright with tulips, weeping for the emptiness I saw ahead. Sitting beside me, she put her arms around me. "Meg, dearest, you mustn't miss me too much. When we set up our establishment in London, I shall ask you to come up for the next season. I shall make certain you go to the proper places."

"Oh, Amelia, you are sweet, but I couldn't intrude."

"It would not be an *intrusion*! I have had a season there, and should find it frightfully boring without having you to introduce. There will be dozens of *suitable* young men, and perhaps a handsome one will offer for you, and then we will live there *together*!"

The picture she created was appealing. We whiled away many hours adding to it until, I am sure, it bore no semblance to reality.

Amelia's wedding in All Saints' was the most magnificent that money could provide. Crowds of town people came to see the daughter of one of their leading citizens marry the son of an important peer. The dinner afterwards at her home was held among huge bouquets of hot house pink-and-white flowers I had arranged. It had been a final labor of love. I was pleased at the effective background the massive sprays created for this loveliest of brides.

I tried not to cry as I watched their carriage, followed by two others filled with baggage and personal servants, disappear up New Inn Hall Lane. In my mind I followed them down the High, past Magdalen, over the Cherwell and—I felt a light touch on my shoulder.

"Miss Castleton."

Recognizing Mr. Knight's voice, I greeted him, grateful for a distraction.

"May I procure a chair for you, or would you prefer to ride home?"

Oh, to ride! Mentally I raced across fields and jumped fences, and. . . "Thank you. Amelia instructed her coachman to drive me home."

He glanced up at the clear sky, then said, as if reading my thoughts, "It is several hours until dark. I'll bring riding horses for you and Bessie to your home shortly."

"How delightful!" I looked over the remains of the wedding party, certain I would not be missed. "I'll leave immediately."

Bessie complained, not liking to ride, but I convinced her she would enjoy it on this lovely day. I was wearing my riding dress, watching out the library window, when Mr. Knight rode up Magpie Lane on Khan, leading Sultan and his own docile mount!

Calling for Bessie, I ran eagerly down to the gate. "I cannot believe Charles let you have *both* his pets! He must have been foxed!"

"He knows I will take good care of them." Mr. Knight lifted me into Sultan's saddle with ease, then assisted Bessie to mount.

We trotted briskly through the traffic on the High into Butcher's

Row and around the ruined castle to Fisher's Row. Ragged children dashed out from squalid cottages to chase us. Drab women looked after us sullenly. With a shiver, I thanked God I did not live in St. Thomas' parish. Turning on Higthe Bridge Street, we reached the Botley Causeway and crossed it at a quickening pace.

The road before me beckoned irresistibly. I took a deep breath. Free! Leaning forward, I gave Sultan his head, paying no heed to Bessie's protesting cry. He galloped down the road, passing plodding country folk and empty farmers' wagons returning from market.

The wind whipped my hair into a tangle and blew my mind clear. I forgot about everything save the rhythm of Sultan's hooves and the rushing road. At last I was alone, all cares far behind.

There was a shout behind me. Looking over my shoulder, I saw Mr. Knight gaining on the distance between us. Sultan's strides slowed as the road wound up a hill and Kahn pulled abreast of us. I was glad Mr. Knight was not one given to useless chatter, permitting the peace of the woods to surround us. Bird songs rose and fell, weaving delicate melodies over the silence.

From a point on the crest, we stopped and looked back. Oxford's spires rose from golden mists, sparkling like precious jewels. Silver rivers branched around her. Hayfields interpersed with meadows spread below the hills.

From below us Bessie called and Mr. Knight answered.

"Lot's wife was turned into a pillar of salt for looking back," I commented.

"Are you fleeing a catastrophe also?" Mr. Knight asked.

Without answering, I nudged Sultan forward, off the road into a clearing. Deep wheel ruts cut the grass. Rubbish and bright rags lay in clumps here and there.

"Gypsies often use this as a camp," Mr. Knight explained, dismounting. After setting me on the ground, he walked Kahn and Sultan to keep them from chilling.

Bessie soon joined us and cast me an angry glance. We had exceeded what she considered a reasonable ride.

"Let Bessie lead them," I said. "They shouldn't give any trouble now."

Idly I shoved at some rubbish with my foot.

The snap of a whip, a man's cursing cries, the thuds of hooves, and the creaking rumble of a carriage caught my attention. A coach passed going towards Oxford, turning my thoughts to Amelia and Oliver. Perhaps they were stopped at some inn for a rest. Oh, that I could be as fortunate as she to ride beside a handsome, wealthy man who adored me! Unwanted tears filmed my eyes.

Mr. Knight pulled me into the circle of his arms. My head rested against his shoulder. Giving in to my emotions, I wept. He stroked my hair, brushing it away from my temples in a soothing manner. Then his warm hand rested on the nape of my neck.

His strong fingers emphasized my weakness. Tingling, frightened, I tensed. What was he going to do? To my dismay, I discovered I was yearning for him to do something!

He released me. "Are you all right now?"

I nodded. Uncontrollable shaking seized my limbs.

"Did you bring a cloak for your mistress?" he asked Bessie.

"Yes, sir." She brought it to us and he placed it around my shoulders.

"I think she has taken a slight chill," he said. "We had best return home."

We went down to Oxford at a dignified pace. All the way I pondered that moment of intimacy, my lonely envy forgotten.

After Mr. Knight departed, Bessie sought me in my room, a troubled frown creasing her forehead, her hands twisting her apron. "Ma'am, begging your pardon, but did Mr. Knight say or do anything to make you cry up there on the hill? I swear I didn't know what to do. I know I was along to protect your reputation and all, but I didn't know what to make of it."

"No, no. I was crying because I will miss Miss Forsythe very much."

"And—and when he—"

"It was all right," I said impatiently. "He was merely trying to comfort me as—as a good friend."

"It had me worried, ma'am, but he is such a fine gentleman, I—"

"Put it out of your mind." I spoke unusually sharply. "We may expect Dr. Castleton very soon. Is the table laid?"

She turned a bright red and curtsied. "Yes, ma'am. I'll go down to the kitchen." She bumped against the table, jarring my flowered pitcher and bowl as she rushed out. I heard her fairly running down the hall to the stairs.

Going to my mirror, I brushed my fingertips from my temples into my hair, then gingerly touched the back of my neck. The memory was thrilling! There was more than friendship in his touch. If he had offered for me at that moment, I would have accepted eagerly. I needed him then. But *not* in the future!

I wanted a lover of fiery passion and great wealth. And, yes, wealth transcended passion. A life as the wife of an obscure clergyman, scrimping on the edge of starvation, was not for me. Mr. Knight posed a threat. If I accepted him in a weak moment, I would lose any chance to live as I dreamed.

A dull canopy of clouds hung from west to east when Mr. Knight next called. I poured tea in the drawing room before the fire. The cheerful flames banished the melancholy atmosphere.

As we visited, I recalled my experience on the hill. I must ask him not to continue calling, but how? He was too kind to be hurt thoughtlessly.

"Something troubles you, Miss Castleton. Would you share it with me?"

I stared into my cup, watching a floating bread crumb.

"Have I offended you?" he asked.

"No, oh, no. Of course not."

He joined me on the settee and took my hand, shaking my resolve. "Please, be frank with me. I will not take offense."

"You are always so kind and thoughtful, so polite, yet so, so *impersonal*." My voice quavered. What was I saying! His *personal* attention created my problem.

"As you know, I have neither fortune nor name. My position as a tutor at Hertford is available only as long as I remain unmarried."

Biting my lips, I tried to regain my composure. Those ill-spoken words sounded as if I *wanted* him to make an offer!

"I cannot think any woman would look with favor on me," he continued. "She would be quite right in thinking me mad if I made an offer."

Withdrawing my hand, I exclaimed, "Yet you waste hours here!" Could I not control my tongue? Each time I spoke I became more involved!

"I had not considered it a waste of time."

My heart beat faster at the warmth in his voice. "It—it keeps you from your studies," I blundered on, "which, as you have pointed out to me times out of mind, is your—your *chief* concern until you pass your doctoral examinations."

He sat quietly a moment, gazing across the room. I saw his jaw muscle flex and his lips press together. "Yes, you are quite right. I have been neglectful of my work of late. It awaits me even now." He placed his half-full cup beside the teapot and rose. "Thank you for your hospitality. Please pay my respects to Dr. Castleton." He bowed and kissed my fingertips. "Good day, Miss Castleton."

When his steps paused partway down the stairs, I rose impulsively to stay his departure, spilling my untouched tea into the saucer and down the hem of my petticoat. His steps resumed. The front door closed.

I felt no sense of satisfaction in disposing of a threatening problem, only a great loss.

Chapter Nine

To fill the void caused by Mr. Knight's absence, I indulged in flirtations with Mr. Fuddleston and Mr. Hammarsley. The latter was the more handsome, the former more witty. Both were terribly immature and unpolished. I found even Mr. Fuddleston's amusing patter did not lift the odd heaviness weighing upon me.

Bessie was late bringing up the warm water for my morning wash. I scolded her at the top of my voice until tears quivered in her eyes. After she escaped in an awkward rush, Father tapped on my door and timidly opened it.

"I thought I heard the sounds of altercation. Nothing serious, I hope."

"Bessie just brought my water! I intended going shopping early. She has delayed me at least half an hour by her laziness!"

"Did you tell her you planned to go out early today?"

"No. I did not decide it until I woke early this morning. I slept poorly."

"Then she could not possibly have known to bring it up."

"She should check. She is lazy, careless, a poor housekeeper. Yesterday I found dust to write my name in on the drawing room table. What will people think if they see that?"

"Did you dust it?"

"No! One ruins servants if one does their work for them. I wish we had a better one. We really need a cook to prepare decent meals. A French cook."

"You know that is not possible. Perhaps you could give Bessie a hand so she can do her work better. She is a good, conscientious girl. If we lost her, I don't know where we'd find one as good."

It was not the least consoling to know he was right. Defiantly, I tied my hat strings and left.

Nearly every step of the way to the Carfax, I was haunted by a tall, sober man. When I passed All Saints, Amelia's wedding, followed by those beautiful moments on the hill, came vividly to mind. I tried to concentrate on the shopping I wanted to do.

Either the shopkeepers did not have what I desired or the items were outrageously dear. Finally, I purchased a length of satin ribbon to keep the trip from being a complete loss.

At home, I looked at the ribbon's bright green color, the one Mr. Knight preferred me to wear. Angrily I thrust it to the back of a drawer.

After dinner I moped about. Although I tried to settle down with a book or my sewing, memories of Mr. Knight continually plagued me. I had not seen him for two weeks. Surely this malaise would pass soon. I should have sent him away long ago, before he became a habit. I *must* put him from my mind!

The doorbell was pulled.

I dropped my sewing and ran down the stairs. As I reached towards the doorknob, I realized I hoped to see Mr. Knight. Firmly I resolved to send him away, then opened the door.

Charles swept me a deep bow. "Come riding with me, my fair dove."

"Oh, Charles! I should *love* to! Did you bring a horse for Bessie?"

"No. Just my pair. I thought she could not keep up with us. Do you think your father will mind?"

"No! You're quite right. We'll have *much* more fun without her. Come in. I'll change in a wink."

Father gave his consent to my hasty request without interrupting a stroke of his pen. Bessie expressed concern over my going off unattended, but what did a stupid serving girl know?

Slowly we rode through Cat Street and north past Wadham. Glancing up at its tower and tall chimneys, I noticed the sun, bright in the morning, was hidden behind dark clouds. Surely it would not come on to rain before we returned for tea!

We broke into a gallop on reaching the Parks, then veered eastward through newly mounded haycocks in the general direction of Headington. Distant grumbles of thunder sounded as we climbed a hill. Black clouds covered the sky. Below a ray of light fell on Oxford and moved slowly across its spires.

"It looks like a magic city, a dream city!" I exclaimed. Then I was struck with its similarity to that day on the hill I wished to forget.

"Funny, Knight called it that a few days ago. He said it was a city of many dreams. Men see them here. Some realize them; for others they fade into gray shadows."

"Let's ride." I kicked Sultan with my heels, starting down the far side. Charles cantered by my side, then burst ahead, leading me in a

merry chase along winding paths and through fields. I became confused quickly. Perhaps we might be lost together! A pleasant idea.

Suddenly Sultan stumbled and slowed. Immediately I pulled him
up and shouted after Charles. He rode on.

I dismounted and led Sultan a few steps. He favored his left fore-
foot. Talking soothingly to him, I ran my hand down his leg and
lifted his hoof. A sharp stone was wedged in the tender center. I tried
unsuccessfully to pick it out with my fingers. Probably Charles could
remove it when he came looking for us. Even then, Sultan should
not be ridden. The best I could do was turn around and head back
the way we had come.

The air chilled and the wind increased, tugging on my cloak.

In a few minutes I heard Kahn's pounding stride overtake us and
Charles jumped down beside me. "Sultan went lame on his left fore-
foot," I explained.

He examined the injury, then carefully pried out the stone with
the point of his dagger. "He can't run now. Up you go on Kahn."

I pointed out that his saddle was unsuitable for me.

Charles looked at the sky. "We don't have time to change them.
Raise your dress high, little dove, and swing your leg over. I won't
look, pon my honor."

I hesitated at being so unladylike. A splash of rain on my cheek
forced action. Once in the saddle, I tucked my petticoats around me
as when I was a child and we walked across the field towards a gate.
As we passed it, the scattering drops became a shower.

Charles swore.

Not one piece of blue sky was visible. A boiling cover of blackish
gray stretched from one horizon to the other. I pulled my cloak
tightly about me, thankful Bessie insisted I wear it instead of my
lighter one. I had been unreasonable of late.

Charles shouted and pointed to the left.

"Where are we going?" I asked pulling abreast of him.

"I noticed a house and barn over there earlier."

We cleared a rise and saw buildings below through heavy rain.
He motioned for me to ride on ahead while he followed at a run
down the grassy slope.

No light shone from the windows of the stone cottage. As I approached the front, I saw the roof had sunken in. Poor shelter that. I
turned Khan towards the barn, also built of stone. It looked secure
enough. With difficulty, I dismounted, catching and tearing my petticoat on the saddle.

Holding Kahn's reins, I pushed open the door. Its loud screech
spooked Kahn, who nearly upset me with his sudden lunge.

The interior was only half-sheltered, there being a gaping hole in the roof. Gently I coaxed Kahn to enter and waited for Charles.

He was badly muddied from several falls. A quick tour of the barn and he declared it adequate for our needs. Using his dagger, he made a cut to guide the water pouring through the roof out the door. The rest was fairly dry save for scattered leaks.

We shook our wet cloaks and spread them to dry. Fortunately they had not been soaked through. Although cold, we were mostly dry. With handfuls of old hay, we rubbed down the horses, talking to calm them while thunder crashed above our heads. When it moved away, we settled to waiting.

The storm showed no sign of ceasing. Early dusk dimmed to early night.

I sat on a pile of hay, running my fingers through my hair. How fortunate I sent Mr. Knight away. The dreams I nearly surrendered would come true, thanks to this lucky happenstance. Everyone knew no young woman's virtue was safe with Charles. After a night together, unattended, with my reputation ruined, he *must* marry me. How much should I resist his advances? Nervously, eagerly, I wondered what it would be like.

Charles spread my cloak over a mound of hay. "Come on, Meg. We'd best sleep. In a few minutes we won't be able to see anything." He sat down and tugged off his boots.

I looked at him dubiously. This was not the invitation I anticipated.

"It's all right. The hay's soft. I'll put my cloak over us. We should be quite comfortable."

Gingerly I followed his instructions, gathering my petticoats close to me.

Charles arranged his cloak across our feet. "Lay down," he commanded. I obeyed and he carefully covered us.

"Meg."

"Yes?" My heart skipped a beat.

"I talked with Knight the other day."

"Oh." Was that man's specter never going to leave me?

"I was shocked when he told me you did not wish to see him again. Is that right? Did you truly *intend* to send him away?"

"Yes."

"And I thought you were well suited, the best girl I know for the best man. You're wrong, Meg. He's stuffy at times, but as steady and loyal as they come. I know you've completely won his heart."

"Please, I'd rather not talk about him," I mumbled, breaking into a sneeze.

"As you say. Lud, but I'm tired!"

As if to prove his words, he was soon snoring. I lay still, stiffling sneezes, weeping, listening to the steady rain and the rustling rats.

Charles shook me awake. "It's stopped. We should leave as soon as possible."

I rose, finding I had more aches than I thought possible. In the morning half-light, I helped saddle the horses. Just as the dawn broke with a washed and sparkling sun, we rode them out.

As we sloshed down the muddy path, Charles whistled a merry tune that grated on my ears. We came on a road and followed it to the London road.

To relieve Sultan of my weight, Charles hailed a farmer who let us ride atop his load of vegetables with the horses tied to the back of his wagon. The trip jarred every bone I possessed. The driver's ceaseless mourning over the damage done his hay by yesterday's storm did nothing to raise my spirits. He took us to the stable where Charles rewarded him handsomely. The man pulled his forelock, gave me a knowing wink and leering smile and departed.

After tending to Sultan's foot and seeing both stallions properly fed, Charles hired a carriage and drove me home.

Bessie greeted us with a cry of relief and summoned Father.

He came to the head of the stairs and stared down at us. His stern voice halted my upward rush. "Margàret, go to your room!"

Stung by his tone, I edged past him. I paused at the bottom of the next flight, straining to hear what he said to Charles. In spite of the disappointing night, this might yet work to my advantage.

"I am waiting, Mr. Heathton!"

"I'm sorry, Dr. Castleton, but Sultan went lame and we were caught in the storm yesterday."

"Where did you spend the night?"

"In an old barn some distance off the London road."

"In a barn!"

"Well, sir, the house had no roof, but the barn did. Partly. Meg may have a sniffle from this, but I don't think her lungs will be inflamed. I took the best care of her I could."

"And who was with you?"

"No one, sir. Remember, we went riding alone."

"I see." There was a long, uncomfortable silence. "Well?"

"I, I don't understand, sir."

"You took my daughter out riding *alone*!"

"You gave your permission, sir."

"You spent the night with her *alone*. Slept with her! You debauched my daughter and you say you don't understand?"

"Debauched! Sir, I did not touch Meg! Pon my honor!"

"Honor! Your reputation belies you, young sir!"

"Dr. Castleton, sir, I have known Meg for—for *years*. She is as precious as a sister to me."

I nearly choked on his kind words.

"I cared for her as best I could with the little we had. In no way has she been dishonored."

"You think so lightly of her and of me that you would shame her name and not offer for her hand?"

"On the contrary, sir, I regard her so highly I would not bring her a life of misery because of a lame horse and a night of foul weather."

"A life of misery. You are consigning her to just that!"

"Not at all, sir. Meg is worthy of better than me. My eye roves too much to give her the happiness she deserves."

"I do not argue with you there, sir, but better than you will not offer after this night. By your irresponsibility you condemn her to a spinster's life! If I were a younger man, I would demand satisfaction from you!"

"But the University regulations—"

"The regulations be damned! My daughter's *honor* is involved!"

I could not bear to listen to anymore and ran to my room weeping. If Charles was convinced he would do me a disservice by offering marriage, no person, no reason under heaven could move him.

When Bessie brought up a tray of food, she found me weeping. Trying to offer comfort, she assured me that Mr. Charles, being a fine gentleman, would surely honor his duty by me. Knowing otherwise, I cried the harder.

Empty days dragged by. Charles did not venture to the house, doubtless avoiding Father. Neither Mr. Fuddleston nor Mr. Hammarsley called. If only I could talk with Amelia, she would spread the word that I was not a loose woman. But she was somewhere on the continent with Oliver. Fearing insults from the bolder Undergraduates, I dared not venture beyond my garden.

The ban against social affairs was lifted for the balls during the week of the Act, but few invitations came to me. I refused all lest I be subjected to snubbing. Sitting at my window, I listened to the bells, voices, music, remembering the annual pageantry, trying to imagine Charles taking his degree.

By the end of the week, my spirits were their lowest. I went into the garden where boredom had driven me to weeding, and attacked a small plot, stripping it methodically. A shadow fell across the ground. A pair of shining boots stood beside me. Charles!

I stood and he clasped me in his arms. "Has it been bad for you, my dove?"

I nodded.

"We had a splendid thing at the college. Yet, amid all the laughter I thought of you, here, alone. And I was saddened."

His exaggerated expression provoked me to laugh. "Charles, you did not!"

"No, I did not, but I thought I should say I did. Now, with a smile, you look far better. Do you understand why I can't offer for you? Why I shouldn't?" he asked earnestly.

I shook my head.

"Father arrived a few days ago and has given me no peace, lecturing me on what I should do. Several times I almost weakened, but I have remained steadfast. It is for both of us. We would not be happy, you and I. Our affection for each other is that of children. You deserve something richer and more lasting." He lifted my chin to look into my face.

"In time people will forget. A fine man will discover you are as wonderful as I know you to be. He will offer for you and you will be happy."

"Oh, Charles, I am alone! I have no friends! Not one!"

"This will pass. I know it will. I brought you this as a symbol of my regard." He gave me a box containing a silver circlet set with tiny diamonds. Clumsily he fastened it to the kerchief at my neck. "There. Think of me kindly, little dove."

I touched it gently, unable to speak for conflicting emotions.

"I'll write of my adventures."

"When do you leave?" I whispered, feeling an agonizing wrench.

"Soon. Today."

"Where will you be going?"

"Oh, Brussells, Paris, Versailles, into Italy, maybe Spain," he answered gaily. "Perhaps even to Hanover to see what our mighty monarch finds worth defending there."

Tears overflowed my eyes.

Charles brushed them away with his handkerchief. "Believe me, Meg, when I return, all this will be past and you will be happy." He kissed me tenderly and left.

Sobbing, I pressed his circlet on my breast.

I moped through the next weeks. For lack of anything better, I copied some of Father's pamphlets for the printers and wrote letters for him. At least those dreary penmanship lessons at Mrs. Spinet's were useful.

My twentieth birthday arrived. I was an old maid. Life had passed me by.

All Father's energies were directed towards absolving the University of any taint of Jacobitism, allowing no thought for my misery. In August he announced he was going up to London and would be back in about two weeks.

"Take me with you!" I begged.

"No. I am part of a deputation. We must see the Vice-Chancellor and give him moral support. It is imperative that we demonstrate to the Crown and the government that the University stands behind Purnell. We intend using every means possible in his, in our defense. There is a powerful move to discredit the University through him."

"Please. I'll not be any trouble!"

"Nonsense. You'll want to see the sights and we shall be too busy.

"But, Father. I shall be completely alone!"

"I should think you would realize, Margaret, I am not going for my amusement. This great University, the greatest in all the world, the product of centuries of scholarship, is being threatened by men of high ambitions and low morals." He paused, adding severely, "Your irresponsible behavior has brought about the rejection of your friends."

"We had no choice. Sultan was injured and the rain had come on heavily. It was too dark to see our way."

"You should have stayed with a farm family."

"We could not find one. We took what shelter we could find."

"You could have continued looking."

"And I might have died with inflamed lungs!"

"I know your fondness for Charles. I've no doubt you rejoiced in the excuse the rain provided. I should think a time of solitude will do your soul good."

Oppressed by the heat, I stared disconsolately at the embroidery in my lap. For the best part of an hour I had not taken a stitch. What was to become of me?

Taking Charles' letter from my bosom, I read it again. Plainly written to amuse me with his misadventures in travel, it emphasized my dejection.

Bessie burst into the drawing room, flushed, panting, her cap askew and her apron twisted to one side. "Mr. Knight has just driven up outside, ma'am!"

"Mr. Knight!" I jumped up and rushed into the library to look out to the front. A carriage stood there, the driver slouching on his seat as if for a long wait. The bell was pulled. "Mr. Knight came in that *carriage*? You must be wrong!"

"Yes, ma'am. I saw him step down. All the world knows Dr. Castleton is in London. He must be here to see you."

"Yes. I'll receive him in the drawing room, of course."

"Begging your pardon, ma'am, but you must change. He's dressed the finest I've ever seen him."

I glanced at my soiled petticoat. "Oh. Yes. Show him up, then come to help me. Only straighten your cap and smooth your apron first."

Quickly I ran up to my room. Green. He liked me in green. I laid out a pale green quilted petticoat and an emerald dress with white floral sprays. Bessie arrived to lift the gown over my head and brush order into my curls, then went to prepare a tea tray. I located the new ribbon in the back of my drawer and fastened it on my best lace cap. He was right. This was the most becoming color with my auburn hair.

I reached for powder to tone down my excessively high color, then paused. It would not do for him to realize I had taken such pains with my appearance when I had sent him away.

With an unhurried pace, I entered the drawing room. Bessie had not exaggerated. Mr. Knight was crisply immaculate. His black suit must be new or nearly so and his snowy shirt was faultless.

"Good afternoon, Mr. Knight. What a pleasure to see you. I am sorry, but Father is away to London."

He bowed low. "Good afternoon, Miss Castleton. You are very lovely."

His sincerity warmed me and I felt a lightness missing these many weeks. "Thank you, sir. I'll ring for tea."

After instructing Bessie, I turned to my visitor. What errand could be so vital that he hired a carriage? Seeing my embroidery in a heap where it had fallen from my lap, I sat in my chair, picked up the material casually and began stitching.

Superficially, no disruption in our friendship had occurred. We chatted about the weather and the University's dilemma should Dawes and Whitmore, now free on bail, come to Oxford. While he seemed solely concerned with this trivia, I found it difficult to refrain from asking his purpose in calling.

I poured his tea, using the scanty amounts of milk and sugar he preferred, and was pleased to note an approving twitch of his eyebrow. His presence was very, very comfortable.

After Bessie removed the tea things, he said, "Miss Castleton, would you, and your maid, of course, give me the pleasure of your company for a drive? I have a carriage in front for your comfort."

"A drive? I shall be delighted! But first I must change into something appropriate."

"No need of that. We are not like to be gone long. I merely wish to show you something." His hazel eyes were bright and an unusual flush touched his cheeks.

"To show me something? How delightful!"

We rattled down the Lane and turned westward on the High. The aquaduct figures were striking as we veered around it and past the ancient, rugged Carfax tower. My curiosity grew as I saw St. Peter's in the Bayly and the little houses around the moat of Roger d'Oilgi's ruined castle from the window.

Mr. Knight said nothing. We crossed several bridges spanning the Isis and continued to St. Thomas'. There Mr. Knight handed me down, then Bessie. I surveyed the churchyard, trying to fathom his purpose in bringing me here.

"Did Dr. Castleton tell you I have taken my degree?"

"No! I heard not a word! Congratulations, _Dr._ Knight!"

He colored deeply. "I am resigning as a tutor at Hertford."

I gaped at him. "This is a day of surprises indeed. I have not heard anything of your activities these two months or more." I looked over the little graveyard, then up the uneven stone walls of the church to its flint roof and the top of its square, battlemented tower. "Are you the curate here?"

He nodded. "Sunday next I preach my first sermon."

"I am so happy for you!"

We passed under the archway of the south porch into the sanctuary, deteriorating through neglect. I remembered Father mentioning that the previous curate was so interested in hunting and fellowshipping in the taverns that the parish had had little care.

"It's quite old. Dates from around 1140 when King Stephen besieged the Empress Maude at the castle."

"And she escaped over the snow?"

"Yes. The people here used to worship at St. George's in the castle. As they couldn't during the siege, they petitioned for a church. At first it was named St. Nicholas. Later it was named for St. Thomas à Becket."

Leaving Bessie to read the inscriptions on the monuments in the church, we crossed the churchyard to the stone and timber rectory.

"My home," he announced, throwing open the door.

The rooms echoed barenness. Instantly I imagined them with a table, chairs, a bench—no, a settee—and, of course, bookshelves. Mentally I placed his desk in a corner for his studies and a bright rug on the floor. Upstairs I found rooms furnished with rolls of dust. I hurried down to the kitchen and began examining the cupboards. "This is a charming place!" I paused to peep through a dining room window at the weedy garden bursting with growth.

"Miss Castleton." He spoke from across the room.

I whirled around. "Yes?"

We faced each other several heartbeats before he continued. "Miss Castleton, will you share this . . . as my wife?"

"Your wife? Here?" I saw myself preparing a meal, picking lovely flowers in the garden, the two of us sitting before a bright fire, he with a book, I with my sewing. After weeks of loneliness, facing the fact that Charles would never marry me, this quiet life held strong appeal.

This man loved me. Father said some day he could become a bishop. Bishops were wealthy, with beautiful homes. What would Father think of my marrying him? Did he know Mr., no, *Dr.* Knight was some earl's illegitimate son? "Have you asked my father?"

"Yes, long ago."

"Long ago?"

"When I asked his permission to call on you."

"Oh." I clasped my hands nervously, staring at a crack between the floorboards. "Have you—have you heard about my tarnished reputation?"

"Yes," he said quietly.

"You warned me not to be careless. I did not heed your warning." Might this glimpse of tranquillity be shattered as my other dreams? Anxiously I looked up. "Do you really want *me* as your wife? Father says I am debauched, hopelessly outcast. Would I be right for a vicar's wife?"

"Miss Castleton," he shook his head, "you have never been debauched."

"How—how do you know?"

"I know you, and I know Heathton."

"That is why they say I *am* ruined!"

Again he shook his head. "Will you marry me?"

At last someone believed me! "Yes! Oh, yes!" Impulsively I ran to him, vaguely expecting to be swept into his arms.

Instead he cupped my face in his hands and gazed intently into my eyes. "You will?"

"Yes, yes. I will."

With great tenderness he kissed my lips, then in passion he held me against him, his lips firm against mine. Stiff with surprise, I felt his passion flow around me. Fire ran through my veins. When he released me, I stared at the blaze in his eyes. "Is . . . is that the way a man kisses a woman?"

"Would you prefer I kissed you so?" He placed a discreet peck on my lips accompanied with a restrained embrace, then stepped back to observe my reaction.

Blood rushed to my cheeks. Dropping my gaze from his face, I whispered, "No."

Again he kissed me with ardor, lifting me off my feet in his intensity.

This time I relaxed, yielding to the pressure of his arms and lips, clinging to his coat. Strange, wonderful sensations filled my body. "And I thought you cold and indifferent!" I gasped.

"Did you indeed?" He bit my ear lobe lightly and kissed the curve of my neck. "Believe me, my dear . . . Meg, I have never regarded you with either, only the *warmest* feelings." Then he added, "Promise me, please, always to speak the truth with me. Under all circumstances."

"Yes, always."

"Next Sabbath our bans will be posted."

"Next!" I drew back to see his face. "I cannot be ready so soon! Father is not here."

"He will be. No doubt he has wondered at my delay. Think carefully, my dear. Do you truly wish to live here? We will probably never have a finer house. The life of a parson has few prospects."

"I was raised in a vicarage."

"I have no powerful friends, and I shall seek no important appointments. My ministry is to the poor."

"It doesn't matter," I answered rashly.

"Next Sabbath our bans will be posted," he said in a voice that precluded argument. Taking a small silver coin from his pocket, he placed it between his teeth and broke it. One half he placed in my hand. "A token to seal our engagement."

Father returned Saturday. He was removing his coat when I told him of Dr. Knight's offer and that our bans would be posted the next day unless he disapproved.

"Humph! You sent him away and all that trouble over young Heathton. He still offered? I should think I'd have no objections! No, none at all! There's not a finer man in all the kingdom!"

On a glorious September day, with the bastings barely out of my new dresses, I met Dr. Knight before the cathedral altar. Dwarfed by the vaulted ceiling, awed by the priest intoning my binding vows, I pledged myself to the solemn man at my side.

Chapter Ten

My new husband carried me over the vicarage threshold. He shoved the door shut and kissed my breath away. "Margaret Knight. We are home."

Stunned by his sudden display of affection, I watched him remove his coat and vest and hang them on a hook by the door. Seeing him in shirt and breeches, I felt embarrassed. Nervously I untied my bonnet and glanced about the drawing room.

Father's deep old chair stood out from the few furnishings in dear familiarity. As long as I could remember, it had been part of my home. Near it was a chair of Dr. Knight's and a small table and chair from Father's house. A similar mixture stood in the other rooms. And a large bed waited upstairs. I swallowed and looked at my husband, then blinked in shock.

He was smiling! Radiant joy transformed his features. He seemed taller, his shoulders broader. "Come. I have some wine in the kitchen." Taking my hands he led me there and poured two glasses. He raised his to me. "To you, to us, to children, to a full life, to joy unbounded!"

I repeated his words slowly, as if making a solemn vow.

After we drained our glasses, he laughed! "Your eyes are huge! You stare as if I were a stranger!"

"You—you are! You've always been so—so cool, so distant. You have changed, Dr. Knight."

He touched my face gently. "Call me Will. Say it. Say my name."

"Yes, Will." I forced a smile.

"We are both different. God has joined us together, and we two shall become one flesh."

I trembled, expectant and a little frightened.

"As in the Song of Songs, I am yours and you are mine . . . forever and ever."

I woke to sunshine in a strange bed. I was married. Dr. Knight and I. *Will* and I. Astonished happiness washed over me. Had he really carried me up here and loved me with a vital, earthly passion? Had he really *laughed*? "Life has been called a 'vale of tears' by some, but I find great joy in that vale as well," he had said.

Will raised to an elbow and leaned over, kissing me with loving tenderness.

"Is this a beautiful dream?" I asked.

He smiled, his face glowing as he caressed me. "It is real."

Deeply content, I lay in his arms. Reality exceeded the best of my dreams.

"Come, my wife, the day is upon us." He rose and pulled me up. Placing a kiss on my forehead, he said, " 'This is the day that the Lord hath made. Let us rejoice and be glad in it.' Can you start a fire and prepare something hot to break our fast?"

"Yes. Bessie taught me," I answered.

"Good. I feared I might need to instruct you." He pulled my laces tight and lifted my petticoats over my head. As I was about to descend the stairs, he said, "Would you set on water to heat, dear? Cold water is fine for washing, but I prefer hot for shaving."

While he dressed, I bustled about carrying up his hot water, heating chocolate and toasting bread. Bible in hand, humming a tune, Will joined me. I poured the chocolate in mugs and set the toast on pewter plates.

"This morning we will sing the 96th Psalm," he announced.

"The 96th Psalm!"

"You do know it?"

"I've read it. You said *sing* it?"

He opened the Bible and held it for me. "We will sing it together. In plainsong. Mr. Law has rightly pointed out that you may *like* a psalm when you read it, but you must sing it to *enjoy* it."

"But—but the food will get cold!"

"Then we will warm it again." With his arm about me, he selected a pitch and began, "O sing unto the Lord a new song: sing unto the Lord all the earth."

The rich tones of his voice drew me into joining him, timidly, then with more assurance. By the closing lines of the psalm, it was truly a hymn of joy.

Will burst into laughter and I did too, being uncontrollably happy. He took me in his arms and prayed, "Father, God, how we joy in Thy great goodness! How we thank Thee and praise Thee for blessings beyond measure! Guide us that we may use this day to Thy glory! Bless this food that we are about to partake of, that it will nourish our bodies. And thanks be to Thee, O Lord, for uniting us as man and wife! Amen." He kissed me, then sat down.

I started to sit also, then remembered to warm the toast over the fire.

As we ate, Will methodically outlined his day. Until dinner he would be working in the study. In the afternoon he would make parish calls in preparation for reopening Coombe's school in the stone house near the church. When we finished, he bowed his head, giving thanks for the food and imploring God's guidance and care for the day.

I began my first day as a housewife with enthusiasm. Fortunately Bessie had planned a week's meals for me, telling me everything required and giving details on where and how to purchase my supplies. In the afternoon I served tea to two shy callers, farmers' wives, bringing gifts of cheese and butter.

As the shadow of St. Thomas' fell before our door, Will returned to a supper of hot soup. He had found a general indifference to his efforts to teach the poor children of the parish. I exerted myself to cheer him.

We drew the drapes over the windows and sat before the drawing-room fire, Will in Father's chair cuddling me in his arms. A phrase from some psalm came vividly to mind: "My cup runneth over."

I rushed through September, marvelling at the depth of my happiness and trying to behave properly as a curate's demure wife. The people of the parish accepted me without either warmth or hostility. Free of the tensions and uncertainties of the University, I found security in the rectory.

At first novel, Will's continual piety gradually became disturbing. At times I resented his daily disciplines. However, I did not voice my complaints as our devotions were not too onerous, being mostly joyous shared moments.

One evening as we sat on the study floor before the fire, Will took my hands and played with my fingers. "I do not think you are at ease during our times of worship. Do you not enjoy them?"

"They are so different. In Father's house we had Bible readings only on saints' days, for serious, soul-searching."

"Did you search your soul?"

"No." I chuckled at the memory. "I sat holding my mouth in a straight line, thinking of other things. I rarely paid heed to the reading. Was that sinful?"

"Do you think of those things now?"

"No." I remembered my promise to be truthful. "Well, sometimes. But not often."

"Do you enjoy our worship?"

"I—I'm not sure. I keep feeling I shouldn't."

He brought a small, worn book from his desk, and lying beside me read, " 'A dull, uneasy, complaining spirit, which is sometimes the spirit of those that seem careful of religion, is yet of all tempers the most contrary to religion, for it disowns that God which it pretends to adore. For he sufficiently disowns God, who does not adore him as a Being of infinite goodness.' "

Looking at me with a smile, he explained, "That is from Law's *A Serious Call*. What can give a person greater happiness than the confidence that God is good? To be sure we should sorrow for our failures and misdoings. But when we worship, we should rejoice in His character and His blessings. Think of the frequent calls in Scripture to rejoice, to clap our hands with joy!"

"I haven't heard those parts."

"We often sing old hundreth. 'Sing to the Lord with *cheerful* voice. Him serve with *mirth*, his praise forth tell; come ye before him and *rejoice*.' Saint Paul wrote to the Philippians from a Roman prison, 'Rejoice in the Lord alway: and again I say, Rejoice!' You see, this transcends our circumstances. Do you like singing the psalms?"

"Oh, yes! Especially when we burst into laughter at the end. I thought it irreverent at first."

"But it is natural, isn't it? An overflowing of joy."

"Yes."

He flipped to the first page of the little book and read, " 'Devotion signifies a life given, or devoted to God.' " Closing the volume, he added, "That is my aim. It includes *all* my life, my serving the parish and teaching, my study, my eating, my rest, and most of all, my relationship with you." He pulled me down for a kiss.

Shortly after Michaelmas term opened, during Father's weekly afternoon visit, he erupted into curses against Dawes and Whitmore.

I jumped and stared at him, shocked.

"Forgive my language, my dear, but my feelings are *very* strong."

"So I gather. What has happened?"

"Those—those impudent young—*fools* started another riot! Right outside Balliol's gates! And this time they recruited others. Some fifteen or twenty. I urged that they *never* be permitted entrance into this town again! They are bent on causing nothing but trouble!"

"What was done about them?"

"Oh, Leigh's expelled them. He was *furious*, I can tell you. Ironic that the Master of Balliol, Whitmore's own college, should be acting for the Vice-Chancellor. They'll not be out on bail so soon this time. In fact, their trial comes up within the month. I should think they'll draw a hard sentence for their irresponsible actions!"

As Father lectured about the University and its difficulties with the Crown, I slipped into thinking of my astonishing husband. Always precisely correct when others were present, he became completely unpredictable when we were alone. Emotions he had restrained many years seemed to burst all bounds.

Arriving from parish calls, he would catch me around the waist for an embrace. Sometimes he sat in Father's deep chair, pulled me into his lap, and told me of the people he had seen or the children in Coombe's school. Then he catechized me on my day, praising my small victories in learning to keep our house. Other days he swung the pot away from the kitchen fire and carried me upstairs for delightful lovemaking.

I thanked God our tranquil life was safe from the University's violent troubles.

As the air grew crisp, I became acutely aware of our straightened circumstances. The tithes were only partially paid and Will refused adding to the burden of poverty by pressing his parishioners for the rest. Therefore we possessed little more wood for burning away the chill than in the summer.

I learned to hoard stubs of sanctuary candles, melting them to make new ones for our home. Using an old cover and blue muslin Father gave me, I created a warm quilt for our bed. Each day I spent long hours scrubbing, while I wished for a servant. We ate fairly well on the cheapest of foods, supplemented by vegetables the former curate planted in our garden and eggs I gathered in our hen house. But I longed for a better life.

As I sliced bread and cheese for our supper, I paused to examine my rough hands and broken fingernails, embedded with garden dirt. Last summer they were soft and pretty. If I was with Father, Bessie would do the scrubbing and I would not be digging in dirt or feeding chickens and the pig Will expected to butcher soon. Amelia and Kate did not do such things. They picked flowers and commanded tasty dishes prepared for them. I was not a lady. I was merely the discontented wife of a poor clergyman.

Will entered the kitchen and circled my waist. He kissed and caressed me as on countless other days.

"Oh, take your hands off me!" I exclaimed. "Must you be forever touching me? Just because we're married is no reason to be less the gentleman!"

His face deathly white, Will held my shoulders a moment, studying my angry face. I saw his eyes cloud, his mouth tense, and his right eyebrow flicker.

Although guilty at hurting him, I choked back words of remorse.

He dropped his hands. "Very well, my dear. Call me when the meal is ready." He went to the study and shut the door.

As usual, we sang a psalm before eating. It sounded like a dirge. Will's prayer was cold, of formal words. In talking of parish affairs, his manner continued politely detached. All evening the icy barrier remained.

When I announced I was retiring, he replied, "Good-night. Sleep well. I intend studying a while longer."

In our bed, thinking of Will, I realized our happiness was as fragile as the beautiful moonlight spread across our new blue quilt. Never should I have spoken so. When he came, I would crawl into his arms, explain my discontent and beg his forgiveness. Slowly the moonlight gathered out the window, leaving the room black. Would he never come?

Unable to wait, I slipped from bed and felt my way downstairs.

Will sat at his desk, reading by the light of two candles.

I touched his shoulder, feeling his muscles jerk. "Will."

He turned calmly. "Yes? I thought you asleep, my dear." Once again he wore his old expression betraying neither pleasure nor annoyance.

"I could not sleep. Aren't you coming up?"

He consulted his pocket watch. "I'm accustomed to studying later."

"You'll be tired tomorrow."

"I'll do very well. Lay down and relax, Meg. You'll soon go to sleep." With a nod of dismissal, he resumed reading.

I watched him make a note on the paper beside his book. Defeated, I turned away. My rash words made us both unhappy. At the door I looked back. "Will," I called softly, discarding my pride.

After a pause he answered without looking up. "Yes?"

I ran to him, kneeling at his side. "Forgive me, please."

His eyes remained on the printed page. "For what? You spoke the truth, as you promised. That is nothing to forgive."

"For speaking a *partial* truth, and hurting you."

He cleared his throat. His eyebrow twitched; his fingers tightened on the quill, whitening his knuckles. "A partial truth?"

"I was—I was unhappy with—with everything. Like Israel in the desert, I've been murmuring all day. So I snapped at you. When I saw how I hurt you, I repented, but I couldn't bring myself to explain."

"I have made too free with you, and I am sorry."

"No! No! You have not. I—I *like* you to touch me. You see, I've found—I've found giving you pleasure gives me pleasure." My face was hot as I whispered, "I *want* you to touch me."

After several moments, he gazed down on me. His hazel eyes seemed to penetrate my being as if he were weighing what I said.

Impulsively I rose, flung my arms around his neck and kissed him. I released him immediately, embarrassed at taking this unusual initiative and feeling no response. "Oh, Will, can you not smile? Have I forever ruined everything?"

"Forgive me, my dear. I am stunned!" He moved back from the desk and took me into his lap, leaning his forehead into the curve of my neck. "Meg, I thought *I* had ruined everything, demonstrating my affection too freely!" He relaxed with a shudder, as if freed of a heavy burden.

"Oh, no! I *crave* your affection! I could not sleep for want of it."

He kissed me again, then raised his head, his eyes shining. With one motion I was eased from his lap and he stood up. "I will repair the situation immediately." He blew out one candle, gave me the other and picked me up.

"You blew tallow on your book," I scolded, nestling against him.

"Good. It will mark my place."

Chapter Eleven

Christmas Eve we were to be with Father. This was the most festive occasion since our marriage, so I decided to wear my green silk with Charles' emeralds. I would powder my hair with wheatmeal and look quite the lady.

Will came upon me as I was stepping outside. "Aren't you getting ready?" he asked, frowning at my old manteau.

"Of course," I laughed, kissing him. "I intend to powder my hair, and I must do it outside, or you could not *breathe* in the house."

He held me close and kissed me again. "I would prefer you *not* to powder. Your hair is far more beautiful in its own rich color."

"But powdering is more elegant and fashionable," I pouted. "I suppose you also prefer me not to paint!"

"I like you better without it."

"Whatever did you think when we met at that first ball?"

"I resolved to dance with you once only."

"But you did not. You reappeared at my side all evening."

"I could not stay away. I remembered other times I'd seen you free of paint and powder."

"If it pleases you, my dear husband, I'll not use them again."

"And would you please wear the blue gown you wore last year?"

"I thought you preferred me in green!"

"I do. However, that dress has pleasant memories."

As I fastened Mother's diamond pendant about my neck, I hoped Will would like the heavy gloves and scarf I'd secretly made for him. It had become so cold these last days, I was tempted several times to give them to him early.

We exchanged gifts in the drawing room hung with holly, ivy and mistletoe. Father gave me a sturdy pair of boots. "The country around St. Thomas' is beautiful for tramping around, but you've nothing suitable for your feet," he said. "You must take some walks, especially out Osney way."

"I will," I promised, scanning the pages of *The Compleat Housewife*, a gift from Bessie. Well she knew I needed its advice.

Father was pleased with the pen holder Will had carved, and Bessie was happy with the shawl I'd knitted.

Will put on his new gloves and pronounced them perfect. Then he presented me with a small package.

I unwrapped a leather box. Inside, sparkling against black velvet, lay an exquisite pair of diamond earrings.

"They were Mother's, the last of her jewels," he explained.

"Oh, Will, they're so beautiful!" Quickly I fastened them to my ears and jerked my head to feel the dangles swing. Dots of color danced wildly on ceiling and walls. Delighted, I kissed Will heartily. "Thank you, my dearest. I *love* them!"

January clasped us in a cold embrace and generously sprinkled snow over Oxford. Constantly aware of the pinch of money, I often thought enviously of Amelia and Oliver, now in London. What they spent on one ball would keep us comfortably many weeks.

One night Will arrived late for supper, looking exceptionally tired, his nose and cheeks stung bright red. He kissed me warmly, then went to the bubbling pot over the kitchen fire. "Is it ready?"

"And extra good. Thornton, the butcher, gave me a meaty knuckle."

"Tonight is a fine night for fasting," he announced.

"What?"

"The Widow Langford has not one thing to eat. Not even for her two children. Hasn't for several days." He spied a loaf of bread waiting to be cut. "And they could use this too."

"But—but what will *we* eat?"

"You do not eat when you fast, m'dear," he said gently. With a thick pad, he picked up the pot, then tucked the bread under his arm. He hesitated at the door. "Have the water boiling for tea when I get back, please. That is permissible."

The kettle was steaming and I was weeping when he returned.

"Meg, you should have seen their faces! They blessed you for your kindness." He placed the emptied pot on the hearth.

"I'm hungry!" I wailed.

"I too. Think, dear," he took my hands in his. "We shared a delicious meal this noon. They have not eaten for days!"

"It has meaning to fast on a holy day. But this!"

"It is written in Isaiah, 'Is not this the fast that I have chosen? to loose the bands of wickedness, to undo the heavy burdens, and to let the oppressed go free, and that ye break every yoke? Is it not to deal thy bread to the hungry?' And he adds later, 'And if thou draw out thy soul to the hungry, and satisfy the afflicted soul; then shall thy light rise in obscurity, and thy darkness be as the noonday.' I am confident God is more pleased when we fast that one in need may eat than when we fast merely because of the calendar."

Taking the teapot to the fire, he filled it and set it aside to steep. "Come, we shall be very comfortable," he said coaxing me to the table.

I sat, rebelling silently.

"We have so much happiness, you and I!"

With a start I realized I had only been considering what we *lacked*.

He began singing, " 'O praise the Lord, all ye nations: praise him, all ye people!' Meg, you must sing too."

Reluctantly I joined him with, "For his merciful kindness is great toward us: and the truth of the Lord endureth for ever. Praise ye the Lord."

As we sipped our tea, Will smiled, scattering the last of my resentment. "I used to think I was born to endure sadness and pain. With you, Meg, I've found joy!"

"Tell me about your mother. Was your father already married when they met?"

"No. He was a student at Christ Church. She lived here, in Oxford. After he took his degree, he married her secretly, knowing his family would oppose them as she was not of the gentry. Her father was a shopkeeper. They lived a short time in a little house near St. Ebbs before going home to face the storm.

"His parents were furious. They had arranged a marriage with a neighbor's only daughter to unite two estates and create a sizable fortune. My grandfather had a stroke and died. My grandmother berated my father, now the earl, with his father's death and made Mother's life miserable. She was skilled at making others miserable."

"Couldn't they leave?"

"Father wanted to. He threatened going to the colonies. Mother dissuaded him. She missed her family and thought he would later regret leaving his for her. As the marriage was secret, pressure was brought on my parents, forcing them to agree to having it dissolved. Father would marry as arranged and Mother would remain in the household as a seamstress. Some months later I was born."

"I wonder if she regretted not going to the colonies."

"I'm sure she did."

"What was her name? Does her family still live here?"

"I don't know. As long as I can remember, she spoke of her father as being dead, and never mentioned her mother. I think they disapproved of the arrangement."

"How could she agree to it?"

"Mother was a giving person, sweet and pliable. Father was kind and strong, but no match for my grandmother. She was a fierce tyrant.

"How she hated me! We met in the garden one day. She threw her fan at me in anger, then demanded I pick it up and hand it to her. I refused. She called for someone to thrash me, but no one came. Not willing to demean herself to pick it up, she had to leave her fan on the path. Before we parted, she said, 'If only you were Sophy's, I could love you. You're so much like me.' Sophy was Father's wife. For years I was terrified of growing to be as hateful as Grandmother."

I covered his hand with mine. "If she was such a tyrant, I can see the resemblance. You are too, at times, but not hateful."

I was immensely proud of the way Will conducted services. He expounded the Scriptures with authority. Rarely did I hear his words or attend their meaning, having learned as a child not to listen while sitting in church. My interest lay in enhancing his appearance.

With care, I mended the least tear in his robes and kept his surplice snowy white. And I hoarded small coins. After months of saving, I purchased a length of very fine French lace and sewed it to the hem of his surplice.

Surprised when noticing it the next Sunday, Will asked, "Is it so important to you that I wear lace?"

"Of course. All proper clergy do."

It puzzled me that his improved appearance did not afford him the gratification I felt.

The second Tuesday in April, Will hired a boy to ring St. Thomas' bell at noon to welcome the trustees of the Radcliffe library to the week-long festivities marking its opening.

As I listened to the bells of Oxford proclaiming this event in friendly dissonance, I hoped Father would be pleased. He set much importance on this week, confident the visiting dignitaries would demonstrate much needed public support for the University. I was content to remain in the parsonage, away from the crowds and long, boring speeches.

Of greater interest to me was a letter from Amelia. Lately she had written of boredom with the endless gaiety of London and homesickness for Oxford. This one began, "The best of news! I am breeding! Our son will be born in the fall. We are both delighted and Oliver's parents are ecstatic over the advent of an heir. We are not even considering the possibility of a daughter!"

I put the letter down and gazed out the window. Beautiful Amelia and handsome Oliver soon to become parents. They had everything! Will and I heartily desired a child, but there was not the least hint of one.

Going to my dresser, I drew out a vial hidden under some clothes. A thoughtful parishioner had given me water from St. Frideswide's holy well at Binsey. It was said to make one fertile, and hundreds made pilgrimages there every year. I looked at it doubtfully. It must be effective if so many believed in it. Quickly I pulled the stopper and swallowed the liquid. A son, I thought. Will must have a son. Perhaps this magic water would cure whatever prevented me from conceiving.

When the spring weather permitted, Will and I took long walks together. The boots Father gave me were perfect for our invigorating tramps. One such time we crossed plowed fields to the ruins of Osney Abbey.

Awed by their melancholy dignity, I ran my hands over the weathered stones. "How old are these walls?"

"About 300 years, or more. The priory was founded a few years before St. Thomas', by the young d'Oilly."

"So long! People used to gather here for worship, didn't they?"

"It was the cathedral. The bells still ring at Christ Church."

"Once grand and beautiful, now plundered and ignored. How sad. Since these were fitted together, generations have lived and died. Do you think anything we will do, you and I, will last so long? Or will we moulder in a forgotten graveyard, leaving barely a trace?"

"I'm not an architect, and buildings seem to last longer than most things." Will turned to look at Oxford's sparkling spires partially dulled by a dark cloud above. " 'Except the Lord build the city, they labor in vain that build.' Our work is with people, people who die in a few years. In that sense nothing we do will have any great permanence. Yet they possess immortal souls. If indeed I am doing God's work, the effects will be more permanent than the Egyptian pyramids."

"If ? As a priest of the Church, can you question that you are doing God's work?"

"I am working *at* it. But whether I am doing what He wants me to do in the place where He would have me, of that I have no great certainty. I long for the calmness of soul that must come with the confidence that one is truly doing God's work. Oh, Meg, how I *long* for a sign!"

"What do you mean by a sign? Do you want a prophet's declaration or a startling display in nature?"

"I don't know. Something that validates my ministry deep in my soul."

"Could I be your sign?"

He stared at me with a thoughtful frown, then took me in his arms. "No. You are a cherished part of my life, an unexpected joy, but not God's sign."

"Your people love you. Many have told me your teaching and preaching have strengthened their faith as none other in their memory. Is not that enough?"

Will looked down with a wistful smile. "Perhaps it will have to do. I may be as the Pharisees, seeking a sign when Christ himself was doing miracles before them."

"This whole quiet countryside speaks to my soul. Its peace seeps into the core of my being."

The cloud passed overhead, dousing us suddenly. Will pressed me into the shelter of the wall, spreading his cloak to cover me. We crouched there through the shower.

Although brief, the rain transformed the fields to sucking mud. Despite my boots, walking was a tremendous struggle with my heavy petticoats. Will scooped me up and headed home.

"It's too far for you to carry me!"

He laughed. "You're a pleasure burden."

Not once did he pause on the way, nor was he excessively tired when he set me down at our door.

The following day, as I started to leave the butcher's, my way was suddenly blocked. An undergraduate faced me, feet planted apart, hands in his pockets, head tipped to one side.

"You must be Miss Castleton," he declared, adding with heavy sarcasm, "I am *honored* at this fortunate meeting!"

"You err, sir. I am Mistress Knight."

He glanced uneasily at the gownsmen beside him. One replied, "Be that as it is, you're Castleton's daughter. I seen you with him."

I said nothing.

"Well, are you?" the first persisted.

Pretending boldness, I answered, "What concern is it of yours?"

"She is, or she'd tell you."

"I'll wager she's trembling in her shoes."

"Madam, your father was instrumental in the disgraceful treatment of our friends. He helped imprison them for a bit of innocent fun."

"Name these abused friends," I demanded, my heart pounding.

"Mr. Dawes and Mr. Whitmore, two fine gentlemen."

"I see." My stomach felt about to turn inside out and the young men seemed to sway before me.

"We'll just teach your father a lesson through you!"

"If you touch me, Mr. Thornton will come to my aid!" I clutched my basket, trying not to faint.

"Ha! That old goat's too afraid of what we'd do to his shop!"

"And you will answer to my husband!"

"Who's he?"

"Dr. Knight, the vicar of St. Thomas'." Speaking his name gave me courage.

"A parson! We're to answer to a parson!" They howled with laughter. "He'd be afraid of his shadow!"

"And I shall complain to Dr. Townson, the Senior Proctor. If you were associated with Dawes and Whitmore, you will be sent down in disgrace should you do anything drawing his attention."

They backed off, slightly surprised.

"Step aside. You're blocking my way!" Feigning disdain, I passed them, my petticoats brushing their silk gowns. What might they do? Students had broken into people's homes on several occasions. I continued buying bread and soap, trying not to reveal my quaking.

Although it was some distance out of my way, I went to the gates of Balliol and asked the porter to see Dr. Leigh. Knowing Father, the Master appreciated my concern, and assured me the proctors would pay special attention to the area around St. Thomas'.

At home, I broke into tears and ran up to our bedroom. Facing eastward, I shook my fists at Oxford, crying, "That wretched University! Leave me alone!" Shocked at my outburst, I fought to control my emotions, telling myself it would likely come to nothing. When I was calm, I decided not to worry Will with the incident.

More important was the suspicion these last days I might be breeding. In another month, when I was certain, I would tell him. I blessed the dear soul bringing me the Binsey water and planned a gift of appreciation.

We were about to retire when there came a pounding on the door. My thoughts leapt to the terrifying scene at the butcher's. When Will rose to answer, I reached out to prevent him, but words stuck in my throat.

Two drunken gownsmen burst into the drawing room. One pinned Will's arms while the other made for me.

I fled around the little table to evade his lunge. No possible weapon was within my reach.

Feinting one way, he reversed, catching my hand before I could dodge his grasp. He jerked me towards him into a swirl of blackness.

A pungent odor and loud voices invaded my consciousness. Will, his face ashen, slowly passed a smoking quill beneath my nose. The Senior Proctor peered anxiously over his shoulder.

"There, she's responding nicely, Dr. Knight," he rumbled in his deep voice. "Only a faint. Females have that tendency. I must say she had ample reason."

I was lying awkwardly on the settee. Will helped me into a sitting position and Dr. Townson sat beside me.

"Better now, ma'am?" He flicked a speck of dust from his purple velvet sleeve. "Sorry to be so late. They eluded us near Quaking Bridge, and we lost time looking in Fisher's Row before coming here."

"It's just a flesh wound, sir," announced one of his Bulldogs from the far corner.

"Flesh wound? What's happened?" I asked.

Will gave me a glass of wine as the Proctor answered. "Two young fools, Bassingwell and Stokebrook, attempted to molest you. Your able husband successfully defended you with Bassingwell's own sword. Lucky for you they ignored the regulation against wearing swords."

"Thank you," I said. "Thank you for saving us."

"Glad to be of service, ma'am. However," he winked at Will, "I gather our intervention rather saved Bassingwell. Quite ferocious you are, sir. I suspect they failed to realize that Dr. Knight of St. Thomas' is also the Black Knight who set this University on its ear over one Mr. Walton some time past.

"I assure you, these young . . . gentlemen will give you no further difficulty. We desire no troublemakers in the University at this time." Dr. Townson rose and nodded to each of us. "Your servant, ma'am. Evening, Dr. Knight."

As Will saw the gownsmen out, I finished the wine, gaining strength from its effects. I heard the bolt slam on the front door.

Will came to kneel before me and grasped my hands.

"Oh, my love," I exclaimed, "once again you have been my champion!"

He bent, placing his face between my palms. "God forgive me," he whispered hoarsely. "I nearly killed that man!"

Word came from Bishop Potter, requesting Will to wait on him.

To me, this could only mean Will's ability was recognized with the offer of a better living, or perhaps a plurality not far distant. In either event, I was sure he was on his way to wearing a bishop's lawn sleeves as Father prophesied.

I wisked through my work singing gaily. Visions of a grand, new parsonage filled my head. Truly God cared for His faithful servants! Using the best meat we could afford, I prepared a tasty stew. We would rejoice in great style!

The moment he entered, I knew Will did not regard his session with the bishop a triumph. When I gave him a welcoming kiss, he held me fiercely in his arms for some time. Ignoring my questions, he swung the pot away from the fire and led me upstairs.

His lovemaking had the quality of desperation. When we lay spent in each other's arms, he said, "I have lost this living."

"But you have been offered a better one."

"Another man will come in three days."

"Three days! But what of us?"

"I am to have a living in Sussex. A place called Tyne-at-the-Crossroads."

"Tyne-at-the-Crossroads? I never heard of it."

"They have not had a vicar for many years."

Fearfully I asked, "It is a poor living? Poorer than this?"

He sighed. "Yes."

I thought of our baby being born in the forsaken wilds of Sussex. That must not happen! I vowed it would not. My son would not be condemned to such a life; I would fight to prevent it. "But why? You served this parish well. The people like you. You deserve better!"

"There was great pressure on the bishop. The parsonage in Sussex will need to be rebuilt and the church repaired."

"You must not go!"

"The people need a vicar."

"Let them have another. You will be forgotten for years! Possibly for the rest of your life! You must *not* go. There will be another place."

"There are far more vicars than livings, my dear."

"Then teach."

"Where? Being married, I could not hold a position at the University, save at Christ Church. If I became associated with a school or started one on my own, this same pressure would be brought against it. Meg, there is no place in the Lord's vineyard I am unwilling to go. The people in Tyne need me." He sighed. "And it is a poor enough living that we might be left alone."

"Who would do this? Why?"

"There are several possibilities. My father's wife has power. She prevented my receiving a fellowship at Merton. Those gownsmen expelled for coming here may have chosen this for their vengeance. Doubtless they have powerful families or friends."

"If only Father was not so vocal, so insistent on using his pen!"

"Don't fret so, my dear. God controls our lives. We know that everything happens to us for the best. Therefore, as Mr. Law points out, we cannot possibly complain for the want of something better."

Despite his words, I sensed a lack of conviction. "Speak to Father," I urged. "He may be able to do something. He could talk to Lord Rockivale and we could go there. Charles would like that."

"Would he?" Will rose and started dressing. "I gave my word. I am going to Tyne."

"It isn't fair! It isn't right!" I nearly told him of our baby, then decided he must change for me, and me alone. "I will not, I *cannot* go to that—that dark hole! Do you think to find the sign you seek there?"

"In three days I leave for Tyne," he said firmly, then added wistfully, "Meg, I want you to go with me."

Separated by a chasm, we packed our belongings. I argued and pled with Will that we live with Father until a suitable place was found. He refused to consider either that or applying to Lord Rockivale. Silently I cursed the forces depriving Will of his living.

Our last night, I lay watching a ray of moonlight move across the blue quilt on our bed. How important that bit of light was in the dark room. Tyne must be a dark, dismal place.

Will pulled me tightly into his arms. I clung to him. He must relent! We had been so happy. For a long time we lay thus, not speaking, his face buried in my hair.

He sighed. "I've arranged for a chaise to take you to your father's house. Ask him for sanctuary."

How could he! Rolling angrily from him, I brushed back my tangled hair. Wet curls wound about my fingers.

Through a sad, misty morning, I watched Will and the wagon driver load our things. Bit by bit my home was carried out.

When all was ready, Will returned to the drawing room. His steps echoed as when we were first here. I had envisioned such happiness that day. And we possessed it, even more, until. . .

A wild desire rose for me to go with him. Even Tyne was more desirable than the emptiness before me. But he would come back. I knew I meant too much to him for him to stay away. He was so loving and considerate, he would *have* to come back. He *must*!

Will fixed his gaze on me until my eyes met his silent, eloquent plea. Words of assent trembled unspoken on my lips.

Taking my hands, he whispered, "If at any time you wish to come to me, my dear, you'll be most welcome." He placed a kiss on each of my palms, then, without looking back, strode out to the wagon.

Chapter Twelve

I waited on Father's steps facing his forbidding door. With a nervous jerk, I pulled the bell a second time.

Bessie opened the door and stared at me, shocked. "Miss Margaret! We thought you had gone!"

"If Father's in, I should like to see him."

"Yes, ma'am, of course. He's in the library."

I went up to the closed door, walking as in a nightmare. Raising my hand, I paused, then tapped in Bessie's fashion.

"Come in, Bessie," Father called.

I entered and hesitantly approached him.

Father sat at his desk, wearing his old red robe and nightcap, its moth-eaten tassel bouncing over his nose. A half-empty wine bottle stood at his elbow; sheets of paper bearing his handwriting were scattered before him and on the floor. "Yes, yes, what do you want?"

Following Will's directions, I said, "Father, I've come seeking sanctuary."

He looked up sharply, almost upsetting the bottle. "Margaret, my child! You've come!" He rose and held out his arms eagerly to embrace me, a tear on either side of his broad smile. "I feared you'd left without bidding me farewell!"

I shook my head, repeating my request.

Dropping his arms, he frowned. "Sanctuary? Sanctuary from what?"

"I—I have no place else to go."

"What do you mean? Where is William?"

"On his way to Tyne-at-the-Crossroads. He left some time ago."

Father pushed his glasses into their proper place, jammed his hands into the pockets of his ragged banyon, and stepped briskly to the far end of the room. There he turned and peered at me over his glasses, which had slipped to the end of his nose. He pursed his lips, then spoke as if repremanding an undergraduate. "Why are you not with him?"

"It's an awful place in Sussex, small, remote. The church and parsonage are in ruins! He'll be buried there, forgotten! He'll never have a chance to gain a worthy pulpit. If I stay, he'll come back and then. . ." My voice trailed to silence, my reasoning foolishness in my own ears.

"I should think your place is with him."

"I come seeking sanctuary," I repeated doggedly.

"If I refuse?"

Never had I thought that possible! "I—I don't know. I . . . Amelia wants me to visit her."

Father glanced at Mother's miniature on his desk. "That our daughter should leave her husband! Katherine, forgive me for failing! What evil have I brought upon William?"

"You must not blame yourself! This is *my* doing."

"There is none to blame save me. On all counts! You are so like Katherine. I denied you nothing, failing always to discipline you properly. And this living that you scorn. *I* arranged it for William through my friend Squire Addleby. The former vicar, now dead, travelled some distance to visit that parish once or twice a year. I wrote Addleby advising him to raise the tithe to a living and recommended William as a man whose company he would enjoy."

"Why? Why would you send your own daughter and son-in-law there?"

"If William was not offered that living, he would be offered no other. There is strong political pressure against him. I don't begin to understand why, but it exists. In an obscure place he will be let alone. Later I will call the bishop's attention to him. Through my work for the University, I have earned a hearing with him. Then William may gain a suitable place in this or another see."

Father rubbed his forehead and paced about as if lecturing. "You say you expect William to come back to you. You humiliated him. He will not come. I doubt he'd have you back if you went to him. A man must trust his wife to be at his side in difficult times. How can he trust you now?"

This could not be! Will loved me! He would come. He *must* come!

"Sanctuary you ask. Sanctuary you shall have. As a vicar of Christ's I may not refuse you. You may have your old room." He waved his hand towards the door in dismissal and turned away.

In the evening, Father sent for me. Wearing his rumpled brown suit, he strode about the library, his cheeks flushed, his eyes bright.

I noticed little wine remained in the bottle on his desk. An empty bottle lay beneath his chair where he had flung his gown, cap and grizzle wig. Dark gray stubble covered his shaven head as a skull cap.

"I have arranged to resume living at the college," he said, clipping his words. Jabbing the air with his right forefinger. "I expected to do so when you married, and was prevented by this lease. Finchwythe expects to be another two years in India. You may fulfill my promise to care for his house and I shall go back to my rooms, which I miss. Bessie may stay with you. I'll make provision for your food and clothing."

"I will be alone? Without your protection?"

"Margaret, you are a married woman. You have the protection of your husband's good name. I trust you live up to it!"

From a window I watched numbly as Father's books and furniture were hauled away. I turned around and stared at the bits of paper littering the library floor. The faint odors of old tobacco and leather clung to the air. Naked shelves gaped behind the glass doors of the bookcases. Horrid words echoed about me. "He will not come. I doubt he would have you back if you went to him."

Bessie entered, her chin quivering, her eyes red and wet.

Sharply I told her to set the room to rights. I never intended to enter it again.

Loneliness enveloped me, binding me as a chained prisoner. Because he needed me, my champion would soon rescue me. Nights I prowled the house, sleeping from dawn to noon, whiling away the afternoons, awaiting. Each time the doorbell was pulled, I ran to answer, stopping at the hall mirror to smooth my apron and hair. He was never there.

The leisure I longed for at St. Thomas' became an onerous burden. In desperation, I cleaned and scrubbed, seeking to speed the hours and exhaust my body.

Discouraged, I went to the cathedral at an hour it would be deserted. I slipped in, crossed to the north aisle and hurried to the far end. As always, the lofty grandeur of the vaulted roof and huge pillars dwarfed me to insignificance.

Stopping at St. Frideswide's shrine, I ran my fingers over the carved clusters of oak leaves. Water from her well had given me our child. Kneeling on the narrow step, I prayed God to send Will to me. Earnestly I vowed to go with him *any* place. If he sent a letter, I would go to him on the next coach. Surely, being made at this ancient, holy place, my prayers and vows would be effective.

The month passed. Father was proved right.

I refused to attend the Act. Father came later and delivered an indignant tirade on the impropriety of the remarks of Terra Filus, who had included him. It hurt me to see him so roused by University matters and indifferent to my misery.

Marketing helped break the monotony of meaningless days. While waiting at the baker's one morning, I heard a large order being given with particular specifications. When asked who it was for, the pert maid replied in a broad London accent, "It is for the honorable Oliver Simpson's table, to be delivered to the residence of Mr. Augustus Forsythe."

I sped there, my errands forgotten.

Amelia received me with joy. Radiantly beautiful, splendidly maternal, she bubbled with news of town life, the latest fashions and plans for her baby. "I would have been here earlier, but I was not well at the end of the season. It was so *very* fatiguing! As it was, we took an entire *week* to come from London, making very short drives. Oliver is so solicitous of my health. *So* solicitous. And Meg, dear Meg, what of you? I've not heard these many weeks!"

When I told her the whole, she took me in her arms and we wept together.

"Meg, sweet Meg, of *course* you couldn't do anything else. Sussex is *most* disagreeable. It's *no* place for you. He *will* come. How could he possibly not? Until then, we will spend our days together. Oliver will not *permit* me to step outside the door, for fear I shall come to grief, so you must come here. We shall *sew* and *plan* for our babies." With a nervous flutter of her hands, quite unlike herself, she added, "He will be *handsome*, my son, don't you think? And Oliver is sure to be *pleased*, isn't he?"

I assured her that with such handsome parents, he was certain to be an exceptional child. How fortunate she was!

Despite her many blessings, Amelia was very tense, retiring every few days to her darkened room with a headache. At these times I sat alone working interlocked hearts and bow-knots on my baby's clothes and dreaming of taking him to Will.

Anticipating his birth in late January or early February, I planned leaving when the roads were safe. As undoubtedly there was no doctor near Tyne, and here I could engage both a midwife and a doctor, I would tell Will it was imperative for our son's welfare that I remain in Oxford. In the joy of having his son, he would forgive and understand. Then I would be happy again.

Bessie shook her head in disapproval as I dressed to visit Amelia late in August. "You should not let yourself go this way, ma'am. Really you shouldn't. I fear we'll have to let out your dresses!"

"I will get larger yet, Bessie."

"You will? Miss Margaret, are you . . . breeding?"

"Yes."

She clapped her hands. "Dr. Castleton will be so pleased! He's often spoken of having a grandchild."

"No! You must *not* tell him. I *won't* have him fussing over me!" Neither could I bear him to remain preoccupied with the University rather than his grandson's advent. Nor did I want anyone to inform Will except myself.

Bessie giggled. "Begging your pardon, ma'am, but it won't be needing to be told. Anyone with eyes in his head can see."

I studied my profile in the mirror. Shawls would not long conceal my coming child. "Then I shall not go out save to see Mrs. Simpson."

In September, Oliver rode to London, leaving Amelia more blue-deviled than I'd ever seen. She credited her fits of melancholy with moods brought on by her pregnancy and Oliver's firm insistence that they soon remove to his Berkshire seat for the birth of his heir.

A week before Michaelmas, Amelia's maid arrived at mid-morning in the Forsythe carriage. "My mistress has been brought to bed. She's sent begging you to come."

"Has Mr. Simpson returned?"

"No, ma'am. And Miss Amelia was quite distraught last night. It's days since she expected him."

I paused only to tie on my straw hat and fling a shawl about my shoulders. As we approached the Forsythe's, we saw the servants strewing hay over New Inn Hall Street to quiet the noise of horses and carriages. The knocker was already padded. Every consideration was being given Amelia's comfort.

She lay on her bed fretting. "He's coming early. And Oliver's not here! It will be all right, won't it, dear Meg?"

"Of course." I kissed her cheek and squeezed her hand. "You will have a healthy, strong child."

"I do hope Oliver won't be angry he is not born in Berkshire!"

"I am confident he will be far more concerned over you than the location of his son's birth."

"Are you *really*? Oh, Meg! you don't know. You just don't *know*!" Tears spilled from her eyes.

Most of the day I sat with her while the midwife and doctor alternated with Amelia's agitated mother. Oliver's arrival was announced, and Amelia sent me down to report how he took the news. As I expected, he evidenced much concern over Amelia and only once mentioned regret they had not removed to Berkshire in time.

Cheered by this, Amelia struggled bravely not to cry out with her bearing-down pains. I wiped her perspiring forehead, gave the midwife some assistance, and watched the doctor work.

The candles were just lighted downstairs when I brought Oliver's tiny son to him. He glowed with pride, then dashed up to his exhausted wife. I rocked the baby gently. In a few months I would hold my own child. And then, what joy when I presented him to Will!

On January 26, a blustery day, I was brought to bed. For two days the vigorous child in my womb had been strangely quiet, as if unwilling to leave warmth and safety for the cold, uncertain world.

Amelia had departed when her little Stephan was a month old, regretting she could not be present for my son's birth. With my time upon me, I wished she might have sat at my side holding my hand.

The midwife, a cheerful, rosy-cheeked woman, bossed Bessie about with an air of confidence. The rhythms of pain increased. My face was wet with sweat and I clung to the knotted sheets and pulled. Would this never end?

Hearing a man's deep voice, I screamed for Will, frantically twisting to see him.

A stranger in shirt-sleeves and a brown wig pushed high on one side came to my side. He smiled kindly and said, "I'm Dr. Cheyney, Mrs. Knight."

An eternity later, I lay exhausted, half-asleep, grateful my travail was over. Rousing, I asked for my baby.

Dr. Cheyney came to my side and held a glass to my lips. "Drink this, Mrs. Knight."

I obeyed. Drowsiness overpowered me.

Forcing up heavy eyelids, I saw the doctor writing at a table by the window, the morning sun shining on his bent head. I tried to speak, but my tongue was thick.

In response to my sounds, he brought me a glass of water.

A few sips of cool water cleared away some of the wool in my head.

He took my hand and stroked it gently. "I gave you a dose of lanaudum so you could rest, Mrs. Knight. Your body needs a chance to regain its strength."

"My—my baby. Let me hold my baby. Just a moment."

He sighed. "You must be brave, Mrs. Knight."

"I want my baby!"

He shook his head. "I am truly sorry, Mrs. Knight. She was born dead."

"No, no! Let me see him! Let me see him!" I tried to raise up, but weakness overcame me.

"You must understand. There was nothing I could do, or the midwife, or you. The," he hesitated, "the cord was around her neck. She was dead before your pains came on."

"Take another bite of the stew, Miss Margaret." Bessie stood at my elbow.

I shook my head. "It doesn't taste good."

"I know, ma'am, but you must get your strength up."

"Why? What is it to any purpose?"

"Two more bites and I'll take it away."

"You're a tyrant," I grumbled for the thousandth time, picking up my fork.

Through a long, gray period I refused to see anyone save Dr. Cheyney. He urged me to weep, assuring me it was proper to show grief. But I had no tears for the baby I neither saw nor touched. He urged me to go outside. But nothing interesting lay beyond the door. He urged me to pray. But who would hear me?

Blocking out all thoughts and memories, I existed in a numb haze.

Jabbing my needle into white satin, I considered how I might best fill the center of this quilted rose. For some obscure reason Bessie had insisted I must use a different design in each of the dozen or so flowers entwined with leaves around the border of a new petticoat.

It took too much effort to argue with Bessie over fashion details on which she was suddenly very knowledgeable. I no longer cared about them. It was easier to think up varieties of stitches. As I'd already used up the common patterns, it must be something unusual.

Surprised, I saw Father in the doorway. Why had Bessie admitted him against my orders? Of course, she was at market.

He bowed unsteadily and took a chair near me. There was the faint smell of port about him. He pulled out his long clay pipe and lit it with elaborate ceremony. After a few puffs, he leaned back and stared at me.

Continuing my quilting, I stole anxious glances at him. If I didn't talk, maybe he would go away.

As always, he began speaking about the University.

I concentrated on my stitches, letting his words flow around me unheeded. Then I realized he was speaking about myself.

"Really, my dear," he was saying, "you should permit me to

write William and tell him. I understand your wish to tell him every-thing yourself, but you have yet to do so. Your husband ought to know."

Long ago I had written letters, many letters, and burned them all. The words were not right on paper. My needle stilled as images of Will crowded my mind, rousing unwanted emotions. The tenuous peace I'd gained by refusing to think was being shattered. I must send Father away.

He was talking again. "Perhaps you would like to attend services at the cathedral Sunday morning. With me, of course. Dean Cony-beare will be reading the homily."

"The cathedral?" That was where I had poured out my heart in fruitless prayer, where we were married. Never could I go there!

"Why, yes, my dear. I should think it would do you good to be among people again, and to hear the dean. He's very uplifting, you know."

I tried to shove aside upsetting memories by talking about the Dean. "He's full of what one must do to live a good life."

"Exactly so. Most people feel better for hearing him."

"I have no need to hear what I should do."

"I should think there is not a person living who does not need to hear such."

"I—I am married. My husband is not here. I should be with him, is that not so?"

He shifted uneasily. "Of course. It would be useless to deny that."

"You—you told me he, W-Will would not have me back. Isn't that so?"

"I should think it would be difficult for a man to take back a woman who refused to go with him. I don't know. William might."

"I pleaded with God to send him here so I could beg his forgive-ness. He hasn't come. I thought to take our—our," my throat tight-ened, almost preventing speech, "ch-child to him."

Sympathetically Father patted my hand.

I recoiled from his touch, sprang up and darted behind my chair, leaving the petticoat in a heap on the floor. "I don't need anyone to tell me what I *should* do. I need to know how to live *as I am*!"

"My dear, God in His mercy—"

"God!" I pressed my forehead, trying to still my raging thoughts. "You claimed it was error to say God left His creation to work itself out. You claimed God was interested in us, His children, and our happiness.

"True, my dear, He is."

"What about *me*? If He is interested in *my* happiness, why did He . . ." The horror in the back of my mind broke loose. "*Why did He kill my child?*"

Father paled. "Margaret, you must not talk that way!"

"It's true! *God* killed my child! He destroyed the one way I could go to my husband. If He is good, why, *why* would He do that?"

"Margaret, my dear, you are overwrought! You cannot say that God killed your child!"

"Then who? The doctor said she—she was dead before she was born. *He* could do nothing. The *midwife* could do nothing. *I* could do nothing. The only one in the whole *universe* who could was *God*!"

"This is monstrous! You cannot believe this! It was an accident!"

"Indeed! Is the great God helpless in the face of accident? Is His 'omnipotent majesty' rendered impotent by a little *accident*? Would I were never born into this—this 'v-vale of t-tears'!"

Father paced the room trailed by a succession of gray puffs. After several turns, he faced me, feet apart, glasses on the tip of his nose. "I should think you must take the next coach to Tyne. You must see William!"

"How can I? Now that she is dead, I have nothing to give him! *Nothing*! He won't accept me, myself, alone. *You* told me that!"

"Perhaps I was in error." Father fumbled in his pockets, pulled out some money, counted it, glanced at me, then laid it on the table, beside my pincushion, thread, and scissors. "There. Your fare."

"And if he turns me away?"

He took another turn around the room, then added to the money on the table. "Your return fare. I don't expect you to need that—"

"But you're not sure!" With both hands I shoved the money and my sewing things from the table. "I don't want your money! You tell me I must go to him. It is not *in* me to make that trip!"

He frowned in puzzlement, his wig tipped back on his head. "But—but Margaret, what else can I do?"

"Go back to your precious common room, to your friends at the Blue Boar or wherever, *and leave me alone!*"

Chapter Thirteen

The loud clang of the doorbell interrupted my reverie.

Since Father's visit I often stood thus at a window. If I concentrated on something outside, I could keep out painful, frightening thoughts. God, the vague, comforting anchor in my life since childhood, was gone. I floated adrift. Having sent Father away, I was left without anyone, anyone at all.

The bell rang again. Bessie was out. I went to the hall. Perhaps the person would go away.

Impatiently the bell was tugged twice. Who could possibly wish to gain entrance here? Curiosity drew me down the stairs one step at a time.

There was another loud clang. Dared I see who this was? It might only be Dr. Cheyney. I took a deep breath and opened the door.

A tall man on his way to the carriage waiting at the gate turned and stared at me. "Oh, there you are."

I blinked, not believing my eyes.

He climbed the front steps, leaning wearily on his stick. His dark blue coat was dirty. Torn lace fell over the slender hand resting negligently on the hilt of his sword. "Charles Heathton to see Dr. Castleton," he announced.

"Charles?" I gasped, weak with relief. "It's really you?"

He cocked his head and scanned my face and gown. "Meg? Good Lord! What's happened to you?"

"Oh, Charles, come in!"

"A moment, my dove, while I send the chaise away."

We left his portmanteau by the door and went up to the drawing room.

Studying me over a glass of wine, Charles shook his head. He took me to the mirror and waved at our reflections. "I know I'm deplorable, but that don't *begin* to describe you!"

Greasy whisps of hair stuck out under my limp, soiled cap. Dark shadows circled my eyes; my pale cheeks were sunken, and my lips virtually bloodless.

With a rueful laugh he said, "We're a sorry pair! What's wrong, little dove? Been sick?"

I nodded.

"Is Will all right, or has he been sick too?"

"I don't know. I—I haven't seen him." My voice broke in a sob.

Charles turned me around. "You haven't *seen* him! When will your father come home?"

I shook my head. "He doesn't live here, and—and Will is in Tyne-at-the-Crossroads. I—I am *alone*!" I leaned against him, weeping.

"Tyne-at-the-. . . Where? Never heard of it." He picked me up. "Lord! there's no weight to you at all!" Gently he placed me on the settee and sat beside me, an arm around my shoulders. "Tell me everything," he said with gentle authority.

Obediently I poured out my tale of woe in a disjointed manner, passing over my child's death as merely sickness.

Charles thought a few moments after I finished, then shook his head. "Meg, my dove, you always were a bit foolish, but I've never known you to act in such a bird-witted manner! You can't possibly expect Will to come back *here*! You *must've* known he wouldn't!"

"Please, don't scold me."

"I won't." He patted my hand. "However, I can't understand why he failed to come when you were sick. Sickness is different."

"He doesn't know."

"Don't know! I was gone too long! There I was, kicking up my heels, having a lark all over the continent, and you were falling into the most shocking tangle! Well, it's unbelievable, that's what it is! I shall have to straighten you out."

"Why did you come back, Charles? And how came you to be in such a sad state yourself?"

"If that don't beat all! Forgot my own troubles. Well, it's a good thing. Been thinking of them too long." He took a deep breath. "They sent old Richard to find me. Took him weeks, following me from place to place. Never was one to write much, you know. Arthur's gone."

"Gone! What do you mean?"

"Just that. He was down in Portsmouth on business. Never could trust anyone else to do things but himself. He was staying at an inn. And he vanished!"

"Do they have any ideas of what might have happened?"

"Arthur was always a steady fellow, but once in a while he would get an odd notion. He might've took it into his head to go out at night. The press gang was working around that time. They might have got him. Or maybe footpads."

"Oh, no! But surely they wouldn't dare touch him, Lord Rockivale's heir!"

"If he was foxed, they wouldn't believe him, especially if he couldn't prove it."

"Oh, Charles, this is terrible!"

"Can't really say I loved my brother—you know how we fought. He was, he is such a prosy fellow! That's the thing of it, not knowing if he was or is. May not know for years. They say when a ship returns to England, the men are often pressed into another voyage. Would to God we knew if he's alive or—or dead, and where.

"Old Richard said Mother's taken to her bed. That's to be expected. Always had bad nerves. But even Rockivale's off his head. Arthur was his favorite, you know, being his heir and all. So they sent for me, Charles the wastral, to pull things together. Can you imagine?" His eyes sparkled at the challenge. "Not that I'm glad Arthur's gone, you understand, but it is nice to be expected to do something important. And I *shall* do it right!"

"I know you will. Poor Martha."

"Taversleigh, our business agent, said she's the only one keeping her wits. I saw him in London. He's the one should've been in Portsmouth. They've found out precious little. Came here to see if Dr. Castleton would go up to Rockivale. They never have taken to Pettigrew. Then I'm off to Portsmouth to see what I can learn."

"Do stay off the streets at night."

"Don't worry, little dove," he patted my hand. "I shall take good care. If it is as it appears, the family name and fame rest with me! I shall have to run the estates. Father certainly can't from all reports. I shall show them all I am not a useless second son!"

He laughed suddenly. "When he found me, Old Richard was so anxious to have me return immediately, he rushed me off without Tutley and but one change of clothes. So you see me very shabby indeed."

I poured him another glass of wine. "You must stay the night."

He raised his eyebrows. "Without either your father or your husband here?"

"I am a married woman," I said with dignity. "Surely it doesn't signify if I choose to entertain an old and valued friend rather than send him off to a dirty old inn!" I snapped my fingers before his nose. "Isn't that all we've ever cared about what people might say?"

"I *am* bone weary. But it would be scandalous to stay, especially after our last escapade. That didn't end too well!"

"Please, Charles. I'm so *lonely*! I shall have Bessie sleep on a cot in my room if that will soothe your sensibilities."

"But Dr. Castleton—"

"Since I failed to go to Tyne, I've sunk beneath reproach in his eyes. I'll take you up to your room to rest before supper. Bessie should be back soon."

For the first time in months I enjoyed my food. I was about to leave Charles alone with a glass of port after Bessie pulled the cloth, but he asked me to stay.

Leaning forward on the polished table, he said, "Tell me, Meg, my dove, where is this Tyne-of-the-tumble-down-church-and-ruined-vicarage?"

"I don't know, precisely. South. In some remote, forgotten corner, far from everything of importance. In Sussex."

"In Sussex! Then it cannot be very far from Portsmouth, which is very important! Tomorrow I shall go to the college and prevail upon Dr. Castleton to go to Rockivale. Do you think he will go alone, or must I go too?"

I blushed. "You will think me very silly, but, what month is this?"

"April. The twentieth day."

I counted off the lost months on my fingers, then smiled. "Yes, he will go alone, I think. It's only if the weather's bad that he balks to travel."

"Fine. I shall send him with a message and go down to Tyne and see Will."

"You will?" My heart began pounding. "You will *talk* with him?"

"Of course, you little goose. I may be able to enlist his help searching for Arthur. Then, when I've learned all I can, I shall go to Rockivale and—"

"No. Please," I laid my hand on his arm, "you must, please, come here first and tell me—tell me all about Will." My vision blurred and I blinked several times to clear it. "It's been so, so *long*! I haven't, you see, there's been no word at all. I *must* know how he is, and—and *everything*!"

Charles covered my hand with his. "Calm yourself, little dove. Another day will not matter. I'll see you before going to Rockivale, and I shall tell you everything."

"Oh, I do hope you will not be long delayed! But you mustn't, please don't tell him about my—my illness."

"But why? He will want to know. He ought to know."

"I'm certain you are right, but—but. . ."

He looked at me sharply, "If he don't know you were ill, he can't be blamed for not coming to see you."

"Yes. And anyway, I'm not sick any longer, so there's no point, I mean, one can't expect him to. . . "

"I'll do as you wish."

Knowing Charles would soon bring news of Will, I took interest again in what occurred about me. Delighted, Bessie stuffed me with food, trying to cover my bones with a bit of flesh.

In a few days, a messenger arrived with several gowns Charles had bought for me in Paris. I held up one of soft emerald silk. If I finished that satin petticoat, they would be perfect together. The gowns were stylish, yet simple enough for a vicar's wife to wear. I tried on a demure one of deep blue sprinkled with white flowers. A quilted stomacher filled in the bodice. It was beautiful! Will's eyes would sparkle to see me in it.

Bessie's clucking sounds of disapproval soon called to my attention that my figure was not adequate to fill it properly. She pinched in seams here and there, trying to decide how to make it fit.

"No, Bessie," I exclaimed, catching her hand. "I will grow into it. I'm eating better. It will soon not be necessary to make any alterations. We will lay these aside until then."

After several weeks, Charles appeared as suddenly as before. I was barely able to withhold my questions about Will until he was properly served with wine and little cakes.

"He looks well enough," Charles said. "Rather more sober than I remember."

"More sober! What can you mean?"

"Just that. He always was a serious fellow, but now there's a heaviness about him. None of that wry humor I liked. It was a good thing I went to see him. He needed livening up. And he was a great help in tracing Arthur. He knew who to see and where to go. He's the most amazing fellow for picking up information of any I've known. Never misses anything and puts it all together to make sense."

"And he is well? What does he look like?"

"Same as always. Well no, there's a slight stoop to his shoulders. He was some thinner, and he was, well, weary. Soul weary. He works hard for his parish, rushing to the sick at all sorts of hours."

"Yes, he would do that."

"He's been given the plurality at Docking too. Insists he must spend a couple nights there each week."

"Docking? Where is that?"

"About an hour's ride from Tyne. A fishing village. Nothing much there beyond a few poor folk. That about sums up his entire parish, aside from the squire and the army that drifts about."

"The army?"

"There's been a deal of smuggling along the coast, and of course quite a bit of highway robbery and general banditry. And it seems a number of sailors choose to jump ship thereabouts and vanish into the countryside. So the army goes there to catch the criminals, then moves on to another place, coming back when it gets too bad again."

"You said he works hard. Too hard?"

"Meg, there's no one to tell him not to make such a hard push to set everything to rights. I daresay that the days we spent looking for Arthur in Portsmouth were like a holiday."

"Did you find out more about your brother?"

He chewed his lower lip, then shook his head. "We determined pretty much that he was pressed aboard some ship. His clothes had been spoilt by some carriage mishap, so he borrowed the innkeeper's. He looked ordinary when he went out and had nothing with him to prove who he was. Can't think why he did that.

"I've started inquiries into all the ships in or near port then. It'll take months to hear back, if we do, and then the answers won't be for certain. He might be dead in some grave in the woods or wandering around out of his mind from a knock on the head." He sighed. "We might never know more."

"I'm so sorry, Charles." After a moment I asked, "What is the parsonage like at Tyne? Is it very bad?"

"Oh, it's unlivable, all right. The roof's fallen in. Will's staying with the squire and his daughter. Right pretty young thing she is." He smiled appreciatively. "High spirited, and er, well, *very* pretty. They all think he's not married, you know. He's fixed up the church right and tight. They're holding services there regular. First time in years.

"Do they, the people, his parishioners, *like* him?"

"That they do. And they ought to. He'd do most anything for them."

"I know. Can't they repair the parsonage?"

"It's a poor parish. Will was barely able to bring the church up to snuff."

"That would be first. If he had the money, would he make it livable, or does he, I mean, is it convenient to—to continue with the squire?"

"If he had the money, he would repair it and move in a thrice."

Tossing in bed that night, I pondered Charles' description of Will's life with the squire and his daughter. Very lovely she was, judging from Charles' smile. Will lived with them and everyone thought he was unmarried. He needed money to repair the parsonage.

Money. I had none. How could I get enough? Had I something to sell? No furniture. Little jewelry. A vision of emeralds came into my drowsy mind. Beautiful stones set in fancy gold work.

Eagerly I lit my candle, went to my dresser and took them out. Green fire flashed in my hands. I always felt like a grand lady when wearing them. Charles bought them for me when I finished Mrs. Spinet's after he had a winning streak at the London gaming tables. He would know their worth. It probably was not proper to ask a man to sell the jewels he gave you, but surely he would understand.

When Charles' late breakfast was cleared away, I took the emerald bracelet from my apron pocket and laid it on the dining table. The sunlight broke into green splinters on the stones. "Charles, if this was sold, would the money be enough for Will's parsonage?"

He looked up in surprise. "Are you tired of this?"

"Oh, no! I love it. But Will needs money."

"I see. No, Meg, I don't think it would."

I placed the matching earrings beside it. "Now, would it be enough?"

He shook his head. "The stone roof fell in some time ago and the whole inside must be redone."

Reluctantly I added the lovely brooch. "Now?"

He picked up the three pieces which he had given me, scrutinized them individually, then dropped them into his coat pocket. "I'll sell them for you. It should bring enough for what he needs."

"I hope so! I do hope so!"

"He'll be pleased to be in his own home, especially considering the source of the money."

"But you mustn't tell."

Charles frowned. "No? It would mean much to him."

With my finger I drew circles on the table. "He might, you see, he is very proud. He might not want to use m-my money."

"Perhaps. Perhaps," he said thoughtfully. "I shall do as you wish. Does this mean you intend joining him when the parsonage is ready?"

"Me?"

"You. His wife."

"Father said I—I have failed him and—and he would not have me. I . . . I . . ." I fled to my room in tears.

After Charles left for Rockivale, Bessie returned from shopping, her chin high, and her lips pressed together. Repeatedly I demanded to know why she was in such a pet.

"If you must know, ma'am, Alvira Huddleton, she's maid to Mrs. Withers, and we known each other since we was babies, well, she said I now work in a Den of Iniquity!"

"What?" I laughed at the charge and Bessie's injured air.

"Taint nothing to laugh at, ma'am. It's all over town that Mr. Charles was here twice for the night, and you living all alone."

"How would anyone know?"

"Like as not 'twas Mistress White down the Lane. She's a very long nose!"

"I see." I shrugged, attempting to treat this lightly. "It doesn't matter what those old gossips think. What did you tell your friend?"

"I told her she oughtn't to say or even think such lies. I told her Mr. Charles was practically a member of the family, and that I slept in your room when he was here."

"Will she tell the others?"

"Oh, yes, ma'am. She wouldn't let a special bit of information like that be hoarded to herself. I don't know's they'll believe it, but it's God's truth."

Determined not to let ugly rumors drag me back into my former state, I busied myself around the house. I was polishing Mr. Finchwythe's silver in the dining room when Father entered, scowling.

His brown suit was in fair shape under his academicals and his grizzle wig was on straight. He pursed his lips, then declared angrily, "I have just been at the Blue Boar!

"*Your* name was being bandied about by some worthless fellows! Undergraduates!"

I bit my lips and kept my eyes on my work.

He glowered at me over his glasses. "I thought after that other affair you would be more circumspect! To what depths of degradation have you fallen, daughter?"

I cringed, dropping my polishing cloth.

"Have you lost *all* sense of respectability?"

"I have done nothing wrong, Father."

"Nothing wrong! I should think entertaining a gentleman *alone* overnight would not be thought precisely right!"

"Charles is my oldest friend. You always considered him as a son, a brother to me." My hands were trembling as I set down the half-polished creamer.

"William was good enough to marry you after your disgraceful adventure in a barn. How do you think he would feel with you *twice* entertaining that *same* man overnight as soon as he returned to Oxford?"

I had not thought of that. "Would you tell him?"

"Of course not. Gossip has its own wings. But I tell you this. If you persist in this behavior, I wash my hands of you!"

With hands clenched at my sides, I cried, "You already have! You've turned your back on me, preferring your precious University!" My voice raised. "Why must you *torment* me? *Leave me alone!*"

Running from the room, I hid in a small closet, weeping quietly. I heard him calling and banging doors, but he would never think of this place among the brooms. When I was certain he was gone, I stepped into the passageway. The only sound was Bessie singing in the kitchen.

Would Father ever forgive me for screaming at him? I thought not.

Wretched woman that I was, even the sacrifice of my treasured emeralds did not ease my lot. Once happy and loved, I was ugly and unwanted, miserable. I was not fit for breathing the air. Yet, I could not quite bring myself to end this hellish existence.

The kerchief I was hemming lay forgotten in my lap. Oppressed by the heavy August heat, I felt unable even to ply my needle. As I wiped my damp brow, I became aware of Bessie singing a strange, cheerful melody while dusting at the far end of the room.

"Breathe, O breathe thy loving spirit into every troubled breast!" she sang.

"What is that you're singing?" I demanded sharply.

"Just a hymn, ma'am."

"A hymn! I've never heard it."

"It's a new one we sing at the meeting house. Mr. Wesley wrote it. Mr. Charles Wesley."

Father had warned that those Methodists were more dangerous than the Jacobites who rioted in the streets, who even attacked me. He said they behaved scandalously. "Wesley! Meeting house! Have you joined those disgraceful *Methodists*?"

"I attend on my evening out."

"What you do your evening out is none affair of mine. But don't sing their songs around me!"

"Yes, ma'am." She dipped a curtsey, her face flaming red.

The doorbell clanged and Bessie rushed to answer.

Bother! Why didn't whoever it was stay away? "I don't wish to see anyone!" I shouted. To my annoyance, I jabbed my needle into my finger and began sucking it to keep from staining the lawn fabric.

A tall figure appeared in the drawing room doorway and I looked away. "I said I didn't want to see anyone! What's the good of having a servant if you aren't obeyed?"

"None whatever, my dove."

Clad in a suit of forest green modestly trimmed with gold braid, Charles surveyed me through his quizzing glass. "Deplorable, Meg. Utterly deplorable! You have fallen back into a shocking state. As you see, *I* am no longer shabby. Why have you not done as well?"

"Charles! I'd given up seeing you!" I rose and held out my hands to him.

"It's been much too long, so I drove the cabriolet down. Made right good time in spite of the heat." He kissed both my hands.

"Have you seen Will?"

"Yes."

"How is he?"

"Let us sit on the settee while I tell you. He's been at Rockivale these last few weeks."

"At Rockivale! Is he, is he the new vicar there?"

"Alas, no. Pettigrew seems much too healthy, and I cannot interest Father in making a change just now. Will had to do most of the work repairing the parsonage. Between that and his parish duties, he fell ill. His churchwarden wrote me and I took him home."

"Is he still there?"

"No. He rode back to Tyne two days ago on my Prince Whist, a more suitable mount for the riding he does than that old cob of his. Really, Meg, you aren't fit to receive a beggar! 'Tis a good thing he didn't stop here before going to Tyne."

"Will, stop here? To see me? Oh, dear!" I tucked some stray hair under my cap. "But he didn't. I am sure he did not care to."

"If he had been confident of your reception, he would have come. I tried to tell him. He insisted as he hadn't heard a word, you had no interest in seeing him."

"Oh." My gaze fell before his. "I'm glad he did not come. He remembers me as I was. I know I've changed; I've become quite, quite ugly."

"Do you remember that sonnet of Shakespeare's you bet I couldn't learn?

'Love is not love
Which alters when it alteration finds,
Or bends with the remover to remove.

O no! It is an ever-fixed mark
That looks on tempests, and is never shaken.
It is the star to every wandering bark,
Whose worth's unknown, although his height be taken,
Love's not Time's fool, though rosy lips and cheeks
Within his bending sickle's compass come;
Love alters not with his brief hours and weeks,
But bears it out even to the edge of doom.'

Such is Will's love for you."

"How I wish. . . But I am no longer the woman he . . . loved. Is he well now?"

Charles shrugged. "He acts very hearty. Had me riding all over Rockivale. I never worked so hard as during his recuperation. Wanted to know all about everything. He's terribly lonely, Meg."

I flinched at the thrust of his words.

"The parsonage will soon be finished. He assured me it will be secure from wind and rain."

"Rockivale is only half a day's ride. And he didn't come. O Charles!" I sobbed.

He put his arm about me. "Hush, hush, little dove. I thought to find you in one of the dresses I sent. You must wear them before they are completely out of fashion."

"Why?"

"Why! Why, er, to please me."

"You're never here. No one comes. No one sees me."

"I should think they would stay away with you looking like a creature to scare off the crows and refusing to see anyone."

"No one cares anyway."

He forced my chin up until I was looking into his eyes. "I care. It pains me seeing you thus. As I recollect, Bessie provides tolerable food. I want to see you eat well tonight."

Bessie conjured up a brace of capons from some unknown source and made them very tasty. In response to Charles' patient coaxing, I ate very well indeed.

He smiled at me over the table. "I like this. It's so peaceful. No one demanding decisions about this or that. If you don't mind, little dove, I should like to stay a few days. I need a holiday from Rockivale."

"You would rather stay here than in London?" I asked.

"Lord yes! Even though the season's over, I'd run myself ragged. London's not a restful place."

I welcomed his company, disregarding any further scandal it might arouse. It could not be worse than before, and ugly gossips could not harm me shut away in my house.

Charles remained a week, drawing me out of myself, making me take pains with my appearance. Bessie dressed my hair in becoming ringlets around my face, pleased I would let her fuss with it. For hours Charles and I sat in a shady spot in the weedy garden while he related experiences in learning to run Rockivale's vast estate.

"Will insisted we see a demonstration of a seed-drill a man named Tull invented. Meg, it's the most astonishing contraption! While a horse pulls it, it plants seeds in rows in the ground! The results are much better than with the common method of scattering. You know, this is a wonderful age! Why, the things men are making, there's no end to them! There's *nothing* we can't do if we've a mind to. Man is truly coming into his own!"

"Do you intend using this machine?"

"As soon as I can. I must convince my tenants that the changes in the fields will be worth the greater yields. Then I shall transform the whole estate!"

Charles' enthusiasm pricked my apathy. When he departed, he said he expected to see further improvement in me when he returned in a few weeks.

Without warning the following afternoon, Bessie brought me an old straw hat with a broad brim.

"What is this for? I'm not going out."

"Yes, ma'am, you are," she said firmly, placing the hat on my head. "I'm taking you to hear a man, a good man. It's not far, just beyond Petty Pont in St. Clement's fields."

What an odd suggestion! Reluctantly I tied the ribbons under my chin. Obviously it would take more effort to refuse her than to follow.

Aside from seasonal changes, the traffic and buildings had hardly altered during my lengthy absence from Oxford's streets. We walked down the Lane to the High, past All Souls', University, and Queens, then out the east gate.

As Bessie hurried me by the physic gardens, memories of Will nearly overpowered me. I could almost hear his voice identifying plants, talking about his students, longing for a sign approving his work.

We crossed the crumbling bridge over the Cherwell with a mass of people. A London coach approached at a trot with blaring horn. The crowds surged to either side allowing the equipage to pass, and I heard a fluent stream of curses from the coachman for being delayed.

At St. Clement's, the greater part of the multitude turned aside with us into the fields. I had not walked such a distance in many months, and was glad to be near our destination.

Richly dressed students laughing loudly, solemn dons, town folk of all sorts jostled each other, some running for advantageous places. A few carriages arrived, scattering those on foot.

The people we joined in the field were singing what I recognized as Bessie's hymn.

"Love divine, all loves excelling.
 Joy of heaven, to earth come down!"

This was a religious meeting! I hung back, wanting no part of it.

"There he is!" Bessie exclaimed. She pointed to a short man some distance away mounting a grassy hillock, probably ruins of fortifications from the time of the Rebellion.

I blinked. He wore a black gown and cassock, as any preaching vicar. But this was not a church! It was an unhallowed place, one frequented by cattle! "Who is he?" I demanded.

"Mr. Wesley. Mr. John Wesley!" she answered in an excited whisper.

"You brought me to a *Methodist* meeting? You have taken leave of your senses!"

"Listen to him, Miss Margaret! Please, listen to him!"

I turned to depart, but my weary legs would carry me no farther. Bessie led me to a crumbling wall to sit near two sour-faced dons. Thank goodness they took no notice of me.

With deliberation, Mr. Wesley looked over the throng facing him as if gauging what sort we were. A breeze mussed his hair, and he smoothed it back with both hands. In a clear voice he announced his text, "The heart of man is deceitful above all things, and desperately wicked: who can know it?"

Wicked! Wicked! The guilt I tried to shut away oppressed me. Weak or not, I would leave. If necessary I'd crawl beyond the range of his voice. I tried to scramble from the wall, but my petticoats caught on the stones.

In a compelling, reasonable manner, Mr. Wesley continued. "He that made man, and that best knows what he has made, informs us that 'the heart of man,' of all mankind, of every man born into the world 'is desperately wicked'; and that it is deceitful above all things, so that we may well ask, 'Who can know it?' "

A hush settled as the audience strained to hear him speak of wickedness and sin. I frantically worked to free myself from the wall.

"We have no need to refer to any particular sins. These are no more than the leaves, or at most, the fruits, which spring from that evil tree. But rather let us look at the general root of all: 'Lucifer, son of the morning,' who cried out boldly, 'I will sit upon the side of the north.' " He pointed to the far side. "See self-will, the firstborn of Satan!"

He was pointing straight at me. " 'I will be like the Most High.' See pride, the twin sister of self-will. When Satan had once transfused his own self-will and pride into the parents of mankind, together with a new species of sin—love of the world, the loving the creature above the creator—all manner of wickedness soon rushed in."

I cringed with "pride" and "self-will" stabbing at me. My hands clenched on my gown as I tried not to hear this awful man. With a jerk I freed my petticoats.

"Hence it is a melancholy truth, that unless the Spirit of God has made the difference, all mankind now, as well as four thousand years ago, 'have corrupted their ways before the Lord; and every imagination of the thought of man's heart is evil, only evil. . . .' "

I covered my ears with my palms, wanting to cry out for him to stop. A trembling seized my limbs. Weakly my hands fell to my sides. Anxious to run from the horrible charges he hurled at me, I wriggled to the edge of the wall.

". . . that nothing less than Almighty grace can cure it. We must turn to the One who knows us, who created us, and cry with the psalmist, 'Search me, O Lord, and prove me.' "

Suddenly I saw my shrinking soul. Love of the world and self-will had taken me from a loving husband. My pride kept me from him. All I thought of was myself. I wanted Will to come to *me*, to make *me* happy. Even the emeralds. I'd given them in an effort to buy *my* peace, to ease *my* guilt. Worst of all, in anger, I dared accuse Almighty God of murdering my child!

With a moan, I slipped from the wall and fell to my knees. My breath came in short gasps. There was no hope. God must turn His back on one so vile as I. A breeze touched my face, chilling the perspiration coursing from my forehead to my chin. Agony of soul became agony of body. Groaning and sobbing, I hid my face in my hands.

How I came to be in my own bed, I know not. For some time I lay alone in torment. Then I heard quick, purposeful steps and the door was flung open.

"I brought Mr. Wesley, ma'am," Bessie announced with a hasty curtsey.

He stepped past her, garbed in a black suit, carrying a broad-brimmed hat. Brown hair streaked with gray fell freely to his shoulders, framing his rather gaunt face. His most outstanding feature was his aquiline nose, until I looked into his eyes. They had the same piercing quality as Will's.

I pulled up the covers and turned away, fearing he might see my evil soul.

Calmly he touched my burning forehead with his cool hand. "Tell me of your distress, Mistress Knight."

Furtively I looked at him from the corner of my eye and saw compassion. He understood! Encouraged, I examined his clear countenance, struck by a serenity and deep joy foreign to me. I began speaking slowly, then more rapidly, baring my heart. Tears flowed. At times sobs prevented my speaking. Then I was done.

He did not withdraw in revulsion, but took my hand in his firm grasp. "Be not afraid, sister. This is the work of the Holy Spirit," he said. "Do you earnestly repent of these your sins?"

"Yes! Oh, yes!"

"Have you asked God's forgiveness!"

"No! How can one as evil as I venture to address Him?"

"We are *all* unworthy. Do you remember the story of the prodigal son?"

"Y—yes."

"The father waited most anxiously for his son's return. So God, your heavenly Father, is waiting for you, eager to forgive if you but ask." He knelt beside my bed. "Ask His forgiveness, Mrs. Knight."

"I don't know how."

"Talk to Him from your own heart. He'll understand, for He *loves* you."

"*He* loves *me*?"

"None is worthy of His love. 'While we were yet sinners, Christ *died* for us,' for *you*. Through Him, Christ alone, you may have salvation. You may be freed from the bondage of a life of sin and have the assurance He has taken away your sins, even as I have gained that assurance."

Clinging to his hand, I prayed, "Dear God, please, please forgive me. Thou knowest how black my heart is. Forgive me for—for holding You responsible for my—my baby. It was wicked to think evil of Thee. Thou only knowest how I've made Will suffer. It's been my sin, my self-will, my pride that's caused us this pain. I know I ought to be with him in Tyne, but I was afraid. Forgive me, please. And, O God, if it can be made right, show me the way! Lord, God, I throw myself on Thy great mercy!"

After waiting several moments, Mr. Wesley prayed, "We thank

Thee God, our Father, for hearing Thy child's humble confession and for granting her pleas."

The tortuous tension flowed from me. Blood ceased pounding in my temples.

"Give her Thy inner witness that she may know of a certainty she possesses Thy forgiveness and fill her with Thy peace. Shed Thy holy love over her and through her. Heal the wounds caused by this estrangement, and give this couple a measure of Thy wisdom that they may again dwell together in love. Amen."

He rose to his feet. "Have you the assurance that your confession was heard and forgiveness granted?"

Amazed, excited, I replied, "I feel right, clean, light as never in all my life! It's gone! That awful weight is gone!"

Chapter Fourteen

I heard Mr. Wesley and Bessie laughing heartily the next morning as I hurried down to receive him in the drawing room.

"Good morning, Mrs. Knight," he said as I entered. Arrayed in a black suit free of any speck of dust or wrinkle, with spotless white tabs, he stood scarcely any higher than I. Had I not heard him preach, I would have doubted a man of his mild appearance could move vast crowds of people.

"Good morning, sir," I replied.

Bessie wiped tears from her pink cheeks and dipped a curtsey before withdrawing.

"I was telling Sister Hoskins about the puppy and his young master at the Kingsley's where I am staying," he explained, his eyes sparkling. "They are a continual delight to me with their avid curiosity. Well, well, I see by your face that your heart is indeed at peace."

"Oh, yes! Everything was at odds with me. Now it's all different! I want to—to hold the world in my heart!" I gave him my hand and led him to the settee.

He nodded. "I too experienced having my life set in order by our gracious Saviour and being released from the burdens of sin."

As we sat down, I noticed Bessie hovering beyond the door. I beckoned her to join us. She sidled in and stood listening, her hands clasped at her waist, her lips parted in a half-smile.

"There is a joy bubbling up from—from my toes," I said.

"An itching to dance down the Lane to the High?" he asked with laughter tugging at his mouth.

"And a few years ago I thought being religious meant a sober countenance!"

"In truth, there is nothing sour, austere, unsociable or unfriendly in religion. On the contrary, it implies the most winning sweetness, the most amiable softness and gentleness. Every believer ought to enjoy life to the full. With God at his side, what could be more delightful?"

"Will, my husband, said much the same. I didn't fully understand what he meant."

"True religion is a heart and life devoted to God."

I thought of Mr. Law's book which Will took so seriously.

"It is loving God with all our hearts and our neighbor as ourselves. Then we will avoid even the *appearance* of evil, and do all possible good to all men. In this there is joy."

I shook my head and stared down at my hands. "I used to ignore appearances. That brought me much trouble."

"Forget what is past. Press on to what is ahead. Seek to grow in grace every hour."

Puzzled, I asked, "How may I do that?"

"In Scripture God has ordained that prayer, reading and hearing His Word, and receiving the Lord's Supper are the ordinary means of conveying grace to men. Therefore, let no day pass without private prayer, reading, and meditation."

"We did that together, Will and I."

"We are enjoined to pray without ceasing. And in souls filled with love, the desire to please God is a continual prayer."

"You mean it doesn't have to fit between 'Most gracious heavenly Father' and 'Amen'?"

"No. He hears the cry of your heart. Fix some part of every day for private exercises; for as the soul and body make the man, the spirit and discipline make a Christian. What is tedious will become pleasant. Therefore, whether or not you like it, read and pray daily. Read a little, pray and meditate much. And do so with expectation. Look for the answer to your prayer and it shall not tarry."

"You speak with such confidence!"

"I speak from God's dealings with me. Pursue perfection. 'Ye shall be perfect as your Father who is in heaven is perfect.' This is Christ's doctrine."

"That is beyond me, for I am filled with imperfection. I'm a very unsaintly person, Mr. Wesley."

"Sinlessness is not what is meant. I have told all the world I am not perfect. I tell you flat, I have not attained the character I draw. This Christian perfection, this sanctification, is pure love—love expelling sin and governing a child of God in both heart and life."

"*Pure* love? I've found mine full of selfishness."

"Let me explain more fully. This is important to grasp, for it leads to maturity," he said earnestly. "In one view it is purity of intention"—he struck his left palm with his right forefinger—"dedicating all the life to God. It is giving God *all* our heart. It is *one* desire and design ruling all our tempers. It is devoting not a *part* but *all* of our soul, body, and substance to God. There are no half Christians."

"In another view," he gestured with two fingers, "it is all the *mind* which was in Christ enabling us to walk as Christ walked. It is a *renewal* of the heart in the whole image of God, the *full* likeness of Him who created it.

"In yet another, it is loving God with all our heart *and* our neighbor as ourselves. In loving God, His love is shed abroad in our hearts by the Holy Spirit. And so it behooves us to express this in doing good to *all* men—strangers, friends, and enemies as well as neighbors. This is not only to their bodies in 'feeding the hungry and clothing the naked, visiting those that are sick or in prison' but also laboring to do good to their souls as God gives the ability."

Will lived this way. And Bessie. Certainly her patient care and concern these months had expressed selfless love. I exchanged a glance with her, feeling a new bond of affection.

"Christian companions are most helpful as we grow, for none can travel this road alone. There is a society of women meeting in a cottage near Merton, under the old city wall. They gather each Wednesday at seven to confess their faults and pray for each other. If you wish, I'll ask Mrs. Bymington, the leader, to take you with her."

Alarmed at baring myself to strangers, I exclaimed, "Is—is this necessary?"

"It is helpful. In fellowship, as we pray for each other, we gain strength and grow. You may be certain Satan will attack you in subtle ways. At such times it's good to know others are praying for you. And they likewise need to know you pray for them."

This picture of mutual support held appeal.

"You will be on trial for two months."

"On trial? Why?"

"To determine your true state. If after that time you wish to continue in this discipline, and no reasonable objection is found, you may join their society."

"I—I don't know."

"They, too, are sinners, forgiven by God's grace. And they have shared experiences similar to yours."

Bessie gave an encouraging nod.

"I—I'll go."

"Fine. Mrs. Bymington is a sensitive sister. Now, I must leave. I am to catch the coach to Bristol this afternoon."

He stood with closed eyes and prayed, "Confirm Thy child in Thy ways, Lord. Give her the faith that worketh by love and let her live by faith in Your Son. May she grow to love Thee with all her heart, mind, soul and strength, and to love every child of man even as Thou hast loved her. Let her daily add to her faith courage, knowledge, temperance, patience, brotherly kindness, and charity that she may overflow with Thy love and joy. Amen."

At the door, he paused with Bessie. "Please excuse me, Mrs. Knight, I must have a word with Sister Hoskins."

I waited a few minutes for him at the head of the stairs, reviewing all he had said. It differed little from Will's teachings. Deep within I felt a stirring, not of pain, but of yearning for him.

Mr. Wesley came soon and we descended together. "If you seek happiness in anything but the Lord," he said, "you must be disappointed. Follow Him closely, Mrs. Knight, and you will never come into any darkness of soul. Nothing but sin can bring you into confusion."

My hand was on the gate when he said, "Mrs. Knight, it is not enough to think, to say, to believe something is true. We must *live* it also!"

The atmosphere in Mr. Finchwythe's rented house had altered radically. When Bessie had returned to my room after seeing Mr. Wesley out the first night, I had embraced her, thanking her with joyful tears for taking me to St. Clement's fields. A dimension of love came into being between us.

Following Mr. Wesley's second departure, I set about cleaning and polishing with a light heart, singing the 96th Psalm from my heart. Dinner was delicious and I ate until I was stuffed, pleasing Bessie.

Feeling impelled to share my new life with Father and to beg his forgiveness for past behavior, I walked around to Christ Church. The afternoon sunshine was the most golden I'd seen. Trees and flowers glowed with vibrant colors. The very stones of Oxford's buildings were friendly. And the crowds of gownsmen and town folk no longer intimidated me.

The porter at Christ Church told me Father was up to town on University business and not expected back for several weeks. This lowered my spirits. There was no one to share this marvelous experience. I thought of Will, longing to tell him of this wonderful change.

During the succeeding days, I came to value the devotional disciplines I found onerous while at St. Thomas'. Each morning and night I read the Gospel of St. John and prayed for Will and myself and Father. During those quiet periods, I considered travelling to Tyne. I'd never gone so far. I'd heard terrifying tales of highwaymen and accidents. And when I arrived there, how would Will receive me?

On Wednesday next, Mrs. Bymington, a woman in her thirties,

called for me shortly before seven. She was shorter than I, plump, with rosy cheeks and sparkling black eyes. As we walked up Long Street, she told me of her five children and her dear, hard-working husband, once a drunkard.

Three other ladies awaited us. The hostess, shy and kind, introduced herself as Mrs. Kent, to be called Suzanna. She led us to her modest drawing room with five chairs arranged in a circle. I sat between Mrs. Bymington and a young girl named Hetty. Across from me sat a superior lady in a fine rose gown, Mrs. Wimple.

Mrs. Bymington hummed a tone and they began singing a song unfamiliar to me.

"Jesus, lover of my soul,
  Let me to thy bosom fly."

The tune was lively and I hummed along, embarrassed, out of place.

The women did not seem to notice my discomforture, intent as they were on making as much noise as possible. Hetty sat with clasped hands, her eyes squeezed shut, as if her life depended on this song. Her voice rang out in sweet, true tones.

"Thou, O Christ, art all I want;
  More than all in thee I find."

They really meant this!

"I am all unrighteousness;
  False and full of sin I am;
  Thou art full of truth and grace.

"Plenteous grace with thee is found,
  Grace to cover all my sin;
  Let the healing streams abound;
  Make and keep me pure within."

This was a hymn for me too.

After the "Amen," Mrs. Bymington inquired, "Hetty, how has it gone with you this week?"

She blushed, twiddled her fingers in her lap and answered, "Things were fine with me until I saw my Johnnie talking to Sarah Wedham. I became jealous and angry, and—and I've still no victory over it."

I remembered seeing Will talking to pretty girls at a ball, and I knew how she felt.

"We'll pray for you, Hetty. Suzanna, how has it gone with you this week?"

Our hostess replied, " 'Twas a good week for me. I've had joyful victory all the time."

A murmur of pleasure went around the circle.

Mrs. Bymington seemed about to ask another question, but instead turned to the lady in rose; "Nellie, how has it gone with you this week?"

Nellie bit her lips and twisted her handkerchief. Tears trembled in her eyes. "I've had a wretched week. I need your prayers so!"

Strange words for a woman of proud appearance!

"My new maid's clumsy. I think she fears me, and—and I've become angry and demanding. Each night I've confessed it and promised to do better, but the next day she'd annoy me in some way and I'd get angry again. Mad, really. I don't know what to do. A year ago I'd have let her go, but now. . . She needs the work. I think she really tries. I feel I must keep her, but I'm *so* unhappy with her."

Mrs. Bymington said, "Thank you, Nellie, for being honest. I know it's hard. We'll pray for you, not only tonight, but every day." She looked around the circle and they all nodded their heads vigorously.

"My girl Jennie and I've been barely speaking to each other this week," she continued. "Anything I say or do's wrong. She can't understand why I won't let her out at night with just any boy. She's taken a shine to the Crammer's son, you know *his* reputation, and she can't understand why I disapprove. A couple times she has sneaked out behind my back. She's pretty and headstrong. I'm so worried she'll get into trouble. And I get angry and she goes upstairs and sulks and won't talk at all. I need your prayers each and every day, very much."

They looked at me. What should I say?

"Margaret, would you mind telling us about your experience when Mr. Wesley was here?" Mrs. Bymington prompted.

"I went to hear him behind St. Clement's." I paused, reluctant to speak candidly. Nellie smiled at me and I plunged ahead. "There, for the first time, I saw myself. And—and my sins. I realized they were causing the misery I've suffered. And I prayed for God's forgiveness and everything's different now. It truly is. I've been happy, really happy. Everything's different, yet, everything's the same."

The women nodded as if they knew just what I meant. Hetty reached over to pat my arm. "I know," she whispered. "It was like that with me."

Then we knelt facing our chairs and leaning on the seats. Each prayed out loud for the others, naming the individual and her problem specifically. I grew hot hearing them pray for me, yet it was pleasant to know they took me seriously and cared about me as a person.

Suzanna's voice broke as she prayed. After a brief silence, she said, "Forgive my pride, O Lord, thinking I'm better than others. Lord, Thou knowest how imperfect I am! Please make me kinder and more understanding. Set a guard before the door of my lips and keep my tongue from speaking evil."

When my turn came, I feared to pray.

Mrs. Bymington broke the uncomfortable quiet summing up our prayers for each one in a sweet way.

We took our seats again and she opened a folded sheet of paper and showed it to Hetty. "I'll need your help," she said. "John Mockleberry brought this new hymn to the meeting and I thought it most appropriate for us."

"Is this another of Mr. Wesley's hymns?" Hetty asked.

"Yes. I don't think it's published yet. It goes this way:

'Forth in thy name, O Lord, I go,
 My daily labor to pursue;
 Thee, only thee, resolve to know
 In all I think or speak or do.' "

She then sang it to a popular tune, her voice wavering. Hetty joined, her pitch strong and true.

We learned it, singing each line after Mrs. Bymington read it, going through the verse twice. Then she read the next verse.

" 'The task thy wisdom hath assigned,
  O let me cheerfully fulfill;
  In all my words thy presence find,
  And prove thy good and perfect will.'

"The words seem so right for us to take with us," she commented. "In all our tasks, in all our speech, we can show our Lord's presence and prove out His will. We'll learn the rest next week."

The women pressed my hand as we parted. I thanked Suzanna for her hospitality and left with Mrs. Bymington. We were not in the house above an hour.

As I retired, I considered the evening. Only with Amelia had I bared my soul, and even then I'd not mentioned envy or anger as if they were sins. But they were. And these women were serious about removing them from their lives. Obviously they benefited from each other's support. I needed that support too, only it would take time to learn to speak freely concerning myself.

Sunday I dressed in a Parisian gown to attend divine service. The cathedral would be more than I could bear. St. Mary's, near the end of the Lane, would be filled with gownsmen, and the sermon would concern some obscure doctrine. The newer All Saints' would be better. I preferred its spacious, simple atmosphere, uncluttered with gothic trappings.

Watching the vicar climb the curved stairs to the pulpit, I recognized him as being from Lincoln. Mr. Wesley himself must have preached here. I tried imagining him beneath the sounding board crowned with urns, but failed. Having seen him in St. Clement's fields, his robes stirred by breezes, this sanctuary seemed a cramped, unlikely setting for him.

The white-wigged priest droned through his learned homily, rarely raising his eyes from the pages before him. In memory, Mr. Wesley took on the significance of a prophet, speaking God's word. Although his hair was not wild and untrimmed, and he had not ranted or raved, as I'd heard rumored, conviction and authority rang in his voice. Priestly garb provided the only point of similarity with the man before me.

Black marble panels above the altar were flanked by cherub heads. While unreadable from my seat, I knew the Commandments, Creed, and the Lord's Prayer were carved there. It struck me how cold and lifeless the service was, even as that marble. The words of God, housed in this beautiful church, were obscured by elaborate ceremonies and empty pomp.

Irreverently, I awaited the benediction and escape from tedium. No wonder the young couple beside me were absorbed in a flirtation. Across the aisle a woman read a book while the man at her side dozed. Next week I would try another church, a smaller one. Perhaps there I would find food for my soul.

The afternoon following my third meeting in Merton Lane, Charles reappeared at my door. Impeccably groomed in a lavender coat of the latest mode, he walked with confidence, swinging his amber-headed stick with a flourish.

"Charles, you look marvelous!" I exclaimed, leading him up to the drawing room.

"As a worthy poet said,

'Act well your part, there all the honor lies,
 Fortune in men has some small difference made . . . '

Dum-da-de-dum . . .

'Worth made the man, and want of it the fellow;
 The rest is all but leather and prunella.'

I was a 'fellow,' now I am a man.

> 'Happy the man, whose wish and care
> A few paternal acres bound,
> Content to breathe his native air,
> In his own ground.'

That is how I am, happy and content."

Over a glass of sherry, he appraised me carefully, then nodded. "You look far better. I thought that dress would become you."

I flushed with pleasure and twirled around. "We had to take it in here and there."

"And you *glow*, my dove. You must have heard from Will!"

"No, I. . ." My old wound throbbed and I faltered. "Charles, a *miracle* has happened! I know, I *know*, my sins are forgiven, and it's *wonderful*!"

"Sins!" His eyebrows shot upwards and he examined me through his gold-rimmed quizzing glass. "Meg, are you tangled in some religious nonsense?"

"It's not nonsense! I heard Mr. Wesley preach—"

"Wesley! That raving fanatic! What does your father say to this?"

"He's been to London on some University matter. I shall tell him on his return. It is *real*, Charles! That was above three weeks ago, and I know it's *real*. I *am* different!"

"I can see you are. Not so downcast. Eating better." He eyed me speculatively, tapping his cheek with his quizzing glass. "I wonder how this will affect Will."

"Will?"

"Your husband, Meg. He lives in Tyne, you know. Is this forgiveness, this happiness, whatever, is this to include *him* as well?"

"What do you mean?"

"I've come from Portsmouth . . . and Tyne. There was a false lead on Arthur." He swung his glass idly on its lavender ribbon. "Found out why he had to go there so often." Charles chuckled. "Had little to do with business. London's the place for that, you know. Didn't think the old boy had it in him."

"He was seeing a woman?"

"A very choice bit of goods."

"But—but he was *married*!"

"A matter of estate and lineage." He wrinkled his nose. "Since he left no heirs, and Martha's certainly not breeding, I suppose it falls to me to save the family name. Most distasteful! All that is neither there, here, nor anywhere. What was I saying? Oh, yes, I went to Portsmouth, and when I finished there, for the present, I went on to Tyne and visited Will in his new parsonage."

"You did?" My heart thumped hard in my breast. "It's finished?"

"It is. He lives there."

"What is it like? Is it snug and nice for him?"

"Hardly big enough to turn around in, though he's added a room. He assured me it's suitable for his needs and tight against the weather."

Restlessly I fussed with a vase of flowers on the table. There was a place for me if. . .

"Well, what are you going do do?"

"Do? Why—why naturally I must go, if—if he'll have me."

"Of course he will."

"Father thought not." Such a long journey through Berkshire, Hampshire and Sussex to Tyne. The magnitude of the trip threw me into panic, and I clutched at formality. "I will write a letter to prepare him."

"A letter!" Charles dropped his quizzing glass.

"Of course. Can you imagine what a shock it would be if I arrived suddenly, without announcement!"

"I dare say he would survive," Charles said drily. "How long will it take to write this letter?"

"Not long. Not long at all. I must compose myself, think how to say, what I should say, and—and write it. Not—not long at all."

"Will it take another year?"

I flushed angrily. "Of course not! I suppose you think I should leave now, this very instant! It takes time to pack. Why, Amelia takes *weeks* to prepare for a trip. Things must be done in order, properly, without undue haste."

"Undue haste! Meg, what *are* you thinking of? You've kept him waiting too long already!"

"Then what difference does another day or two make? I must think." I stamped my foot and flared out, "Don't *stare* at me that way. Who are you to sit in judgment on me?"

"A friend. I'm not sitting in judgment. I thought you would. . . Never mind. Apparently there is less change in your life .nan you think."

His words shocked me. Regaining control over my temper, I said more calmly, "We'll talk over supper. I'm surprised the parsonage is ready so soon."

"I'll not stay. I came to tell you the 'good' news. I'll be on my way. My coachman awaits."

"You went by coach?"

"Yes. I always go to Tyne that way. It's, er, more comfortable. Regardless, I do not intend to keep him waiting for nothing!"

"For nothing! Why, pray tell, is he waiting?"

"Either to help load your things for Tyne or take me to Rockivale. I am needed there."

"To load my things! Did you expect me to begin a journey of this consequence *immediately*? Now? At *teatime*?"

"Good-bye, m'dear. I must hurry home. The rocks may fly away if I'm not there to watch them." He bowed with an exaggerated flourish and left.

Stunned, I heard him descend the stairs quickly and shut the front door. He thought I was making excuses! This very night I would write a letter. Tomorrow I would begin packing. Probably I should wait for a reply in the event Will should not want me. But he must. He must.

I searched through several drawers until I found paper, quill and ink. It took more rummaging to locate my penknife. I sat down, sharpened the quill carefully, and wrote, "Dear Will." No more rational words would come. I chewed on the end of the quill, thinking.

Late that night, in my room, I completed my letter and burned it. The next day I struggled to compose a proper message. Everything, being excessively stiff or sentimental, ended as ashes in my grate.

As I watched the last attempt curl and blacken in orange flames, I shivered. It might be necessary to make that awful trip without writing Will, not knowing if he would have me.

Saturday, a young footman, splendid in sky blue livery, pulled the bell. Bessie brought me a note, exclaiming over his fine appearance. While I read it, she stood before my mirror, fussing with her mob cap and gown. "He's quite handsome, ma'am," she confided. "And from London!"

"He told you that?"

"No ma'am. He has that sound in his words. Very plain it is."

The note was from Amelia. She had taken a rented house and asked me to call soon. Excited to see her again, and mystified at her sudden return, I went with the footman to see her immediately.

Amelia was directing the removal of dust covers and cleaning an elaborate ballroom when her haughty butler announced me with an air of disdain. She embraced and kissed me enthusiastically, then led me into a small salon to be alone.

"You can't *know* how happy I am to see you, Meg. You are my *one* comfort! I've *left* Oliver!" she announced. "And it's *such* a relief! I feel *young* again!" Her eyes were over-bright and her color high.

"Amelia! But why?"

"Life was *intolerable* with him. He has a *mistress,* you know."

"I didn't know."

"Well, it's *common* knowledge in town. He took up with that—that *woman* while I was carrying Stephan and couldn't satisfy his needs. He even *left* me to ride up to London to see her just before his *son's* birth. When he belonged here, with *me!*"

I remembered her great distress.

"She's pretty enough, I suppose," she added.

"You *know* her?"

"Oh, yes. He's quite *open* about it. I think it would not have been so *humiliating* had he tried to keep it *from* me. I simply could *not* tolerate it any longer. I hoped with the birth of his son, his *heir,* the flirtation would die. But it hasn't," she finished weakly.

"Oh, my dear Amelia!" I took her hand to offer sympathy.

She pressed her trembling lips together and raised her chin defiantly. "Mother told me I should *ignore* this. *All* men have affairs some time or other, usually *many*. It's the way *they* are."

All men? Arthur, now Oliver. And the squire in Tyne had a pretty daughter, and everyone thought Will unmarried.

"She may be right," Amelia continued. "*I* don't care. I won't be second to *any* woman! I never did like London. It's crowded and *filthy*. I prefer living here. Maybe I'll divorce him and make the break complete."

"Oh, Amelia!"

"Its been done, you know. I'm here to live my *own* life. And to begin with, I'm giving a *ball!*"

"A ball?" This new Amelia puzzled and shocked me.

"To celebrate my *freedom,* my new *life*. And *you* must come. You've been *too* quiet, *too* solemn. Actually living like a *widow*. But, if you were one, as pretty and slim as you are, I think you'd have more *fun*." She paused. "Or, have you heard from your Will?"

"No. Charles visited him and says he is doing well."

Kindly she said, "Stop pining for him, Meg. Come to my ball next Wednesday. Make it a new beginning for you too."

"Wednesday?" I thought of the praying ladies in Merton Lane. "I don't know. I haven't been to a ball in ages." An evening of gaiety and music was tempting. It would dispel the malaise Charles left.

"Please, Meg!" Her earnest appeal won.

"Yes, I'll come."

"Good. Now, you *must* arrange my bouquets. No one does it half so well as *you*."

I agreed readily, shoving aside a few stubborn doubts.

Wednesday morning I supervised placing the bouquets I arranged from the mounds of pink and white blooms Amelia provided. They reminded me of the ones I worked with for her marriage banquet. What happened to the love and happiness shining in their faces that day?

Bessie said little as she pulled my laces tight. I knew she thought I should go to Merton Lane. No matter. I could go next week. Tonight I would be gay again and wear my blue satin gown. I scrutinized my reflection critically. Since we restyled it in the mode of the new French dresses, it looked quite fine.

The doorbell interrupted my preparations and Bessie went down to answer. I heard Mrs. Bymington's voice and felt a guilty twinge. Next week, when I explained, at least Hetty would understand. The rest might be shocked at my preferring frivolity to their meeting. Amelia was right. I needed this evening. Tonight's laughter and music would be a welcome diversion from the problem of my unwritten letter.

It was exciting to mingle once more with people in beautiful clothing. All around me were bright colors, flashing jewels, sharp laughter, and witty words. It was so familiar, I kept expecting Will or at least Charles to appear.

Strangely, no dons were in attendance. A constantly changing throng of youths, many in black silk gowns and caps with gold tassels, surrounded Amelia. She flirted outrageously. Her lively laughter and carelessly blown kisses seemed to infect everyone. The other women, evidently new friends, also behaved in a bold, disquieting manner. I had been a recluse too long. Or was it because Will was not at my side that everything seemed a gaudy pretense?

A young man in puce satin and frothy lace danced me out of the room into a small, vacant salon. Distrusting his familiar manner, I suggested we return to the others.

Holding my arm firmly, he pulled me close. "I've heard of you, Mistress Knight," he whispered, "but the stories don't begin to do you justice." And he kissed my cheek.

I whirled to slap him, but he dodged with a laugh.

"Ah! I prefer spirit to demurely downcast eyes! You *will* permit me to escort you home tonight—and *remain*."

I gasped, speechless.

"Oh, come, come, madam. Heathton need not know. Anyways, surely he wouldn't mind while he's out of town. In fact, you must be quite lonely."

"How *dare* you address me in this fashion!"

"Such indignation! Everyone in Oxford knows of Mistress Knight. I, for one, admire your taste, your flare for mystery and seclusion."

"You misunderstand completely!" I broke from his grasp and dashed to the door, nearly colliding with Amelia and a brash young man. Before my eyes he took her in his arms and kissed her! And she embraced him!

I fled to the ballroom. One of Amelia's older, more reserved, admirers requested I stand up with him. His proper attitude soothed my feelings. Later he took me to dinner. At its conclusion, anxious to depart this bewildering affair, I asked him to summon Amelia's carriage for me.

On his return, he bowed and kissed my fingertips. "It is at the door, fair lady. May I await on you tomorrow evening?"

I stared at him. "What?"

"May I call?"

"Sir, I am a married woman. I do not receive evening callers. I am present tonight only as Amelia's friend."

"I understand perfectly, dear lady," he answered smoothly. "However, all the world knows you receive. One gentleman in particular. Since he is not now in residence, surely there would be no objection if I—"

"Sir, I will *not* receive you!" The footman barely had time to hand me my cardinal as I ran down the steps to the carriage. I felt like to vomit. Leaning back on the pink satin squabs, I gulped the night air and fanned my face briskly.

Mrs. Bymington called the next afternoon. Hot with embarrassment, I met her in the drawing room. She settled primly on the edge of a chair, her stiff, white stomacher a sharp contrast to her dark brown gown. Nervously I poured her a dish of tea.

"We missed you last night, my dear."

"I attended a ball given by Amelia Simpson, a dear friend of mine."

"I heard she was in town. It must have been a lavish affair."

"It was. She always does things in a high style."

Mrs. Bymington stirred her tea and sugar slowly. "And did you enjoy it?"

"No." I was shaking so badly my tea spilled into my saucer.

"I see." She sounded sympathetic.

I looked up at her. "I wanted some fun. It's been so *long* since I attended a party. Do you *understand*?"

"Of course I do, my dear. But why didn't you enjoy it?"

"At first I did, except—except I missed my husband."

"Of course. And then?"

"They all behaved in—in an unbelievable fashion! I. . . Two men had the effrontery to. . . It was *mortifying*!"

"You mentioned missing your husband. Please don't take offense at my familiarity, but I'm confident you won't miss him much longer."

I raised my eyebrows in surprise. What did she know I did not?

"You told us he was repairing his parsonage. No doubt it will soon be finished, and you can go to him. Then your lengthy separation will be over. Let us pray for its speedy completion." Promptly she set down her empty cup and knelt by her chair.

I followed her example, my mind in a turmoil.

She prayed with her customary fervor. Not one word penetrated my mind.

She was assuming I would go to Tyne immediately when the parsonage was ready. As Charles had. Fear blocked my way.

When we rose, I wiped tears from my lashes. "Thank you," I managed to whisper.

"My dear, are you fearful of making this trip?"

I nodded.

"At times I too fear to follow what I know is God's leading. When I hang back, I am reminded of a promse in Isaiah. 'Fear not; for I have called thee by thy name; thou art mine. When thou passest through the waters, I will be with thee; and through the rivers, they shall not overflow thee; when thou walkest through the fire, thou shalt not be burned; neither shall the flame kindle upon thee. For I am the Lord thy God.' Remember, my dear, fear not."

That night I gave strict orders to Bessie to bar the outside doors and admit no one unless she knew for certain it was a friend. The bell was pulled repeatedly, its loud clang carrying up two flights of stairs and penetrating my closed door. Each time I winced, appalled at its significance. This came of my heedless flouting of appearances.

Dressed for bed, I sought comfort in my Bible. Having finished John's Gospel, I had turned to the epistles. I began reading near the end of Ephesians, where I had left off in the morning.

Words seemed to leap from the page and fasten themselves to

my heart. "Wives, submit yourselves unto your own husbands, as unto the Lord."

I had submitted to Will. Our shared, joyous loving surged into my mind. Pained, I read on quickly.

"For the husband is the head of the wife, even as Christ is the head of the church."

I had not yielded to Will as my head, or I would have accompanied him, would even now be in Tyne. Impatiently, I brushed away the tears blurring the print. Skipping several lines, hoping for a safer passage, I read, blinked and read again.

"And the wife see that she reverence her husband."

I *did* reverence Will. I *loved* him. I would gladly welcome him to my arms and submit to him if he were only here. Mr. Wesley's last words came back clearly. "It is not enough to think, to say, to believe something is true. We must *live* it also."

I was Will's wife. I knew it. I said it last night, but those men did not believe me. Even Amelia called me a widow. Unless I was with Will, I could not be a good wife.

But would he want me? Long ago Father mentioned scars from past hurts. I, whom he loved once, had added to them. When he left, Will said I would always be welcome. Was this still true? Or had I caused so much pain he no longer wanted me? Might he have changed that much?

Snapping my Bible shut, I jumped up to place it on my table, tripped on my nightdress, and tore it. Disgusted at my carelessness, I examined the rip. If not mended promptly, it would grow during the night.

Needing a needle and thread, I removed the tray of my sewing box to take it to my bed where I would sit to repair my gown. The candlelight shone on a misshapen bit of metal in a corner of the bottom section. I picked it up, holding it near the flame.

Will's teeth marks were still plain where he had held the coin to break it the day I agreed to marry him. He used to carry the other piece in a pouch over his heart.

Fear not.

We must *live* it.

I dashed into the hall shouting, "Bessie! Bessie!"

She opened her door in wide-eyed alarm.

"Where is Father's money for my ticket to Tyne? I'm going at once!"

Chapter Fifteen

The coach came to a rocking halt. Almost immediately the guard flung open the door and dropped the steps, bawling, "Tyne-at-de-Crossroads!" He helped me down and pointed across the road. "Dat dere's de Curling Horn, ma'am. De onliest one wud rooms to let here abouts."

His odd speech grated on my ears. I hoped the people here spoke more plainly.

While the driver handed down my things, I glanced around at the cluster of buildings comprising the village. It was far from Oxford's grand style. No wonder the man at the coaching office had grumbled, " 'Taint a regular stop. No one goes there."

The guard touched his hat, leapt up on the box and the old coach rumbled off, leaving me alone with my trunk and boxes at the foot of a gallows. I watched the coach up the road curving between thatched cottages until it rounded a bend and was no longer visible. It would be several days before another came.

Some yards beyond me, another rutted track crossed the road. Above this crossing, on a rise, stood the church, its gray tower showing between the branches of several elms. It looked sturdy and aged, as if it watched life between these hills long before the foundations of the village. Perhaps it dated from Saxon days. On the far side I saw the corner of a cottage with a large, gracefully weeping willow trailing over its garden wall. That must be the vicarage, Will's home.

I started towards it, eager to see him. A man's hail from the inn detained me.

Roughly dressed in a short, buff jacket, his shirt sleeves rolled to the elbow, he stood in the open doorway. His flaxen hair was neatly pulled back from his ruddy face into a queque. Above him hung a cracked wooden sign bearing the faint, peeling picture of a ram's head on a bluish background. A small, leaded window on either side of the door faced the road out of a dirty white, plastered wall. The overhanging upper stories, faced with gray flint, were capped with a steep red-tiled roof. The building towered over the rest of the village huddling against the hill beyond it.

I became aware that I was the object of several people's attention, in the smithy next to the inn and standing in the doors of the few shops along the road. Never since my first days at Mrs. Spinet's had I been scrutinized by so many strangers. I must escape them. Will's church and the inn offered refuge. At the moment, being nearer, the inn looked more inviting.

"I reckon ye'll be wanting a place to stay, ma'am?" the man asked coming towards me. "Dere be naunbut dis inn here." He bowed. "We'd be pleased to serve ye, ma'am."

Anything was preferrable to those stolid stares. "Yes. I—I need a place to stay."

He approached briskly and offered his hand to help me across the deeply rutted road. At the inn's door, he shouted, "Lookee sharp, Nancy! We've a lady!"

I stepped over the threshold into a long room spanned by thick oak beams. Several deal tables and four-legged stools in the center were littered with dirty earthen dishes and bits of food. At the farther end was a large stone fireplace flanked by high-backed settles. A woman sweeping the crimson tile floor set aside her broom, wiped her hands on the stained apron over her blue-and-green ticken petticoat and bobbed a curtsey.

"Ye be welcome, ma'am," she said. "Ye'll be wanting a bite to ait and tub to freshen in," she stated, giving her mob cap a tug.

"Er, yes, please." I could hardly understand these people.

"Foller me up. I'll bring up your tray dracly minute. Mus Wilmot, he'll tote up your things and show your maid to a room down de hall."

"I—I have no maid. I'm travelling alone."

She eyed me up and down speculatively. "Oh. Yes, ma'am."

I was led to a room titled "The Lamb." Against two walls stood a narrow bed, chest of drawers and wardrobe, all of plain oak, badly scratched. A marble-topped table held a white basin and pitcher. The bentwood chair beside the chest had a seat of green tapestry. A frayed, orangish-red bellpull hung near the door.

With relief, I shed my dusty garments and soaked off travel grime in the tepid hip bath. While I devoured thick slices of bread and cheese, washing them down with brown ale, I looked at the bed with longing. To be at my best when meeting Will, I must rest.

Refreshed by a nap, I prepared carefully for this vital meeting. I chose a green dress of Holland cloth and brushed my hair around my trembling fingers into ringlets.

Already the exhausting journey was fading like a bad dream. The tales of hazardous travel and dirty inns had always seemed exaggerated. They were not. We had suffered a broken axel, a drunken driver, and Hampshire highwaymen armed with pistols. Had I not carried most of my money in a packet next to my skin, as Amelia advised, I should have arrived here destitute.

The Sussex roads, pitted with bone-jarring holes and ruts, crossed endless treeless hills, most of which we passengers trudged up leaning against the eternal wind. Had I known all this before, I should have preferred to chance riding across country, leaving my things for Charles to bring later.

How could he consider a *coach* more comfortable than his cabriolet or riding Kahn? "I always go to Tyne that way," he said. Was he coming oftener than I knew? He might be seeing that woman of Arthur's whom he called "a very choice piece of goods."

I paused at the door to rehearse my speech for Will. It sounded shabby. The hope riding on my shoulder as we crossed Folly Bridge had deserted me along the road.

"The rivers will not overflow me," I whispered for the hundreth time. Words, only words. Anxiously I recalled a hymn sung in Merton Lane:

Men, devils engaged, the billows arise,
And horribly rage, and threaten the skies;
Their fury shall never our steadfastness shock
The weakest believer is built on a rock!

My steadfastness was shaken. I did not feel secure or built on the Rock. Nor could I give "thanks never ceasing," as instructed in the next verse. Rather, my new faith seemed to have spent itself along the way, leaving me isolated, apart from God's presence. Was I even beyond the reach of the Merton ladies' prayers?

Having come this far, I could not turn back now. Resolutely I descended to the common room.

The sun streamed through the western windows onto the freshly scrubbed tables and stools, leaving the fireplace and settles in semishadows. Everything looked mellowed from age, but clean. On the whole, it was better than most of the crowded inns I'd seen along the coaching road. Voices came from a door across the room, leading, I assumed, into the taproom.

I was crossing towards it when the woman who greeted me bustled out, giving me a glimpse behind her of several men in laborers' smocks, drinking from tankards.

"Oh, ma'am, I didn't know ye be about. Be ye rested?"

I cleared my throat and licked my dry lips. "Yes, thank you. I—I will take a walk about the village, to see the church."

"Dere be naun bettermost to ourn, no-one-wheres-de-wurreld. De new parson, he brung it up to snuff to year, fine as ever it were. Now he holds services dere every Sunday as regular as regular."

"I noticed it when I arrived."

"Begging your pardon, ma'am, but ye'd be best be back dis side o' de dark. Ye hadn't ought to be later. Lamentable unsafe it be."

"Thank you. I'll remember."

I walked under the stately old elms in the churchyard, past the tipsy table monuments with bulging sides, to the gray flint church. Just below the top of the square tower protruded a row of carved faces. Gargoyles, I thought, robbed of their ferocity by the patient erosion of time.

The stone arch above the south door was patched in two places with freshly squared stones. Black beaten bands and large bright nails studded the heavy oak door. A large plate of curious scrolled design, fashioned by an artistic blacksmith of long ago, surrounded an enormous keyhole.

Inside stood an ancient marble font encircled with carved oak leaves. Above the oaken alms box close by, there were several crude geometrical carvings in the stone doorjamb. I wondered at their meaning. Benches with narrow seats and straight backs flanked the single aisle leading to the iron rail before the stone altar incised with five crosses. Stray beams from the low sun glowed on the brass cross and candlesticks. The musty smell of ages seemed to creep from the dimming corners of the freshly whitewashed walls.

Everything bore the heavy simplicity of poverty. Often Will complained that we neglect the poor and preach to the rich when our Lord said preaching to the poor was a sign His kingdom had come. Will should feel comfortable here.

Three tall, narrow windows on each side admitted little light. Their colored panes formed scenes of the nativity, Christ in the temple, with the woman at the well, as the Good Shepherd, healing Bartimaeus and holding a fair Saxon child on His lap. Over the altar His pale countenance was raised heavenward, His hands lifted in benediction or prayer as fluffy clouds bore Him upward from green hills very similar to those of Sussex.

I approached the chancel slowly, awed at being in this place of Will's ministry. Three new steps of wood led to the stone pulpit high on my left. His hands would rest on its edge as he spoke forth God's word. Above, massive wooden beams, dark with age, formed the chancel arch. A large black hook, which once held a crucifix, protruded from it.

I knelt on the stone floor and bowed my head, my face in my

hands. Incoherently, I begged God for wisdom, for strength, for courage, and mostly that He would make Will receptive to me. At last, ready to seek him at the vicarage, I rose to my feet.

I was dusting off my petticoat when the north door opened and I saw a man's silhouette. "Are—are you the vicar?" I asked, my heart beating wildly.

"No, ma'am, I am Edward Smythe, at your service. Do you wish to see him?"

"Yes, if—if he's not too busy."

He closed the door and approached me deferentially. "I'm sorry, ma'am, but he was called to see old Goody Hawkson but a short while ago. He'll likely be quite late."

I clasped my hands nervously. Should I await his return, possibly beyond the coming of dark, or go back to the inn?

"May I give him your name and your direction? He could call on you tomorrow after the services," he suggested.

Of course, that would be best. "Tomorrow is. . .?"

"Sunday, ma'am."

"Thank you. I've—I've lost track of the days. I've been travelling. From Oxford."

"And your name?"

If I said "Mrs. Knight," he would assume I was related to Will. That might prove embarrassing to him if he didn't. . . "Er, Castleton. Miss Castleton," I answered. "Please tell him Miss Castleton was here. I'm staying at the Curling Horn, and will attend service tomorrow. Ah, what is his name?"

"Dr. William Knight, Miss. And a fine man he is. Also from Oxford. I know you'll enjoy the service right well."

"I'm sure I shall, Mr.—Mr. Smythe."

We went through the south door into the twilight. I saw him to be dark-haired, slightly shorter than Will. He seemed solid and trustworthy, a comfortable man with a mouth curved for humor.

Shadows from the hills were deepening on the village as I walked to the inn, dejected by another delay. However, if Mr. Smythe delivered my message and prepared Will for my appearance, this might be better after all. It would not be fair to catch him unawares in the service.

"Rend your heart, and not your garments, and turn unto the Lord your God: for he is gracious and merciful, slow to anger, and of great kindness, and repenteth him of the evil," read Will.

I thrilled to the sound of his voice, to seeing him again in vestments, leading the worship.

Sunlight touched his wigless head, gilding his fair hair. Two new creases crossed his forehead. His face was tanned, as if he spent much time outside. The hump on his nose seemed more accented and his cheeks a little hollowed. Either he was not eating well, or he was working too hard. As he moved his hands, I noticed fraying on his cuffs. I should mend them soon. Only once did his hazel eyes meet mine briefly. My heart turned over with a great thump and my cheeks must have flamed red.

Fervently I prayed the collect with him. "O Lord, our heavenly Father, Almighty and everlasting God, who hast safely brought us to the beginning of this day; Defend us in the same with Thy mighty power; and grant that this day we fall into no sin, neither run into any kind of danger; but that all our doings, being ordered by Thy governance, to do alway that is righteous in Thy sight; through Jesus Christ our Lord. Amen."

As the congregation filed out behind a portly gentleman, several of them threw shy glances my way. Of the fifty or so fair-haired, blue-eyed people present, I was probably the only stranger. Simple though my lutestring gown and straw hat were, they must have looked costly to most of the women.

With a formal nod Will greeted me. "Miss Castleton? Mr. Smythe informed me of your arrival. I regret I was out last evening."

Sense and composure deserted me. I trembled as a foolish chit not yet out of the schoolroom. "I . . . yes . . . it—it was wonderful to—to . . . worship with you this morning."

His eyes remained disturbingly blank. Tiny tension lines framed his mouth. "Will you be with us again?" he asked coolly.

"Yes. I'm—I'm staying at the Curling Horn."

"So Mr. Smythe said. I trust you enjoy your stay." He turned to a middle-aged man waiting to speak with him.

Rebuffed by his manner, I walked away, biting my lips to keep back my tears. After all my anticipation, this meeting had turned out all wrong.

"Ho there, Miss Castleton!" called the rotund gentleman. He hurried to me with a limping hop and waving his beribboned stick. His white full bottom wig and the skirts of his brown camlet coat bounced with each hop. "Miss Castleton, Miss Castleton," he began breathlessly, his ruddy complexion beaded with perspiration, "Squire Addleby at your service. I understand you arrived yesterday from Oxford."

"Yes. I left there a few days ago."

"Fine, fine. And are you acquainted with Dr. Philip Castleton of Christ Church College?"

"My father."

"Is he indeed! A fine man. A fine man. I see him when I go to Oxford. Perhaps he's mentioned me?"

"Yes, several times."

"We would be honored, my daughter and I, if you would dine with us today."

"Thank you, sir. I shall be happy to do so."

"On Sundays we dine late, at five. And, of course, we would like you to stay for tea and supper, if possible. As Colonel Snyde and his aide will be with us, we must be formal. I shall send my coach for you about half after four."

"Thank you. You are very kind."

"I am eager to hear of your fine father. He is so stimulating! An exceptional intellect! Always so kind to me. We must make your sojourn in our quiet village enjoyable."

"I'm sure it will be," I answered with a confidence I did not feel.

On leaving the churchyard, I encountered Mr. Smythe. In the bright sunshine, his attractive features were dominated by laughing eyes. His light step and gay smile reminded me of Charles, and I was drawn to him. A slim girl with yellow curls hung on his arm.

We exchanged bows.

"Good day, Miss Castleton. May I present Miss Cowper? Next Sunday Dr. Knight will post our bans." They looked lovingly at each other.

"May I wish you happy. Have I seen you before, Miss Cowper?"

"I help at de Curling Horn, ma'am."

"Oh, yes. I remember. Last night I had a glimpse of you in the taproom."

They hurried off down the road, leaving me in a pensive mood.

As I requested, Anne Cowper roused me from a deep sleep to help me dress. Though unused to having a maid, I hoped to learn about Will and the people of Tyne through her.

Chattering happily in heavily accented speech, she arranged my hair with surprising skill. Her blue eyes sparkled as she worked, her tongue keeping pace with her fingers. She confided she once hoped to better her position through some foreign lady stopping here, but now definitely preferred being "Mistus Smythe."

I questioned her about Mr. Smythe, seeking to draw her out.

"He justabout be an upstanding man, ma'am. He be kind and good, for all he be a King's man."

"A King's man?"

"He be de Prevention Officer, ma'am. It were lamentable evil in

Tyne wud robbers and murderers. 'Twas hardly safe to leave your door. Den Mus Smythe come. He catched and hung four of dem. 'Tis safe now daytimes. But not by night. Ye hadn't ought to goo out arter dark. Den de *Devil* hisself roams."

Her tone was so serious, an ominous chill made me shiver. "Your Mr. Smythe seems to have done well."

"Aye, dat he has. Not like de Colonel. How he do goo on! 'Twill be most comfortable when he goo away."

"Oh?"

"Him be a contrary, ill-conditioned man. Dere be naun as is partial to him. Naun at all."

"I see. I met Mr. Smythe at the church last night."

"Yes, ma'am," she exclaimed proudly. "He be a God-fearing man. Him and Dr. Knight do be neighbors together."

"And your vicar, do you like him?"

"Oh, yes, ma'am. He be a still man, and a'most a saint. 'Tis miracles he's worked! It's not yet two year since he come, and de changes we've had! We'd no vicar since I be leetle. Ye seen our fine church. 'Twas his work. And he built de vicarage a'most from de ground. It were tedious bad! We've services as regular as de sun, even in Docking. And, like Goody Hawkson says, he loves us all. And he's teached Mus Smythe some of his learning. He says he'll goo far in de King's service."

"I'm sure your vicar is right. I mean, he seems a very astute man. And he is good looking too, don't you think?"

"Dat he be. All de 'oomen be arter him, him not being married, you know. But him's lost his heart to Miss Elizabeth, de Squire's daughter. She be purty and of de quality too. He lived wud de squire 'til de last weeks, de vicarage being justabout rattleboned. It were Fate, her being purty and all. But de Squire, he wants better'n a parson for his only daughter."

"Pull the laces as tight as you can," I directed, not wishing to hear more such gossip. "The Squire said this is a formal dinner. I must look my best."

She obeyed, tightening my corset until I could barely breathe. Carefully she lifted my green silk gown over my head and arranged the back folds over my panier. I fastened Charles' little circlet of diamonds to the ecru lace on my bosom, then hung Will's earrings on my ears. Would he attend this dinner instead of a colonel?

The squire's footman in startling orange and blue livery took my cloak at the door. The old butler led me through the central mahogany panelled hall, past a curving staircase to the salon in back.

"Miss Castleton," he announced and withdrew.

Quickly the squire came with an effusive welcome and led me to an attractive young lady. "Miss Castleton, my daughter, Elizabeth."

"Miss Castleton, we are most happy to have you in our home." Her smile lit her dark brown eyes flecked with gold and brought a becoming flush to her cheeks. Her brown hair was prettily curled and the cut of her crimson and cream gown displayed her slender figure to good advantage. She radiated youthful exuberance. Any man could lose his heart to her.

"I am delighted to be here. Please call me Margaret, or Meg. My friends do."

"Meg it shall be. And you shall call me Elizabeth."

"Colonel Snyde, may I present Miss Castleton," said Squire Addleby. "Miss Castleton is the daughter of one of the leading dons of Christ Church, Oxford, and, I am proud to say, one whom I count a friend."

Glittering with gold braid and lace on the scarlet cuffs and lapels of his blue coat and ornate gold embroidery on his buff waistcoat, the colonel bowed. His bold eyes swept me from head to hem. Raising my hand to his lips, he pressed a flabby, moist kiss on it in an excessive display of gallantry. A large man, he spoke with self-assurance in a deep voice. A silvered scar crossed his right cheek to the bridge of his nose. Arrogance and power showed in his stance. His look and tone implied he and I must make the best of being among social inferiors. He seemed the kind to heap flattery upon any woman catching his attention. New and alone, I felt marked as his next target.

"And this is Lieutenant Stevenson," Elizabeth said, indicating the handsome young officer at her side.

He bowed low over my hand, murmuring something so softly I could not hear it.

"And behind you. . ."

I began turning at the squire's words.

" . . . is our beloved vicar, Dr. Knight."

I saw Will as his name was spoken. Light-headed, darkness swirled in from the sides. Fortunately a settee was at my side and I sank onto it.

"Are you all right, Miss Castelton?" my host inquired anxiously.

Colonel Snyde sat beside me solicitously and began chafing my wrist.

"Oh, yes, quite," I answered, fluttering my fan with my free hand, trying to draw the other from the colonel's grasp. "Just a little dizzy. I'm still fatigued from my journey. Forgive me, please. Dr.

Knight, it's a pleasure to see you again."

He bowed and moved out of sight behind the others.

"You're sure nothing's wrong, Meg?" Elizabeth asked.

"Very sure. It's just a bit of dizziness. I feel so foolish!"

Will brought me a glass of deep red liquid, his eyes avoiding mine. "Drink this wine. The squire's specialty."

"Yes, yes, my dear. That'll put color in your cheeks," Addleby assured me. He watched attentively as I sipped it. "Perhaps you met our good vicar in Oxford. He was at St. Thomas' before coming here, and a fellow at Hertford College before that. In fact, your father recommended him to me. Very highly, he did. And I'm glad I listened."

"Yes, I knew Dr. Knight there. A mutual friend introduced us, Mr. Charles Heathton."

"Ah, yes, Lord Rockivale's son. He's paid us several visits. A fine young man. Not a featherheaded fool as so many of his age. It's a pity about his brother."

The butler announced dinner.

"Please do not delay because of me," I said attempting to rise. But my knees would not support my weight.

"Humph. Well, well, no need to hurry. Dr. Knight, will you please escort Miss Castleton in when she is able?" Squire Addleby asked.

"Gladly, sir." Will spoke with polite restraint.

"You must have much in common. Come, come, everyone. Mustn't delay or the food will cool," urged the squire, leading the others from the room.

When the door closed, I looked at Will. His back was to me, his attention focused on the sideboard.

"Will, I'm so *glad* you're here. I'm most anxious to talk with you."

"Now is neither the time nor the place." His words were like a stinging slap.

"No, no. Of course not." I finished the wine and, leaning on the settee arm, managed to regain my feet. Half-fearing another set down, I placed my glass before him and touched his sleeve. "Look at me, please," I said, yearning to see tenderness and love in his eyes again.

"You are very lovely," he said politely, moving the glass beside a cut glass decanter.

"I—I did not mean that."

Slowly he faced me. "Yes?"

Words froze on my tongue as the chill from his eyes went to my toes. I stared at the floor, trying to regain my composure.

After a long silence, he said, "We had best be going. Squire Ad-dleby will send for us if we delay longer." Guiding me with a slight pressure on my arm, he led me to the door. Before opening it, he spoke in a kinder tone. "Unless you desire a military escort, I suggest you wait until after the colonel leaves before departing for the inn."

"Oh. Thank you for the warning."

During dinner I strove to feign appreciation for food I could not taste. It was a constant battle to keep from watching Will seated at Elizabeth's left or straining to hear his remarks to her. I tried to concentrate on conversing intelligently with the squire at my right while responding moderately to the colonel's heavy barrage of flat-tery from across the table. Finally the port was brought in, enabling me to escape with Elizabeth to the drawing room.

Eagerly she questioned me about Oxford society and styles. Hav-ing been a recluse, I was hard put not to appear a dullard. For once I had reason to be glad I attended Amelia's ball. I described the gowns I saw there and repeated some of the gossip I'd heard. The men's en-trance brought welcome relief.

Lieutenant Stevenson promptly engaged Elizabeth and me in conversation, then skillfully drew her to a corner of the room. Will and the squire became absorbed in a chess game, leaving me to Col-onel Snyde. From his manner, I feared he had a non-military con-quest on his mind. Pleading faintness, I rejected an invitation to see the squire's famous gardens by the setting sun. I settled myself beside the fire and refused to be enticed away.

The arrival of the tea tray broke into a tactical description of Culloden. Elizabeth invited us to have refreshment and insisted her father and Will interrupt their game temporarily. Gracefully she pre-sided over the pretty china pot with matching thin cups and plates holding cakes, bread and jam.

"Well, Dr. Knight," said the colonel, "did you notice anything amiss on your way to Docking this afternoon?"

Will shook his head. "I took the main road and saw no one at all either way."

"Too quiet. Something's afoot. I can feel it. These clear nights lately have kept the smugglers at home. They'll have to move their goods soon to take a shipment at the dark of the moon. When they do, we'll be ready for them. And we'll even put a stop to that damned Red Demon before long. Beg pardon, ladies."

"I hope you will. I hope you will," our host replied, holding out his cup for Elizabeth to refill. "He's far more dangerous to us than smugglers."

"Do you think he's real?" Will asked. "Everyone who's claimed to see him was drunk at the time. Personally, I think Dick Hanford made him up to explain himself to his wife."

"No, no. He's real enough," affirmed Colonel Snyde. "The worst of scoundrels! A murdering thief to whom nothing is sacred! Believe me, we'll soon have him kicking his heels high in front of the Curling Horn."

I remembered standing at the foot of the gallows on my arrival and shuddered at the thought of a man hanging there.

"Have you any idea where or how to catch him?" Will asked.

The colonel laughed. "You are so naive, Vicar! I keep my ideas to myself. He has cohorts everywhere. Every household is thick with smugglers. Why, they even have tunnels under the village, though I've yet to find them. A very unsatisfactory state of affairs. If I told you my plans, I would lose the element of surprise."

"Surely no one here would reveal your confidence outside this room!" the squire protested.

"I am confident you're quite right. But he does not work alone. Some of your servants, possibly your most trusted, may be in league with him. The village swarms with his spies. How else could he know to rob the most richly laden coaches and messengers? How else could he continually escape from our carefully set traps?"

"Mr. Smythe has already captured and hung several highwaymen. None of them was connected with the Red Demon." Will took a swallow of tea. "Perhaps all the deeds he is credited with are the work of many men. Or else he is superhuman. It stretches the imagination to think that he can rob a coach near Brighthelmstone and kill a man this side of Lewes at virtually the same time."

"Oh, without a doubt many men are involved," the colonel agreed. "*His* men. I find it most interesting that Smythe has been unable to apprehend one smuggler although they are very active. The few felons stupid enough to fall into his crude traps *claim* not to be working with him, but *I* didn't believe them."

"Not even when they denied it under severe . . . questioning?"

"Vicar, the people here do not understand the art of interrogation. When *I* make my capture, *I* shall turn him over to Sargeant Hillyer. He will tell us *everything* we wish."

"Gentlemen, gentlemen, enough of this," interrupted the squire. "Such talk cannot be amusing to the ladies." He then took Will back to the chessboard, saying, "Now, sir, I shall turn the tide of fortune and defeat you."

Elizabeth proposed a game of whist for the rest of us. For several dragging hours I tried to apply my mind to my cards with indifferent success.

Following a light supper, Colonel Snyde announced, "Come, Stevenson, we've work to do tomorrow." He thanked his host, then bowed to me. "May we escort you to the inn?"

"Thank you, but I should like to visit longer with Elizabeth."

"*Dear* lady." He raised my hand to brush his lips over my skin. "I hope to see you soon. Your presence is a fair addition to this district."

I replied civilly, resisting the temptation to wipe the back of my hand on my gown.

After the military men departed, I conversed with Elizabeth until I thought a reasonable interval passed. Then I thanked her and her father for their gracious hospitality and prepared to leave.

To my surprise, Will broke off the chess game, saying, "No need to disturb your men, Addleby. I drove over in my trap and can take Mistress . . . Castleton to the inn on my way home."

"Very thoughtful, Vicar. I'll send Johnson along as a moon."

"No need, sir. Prince would take me home safely on the blackest night. And, despite all the evil done here, I've never been troubled by anyone."

"I'm grateful they at least respect the cloth," said the squire. "There's naught else they regard hereabouts."

Will drove in silence until we came to a crumbling tower I noticed earlier on the drive to the manor. He pulled onto its shadow and stopped.

"What is this ruin?" I asked.

"The villagers call it 'Addleby's Folly.' He built it a few years ago to add 'charm' to the landscape."

"Oh." I waited tensely. Now was the time and place for our talk.

"You are thin," he observed. "Have you been well?"

"My—my appetite hasn't been good."

"So I noticed. Had you eaten less, Addleby would have been offended."

Encouraged by his attention, I asked, "And you? How have you been?"

"Fairly well. I spent several weeks at Rockivale in July."

"So Charles told me."

"*Did* he!" His voice took on a strange edge.

"Yes, I . . . I wish . . . you had . . . come. . ."

"There seemed no reason. I hadn't heard from you."

"I—I did write, but—but I burned the letters."

In strained silence we watched half a moon rise over a distant hill. This was not as I anticipated. My carefully rehearsed words would certainly be brusquely rebuffed by this cold man.

"How long will you be here?" he asked.

"I—I don't know," I murmured.

After another silence, he spoke spacing his words carefully. "Have you been happy?"

Emotions strangled my answer. Traitorous tears crept down my cheeks and I barely kept from sobbing.

After waiting some time for my reply, he reached over to touch my wet cheek.

Suddenly we were in motion. By the time we reached the inn, the air had dried my tears and I regained a measure of control. Mr. Wilmot came out and helped me down. I bade both men "good-night," and hurried upstairs.

In the safety of my room, I fell across my bed and wept. Not even when we were alone had Will shown the slightest warmth towards me.

Chapter Sixteen

Most of Monday I slept. The next days I browsed in the few shops, watched the wheelwright shrink a red-hot iron tire onto a broad wagon wheel and tramped the several roads and lanes meeting at the church. Always I watched for Will, without reward.

The village clustered around the intersection of the rutty roads to Lewes and to Docking. The latter was scarcely better than a lane. Being used to the hurrying bustle of Oxford's traffic, this place seemed too quiet. Only a few broad-wheeled carts moved the heaviest things. Pack trains, horse, and foot traffic carried most items. The only one having a carriage was apparently the squire, and his was not evident during the week. But then, the roads were such as to discourage wheeled vehicles.

Along the Lewes Road were the shops. Brick and flint cottages with steep thatched roofs and mellowed stone walls decorated with an assortment of plants and vines edged the Docking Road a few yards in each direction and the several other lanes meandering across the main road. A number of cottages were scattered randomly along the bottom between the hills.

The highest hill rose behind the Curling Horn. At its foot was a large, spring-fed fountain where women, girls, and boys gathered morning and evening with buckets.

People greeted me courteously, but with restraint. None was given to visiting with a stranger. By Thursday morning, I was desperately lonely and bored to distraction.

After some argument, I persuaded Henry Wilmot to permit me the use of his horse, Black, for riding. This docile beast was easy to manage and basically lazy. I ventured beyond the squire's manor and followed a dry streambed winding between the hills to the ocean.

Under a cloudless sky, the channel was bright blue. I was awed by the shining expanse of water. The shoreline curved westward into a distant blue-gray. It blended into what I guessed to be the Isle of Wight. The eastern view was cut short by sheer, white cliffs looming over the narrow strip of shingle at their base. An endless succession of waves lapped the wet sand below the shingle.

I urged Black to a fast canter along the dark band just above the foam. Wind stung my face and tangled my hair, producing a joyous sense of freedom and exhilaration, lifting my burdens.

Finally I reined in Black and stared up at the white cliffs rising from a rubble heap of boulders. Majestic. Beautiful. And I knew, obviously, I must seek out Will. No matter how distant and cold he was, I must tell him what lay on my heart, provided I could find him.

Returning to Tyne, on impulse, I took a different path, wandering in the general direction of the village around another hill. Against the sheltered side I came on an isolated flint cottage. A thin curl of smoke rose from its chimney. The shaggy roof looked to need new thatch and a shutter hung at an odd angle. The few plants in the kitchen garden appeared well tended.

As I approached, a young woman, great with child, came out to the well near the door. She stared at me, her hand shielding her eyes. I pulled Black to a halt before her, dismounted and introduced myself.

Shyly she answered, "I be Mistus Richards." Her plain face was browned with freckles. Bright red hair fell about her thin shoulders. Her shapeless, drab bodice was neatly mended in several places and her dark skirt hung limply to her ankles above bare feet. Hunger for company overcame her reticence as we talked. Twisting her apron in her fingers, and with frequent nervous glances over her shoulder and to either side, she confided her concern over being alone when her baby, her first, was born.

Remembering my own apprehension, I inquired, "Are there no near neighbors?"

"No ma'am. Dere be naun."

"Have you no visitors? Doesn't the vicar call?"

"Oh, yes, ma'am. He be that good! And brings de news. Mass Richards, I doant know as when he come. He drive de pack train into Lewes. De days do be tedious long."

I promised to see her when next I rode this way, and continued back to Tyne. There had been a large, scowling man with a crooked nose in the taproom one night answering to the name of Richards. Anne Cowper plainly feared him. What a life this poor woman must live!

My room was in gloomy near darkness when I awoke from my nap. Stretching, I idly pondered whether I should go down to supper now or later. The noise of many voices and laughter below pricked my curiosity. At length I donned my green holland and investigated.

The common room was filled with local men and women drinking ale. A few ate supper at a long table. All were in high spirits.

As I took a seat at the table, shouts of welcome burst about me. Will stood in the door. He removed his cloak glistening with drops of moisture and made his way through the throng, speaking with each person he passed. Mrs. Wilmot hastily laid a cover opposite me.

When he was seated, I passed him the tasty game pie.

He acknowledged my presence with a pleasant nod. "Mistress Castleton, good to see you," he said, scooping out a generous helping.

"How be Docking?" someone called out.

"Fishy!" Will responded.

After a roar of laughter died, Mrs. Wilmot said loudly, "Let de parson ait. He'll best answer questions arter he's lost his hunger."

I studied him in quick glances across the narrow table. His face glowed from the ride. Once our eyes met and I felt my cheeks grow hot.

When his meal was completed, he moved to the settle by the fire on the great stone hearth. I joined the fringe of those crowding about him. Will took out his long churchwarden's pipe, filled it with tobacco, lit it, and leaned back to enjoy a few puffs before speaking.

The people waited respectfully, whispering and shuffling their feet.

"I had a good ride to Docking. 'Tis a pleasant enough place, but I'm glad to be home."

A murmur of approval rippled around the room. Noticing Edward Smythe leaning against the wall behind me, I asked him where Docking was.

"A few miles down the road. It's a fishing village. Dr. Knight goes there every Sunday afternoon for services and every other Wednesday and Thursday."

Will launched into a recital of everyone he'd seen during his trip. The common room's hush was broken by general comments after he announced the birth of a baby, the broken leg of Captain Beck, the return of old Mrs. Hurst and the good health of the old crone Goody Akehurst. As he continued, I realized he was the main source of news between these villages.

At the conclusion of his report, the crowd quickly dispersed. Most left in groups for their homes. A few men went into the taproom, shouting for Henry Wilmot and Anne to fill their tankards. Mistress Wilmot extinguished the lamps, except those near the fireplace and hurried out to the kitchen.

Two old men remained with Will, smoking their pipes and gazing into the fire licking hungrily at a beech log. A proper woman would leave the men alone, but I could not bring myself to go to my room. Thinking I might be unnoticed, I took a seat at the dim end of the room and sat quite still, absorbing Will's profile, remembering our life together.

From time to time one of the men muttered something in a low voice, bringing a grunt of assent or chuckle from the others. At last the two emptied their pipes, shrugged into their coats and left.

Will stayed, staring at the flames. "Mistress Castleton, would you like to play a game of chess? Wilmot has a set we could use."

"I," my palms became moist, "I haven't played since . . . for a very long time. If you don't mind a poor competitor, I'd enjoy playing."

"Come up by the fire. I'll speak to Wilmot." He left without once glancing at me. Soon he returned with a box and board which he set up on a table before the hearth. He turned it to give me the white men. When we were settled, he looked at me with the masked expression I remembered so well. "Ready?"

I smiled and moved out my king's pawn. After the first several opening maneuvers, I relaxed a little, feeling easier with him in the familiar game. Being out of practice, I recognized his traps too late to avoid them. The first game quickly went to him. It took longer for me to lose the second game.

The third was well under way when I realized he had either deliberately opened himself to attack or made a mistake. Neither seemed possible. Cautiously I pursued my opportunity. As he let me place my men in a position to checkmate his king, my periods of deliberation between moves stretched. How often I longed to beat him just once! Now, with victory but a move away, I feared it. After lengthy thought, I purposely wasted a move, throwing away my opportunity.

He looked at me quizzically and broke his habitual silence. "Are you sure?"

I smiled sheepishly. "No. But it's done."

He studied me, then the board. Efficiently he captured several of my men and checkmated me. "You shouldn't have lost that one," he said, putting the men into the box.

"I know. It was a foolish move. I—I do many foolish things."

"Perhaps we can play again," he suggested turning away towards the door.

My heart skipped a beat. "I should like that very much. Must you leave?"

"Yes. The hour is late." He swung his cloak about his shoulders. "Thank you for a memorable evening."

For a moment we faced each other over the deserted tables and benches, his face hidden in shadows. He bowed. "Good-night, Meg," hung softly in the air and he was gone.

Humming to myself, I relived the pleasant evening with Will the previous night, while fastening a green ribbon in my hair. There was a light tap on my door and I called, "Come in."

Anne Cowper entered to announce, "Miss Addleby be here. Her asked ifn ye'd see her."

Feeling my room inadequate for entertaining, I quickly smoothed my holland petticoats and descended to the common room.

Elizabeth was cool and lovely in a sapphire riding dress. Her matching tricorn sported a snowy plume. "I'm sorry I could not call earlier, but things at the manor keep me very busy. Since Mother died last year, I have the running of the house. And you know how servants are. They are so stupid I spend half the day repeating instructions already given." She sighed. "When one gets the least trained and begins working in a proper manner, she's off to Town thinking to find a better position."

I nodded sympathetically, thinking how common this complaint was in Oxford.

"All that is neither here nor there. Meg, I came begging your aid. Father is giving me a ball on Friday next, a week from today, my nineteenth birthday. This will be our first social event in over a year, as we are just out of black gloves. Naturally the invitations have long been sent. But, you see, there are many details I don't know how to handle, and I know no one to consult. Surely you can help me after all the gay parties you've attended at Oxford. Please say yes."

"I shall be delighted! I love a party."

"Would you ride up to the manor now, so we can begin?" A mischievous smile played about her lips as she added, "I was given to understand you are a neck-or-nothing rider."

"Oh? I am found out!"

"Father and several of our servants saw you on the beach yesterday. By now all the village knows. You should realize everything you do is common knowledge in a place like Tyne."

We spent the afternoon in the ballroom and garden discussing food, furniture arrangement, and flowers. The rooms of this ancient fortress were austere by modern standards, but an abundance of Michaelmas daisies with some silver honesty from the walled garden would transform them.

Over tea, Elizabeth told me a bit of the history of the manor. Originally it was built to defend the coast from the Danes and added to over the years. It had come into her family when the squire's father bought it. At the time the Pretender threatened invasion, it had nearly reverted to its first purpose of defense, but nothing of moment had occurred since.

The squire joined us and listened with interest to our plans. He gave enthusiastic approval and assured Elizabeth everything necessary would be ordered from Lewes promptly, and extra servants would be hired to help with cooking, cleaning, and decorating. For all of his rough ways, I could see he held his daughter in deep affection, indulging her every desire. And, while he lacked polish, his manner towards me was marked with genuine thoughtfulness.

As I rode back to the inn, I thought hopefully on the evening with Will. His manner was not so cold as on Sunday. Perhaps my sudden appearance had been an oversetting shock. If he came again this night, I would speak to him without fail, even if I had to behave unseemly to do so. He might have called while I was gone, could even be at the inn this very moment. I kicked Black into as rapid a pace as he would go.

Bursting into the common room, I found it empty. Disappointed, I started up the stairs. The taproom door squeaked.

"Meg, my dove! Don't fly away!"

I spun around.

Charles caught me about the waist and swung me off the stairs. "You've been riding alone, shocking everyone for miles around," he chided in a sing-song imitation of Lord Rockivale. "I fear you will never behave like a lady."

"Charles! I can't believe my eyes! What brings you here?"

"You, of course. I stopped in Oxford, and Bessie said you were here to—"

I placed my fingers on his lips, glancing at Mrs. Wilmot who had entered in the back and was watching our reunion with interest. "Hush," I warned in a whisper, leading him to the table farthest from her.

"What's wrong?"

We sat down. "No one knows I'm Will's wife."

"What?" He waved to Mrs. Wilmot. "Two glasses of your best wine, Nancy." When she left, he said, "I don't understand. She said you were coming to live here, with him. I was about to call on you at Will's."

"She was right, but—but on the way," I paused to fight back tears, "on the way I thought about it, about appearing at his door without a warning after so long. He might hate me."

"He doesn't, Meg."

"How can you be certain? His manner is so cold! Like ice! He wouldn't tell anyone how he truly feels. I was afraid he. . ." I looked down at my hands, clenched in my lap, and took a deep breath. "So I'm staying here. And I'm using Father's name so people won't ask questions. Then, if Will doesn't want me, I won't be an embarrassment."

"Oh, Meg, you foolish, foolish girl!" Charles put a sympathetic arm about my shoulders as Mrs. Wilmot brought the wine. "Thanks, Nancy. This is a celebration. Meg and I grew up together. I've not seen her for some time."

"Be you wanting some refreshment, Mus Heathton?"

"No. I'll be leaving soon for the vicar's." He waited until she went into the kitchen, then said, "I've told you times out of mind that he loves you and wants you."

I shook my head. "Sunday I saw him. He was so, so cold! I was sure he hated me."

"But Meg, what must he think when you arrive using your father's name? Have you explained?"

"I couldn't talk to him while he was like that. I just couldn't. Last night he came—"

"There, you see—"

"To report on his trip to Docking."

"Oh."

"And we played chess afterwards. Oh, Charles, it was just like, just like—"

"And you said nothing?"

"I was about to, and he left."

He patted my hands. "Drink your wine, my dove." He drained his glass. "What a tangle you've worked! Have no fears, I'll set everything straight. After I dine with him tonight, instead of reciting my progress with Rockivale's harvest, I'll speak for you."

For hours I waited anxiously in my room, alert for Charles' footsteps down the hall, anticipating a summons to a reunion at the vicarage. I moved from the chair to the bed, back to the chair. Nervously I brushed out my hair, changed my clothes, rearranged my gowns in the wardrobe, still he did not come. Sitting on the bed, I debated whether to go below or even risk walking down the road to meet him.

The sun shining in my eyes roused me. Painfully I rose from my cramped position on the bed. Through the window I could see the morning was well advanced. Hastily I straightened my hair and dress and went downstairs.

Anne Cowper greeted me and poured a cup of hot chocolate. "Has Mr. Heathton come down yet?"

"Yes, ma'am. He be gone afore dere was light."

"He was!"

"Oh, yes, ma'am. Him has far to goo and doant like travelling arter it be dark."

Strange. In Oxford he never liked being roused before noon. Night travel was common to him. "Did he leave a message for me?"

"No, ma'am."

I nearly wept into my chocolate. Charles never had been able to admit a failure gracefully.

Chapter Seventeen

Aimlessly I wandered past the blacksmith and wheelwright's forge, the bakery, the spice shop, and the candlemaker, pondering Charles' failure on my behalf. The church stood on a rise ahead, the vicarage beside it. Gathering all my courage, I went to each looking for Will. I could not find anyone.

After dinner, I decided to shake my gloom by riding out to the beach and then visit Mrs. Richards. She was pathetically happy to see me and insisted I have some ale and a bit of bread. Her dented tin plates were brightly polished and the rough oak table scrubbed clean. Sensing food was in meager supply, I ate as sparingly as I could without giving offence. Starved for companionship and news, she held me there talking. The baby had slipped lower and was heavier to carry, the only indications he might come soon. I promised to return early in the week.

On a whim, I rode up the twisting path to the top of the hill behind the Curling Horn. There I found scattered stones nearly hidden by tall grasses. They seemed to form the general outline of some building, probably an ancient Saxon or Norman structure long forgotten. Dismounting, I felt the weathered, hewn surface of one large block. Who had made these and who had thrown them down?

I tied Black to a scrubby bush leaning northward. Moodily I walked across the springy turf among the rubble of the past, one hand on my hat to prevent the wind's stealing it. An uneasy sadness descended on my spirit. Someone's hopes and plans had met with total destruction.

Ahead, glimpses of the channel shimmered between the hills. In the other direction dreary swells of parched, yellow land faded into blues and grays towards Surrey. Neither human nor animal was visible. I was depressingly alone in a remote place. As the horizon deepened to purples, I felt wizened men clad in skins peering at me from the mysterious past, as they had peered at the Romans and other invaders. A single swan flew over a near hill, its long neck stretched forward, its wings beating heavily. Its pure body against the vast sky emphasized the utter loneliness of this place.

On a lower hill across from me stood a tall windmill, its sails spinning in the breeze. Neither man nor beast was near it. The only sign it was not deserted was the smoke drifting from the cottage adjacent to the mill.

Gloomy silence cast a heavy mantle around me. I missed the rattling wagons and carriages driven by noisy men, the Oxford hawkers shouting their wares from dawn to dark, and, above all, the bells. This stillness was unnatural.

Then again, it was like long ago, when I was young at Rockivale. The tension building in me since my decision to come here oozed away, and I took a deep breath. Flinging my arms wide I turned around slowly several times, my head back, as I had done when little and alone on top of a Rockivale hill.

There were fresh, sweet scents and a flat tinkling of distant bells carried on the prevailing southwest breezes. Somewhere above me, like a fragile, happy spirit, rang a bird's rippling song. I stopped and scanned the revolving golden sky, but could not locate this joyous, free creature.

Dwarfed by the immensity of the downs, and a little dizzy, I staggered a few yards and sat down on an upended stone on the village side of the hill. Below lay Tyne. It was a far cry from the majestic spires of Oxford. Neat thatched cottages clustered about the hill with here and there a steep red-tiled roof or one of gray stone. Thin columns of smoke rose straight, then bent into northern, winding trails. Soft lights glowed in the windows. A few people moved about in the twilight of the lanes brightened with yellow splashes of autumn foliage.

I watched Will leave a cottage and ride out of sight to my left. How might I reach him? O God, give me wisdom! Give me courage! O God, I don't know what to do!

Filling my lungs with fragrant air, I forced myself to consider Tyne and its inhabitants. It was truly a poor place, but not as horrid as I had imagined. An aura of peace hung over it, welcome contrast to the suppressed violence and tensions of Oxford. Squire Addleby was nice enough. Elizabeth was pretty and willful. The Wilmots, Anne, Mr. Smythe and Mrs. Richards seemed quite pleasant. Mr. Richards and Colonel Snyde struck the only discordant notes, and the legendary demon. I would be happy here, if only Will would have me.

Mr. Smythe rode to a cottage, talked with a man, then galloped to another. Perhaps he was seeking Will.

Hoofbeats upon the path interrupted my thoughts. Will emerged, riding the magnificent chestnut stallion Charles gave him.

He had come to see me! An answer to my prayers! I could tell him what was on my heart!

"Will!" I ran towards him.

"Good day, madam." His tone was aloof, as if speaking to a total stranger. "Mrs. Cowper sent me."

I stopped, feeling I had collided with an invisible, icy wall.

"She thought you should be warned of the nuns' ghosts that walk here at dusk."

"Ghosts? What sort of place is this that ghosts would inhabit it?"

"There may well be many ghosts here." He dismounted and tied his mount beside Black. "Some think that centuries ago men buried one of their great leaders in this mound."

"Oh." I shivered as if an ancient spectre had breathed upon my soul.

"The Romans may have used it as an outpost. Early church leaders considered it a strategic site and built something here. Eventually it became a nunnery. Cromwell's men tore it down, as you see, not leaving one stone on another."

"A hill of many sorrows, where the air is sweet and fresh."

"That's the thyme. It grows everywhere."

"And so you came at Mrs. Cowper's request. She is very kind."

"Everyone in the village knows you're here. She said I should pay more attention to the foreigner in our midst than merely play chess with her, which must be boring to any woman."

"But it was not. Not to me." I sank down on my stone seat and grasped at commonplace talk. "You look very well. Do you ride a great deal?"

He seemed to relax a little. "Yes. More than I study, I fear. I make regular rides to Docking, often to Lewes, occasionally to Chichester and beyond to Portsmouth. There is a legend that St. Paul visited Chichester."

"Really? When?"

"After being released from Rome. They suppose that the Pudens mentioned at the end of II Timothy was later in command of the Roman soldiers stationed in ancient Regnum, now Chichester. St. Paul is said to have come at his invitation."

"Do you believe that could be true?"

He shrugged. "It is possible. I doubt we will ever know. A later saint did indeed live there. Saint Richard, Bishop of Chichester. He ministered faithfully to every corner of his diocese and gave liberally to the poor. Half a millennium ago he died. In 1253, to be precise. He left this prayer:

'Thanks be to Thee, my Lord Jesus Christ,
For all the benefits which Thou hast given me,

For all the pains and insults which Thou hast borne for me,
O most merciful Redeemer, Friend, and Brother,
May I know Thee more clearly,
Love Thee more dearly,
And follow Thee more nearly.'

That is the most a person can desire."

"Like a new hymn I learned. 'Thee, only thee, resolved to know in all I think or speak or do.' " Taking heart in this sharing, I rose and approached him slowly.

He stared down on his parish and frowned as if facing an unpleasant duty. "Your father wrote soon after I arrived telling me he had moved back to his old rooms at Christ Church." He paused before asking, "Is he still there?"

"I suppose so. He was in London on University business when I left."

His attention remained focused below and his lips tightened into a straight line. I saw his jaw muscle flex.

I took a deep breath and reached out to touch his arm, asking, "Last night, did—did Charles speak to you of—of the reason I came?"

His fingers closed into a fist. "We had *important* matters to discuss."

"I—I don't understand."

He faced me, his expression set.

Dismayed, I stepped back a pace.

"Do not blame him. He tried. I would not permit him to talk about you."

"But why? Is the raising of cattle and crops at Rockivale more important? I came from Oxford to see you, Will, to *talk* with you."

"I've been aware of that since Smythe mentioned your arrival. Do you think I would allow *him,* or anyone else to speak on your behalf? What you came to say to me must be said by *you!*" His lips clamped together firmly; his eyes were hard.

I quailed before him. "But—but I have not seen you to—to talk with you," I protested weakly.

"We are together now."

"Will, don't be this way. Please."

A discrete cough startled us. I whirled around to see who it was. Will turned away.

"Dr. Knight, Mistress Bradford's sent for you." Mr. Smythe sat astride his horse, his face bright red, his eyes fastened on Will's back. "Her husband fell at the old quarry and is grievous hurt."

Several seconds passed before Will turned around with his usual calm manner. "Where are they?"

"Either at the bottom of the quarry or the Bradford's cottage."

"Thank you, Smythe." He untied his stallion. "I'll go immediately. Would you please see Mistress Castleton to the inn? It's coming on dark below."

"Gladly," Mr. Smythe answered, dismounting. "God speed."

I stared after Will, badly shaken.

"Are you ready to go, ma'am?"

Mr. Smythe's kind voice recalled me. What had he heard? I dare not ask. He helped me mount and we went down to the Curling Horn.

Sunday Will preached in a forceful, simple style, much like Mr. Wesley's. He exhorted us to live godly lives appropriate to our Christian profession, avoiding even the appearance of evil.

His words struck my heart. In my old pride I had laughed at appearances. My behavior caused Father and Will needless hurt. Perhaps I had done some thoughtless things again, making him angry with me. Even angry with Charles. I prayed earnestly that his anger towards me was evidence of love.

After the service, his greeting was correct and impersonal.

Elizabeth approached to invite me to attend the manor for dinner. I accepted eagerly, my mind flying ahead to driving back to the inn with Will. If only his anger had cooled by then.

I dressed carefully in my green silk, hoping to please him. As I started to fasten Charles' pin to the lace on my bosom, I decided to wear only Will's earrings. Whatever caused his anger, I wanted nothing to arouse it again.

Once more Lieutenant Stevenson and Colonel Snyde were present. The colonel immediately took charge of me. Short of unforgivable rudeness, I could not escape him.

The squire and Will had barely begun their after-dinner game when a boy arrived. Goody Hawkson had taken a bad turn and wanted the parson at her side. Will apologized to his host for interrupting the game and departed promptly. I watched him go with a sinking heart.

The colonel's overly familiar air and excessive compliments unsettled me further. Without visible male protection, and being neither squint-eyed nor pox-scarred, I must have appeared as fair game to him. I determined to outstay him, not wanting his escort to the inn.

The hour was very late when he said, "Miss Castleton, if you are ready to leave, I shall be happy to take you to the Curling Horn."

"Thank you, Colonel, but there are things I must discuss with Elizabeth concerning her party Friday."

"Go on, Meg. We'll talk tomorrow," she said. "You must not be alone after dark. Colonel Snyde and Lieutenant Stevenson will bear you good company."

I looked to the squire for the offer of a servant later, but he did not join in the discussion. Reluctantly I made my farewells.

As he handed me into the squire's carriage, the colonel commented, "You are a very adventurous woman, driving and riding about as you do." His voice dropped to an intimate level. "I *admire* adventurous women!" And he flashed a bold smile.

Will arrived suddenly and cantered to a halt before us. He dismounted, leaving his stallion under the noses of the squire's horses, blocking our passage.

"How is Goody Hawkson?" Squire Addleby inquired from the doorway.

"Sleeping when I left," Will answered. "It was a bad spell. She thought she was dying, but she'll live to see many a dawn. Have you seen my Bible? I went in such a hurry, I seemed to have left it here. On the hall table, I think."

Elizabeth stepped inside to look for it.

From his mounted position beside my window, Colonel Snyde snapped, "Move your nag, Vicar! You're blocking our way!"

Will looked around in surprise. "Oh, I beg your pardon, sir." Taking the bridle, he led his horse forward one step, still blocking our passage.

The colonel shouted, "Move that wretched nag out of my way!" as Elizabeth came out on the top step.

"I'm sorry, Dr. Knight, but I could not find it in the hall or the drawing room."

"Thank you. I must have left it at the inn this afternoon. Mistress Castleton, may I accompany you there?"

"Sir, *I* am taking the lady home!" said the colonel haughtily. "If you will just remove that nag—"

"But Colonel Snyde," I interrupted, "your garrison is in the opposite direction, I believe. You are most thoughtful to put yourself out so much on my behalf at this hour—"

"*I* am taking you to the inn!"

Will shrugged. He waved to the Addlebys and mounted.

Arrogantly the colonel ordered the driver ahead.

Will guided his mount to the far side of the carriage. Lieutenant Stevenson served as an outrider.

"Where does this Goody Hawkson live?" I asked sliding across the seat to Will's side.

"A mile toward Docking," Will answered. "She's very old. On nights like this, when the fog's in, she has trouble breathing and feels like she's dying. Then she sends her grandson in to me. I sit with her until she goes to sleep."

"Don't let us delay you in searching for your Bible," Colonel Snyde sneered.

"Oh, you're not delaying me," Will replied lightly.

"Are you quite comfortable, dear lady? I did not see a robe for you."

"Thank you, Colonel. My cloak is adequate. The night is not overly chill."

"I trust you do not find life in this remote village too dull."

"Oh, no. Bye the bye, Vicar, I had an interesting visit with Mrs. Richards yesterday." Deliberately I extended the account until the inn was in sight.

"Vicar, roust out that lazy Wilmot to take care of his guest!" the colonel interrupted brusquely.

"Certainly. Excuse me, madam."

"Perhaps you will go riding with me one afternoon this week, Miss Castleton," the colonel suggested. "I am able to provide a lively steed for your use. You may wish to investigate some of the less known byways, being of an adventurous turn."

"You're most kind. With Elizabeth's party coming, I'm required most of the time at the manor. Perhaps the following week?"

Mr. Wilmot and Will came out as the colonel was handing me down. The innkeeper bowed respectfully to the officers and held the door for me.

Smiling my sweetest, I gave the frustrated colonel my hand. "Thank you for your kindness."

He bowed low, his gold braid flashing in the light from the lantern over the door, and kissed my fingers. "My pleasure," he said sourly.

I entered the deserted common room with Will behind me. Making sure we were alone, I whispered, "I came so far to see you! Can you not make some time to see me?"

"My congregation is small, but their cares are many. I must spend my time with them when I am not working my field."

"Will, please!"

"Ah, there it is!" He strode to a table at the far end before the hearth and picked up a book.

I trailed him, hurt he should treat me thus. He flipped it open. Over his arm I read in Father's large hand, "To a most promising scholar."

"He gave me this when I started my doctoral work. I'm glad I found it."

"I can't recollect your ever mislaying anything!"

"Perhaps, *Miss* Castleton, I've changed. Good-nght."

Determined to put the puzzle of Will's behavior from my mind, I rode to the manor Monday noon despite a gray drizzle. I felt rather fagged, having lain awake much of the night worrying if he had indeed changed and in what way.

Elizabeth tried on her new gown, an elaborate creation of pink satin and silver lace over an enormous hoop. I thought the bodice shockingly low. She assured me it was perfect for showing off her mother's diamond necklace. I felt far more than a necklace was displayed, but kept my opinions to myself. Her hem dipped slightly in front, threatening to trip her, so I stitched it up.

The squire joined us for dinner, wearing buckskins and muddy boots. "Ah, this is the weather we need. Our rains are late this year."

"Oh, no!" Elizabeth wailed. "My guests! If it rains hard, how will they manage the roads?"

"Perhaps it will hold off a few days more until after your big day. We've had an uncommon dry spell," he informed me. "It's been good for the roads and little else. They do get impassable at times." Then, noticing how little I was eating, "My dear Miss Castleton, you must have some mutton. I raised it here, the best in all England." Next he insisted I spread blackberry jam on my bread and urged me to taste the tart.

Bewildered by his attention, I looked to Elizabeth and saw she was amused.

"My dear," my host said as we rose from the table, "we have many unused rooms in this old house. You should stay with us, and then you would not need to run back and forth between here and the inn. Such an inconvenience."

"You are very kind, sir, but I could not put you to that trouble."

"No trouble. No trouble at all. A pleasure, really, yes, indeed, a rare pleasure you would be allowing us. Why, the vicar lived here for over a year and we were hardly aware of his presence. You'd bring us a great deal more pleasure, believe me, Miss Castleton."

I laughed at his persistence. "You will need every room you have for your party guests. An unexpected addition to your household now would try your staff beyond endurance."

"Humph. I suppose. After all this is over, we'll talk again."

The night winds moaning about the corners of the inn had shined the sky to a deep blue. I leaned out my window to see all nature sparkling in the morning sun. On such a lovely, crisp day, everything must work out well.

Elizabeth did not need me at the manor, so my time was free. Rather than sit in my room or seach for Will, I decided to visit Mary Richards again. Thinking she might enjoy a special treat, I purchased tea in the spice shop and little cakes from the baker, then rode out with a basket tied behind me.

As I approached the cottage, I was surprised Mary did not come out to greet me. Leaving Black tied to a tree, I rapped on the door.

A low moan answered me. On entering, I found her on her knees, bending over. "Thank God!" she cried. "My baby. . ."

Anxiously I knelt at her side. When the spasm subsided, I helped her onto her bed. With a wet rag, I wiped the sweat from her face, then did my best to make her comfortable.

"Thank God ye come!" she whispered. "I be hem afeard!"

"I'll ride to Tyne and find the doctor, or at least a midwife."

"No! No! Please, bide wud me!"

"But I don't know what do do! I've never mid-wifed!"

"Mass Richards, he'll not come 'til late in de night. Please, please doant leave me!"

Reluctantly I promised to stay. I prayed for someone to come, then for wisdom to know what to do. For the first time I tried to remember my travail and what was done for me and for Amelia.

In the yard I found two lengths of rope which I tied to the bedposts at the foot, and gave the ends to Mary for pulling. I took an old blanket from a shelf to wrap around the babe. There had been basins of hot water, so I carried in some from the well, put on the kettle and stirred up the fire.

Through the long hours I cared for Mary. Sips of newly brewed tea and bites of cake refreshed her. I silently prayed for her when we were not talking of her work spinning wool and, of course, her baby. As shadows from the hills engulfed the cottage, her pains became more severe. Witnessing this brought back my fruitless experience vividly. With the memories came the sorrow I had fought to shut out.

Harsh grunting sounds from Mary jerked me to the present. As my midwife had done, I placed my hand on her abdomen and felt her muscles knotting to force out the baby. When the head appeared, I thanked God it was coming right. As firmly as I dared, I pulled on it to aid Mary's waning strength. Then he was in my hands, covered with a bloody, cheeselike substance. A boy! A warm, live baby!

Quickly I cleaned off his face. His wail was welcome to both Mary and me. Clumsily I cut and tied his cord as they did for Amelia's Stephan. When he was cleaned up, I wrapped him in the blanket and gave Mary her tiny son.

Although white and exhausted, her plain, freckled features were transformed with a joy I had not seen since we met.

"John. He be called for hisn father. Him be a brave son. Mayhap Mass Richards, he be pleased."

"He's a fine boy. I'm sure he'll be very proud of him." Tenderly I ran my forefinger down the thin little arm and over his tight fist. This tiny baby was mine also. I too had labored for him, and, praise God, this time my labor was not in vain.

Concerned that she eat, I sliced a bit of cheese from a chunk in her cupboard and brewed fresh tea. In the midst of eating, she dropped into a deep slumber.

My own weariness welled up. I stepped into the yard for a breath of air before straightening the cottage. The crescent moon was low in the west. It must be past midnight. A soft nicker welcomed me. Quickly I brought Black a bucket of water, apologizing for forgetting him.

Mother and child were sleeping, impervious to the noises I made. Should I remain, a guardian to that new, helpless human? In a few hours morning would be here. John Richards was expected late tonight. From the little I had seen of him at the inn, I had no desire to be present when that big, rough man arrived. Putting things to rights as rapidly as I could, I left with a silent promise to send out the doctor and some food come day.

The chill air pierced my cloak. The moon had set, leaving only uncertain starlight. Tired, exhilarated with the successful birth, I turned Black down the road. My one desire now was to sink into my bed for hours and hours.

Rounding a curve, I saw the shimmer of starlight on black water. Confused by the dark, I must have taken a wrong turn! I pulled Black to a halt and stared at white, foamy crests surging onto the beach below. Between the pounding waves, a gentle breeze wafted nocturnal sounds to me, soft as the murmur of voices. The beautiful, peaceful scene served as a blessed balm to my spirit.

Above stretched a black canopy decorated with stars set in their eternal patterns. The words of Amos came to mind as Will would quote them when coming home to St. Thomas' on a clear night. "Seek him that maketh the seven stars and Orion and turneth the shadow of death into the morning and maketh the day dark with night: that calleth for the waters of the sea and poureth them out upon the face of the earth: the LORD is his name."

The deep silence about me seemed a link with the ages long past. I was awed and exalted by the majestic sweep of sea and sky. How great and wonderful it all was! There was another fragment from the prophet appropriate for this moment. " . . . He that maketh the morning darkness and treadeth upon the high places of the earth, The LORD, the God of hosts, is his name." He must be in this place, close beside me, above me. Raising my right hand, I reached towards the pulsating stars. My hand, raised to God—my hand that helped bring a new life into this world. Praise God this travail was fruitful!

"Give unto the Lord the glory due unto his name," I exclaimed aloud. "Bring an offering, and come into his courts. O worship the Lord in the beauty of holiness!" From a full heart I burst into song. "Praise God from whom all blessings flow! Praise Him all creatures here below! Praise Him—"

A light flared below, swung as a signal, then vanished, leaving me in prickling silence. Smugglers? Whoever it was *must* have heard me. As if to confirm my fears, I heard the soft, rapid thuds of a running horse.

I turned Black and urged him into a trot away from the sea. Surely he knew the way home. Letting the reins fall slack, I leaned forward to whisper, "Go home, Black. Hurry! Oh, please, dear Father, guide him and don't let him stumble or fall!"

No flicker of light offered the hope of sanctuary or guidance. Every warning I'd heard about danger after dark and the terrible lengendary demon went through my mind. Anxious to flee the unknown horseman by the sea, I kicked Black into a reckless gallop.

When I was beginning to hope we had escaped, I heard hooves now pounding in pursuit. I pressed my legs against Black's side and dug my fingers into his thick mane, yelling for him to run. Responding to my panic, he broke into a neck-or-nothing pace.

Louder and louder grew the hoofbeats from the other horse. The rider came abreast of me. I glimpsed a hunched figure, a flapping cape and then an arm reaching towards me.

I struck him away.

He moved closer. His hand gripped my waist and I was pulled from my saddle.

Screaming, I hit at him. Then I was falling, falling into inky blackness.

Stars winked through interlaced branches partially stripped of their leaves. I lay on hard earth. My cloak was tightly wound about me, warming me from the chill air on my face and effectively preventing any movement. Involuntarily I sighed.

A hunchbacked man approached, walking as one trying to conceal a limp. His wide-brimmed hat threw black shadows across his face. "Ye be an unaccountable nosy wench," he rasped in a vicious, inhuman voice. Squatting beside me, he gripped my shoulder, causing a stab of pain. "Who be ye? How be ye out in de dark?"

I cowered under his rough grasp and horrible voice.

"Who be ye?" he demanded.

"M-m-mistress Knight. Who, who are you?"

"Dey calls me out of my name as de Red Demon."

"I thought—I thought he wasn't real," I quavered.

He cackled an unearthly laugh. "Den why be ye squintin' arter me?"

"I—I wasn't. I was going to—to the Curling Horn."

"I doant know as dis be no way to de inn, I bluv."

"I missed my way in the dark."

"Be dere naun to tell ye I take my own in de dark?"

"I—I was with M-Mrs. Richards. Her baby was b-born and I tried to—to help her."

"Think ye I be ardle-headed? Ye'd be wud en still. Ye be squintin' out for de excise, dat Smythe, surelye."

"No, no!" My voice caught. "I was going to the inn."

"So ye say!" he scoffed. For a while he rocked on his heels, as if thinking. "Being as yer a foreigner and neighbor wud de squire, dered be a lamentable pucker should ye not goo to de inn." He paused again. "Be ye kin to de vicar?"

"The vicar?" I licked my lips. "What has the vicar to do with me?"

"Ye say ye be Mistus Knight. Spik de truth now!"

"Oh!" I groaned and shook my head. My befuddled brain must not betray me again. How might I reply and protect Will?

"It queers me who ye be. Be ye wed to en?"

I tried to deny it, but could not.

"Spik de truth!"

"Y-yes. We are wed."

"Yer not wud en. Mayhap ye'd like en dead? I doant know but ye'd keep yer clapper still should I make en die, surelye."

"No! Oh, no! Nothing must happen to him!"

"No?"

"He—he's a good man."

"A good man!" the raspy voice whined. "Nary be so good as dey say. I'd justabout like to have en dead. De vicar do put me in a gurt moil now and agin."

"Please, please don't harm him!"

"And what might ye be agreeable to do for en?"

"Anything! Oh, anything!"

"Wud ye hold your clapper? Wud ye no goo nabbling about what ye see dis night?"

"Yes, yes!"

"Ifn ye doant, ifn ye says whatsumever to *nobody*, e'en de vicar hisself, den I spik to de magistrate. Dis here *good* man, he help criminals flee de king. Ifn I spik, he be hung, surelye."

I gasped.

"One lettle word an' de vicar, he die."

"I'll tell *no one*! I—I give you my word."

"Ye be agreeable to anything for en?" He bent over me for a long, terrifying moment. "*Anything?*" He scooped me up and began carrying me away.

Helplessly I squirmed and wriggled against my tightly wrapped cloak, screaming.

"Shruck as ye can. Dere be naun to hear."

Again I plummetted into tingling darkness.

Cool air fanned my face. My cloak fell in loose folds about me. I sensed motion, then a few bumps. I was in a cart! Where was I being taken? Cautiously I opened my eyes, then slowly turned my head until I could see the driver.

His coat concealed his form. Although he was not wearing a floppy broad hat, there was no light to reveal his features. Glancing at me, he asked, "Are you all right, Meg?"

"Will!" I flung myself at him, sobbing uncontrollably.

Bringing the cart to a halt, he took me in his arms, stroked my hair and rocked me. The familiar security of his arms and the soothing of this touch gradually dispelled the night's terrors.

"What happened? Why are you out alone at this hour?"

"I'm—I'm so frightened!"

"Easy. I'll take care of you. Tell me what happened."

"I—I went to see Mrs. Richards this—this afternoon. Her travail was upon her. She wouldn't let me go for help, so I stayed to help her bear her son. Oh, Will, he's a beautiful baby! When all was over, I left for the inn."

"You should have stayed with her."

"I'm afraid of John Richards. He's a big, ugly man."

"I understand. Then?"

"I—I—I lost my way. Black began running. I couldn't stop him. I—I fainted. How did you find me?"

"I was returning from a late call. Black was grazing beside the road and you were on the ground, unconscious. I'm taking you to Wentworth, the apothecary."

Leaning comfortably against his shoulder, I wished we could stay thus forever. "I feel all right now, truly I do. There's no need to bother him."

The pre-dawn chill caused me to shiver. He opened his coat and spread it around me. I cuddled against him comfortably. Did I feel his lips brush my hair, or was it only wishing?

"Then I'll take you to the inn."

"Now? So soon?"

"It isn't safe for you to be out at night, even with me. You're fortunate you weren't accosted. You must *not* go out like this again," he ended sternly.

"I won't, you may be sure, I won't."

When Will helped me down from the cart at the inn, my knees buckled, and I swayed against him. He picked me up and carried me inside. Henry Wilmot was dozing by the embers in the fireplace of the common room.

"Wilmot!" Will called, "Bring a glass of brandy and have your wife prepare something hot. Mistress . . . Castleton has had a fright and needs care."

Mr. Wilmot jumped up. "Yes, sir. I be dere dracly minute, Vicar." He rushed into the back shouting for his wife.

Will bore me up to my room and laid me gently on my bed. Wilmot came lumbering after us.

"Me wife'll be up dracly minute wud hot broth," he announced, his chest heaving from the unusual exertion. "Ye hadn't ought to goo out in de dark when de Demon be about, ma'am," he reproved, pouring a generous glass of brandy.

"Black spooked at something and ran away. Mistress Castleton fainted. I found them beside the road," Will explained, taking the brandy. He sat on the bed and held the glass to my lips.

The liquid burned my throat. I made a choking cough and my eyes watered as a warm glow spread through me.

"But 'tis e'en a'most day!" Wilmot said, hovering anxiously in the door.

"Mrs. Richards had her baby. I stayed with her. Black ran away on my way back here."

"Ye should bide de night, ma'am."

"I—I was afraid her husband would come."

"He be sidy and tempersome ifn he be tight, alright. Howsumdever, nohows in de night—"

"Please send the doctor to make sure she's all right," I interrupted.

"De doctor, he be in Lewes, ma'am."

"Then a midwife, please. It was a hard birth, and I've not done this before. And send some bread and meat with her. Red meat. Put it to my account."

"Yes, ma'am. I'll send Anne to Mrs. Springer." He clumped heavily down the stairs.

"Better?" Will asked.

I nodded, basking happily in his tender concern.

He rose and went to look out of the window. "Then I'll leave."

"Oh, please don't." Then, to delay him I asked, "Are you off to Docking?"

"Not this week. I hold vespers here tonight. Next Wednesday I hold them in Docking."

"Can't you stay? Please? There is so much I have to tell you. Can't we talk now?"

He whirled about and stared at me. I sensed the new, warm bond snap.

His stance stiffened and he answered coldly, "You're in good hands. I trust a rest will restore you."

Mrs. Wilmot soon appeared with the broth and found me weeping. In her good-hearted way, she fussed about helping me into my nightdress and promising to look in on me during the day.

In a sleepy fog I was again in our happy home near St. Thomas' with Will. Then the Red Demon's horrible laughter shattered the scene. Suddenly I saw a blood-red devil hang Will. I awakened with a start, trembling.

When Mrs. Wilmot brought up a tray of dinner, she reported that Mrs. Springer found Mrs. Richards quite well, albeit very weak. Mr. Richards had not returned, but surely would tonight.

I could have remained there safely!

" 'Tis a shame ye be put out of your way to birth her, ma'am."

"Put out of my way! I'm *glad* I was there. She was frightened to death and had a long, hard travail."

"Ye be kind, ma'am. I doant know as de foreigners concern demselves wud us." From her matter-of-fact tone, I could not determine whether she approved my actions or not.

Over the Wilmots' objections, I insisted on walking to the church for vespers. I sat near the back of the sanctuary. An old woman in shabby black and Mr. Smythe were the only others present to hear Will read the service.

Led by his clear, resonant voice, I prayed earnestly, " . . . give unto thy servants that peace which the world cannot give; that both our hearts may be set to obey thy commandments, and also that by thee, we, being defended from the fear of our enemies, may pass our time in rest and quietness."

A measure of that peace calmed my troubled heart. Had not Will comforted me with tenderness? His love could not be dead. He would understand and forgive and take me back. And somehow God would protect us both from that evil man. It would come about in God's own good time.

Chapter Eighteen

Thursday I rose early and opened my window wide. The gray mists were rising early and it promised to be a beautiful day. With this bright prospect, the terror beside the sea faded to nothing more than an ugly dream. Larks sang. Warm air sweet with thyme caressed my face. I hoped for Elizabeth's sake the world would be as beautiful on the morrow.

I examined my old brown riding dress with distaste. It was in a sad state from my frightening experience, and I was tired of wearing it. However, preferring to ride Black rather than walking to the squire's, I put it on. Then, on inspiration, I packed my green sprigged calico gown for a change on arriving at the manor. And I would leave it there for tomorrow as well.

Singing "Forth in thy name, O Lord, I go," I rode to the manor. Together, Elizabeth and I directed the servants in cleaning and cooking until the upper floors shone and good things filled the kitchen. From time to time some naïve remark of hers impressed me with how much older I was than she. Her main concern seemed to be going to Tunbridge Wells or Lewes for parties now that she was out of mourning. Life was before her, waiting to open its marvelous treasures.

The sun was setting when I returned to the Curling Horn. I put down the urge to see my dear little John in the Richards' cottage. At all costs I must avoid being out again after dark. The spectre of that misshapen man and his rasping voice made me kick Black to a faster pace. "O Lord," I prayed, "please protect Will from that evil man's power. Whatever he's done, don't let him be hanged!"

On the way to the manor the following morning, I stopped at a yew hedgerow thickly tangled with clematis, finer than that in Elizabeth's garden. Leaving the feathery ones she called "Old Man's Beard" to produce next year's beauty, I picked as much of the silvery, trailing plants as I could manage. These would add grace and contrast to her daisies.

Elizabeth greeted me joyfully, her cheeks flushed, her eyes

sparkling. Unable to settle to any task, she fluttered here and there like a nervous butterfly while I changed to my calico gown. Together we went into the gardens to pick flowers before the heat of the day. I paid scant heed to her incessant chatter, concentrating on selecting the choicest of the Michaelmas daisies.

One of the maids appeared, requesting Elizabeth's guidance in the house. They took in all we had picked and left me alone.

Shining, dark green ivy leaves caught my eye. They would be just the thing to emphasize the purple and silver. Happily I began cutting it, singing softly to myself.

In response to a crunching step on the gravel path, I said, "Are you back so soon?" and turned around.

Scarlet flooded Will's cheeks. For several heartbeats we stared at each other, the daisies and ivy tumbling from my hands.

We both set about collecting the scattered blossoms hastily.

"Addleby said Elizabeth was out here. I came to wish her happy."

"Of course. Yes, she was here. One of the maids asked for her inside. Will, please, I—we *must* talk."

He raised an eyebrow and looked at me strangely, as if disappointed.

"Oh, there you are, Dr. Knight! Father said you were out here," Elizabeth exclaimed, running down the path, her apricot petticoats billowing. She was so charming, young and glowing, I suffered a twinge of jealousy.

Will gave me the remaining flowers. "I believe we have them all, *Miss Castleton.*" He bowed to Elizabeth, saying warmly, "I came to extend my felicitations on this joyful occasion." And he kissed her hand!

Elizabeth giggled and thanked him.

Looking over his bent back at her glossy curls, clear complexion and trim figure, Anne's words came back to me forcefully. Could Will really have lost his heart to her?

"Excuse me," I murmured. "I'll take these inside." My heart was thumping, my hands shaking as I fairly ran to the manor. By setting my mind to arranging bouquets, I was able to calm myself before I needed to speak with anyone. The effect of mingling clematis and ivy with the Michaelmas daisies was graceful and pleasing.

Squire Addleby stopped to admire my efforts. "I believe a small flower would look festive on my coat. Please select one for me, my dear."

I chose a newly opened daisy and pinned it to his dark blue coat. Acutely conscious of his attentive smile, I wished Will had looked at me thus. No doubt I offered no competition for Elizabeth's young charms. My calico dress was modestly becoming, so I should have looked at least pleasing to him.

When the vases were filled to my satisfaction and strategically placed about the manor, I declined Elizabeth's invitation to dinner. Her overnight guests would soon be arriving, and I needed to return to the inn for a rest. I changed back into my riding dress, packed up my calico, and departed.

Black trotted lazily along the road while I tried vainly to keep from comparing Will's coldness towards me with his warmth towards Elizabeth. To counteract the dismals, I decided to visit Mary Richards and dear little John. She might permit me to hold him as I had done so briefly when he was born. Surely then I could put Will from my mind.

Again she did not come to greet me. There was not the least whiff of smoke from her chimney. Vaguely worried, I dismounted in front near the well. Black whinnied. A horse answered from the side.

"Mary!" I called, pushing open the door standing ajar. "It's Meg. I've come—"

Outside light fell on her bloodied face staring blankly at me from the floor. In the dim room I saw a figure move towards me. I shrank back screaming, then whirled and ran to Black.

A hand grabbed my right arm, jerking me around.

It was Will, angrier than I had ever seen him.

In relief I clung to him. "W-what's happened to Mary?"

"She's dead."

"Dead!" I stared at him, hardly believing my ears. "Dead? The—the baby! Little John! I must go to him!" I tried to pull away, but his grip held firm.

"No!"

"I must! He needs me. He's so tiny. Please! He's mine too!"

"No, Meg. No. He's dead."

"He can't be! He can't be! He was just born!" My voice rose. "Let me go to him!" A stinging slap on my cheek silenced me.

"Woman, obey me in this!" His stern tone forbade further argument. "You are *not* to go into that place again. Mary Richard's baby is dead, as she is. There is nothing you can do for either of them. And—and the sight is not . . . pleasant."

"Dead? My—the baby dead?" Grief overwhelmed me. "Not again! O Lord, please, not again!"

For a few moments he held me, giving comfort. Supporting me with his arm, he led me to Black. "Can you ride?"

I nodded, choking back my sobs.

He helped me mount. "Stay here," he commanded curtly. He strode to the cottage and closed the door tightly, then took Black around to his fine stallion tethered on the side. "Easy Prince, easy," he said to the steed nervously eyeing Black and me.

"Stay with me," he ordered. We rode at a gallop back to the manor. I was left in front with instructions not to dismount while he reported to the squire. Then we rode to the Curling Horn. In a few terse words he explained to the Wilmots and again entrusted me to their care before leaving to find Edward Smythe.

Anne Cowper calmed me and put me to bed. As she pulled the curtain over my window, she said, "Dere, ye'll be needing a proper rest for de grand ball tonight, surelye."

"Ball!" I sat up. "No! I can't go! I've no heart for merrymaking this day!"

She smiled, her tone soothing, as to a child. "Mrs. Richards' dying be lamentable sad. Howsumdever, Miss Elizabeth herself expects ye. She be justabout unhappy ifn ye did not goo. And we hadn't ought to put de squire in a niff, surelye."

I lay back and she came to smooth the covers.

"Ma'am," she said earnestly, "Mrs. Richards, she doant care about nothing no how. Her and her babe, dey be happy. De vicar, he says so."

"I know." I sighed helplessly. Anne was right, but I rebelled at the callousness of gaiety this day. I tossed on my bed until oblivion rescued me.

With a shake of my shoulder, Anne tugged me back to reality. "Beg pardon, ma'am, but it be time ye was up."

I wanted to tell her to go away and let me sink back into that peaceful nothingness. However, I rose and donned my morning robe. While I sipped the hot, strong tea she brought and nibbled at buttered bread and thin slices of beef, she straightened my bed and laid out my blue satin gown. When I thought I had eaten enough to keep her from fussing, I put on my corset and she pulled the laces tight.

Anne chattered continuously about the fine carriages passing through Tyne going to the manor.

I hardly heard her. Tyne had presented a pleasant face to me, yet beneath it lurked violence as hideous as any in Oxford. Or even London. Maybe there was no safe, peaceful place in the world. So much had happened these last days, I seemed numbed to anything more.

Anne tightened my laces again. "I doant know but ye ought to powder yer hair. It be right fitting for de grand party."

"No. I never use powder."

"Yes, ma'am," she answered taking up my gown.

My appearance mattered little. After a suitable stay to please Elizabeth, I would return and retire, my duty done.

I glowered at my reflection in the mirror. Anne had done very well with my hair. At her insistence, I placed a small star patch at the outer corner of my right eye. As I hung Mother's pendant about my neck, I thought of the ball when I met Will, and the one at Rockivale when I was first confident of his affection. What a thoughtless, giddy chit I was!

Will's earrings provided the finishing touch; I did look a lady. Little that mattered. Since he brought greetings this morning, I expected Will would not attend the ball. He might even be involved in the search for the murderer. In any event, I would not need to endure his coolness publicly.

As I gave a final glance at the mirror, it struck me that I had looked much like this for Amelia's ball. I winced, remembering the sickening remarks I heard. Thank goodness there would be no repeat of that at the squire's daughter's birthday ball.

When the squire's carriage arrived, I descended into the common room. A group of dusty men entered talking loudly.

"Dat be a nasty business!"

"Aye. I justabout glad we catched him, I be."

"And saying he do dat on account of his son doant favor him! Ye can't never make no sense of such a one!"

"Him's more de fool. Ain't naun o' mine favored naun at all for a sennight, surelye. Now de wurreld know at one leetle look dey be mine, dem what's lived."

"And chastising de vicar hisself!"

"Aye, dat be de wust."

"Howsumdever, de vicar, he be alone. And he be a man. He just about need an 'ooman same's nobody."

"And all de wurreld know Mistus Richards she be lonely as a milestone."

Seeing me on the stairs, they promptly hushed each other. With shouts for Wilmot to pour up his ale, they crowded into the taproom.

Without conscious volition, my feet carried me across the room to the waiting footman and into the carriage. So John Richards had been caught and had confessed to the terrible murders. And he said Will. . . . Now *two* evil men threatened him. And I was going to a ball.

Inside the manor, a gay fever pervaded the air, jarring rudely against my mood. Girls giggled and rustled above. Officers in full dress uniforms wandered about laughing and casting speculative glances my way. Fiddles and flutes tuned and ran scales in the drawing room.

Upstairs, I found Elizabeth, properly powdered and painted, with pink petticoats swishing gracefully. She embraced me in delight. "Meg, dear Meg, you're elegant! I can't thank you enough!"

"Your happiness is my reward. Let me look at you." I stepped back. "You are beautiful! The dress is perfect!" Diamonds sparkled on her breast. The necklace did look very lovely against her creamy skin.

She asked with concern, "Don't they powder any more in society?"

I flushed. "Yes, they do. In this I don't follow the fashion."

Relieved that she had not erred in her toilet, Elizabeth took my arm and said kindly, "Really, you are much more striking as you are."

She led me to a group of girls and began introducing her many young friends. Pretty or plain, they were excited, a little awkward, eager for whatever the night held. Their mothers tolerantly herded everyone below, then settled to dividing their attention between gossipping and watching the dashing young officers, making the barest effort at civility with me.

Lieutenant Stevenson presented himself as my first partner. Despite his suave airs, he lacked Will's smooth, effortless dancing skill. What a joy if I could dance with him again!

"Miss Castleton," the lieutenant said, "I must express my admiration for your wonderful behavior towards the colonel last Sunday."

"I don't understand."

"When we escorted you to the inn."

"Oh?"

"He pride's himself on his conquests. Your indifference to his boasted charms was a delight to behold."

"I see."

"And the vicar! He was a marvel! Believe me, everyone in the barracks knows the parson outmaneuvered our colonel."

"I trust he is not offended."

"Oh, but he is. So offended he refuses to dine here Sunday."

"He will not hold it against Mr. Knight, will he?"

"Very likely. But that gentleman seems capable of handling himself quite well."

A shiver of uneasiness passed over me. My thoughtlessness had created yet another enemy for Will. "Why is that girl, Miss, ah,

Miss . . . over there, standing alone?" I asked nodding to one of Elizabeth's plainer friends. "I thought there would be partners for all."

"One of the men came ill this afternoon. But, have no fear, all are eager to dance with you. You'll not be unattended."

"With me? Why?"

"As I said, you're famous in the barracks."

The prospect of dancing the remainder of the evening with gay young officers seemed tiring. To the next one who requested my partnership, I explained I would like to rest and pointed out the girl in need of a partner.

Escaping to the dining room, I sampled the shrub. The rum and citrus mixture was just right. Now, where could I go? If I went back to the ball, I would have to face more partners. I must be aging to find that prospect distressing instead of exciting.

Visiting with the mothers would not answer. I was not *that* old. Obviously they were puzzled by me, being neither a girl nor a matron, and alone. They likely thought me very loose, as did Amelia's friends. And they would resent the attention given me, if the lieutenant's prophecy was correct.

Stepping into the main hall, I noticed the library door was closed. That might provide a refuge. I eased it open enough to see the cases of books illumined by flaming candles and pulsing firelight. I heard no sounds. It must be deserted. With a sigh of relief, I slipped in and closed the door behind me. The familiar odors of old books and tobacco were signs I had reached a quiet haven. I relaxed and moved towards the cheery blaze on the hearth.

A stir at the far end of the room startled me. Squire Addleby and Will were rising to their feet, a chessboard between them.

"Good evening, Miss Castleton," they said.

"Oh, gentlemen, please excuse my interruption. Continue your game. I stole in here to sit quietly for a while. Pray, pay me no heed."

They murmured something polite, sat down and resumed their game.

I sank onto a settee. Will was here! He might even accompany me to the inn. Leaning back, I stared at the flames leaping about a great oak log and contemplated the evening's possibilities. Lulled by the muted music and laughter, I imagined what I would say to him when we were alone. This opportunity would *not* pass as the others.

"Aha!" exclaimed the squire. "I've caught your queen! Now, sir, I finally have you at a disadvantage!"

I hoped my presence disconcerted Will.

The game continued at its usual slow pace. Occasionally the

squire made some soft sound. Will made none at all.

After a while, I moved to a chair where I could casually observe the men as they played. The older man hunched over the board, drumming his fingers, squirming about in his seat from time to time. Will's relaxed posture belied the intense concentration I knew he must be focusing on the game.

"Check," Will said. The squire might as well resign.

"Uh."

"Check." A long silence, then, "Check."

"Never let up, do you?"

"Check."

"I've no place to move. Another game to you, Vicar. At least I had you at the disadvantage for a time tonight. Next time will be better. Ah, well, I must make an appearance at the ball for a few minutes, then I'll retire. This foot won't permit me to stand for long. All that fuss this afternoon made it worse. Thank goodness my cousin, Mrs. Montgomery, will make a proper hostess whether or not I am there."

Squire Addleby limped over to me, splendid in black velvet with silver lacing and a curled, snowy wig. He bowed, saying, "Miss Castleton, I am deeply in your debt for your kindness to my daughter. It has meant a great deal to us both to have you here, a gracious, beautiful woman who understands these affairs. Its success is yours entirely."

"You're too kind, sir. I merely made a few suggestions and carried out Elizabeth's ideas."

"Your modesty is but one of many attractive virtues. Lovely lady, I hope you will honor Tyne with a long stay, a *very* long stay. Good-night." He kissed my hand and left.

Will rearranged the chessboard, then moved to the fire and held his hands to the heat.

The tense silence threatened to pull me apart.

Leaving the fire, he came near me and said, "I'm glad you came, Meg."

"I've no heart for this party."

"I thought not."

"Anne Cowper pointed out that my mourning couldn't help poor Mary Richards or—" I took a deep breath to prevent my voice from quavering. "And my absence would hurt Elizabeth."

"Quite true. I'm very sorry you were there."

"Yes. I doubt I shall forget. They've caught John Richards, just before I came."

"I heard."

"You know that he confessed?"

"Yes."

A weight pressed me down, smothering my thoughts.

After a pause he added, "And I know of his charge against me."

"His charge?"

"That I fathered his child."

"Oh." I wanted to put those ugly words from my mind.

The log popped noisily and showered sparks onto the hearth.

He asked, "Do you believe it?"

"What?"

"John Richards' charge against me."

"That." My eyes dropped to the ivory fan in my lap which I was spreading and closing rapidly. Chinese ivory from half way around the world. "*He* must've believed it to—to do what he did." The still room closed in about me. My heart raced fit to burst my stays. "Mary was terribly lonely. I'm sure she was not the only lonely person." I ran my tongue over my lips, then looked up at him. "Please, tell me what to believe."

"If I were guilty of that sin, do you think I would admit it?"

"You would not lie."

"What do *you* think?"

"I don't *want* to think!"

He stood gazing down at me, waiting.

I could not bear the silence. "You are not that kind of man. Yet," I tried to swallow the lump in my throat, "whatever you say, I'll believe you," I whispered.

"You honor me with your faith." His tone was cold. "I visited her often because of her isolation and her need to talk to someone. I did not father her child." He added bitterly, "Nor anyone else's."

The horror of the day faded as relief blossomed within me. "Thank you for telling me." I looked up, meeting his eyes and smiled, feeling my anxieties slough off.

A familiar waltz floated in the air, trailing dear memories. As in a dream, he extended his hand. I took it and rose, tingling at his touch.

We danced in the center of the room, at one with each other and the music. As at Rockivale, a lifetime past, he held me in a firm embrace. What ecstasy! Too soon the music ended. We stood together, my heart so full of joy I could not speak.

I felt his lips press against my neck, then my lips. His passionate embrace fairly crushed my ribs. When he loosened his hold, his eyes were glowing, his face flushed. A ghost of a smile played at the corners of his mouth.

Choked with emotion, I clung to him, panting.

He lightly touched my hair, and laid his hand on my neck in a gentle caress. Tenderly he kissed me again.

"Will, I—"

Laying a finger across my lips, he said, "Not now. I'll bring our supper here."

"Oh, yes! Please do." He had turned towards the door when I added, "And then, oh, there is so *much* I have to tell you."

He froze in stride. His shoulders slumped slightly. Levelly he asked, "About what happened in Oxford?"

"Yes. I am so anxious to talk with you."

He left quickly without a glance.

Puzzled by his change, I determined to set things right immediately on his return. Here, in this library, confident of his love, I could open my heart to him fully.

The clock over the fire ticked off the minutes. I paced impatiently, tapping my fan in the palm of my hand, rehearsing what I would say.

At length the door opened and an officer entered, bearing two plates of delicacies. For a moment his figure blurred as I forced a smile.

"The vicar asked me to bring you this. He begged your forgiveness for leaving so abruptly, but he lost track of the time."

I thanked him for his kindness and said I hoped this was not an imposition. To make conversation, we talked of the places he had served and his ambition to cross the ocean and see the American colonies.

When I finished picking at my food, I allowed him to prevail upon me to endure several wearisome dances.

Finally, Lieutenant Stevenson presented himself, bowed with a flourish and said, "I am sorry, but we must return to the barracks. We will be happy to escort you to the Curling Horn."

"You are very kind. I will be ready as soon as I bid Elizabeth good-night."

As he walked me to the squire's carriage, the lieutenant explained, "The vicar asked me to make certain you arrived there safely. He said you had a frightening experience earlier this week."

"Yes. Your escort is much appreciated." Was it only three days since that horrible encounter with the "mythical" man?

The officers, gay from the punch, sang lustily all the way to the inn. They saw me safely inside. From my window, I listened to their singing diminish as they rode away.

The company of one quiet man in a black frock coat would be more exciting than all King George's most handsome officers.

Chapter Nineteen

I rose late and faced, without enthusiasm, the problem of what to wear. Surrounded with her friends, Elizabeth had no need of me at the manor. Mary Richards was dead. And Will? Confused by his sudden changes, I was of two minds whether to seek him out or await his call. Would I could sleep the day away!

With a handful of women, I attended the burial services for Mary Richards and her baby. Although I knew her briefly, this represented a great loss to me. I tried to speak with Will at the conclusion of the graveside prayers, but Mr. Smythe reached him first. They left together in deep conversation.

Frustrated by inaction, I walked about the village. It was cheering that those I met smiled when greeting me and some even used my name.

I passed a few women sitting before a cottage busy pulling whitened straws through their mouths and plaiting them. Bundles of bleached straw and finished plaits lay about their feet. I supposed the plaits were destined for someone who fashioned hats or baskets. One woman smiled shyly at me as she bent to pick up a grooved wooden roller.

"Good-day, ladies," I said.

They responded politely.

Receiving no invitation to stay and pass the time with them, I walked on, my idleness a heavier burden for their industry.

With weighted feet I climbed the meandering path to the ruined nunnery. Below I saw Will on Prince stop at a cottage. Edward Smythe left the inn with Anne on his arm. At dinner she said they would be wed in two weeks' time. I watched them stroll down a crooked lane under trees bared of all save a few tatters of foliage. They entered a cottage, no doubt her parents' home.

Across the way the miller and a man were loading sacks into a broad-wheeled cart before the mill. Farther up the bottom, a pair of red oxen pulled a plow in a narrow field followed by a ploughman. A boy walked beside the slow animals with a long stick. His whistles and shouts mingled faintly with the miller's voice, punctuated with sharp blows on the anvil beside the inn.

Everyone within range of my vision was doing something with or for another. They all had a place in this community. I was a foreigner. If I left, my absence would barely be noted. The Wilmots would miss a paying guest. Elizabeth and the squire would miss my company a little.

And Will? For a few precious moments last night I thought, I hoped. . . But his life seemed complete without me. I almost wished he had fathered that poor, dead baby. It would have shown a need for me.

He left the first cottage and rode to another of the scattered outer dwellings. Later he would go home to an empty house. Did he have a housekeeper to do for him? What was the parsonage like inside? In fancy I went there, swept it, and prepared his favorite kidney pie.

"O Lord, God in heaven, who treads the heights of these downs, help me! Help me find my way out of this muddle. I came. I believed this was what You wanted me to do. But everything's so confused! At times Will shows he cares, yet he doesn't want to hear what I long to tell him. I have no place here. I have no place in Oxford. In all the world is there a place for me?" In desperation I thought of the colonies the young officer described as filled with opportunities and savages.

"O Lord, what shall I do? Give me a sign, please. Some direction. Some way of knowing what I should do."

I sensed a kinship with the shades of the nuns once living here. They, too, must have felt as I when they were driven out by Cromwell's men and their home destroyed. Where had they gone? What did they do? Perhaps the soldiers killed them. That was better than to live without a place where they belonged.

As the sun neared the horizon, I left my seat and made my way down to the inn. Will might come tonight for food, maybe even to see me. It was a slender hope, but, if so, I must look my best.

A letter addressed to me in Charles' hand lay on the chest in my room.

My Dear Little Dove,
    I hope by now you have spoken with Will and made up sensibly. I will arrive on Tuesday next and spend the night at the inn. I shall expect to see you happily installed in the parsonage.
    In the event you are not, I will speak to Will. As you know, I failed in my first attempt. This time I will not permit him to draw me off into other matters before I have made it plain to him why you are in Tyne. However, you will be wiser to act before I arrive.
                                                            Yours ever,
                                                            Charles

A sign. I had prayed for a sign.

I pondered its interpretation while I changed to my prettiest calico dress, brushed my hair and tied it with a green ribbon.

Few were present for supper. I visited with Mrs. Wilmot, trying to prolong my presence in the common room. There was guarded excitement over the successful landing of contraband in the fog early Monday morning and its subsequent removal only last night under the very noses of the army. Once again the proud colonel was foiled.

Will did not come.

Discouraged, I went to my room. What should I do? I longed to run to the parsonage, to pound on the door and beg him to take me.

Why not? If I'd run after him when he left Oxford, or come long ago, or sent one of those letters. . . Every impulsive move prompted by my heart was squelched as unbecoming behavior. What did it matter if I could repair our lives at the cost of my dignity?

There was Charles' letter urging me to act before he came on Tuesday. A sign. The church and parsonage were only a short distance from the inn. Will would be there preparing for Sunday's service. Even a demon would not venture near the homes of decent folk. Surely I would be safe for the few minutes it took me to run there. It was worth the risk.

I pulled on my boots and threw my cardinal about my shoulders. Men's laughter came from the taproom as I slipped through the deserted common room. Outside in the cool, light air, I hurried down the road. Several times I was nearly overset by the wind tugging on my petticoats or by tripping on the uneven surface.

The unlit church loomed before me, an ominous mass amid the elms. I veered towards the parsonage, Will's home. Over the low garden wall I saw it, too, was dark! Might he be gone? What would I do? A small stone caught my toe. I stumbled, regained my balance and stopped beneath the willow. Having come this far, I would not turn back. Perhaps he had dozed off over a book and his candle guttered out.

"Please, let him be here," I prayed. "Please, let him be here."

A gloved hand clamped across my mouth and I was roughly dragged to a clump of bushes and thrown to the ground. My assailant's body pinned me there. A few vain efforts to struggle free convinced me I was unable to move.

A horse clopped softly through the churchyard and passed a few feet from us. Could that be Will, and I unable to cry for help?

Some long minutes after the rider passed, my attacker raised his head to look after him. I pushed against the man and beat with my fists, but he held me down firmly.

In an ugly, rasping voice he said, "Purty lady, ye be out in my night. Ye be unaccountable eager to see me, do ye not?" He placed a hand around my throat. "Ifn ye shruck, ye'll shruck no more, surelye."

In despair I ceased struggling.

He removed his hand from my mouth.

Fighting panic, I gulped in deep breaths. "Let me go!"

"Why? De night be mine. Everyone in de night be mine." In the shadow of the broad brim of his hat I could barely make out a cloth pierced with two holes covering his features.

"And that rider? If he was yours, you wouldn't have hid."

"Him be de Devil's aright. Dere be no cause I should share my catch wud him." The creature stared down at me. "Ye be goan to see de parson. I dunno but what I said ifn ye do he dies."

"No—no! I have kept my word."

"Den why be ye here?"

"P-personal reasons. They have nothing to do with you."

He cackled. "Lies! Lies! Ye be goan to de vicarage. Dere be naun else to bring ye abroad in *my* night."

"Let me go! I swear I'll tell him nothing about you."

"In de morning, I give certain things to de Prevention Officer. Den de vicar, he hangs."

"No! No! Kill *me* if you must!"

"*Kill* you?"

He laughed. "I seen you walk about. Ye be a prime 'un. Kill you? No, no. Dere ain't no call for dat. Dere be better den dat to do!" He leapt to his feet, pulling me up by my wrists.

Bent and twisted, he stood little taller than me. Suddenly he spun around, dropping one wrist. "Who dat?" he whispered.

Jerking free, I stumbled across the Docking road to huddle in a friendly shadow. What a blessing the moon was not yet up!

I heard uneven steps in pursuit. He came near. Cautiously I picked up a stone and hurled it towards Lewes. He paused, then went after the sound. I offered a silent prayer of thanks.

After some time, I heard a low whistle, then hoofbeats growing faint. I waited, trying to decide if this was a ruse or if he had really ridden off.

The tip of the crescent moon appeared over a hill. I darted back to the inn before its light should betray me.

In my room, I examined the damage from my fruitless adventure. My dress was muddied and the bodice torn beyond repair. Fortunately the rips in my cloak were minor and could be mended.

Leaves, twigs and dirt were caught in my hair. I labored for hours cleaning and mending.

Every effort to go to Will was thwarted. Might this be a sign it was not God's will that I should rejoin him? Selfish fear and pride drove me from Will. My loneliness for him brought me to him. Always I thought of myself. Rather I should think of the man I had wronged. What would be best for him? Could I add anything to his ministry? The people liked him as he was; they might resent a wife. And what of that evil man's threat? If I left, that danger would be lessened.

I should leave Wednesday with Charles. That was the meaning of my sign.

Before retiring, I laid my small store of money on the table to count. There was little more than what I owed the Wilmots. The only way I could leave would be with Charles.

The church was nearly filled, primarily because a large group of officers augmented the regular congregation. Doubtless this was their way of applauding the parson for embarrassing their colonel.

Eloquently Will preached on forgiveness, using God's love and mercy in forgiving our sins as the basis for us to forgive each other. It seemed a message from him to me. However, after the service, he only spoke a few formal words to me.

Neither Mr. Smythe nor Anne Cowper were present. As I had left the inn, she told me earnestly that they could not attend so long as they were being "church bawled." "Ifn we does, ma'am, it's certain sure our children, dey be born deaf and dumb."

Squire Addleby hailed me with an invitation to dine with him and Elizabeth. "I am happy to say that Colonel Snyde will not be with us, so dinner will not be formal. We consider you practically a member of the family."

In keeping with the squire's suggestion, I chose my green calico with white bows down the stomacher and fastened a green ribbon in my auburn curls. This could be the last time I saw Will. His memory of me must be pleasant. Although they were not suitable with my gown, I decided to wear his mother's diamond earrings.

The dinner of trout, roast beef and chicken was served simply. Although Elizabeth plainly missed the stimulus of the lieutenant, she was an attentive hostess. She gossiped brightly with me about her friends and the ball. Will sat opposite me, discussing the improvement the planting of turnips had brought to the economy of the whole district. He was bent on urging the squire to incorporate further changes.

Squire Addleby dismissed the subject with a wave of his hand. "Elizabeth's ball was a great success, thanks to you, my dear Miss Castleton. With the guests gone and things normal again, surely you will grant us the joy of being our guest. You would be no trouble at all in this rambling place and your presence would give us great pleasure. Do say you will come."

"You are very kind, sir; however, I intend leaving for Oxford on Wednesday."

Will glanced at me in surprise.

"So soon?" the squire inquired anxiously. "My dear Miss Castleton, we must try to change your mind."

"I should miss you dreadfully!" Elizabeth exclaimed in reproach.

"How will you go?" Will asked. "The coach passes here Tuesday, Thursday and Saturday."

"Yesterday I received a letter from Charles Heathton. He said he was arriving Tuesday for the night. We're old friends. I think I can persuade him to take me to Oxford."

Will's expression froze. "And if he is taking another direction?"

"Then I shall take the Thursday coach," I replied, trying not to think of my inadequate funds. "Please, let's talk of other than my dull plans."

Elizabeth obliged me by describing her preparations for wintering in Greece.

"I expect to bring back another sarcophagus for the garden," the squire stated. "And I've thought about getting one of those obolisks. Lord Hillary has one in his garden. But I can't decide where it should go. Some place where I could see it from the house. No point in getting a thing like that and hiding it where no one will see it.

"By-the-by, Dr. Knight, are you going to Docking as usual Wednesday?"

"Yes, sir, and tomorrow as well."

"Tomorrow!"

"Goody Ensworth died last night. I promised to lay her to rest tomorrow. The people are expecting me."

"There are some parish affairs we should discuss. The Richards' affair, you know."

At that, Elizabeth rose and she and I withdrew to the salon. There I listened to her elaborate on the glories and trials of travel on the continent.

When the men entered, the squire suggested they forego their usual chess and we all play whist. He paired Will with Elizabeth, seating me with a gallant flourish as his partner. As we played, he favored me with frequent smiles and compliments.

However, I was more aware of the few expressions crossing

Will's face and his manners towards Elizabeth. Naturally she flirted prettily with her partner. Jealous twinges provided a continual distraction from my cards.

Will drove his cart slowly to the inn. I sat stiffly beside him staring ahead, trying not to dwell on the finality of this short trip. Again he pulled into the shadow of Addleby's Folly.

My fingers pressed into the backs of my clasped hands. Urgently I prayed that the evil demon not see us here and misunderstand.

The moon hung like a handleless scythe over a black hill. Into the nocturnal quiet dropped a few low "chook-chook" bird notes. The song ascended easily, hovered, then burst into a passionate outpouring of cascading melody. A sudden silence was splintered by another song more acrobatic than the first.

Hardly daring to take a breath, I listened to the beautiful warbling trills, amazed at the richness of the music. "What is that?" I asked.

"A nightingale."

It made a fluttering in a nearby bush, then I saw it hop to an upper branch. Head lifted, its silvered profile quivering with intensity, it sang a magic spell. Then it was gone.

For a few precious moments I savored the beautiful sounds. I felt part of the moon, the hills, the night.

"You are determined to leave this week?" Will inquired softly.

"Yes."

"Why? Why are you leaving?"

I could only manage a whisper. "There seems no reason to stay."

After a long pause he asked. "Will you return?"

"I—I don't think so."

He broke the next silence speaking harshly, bitterly. "You said you came to talk with me. Will you leave without accomplishing your purpose?"

My long prepared speech trembled on my tongue. Then I realized that awful creature would have Will hung if I stayed.

"Why are you leaving?" he persisted. "Tell me the truth."

Nervously I glanced over my shoulder. "Because, because I am a danger to you."

He peered at me through the dark. "How can *you* be a *danger* to me?"

I kept silence.

"Tell me how!"

"I can't. Please believe me, I can't," I pled in a shaking voice.

The pressing questions I feared did not come. Instead he set the cart in motion.

When we came to the Curling Horn, Will lifted me down, his hands on my waist. He left them there, quickly checked the door for Wilmot, then asked in a low voice, "Meg, do you *want* to go?"

Blinking back tears, I shook my head.

The door creaked. As my host joined us, Will spoke pleasantly to him, then climbed into his cart and drove off without a word of parting to me.

I mounted the stairs with leaden feet. My hopes had come to naught. If only I could go back to the day he left Oxford! We could have shared grief for our baby. By now we might have had another child. I expected God to remove the results of my sins, to make everything right. He had not. Because of my actions, I must live on empty and unfulfilled.

Without removing my cloak, I fell across my bed. The too-familiar black gloom of past months pressed about me.

Chapter Twenty

A cry of alarm roused me. Anne stood at my side with a tray of hot chocolate and rolls. "Oh, ma'am, ye give me that gurt a start!"

I looked at my clothes, then the sunlight, puzzled. "I, I was tired."

"Ye do look to be beazled and a bit peaked, ma'am." She took my cloak to hang up, then my dress. As she gave me my robe she asked, "Be ye wishing to bide abed?"

It seemed easiest, so I said yes, and asked not to be disturbed before I went downstairs. Bessie would not have allowed this, but she was not here to prod at me.

As I lay abed, listlessly watching the sunlight move across the floor, I remembered Mr. Wesley on his knees praying for me. He spoke of an inner assurance of forgiveness and peace. I no longer possessed them. Were they real?

I took up my Bible, unopened since my arrival. Flipping through its pages front to back, back to front, I looked for something, I knew not what. More slowly I leafed through it again, through the Old Testament into the Gospels. Surely in all these words there must be something for me. Then my eye picked up the word "peace."

"Peace I leave with you, my peace I give unto you: not as the world giveth, give I unto you. Let not your heart be troubled, neither let it be afraid." I knew that peace in Oxford when I began my trip. Fear and uncertainty had edged in, replacing it. And so I had chosen to live a lie instead of trusting God and going directly to Will.

On the facing page I read, "If a man love me, he will keep my words, and my Father will love him, and we will come unto him, and make our abode with him." I had not obeyed fully because I did not love fully. What had Mr. Wesley said about fear and love? Something about love casting out fear.

I knelt beside my bed to pray as I had not since leaving Oxford. In confessing my lack of love and my lie, I found anew the cleansing of forgiveness and deep peace. My circumstances were still in confusion, but an underlying security in God kept me from panic.

Anne bustled up in the common room to lay a cover before me at the supper table. "De rest done you good, ma'am. Ye looked tedious down dis morning, and now ye be shining like."

Mrs. Wilmot had just served me when a stout village woman sat opposite with a pewter tankard. She took a deep drink of her ale, wiped her mouth with the back of her hand and addressed Mrs. Wilmot. "Like I says, it must a been her brother. Ain't nobody else. Jimmie Caird, he says he doant know nothin'. Nobody came. Nobody went. But John Richards, he be dead."

"Den he killed hisself, surelye," Mrs. Wilmot concluded. "Him be a larmentaable evil man. Mayhap he be de Red Demon hisself."

"Mass Padge, him's my man," she explained to me. "He says he bluv Richards ain't one to cut open hisn belly hisself. Like as not he be murdered and Jimmie, he knows and ain't sayin'. Or mayhap he be otherwheres and he be afeard it be known. He do fornicate every chance, he do."

"More'n likely wud de Croft girl. Now dere's one's too footy by half." Mrs. Wilmot nodded sagely. "I seen her making calves' eyes at dat Jimmie, trying to nurt him."

"Him's not de only one. What d'ye think? *I* seen her looking at de *parson*! A-pouting her lips, a-wiggling her hips! She no ought to act dat way. She be most a draggle tail."

"Chuckleheaded girl! De parson's an upstanding man, like gentry, I'd say, wouldn't you, ma'am?" Mrs. Wilmot asked me.

I nodded.

"De likes of her hadn't ought to interest him. Now Miss Elizabeth, *she* be like him."

"I be dubbersome de squire'd be partial to dat, hem-a-bit, Nancy. Him be very choice who she be church-bawled with. Him be set on Miss Elizabeth finding a gentleman to rule hisn land."

"Ain't nobody nowheres bettermost to Dr. Knight, surelye. He be a nice still man. And he know de land, for all he's a foreigner. Lookee how he done hisn field."

"But de parson to be master to de squire's land? I allow dat doant be fitting."

"Ye see him and Miss Elizabeth together and ye'll alter yer thinking quick enew. And, mayhap he marry her, he'd no. goo off and let de church goo rattlebone agin. I tell ye, dat marriage'd be a blessing to us all, surelye."

All this brought back seeing Will kiss Elizabeth's hand in the garden and their interchange as partners last night. Agitated, I rose. "Excuse me, please. I must retire."

"Ma'am," Mrs. Wilmot called as I walked away, "I most disremembered! And oh, de squire, he be miffed! Brookes, hisn footman, brung a letter whiles ye be abed." She gave it to me and stood twisting her apron, frowning anxiously.

I opened it saying, "I'm sure it is nothing you need worry about." The message was brief. "It's only an invitation to dine tomorrow. I'll send a reply in the morning."

"Such a relief, ma'am! Ye can't know!"

Immediately upon arising, I sincerely thanked God for the new day and earnestly asked Him to guide me through these last days in Tyne. Something would have to be done about my lies. Whatever it was, He would show me at the right time.

A depressing fog shrouded the village beyond my window. Dutifully I wrote and sent my acceptance note to the squire. Then, with a sigh, I turned to packing.

First the blue satin, then the green silk were folded and laid in my trunk. I surveyed my few remaining belongings. They could easily be done tonight, or tomorrow. Despite my resolution to depart, I was loath to make the necessary preparations.

By noon the fog withdrew to the horizon, leaving the sky clear. It was a perfect day for riding. Stopping at Addleby's Folly, I regarded the contrived ruin thoughtfully. Oh, that different words were spoken that night, tender, passionate as the nightingale's song.

It was beyond my power to relive the past. My future was entrusted to God's hands. It seemed I might dispel some of the evil hovering over Will by leaving. Only truth could repair a lie. The Addlebys must be told, no matter how embarrassing it might be. I should trust the Lord to guard my lips from any indiscretion harmful to Will.

Elizabeth greeted me affectionately. Squire Addleby, elegant in a rich brown coat with a floral embroidered waistcoat and ruffled shirt, sought to anticipate my every whim. At dinner he urged me to try a bite of everything and insisted on my being served large portions. It was difficult to avoid offending him and not be in agony from my corset.

"You must have a wheatear, my dear Miss Castleton," he insisted. "I'll wager you've never had the like before."

"What is it?" I asked, cutting at what looked to be a small chicken.

"A special delicacy here. It's a bird, more tasty than lark, I think. Old Michael brought these in only last night. They must have been in a late flock, for the season's quite over."

I found the wheatear fully as delicious as he promised, and said so.

Satisfied at pleasing me, he said, "I wish you could go with us to Greece. You'd find it most enjoyable, and it would be more amusing for Elizabeth with you as a companion. In any event, I insist you return to Tyne next spring. We have beautiful springs, haven't we, Elizabeth?"

"Yes, Papa."

"And you must plan on a long stay. Here at the manor. With us."

"You are very kind," I answered, touched by his hospitality.

As he pared an apple, he added, "We'll miss you sorely, Miss Castleton. You've enriched us all these few weeks. I cannot understand how you managed to remain unwed so long. You're a comely woman."

"Papa!" Elizabeth exclaimed, blushing.

"She is, daughter. It's naught but the truth. The men at Oxford must be blind. Blinder than in my day."

I took a deep breath. "Well, you see, sir, I am wed, to a fine man."

His knife clattered on his plate. "Are you not Dr. Castleton's daughter?"

"Yes, sir. I chose to use his name when I came here instead of my married name."

"But why?" He stared at me intently, his face growing scarlet. "Why did you do that?"

"I was, you see, my husband. . . It was to spare him embarrassment."

"To spare him!" He flung himself back in his chair. "But how would you embarrass him here in *Tyne*?"

"Papa, these are matters not concerning us," Elizabeth interjected.

"Beth! You forget yourself!" The squire glared at her but she did not flinch. He gave a short, explosive laugh and relaxed. "You are quite right. Forgive my questions, dear lady."

"Rather I must ask your pardon in being untruthful."

He dismissed this with a wave of his hand. "No matter who you are, Miss Castleton, you have been a refreshing touch to our home. Most refreshing. Excuse me, ladies. My businessman awaits. I wish you a safe journey." He bowed, leaving the half-pared apple browning on his plate.

"Meg, let's go into the garden," Elizabeth suggested.

Arms linked, we strolled to the far end denuded of its Michael-mas daisies. There, between the pillars of a small domed structure aping a Grecean temple, I pledged her to silence and proceeded to relate much of my history, omitting Will's identity and my reason for coming to Tyne.

Elizabeth considered it most romantic. "Meg, dear Meg, I wish you did not have to leave! But I'm sure that your husband, wherever he is, will be delighted to have you back."

I shook my head. "No, I'm afraid not," I said sorrowfully. "Believe me, Elizabeth, I must return to Oxford," I concluded.

As the sun was nearing the top of the garden wall, Elizabeth begged me to stay for tea, but I declined. Charles might be at the Curling Horn, and I must tell him of my intention to travel with him.

I departed, still wondering if, in my attempt to do the right thing, I had muddled it forever. Truly it would have been better for Will had I never come to Tyne.

A distant horseman descended a golden hill in my direction. Vaguely he resembled the wild-riding Red Demon. But surely he could not be this bold in daylight when he might be seen! I looked back towards the manor. It was hidden by a curve of a hill. No one was visible!

Frantic at being accosted yet again, I slapped Black's rump repeatedly until he broke into a gallop. A quick glance showed the rider swerving to intercept me. I looked again and recognized Will's magnificent chestnut.

Will waved.

Trembling with relief, I reined in Black and waited.

As he approached, Will slowed to a trot, then a prancing walk. He sat his horse easily. Pointing back along the road, he said, "Follow me!"

Obediently I turned Black and cantered at his side. He turned into thick bushes and led me along a trail depressed more than a foot below ground, densely screened on both sides with arching bushes and trees. Confident not even the Demon would see us here, I relaxed and turned to considering what important matter caused Will to seek me out.

We emerged on chalk cliffs overlooking the stretch of beach I had galloped upon freely. He lifted me down beside a sparse growth of young beechs onto a patch of grass edging the cliffs. As he tethered the horses, he said, "I thought we could best talk here."

I asked, thinking more of the Demon than the villagers, "Won't this cause a scandal?"

"According to Wilmot, all the village thinks you are at the manor and will remain into the evening. As you see, this is a very private place."

Spreading his cloak near the trees, he said, "You may sit, if you wish."

I did so, arranging my petticoats modestly.

He sat at my side and stared at the channel covered with a puffy bank of light gray fog.

"Are you returning from Docking?" I asked to break the silence.

"I came back yesterday afternoon." He broke off a blade of grass and began pulling and twisting it between his fingers. He seemed troubled and strangely uncertain what to say.

"What are those furrows?" I babbled on, pointing to the area near the brink of the cliff where chunks of turf lay overturned in a regular pattern.

"Those are traps for the wheatears."

"Oh. The squire had them for dinner. They were very delicious."

"And plentiful. The shepherds catch them on the high downs and sell them at a penny each. Since they often get several dozen a day, it makes an important addition to their income. These probably belong to Old Michael."

"How is a clod of earth a trap?"

"When the skies are overcast the birds evidently are beset with fears. They land and try to get under a rock, anything."

"Like a clod of earth?"

"They hide there for safety. Under each clod is a noose to snare them." He turned to look at me. "Fear makes us do strange things. Senseless things. People as well as birds and animals are its prey."

"How I know! But I've never known you to be afraid of anything or any person."

"All my life I've feared losing the things, the people I valued most. Like the wheatears, I've tried to hide by not showing how much I cared."

He broke the blade of grass. "Meg, you said you came expressly to see me. To talk with me. I've avoided this, prevented your speaking."

His admission surprised me.

He remained intent on the broken blade of grass. "If you didn't actually say it, then, I thought, I hoped, you might change your mind. Each time I thought you'd changed, you emphasized wanting to talk with me. Nothing I did could sway you." He tossed aside the grass and looked at me. "You're determined to leave shortly. So say it. You see, I know why you've come."

"How could you possibly know?"

"I know you. And I know Heathton."

"Charles? What has he to do with us?"

"Since he returned from his tour, he's had little to talk of except you and Rockivale . . . and you." He paused. "He told me of staying with you, not knowing I knew Dr. Castleton had moved to Christ Church." He sighed. "When I left Rockivale, I went to Oxford to see you."

"You did!"

"I stopped at the Ark first for dinner. There I heard," he paused again, "I heard several smarts linking your name with Heathton's."

"Oh, no! What, what do you think I came to—to say?"

He faced the sea and stared with frowning concentration at the fog bank, hands clasped around one knee, his knuckles white. He pressed his lips together and a muscle flexed under his ear. "You may rest assured I expect neither an apology nor for you to beg forgiveness. That is not done now. You are quite in the mode of the times."

Shock twisted my stomach. "Will!" Gently I said, "That gossip was baseless. Every night Charles was in the house, Bessie slept in my room. Nothing, *nothing* improper occurred."

He glanced at me skeptically, then stared ahead.

"I'm speaking the truth. You must believe me!"

"Do not protest over much."

"Will, please, what did you expect when I first came?"

His expression became set, his eyes blank as he turned to me. "You surely have no wish for this marriage to continue."

I gasped. "No wish. . . " I covered my mouth with icy fingers. "Is—is *that* what you want?" Pride rescued me. Recovering my dignity, I said, "Of course. Then you would be free, free to court Elizabeth."

He regarded me with a puzzled frown.

"Anne Cowper says you dance continual attendance on her. Mrs. Wilmot says you're quite smitten with her." I was chagrined at the bitterness in my tone betraying my hurt.

"Do they?"

"Are—are they right?"

"Have you not learned to distinguish village gossip from facts?"

"No more than you. But, remember, you have never been the one to act in vain flattery, kissing the hand of every woman coming your way!" I retorted sharply.

"The garden," he said, remembering. "I must apologize for such dissembling." He added soberly, "There is much I should ask you to forgive."

"Is—is there another woman, who has—has engaged your affections?"

"Of course not! However, I will not stand in the way of your happiness."

To conceal my relief, I adopted Amelia's lofty manner. "I have no wish to be involved in a scandal with nothing to gain."

"Nothing?" He raised an eyebrow. "Not even Heathton?"

"I told you, nothing happened!"

"You've always loved him, Meg. When first we met you told me you would do anything for him."

I gasped. "You think that? Even at St. Thomas'?"

"He was abroad then. I hoped to win your heart while he was absent. I failed. Why did you come?"

If he felt this way, it would be too humiliating to tell him the truth. "It matters not since I am leaving tomorrow. And I will not return. Ever!"

"And you leave with Heathton."

I bit my lower lip.

Angrily he said, "After coming so far, *say* what you wanted to say!"

"It was a fool's errand!" I jumped up and ran to Black. Tears blinded me as I tried to force my shaking fingers to untie the reins.

Will pulled my hands from their tangle.

"Let me go!"

He held me firmly. "No. We must part honestly."

"I'll not have you mock me! I have some pride!" And then all I'd heard and read about pride and humility flooded into my mind.

"Meg." His tone carried gentle reproof. "I'll not mock you. Have I," his fingers tightened around my hands, "have I been in error?"

My legs weakened and I swayed against the tree. Taking several breaths to steady my voice, I fastened my attention on the white bands hanging against the front of his black frock coat. "When I came, if—if. . . " I took another breath. "If I had gone to—to the vicarage, to you, and. . . " I faltered, unable to finish.

"And?" he prompted gently.

"Asked to—to stay, what . . . would you . . . have . . . done?"

His voice was husky as he said, "Welcomed you home."

"Truly? I was . . . afraid."

His kiss was warm and demanding.

I surrendered, clinging to him. "Oh, my dearest, my beloved. I was afraid you wouldn't forgive me for—"

"Hush," he interrupted. "There is a cave just below us. Will you come?"

"Yes! Yes!" I took a few steps, then recalled the Demon's warnings and stopped. "I—I can't."

"Why?" he demanded.

"I—I *must* go away. It will be best." Tears crept down my cheeks.

With surprising understanding he asked, "Because you fancy you place me in danger?"

I nodded.

"Meg," he tilted my chin up.

I looked into his hazel eyes filled with the loving tenderness I had yearned to see.

"Believe me, you place me in no danger at all."

"You don't know."

"Rather, I am a danger to you." Stepping carefully between the wheatear traps, he took me to the brink of the cliffs and pointed to the channel. "From time to time a navy ship passes with illegally impressed men aboard."

I moved back from the edge, dizzily conscious of the waves and rocks below. "Like Arthur Heathton?"

"Yes. Occasionally one escapes. Late one night, after seeing a sick parishioner, I passed below. I came across one nearly dead from exhaustion. He revived enough to beg for aid. I cared for him and arranged his escape from this district. There have been others. This activity is a hanging crime."

So the Demon had spoken the truth!

"Many parsons have done this. Some have died for it. You see, the danger I face is of my own making, though I am unlikely to be caught."

"But if—if someone had seen you, had proof that you had done this?"

"The person claiming that won't turn me over to Mr. Smythe. It was an empty threat."

"B—but you can't be certain."

"I am certain. I know."

His confidence broke the outlaw's chains of fear.

"Meg," he took my hands and kissed them. "Living with me will place you in the shadow of the gallows. If I am caught, justice would be swift. My guilt might spread to you."

"That is nothing. Without you life has been unbearable!"

"Think carefully. I could not endure losing you a second time."

"I am positive."

Holding my hand, he guided me down a narrow path on the face of the cliff.

Seeing the ground fall away sharply beneath my feet, I closed my eyes and inched my feet along, fighting lightheaded dizziness. When we stopped, I opened my eyes cautiously, careful not to look below.

Will shoved back a bush clinging to the sheer rock, raised a dark cloth behind it, and led me into a dim cave. "Stand still," he commanded.

I heard him move about and strike a flint. Light flared as he lit a lantern having only one side unshuttered. A rolled blanket and bundle were faintly visible in one corner.

"A smuggler's cave?" I asked brightly, relieved to be safely off the narrow path.

He looked about and shook his head. "There is much for you to forgive. Too much."

I embraced him. "Nothing is too much. Are you the secret captain of a whole band of smugglers?" I teased. "Remember, Charles once said," I paused, embarrassed, "that you—you would be successful as such."

"No. Not that. Meg, I am the Red Demon."

I gaped at him and laughed shakily. "You're hoaxing me!"

"No, Meg, it's true."

I drew back. "You can't be! It's impossible! He—he's horrible!"

"But I am, my dear, I am."

"You're too tall. He's short. He's misshappen. He has a bad foot. And his voice is hideous!"

"Illusions, my dear. I stoop," he demonstrated, "place a pad here," patted his back, "and walk thus." He took a few steps as one trying to conceal a limp. "Now, be ye believing, purty lady?" he rasped.

Terrified, I shrank against the damp wall.

"I were at de sea and in de road agin de church."

I shuddered at the memories the inhuman voice revived. "But—but why?"

"The first time another's life depended on your silence. The second time it was your life. This area abounds with thieves, highwaymen and murderers. Since you ventured forth a second time, I thought it necessary to frighten you badly enough to prevent your doing it again, to give you a taste of what might well happen." Looking into my face he continued, "Except for that rider, I would not have touched you. Had he seen you, he would have raped you and slit your throat."

Instinctively I touched my neck.

"I let you escape when you were safe. I watched until you were inside."

"But I ran across the road and hid."

"Not very well. My threats were empty, of course. However, if you mentioned what you saw to Colonel Snyde, or, worse yet, to Edward Smythe, I would be caught and executed."

"How can a man as good as you be evil?"

"I quote, 'Nary be so good as dey say.' "

"Or evil ones as evil," I countered.

"Perhaps I'm not the person you think. Perhaps I've really changed."

Could this be so? My beloved, the Red Demon? Impossible! Yet he would not lie. Numbly I tried to understand, but my mind refused to function.

After several minutes, he held out his hand. "Come. I'll take you up the cliff."

"Up the cliff?" I asked blankly.

"Surely you've no desire to remain with me, a criminal!"

Placing my hand in his, I said, "But I do."

His face was invisible in the dim light. "Can you forgive me for terrorizing you?"

"Yes. I forgive you. I belong with you. I love you.

'Thou art my life, my love, my heart, The very eyes of me,
And hast command of every part To live and *die* for thee!' "

He turned away. "You said that to Heathton."

"I said it to you, the man I love."

Gently he explored my face with his fingertips. Thin streams of fire raced from my cheeks to my toes. He said softly, "I may be hung."

" 'Whither thou goest I will go.' I only fear being without you."

With a sigh that was nearly a moan, he embraced me, his mouth pressing mine fiercely, hungrily.

Climbing up the narrow trail with a light heart, clinging to Will's hand, I experienced few of the fears of the descent. The world was beautiful. No evil could befall me when I was so attune with the universe!

Safely on the grass, he embraced me again. "We will fill the parsonage with greater joy than has ever been known under its roof, and many, many children."

"Will, my dearest, I, there, there is something I must tell you."

His arms tensed, as if steeling himself for a blow.

"Last January. . . last January our baby was born."

"A baby! We have a child!" Surprised joy radiated from his face.

Anxiously I began explaining. "I was selfishly hurt when you left. I kept expecting you back, thinking to tell you then. I wanted you to come just for me. L-later I thought to bring you our child, hoping you would not turn me away."

"I would not turn you away any time."

"I—I was not certain."

"Where is our child? Have we a son or daughter?" He chuckled. "Or both?"

"S—she was d-dead e'er she was born. S-strangled by the cord." My old grief rolled over me and I leaned against him, weeping.

He held me tightly. "Would I had been with you!" he whispered.

"I was too proud to. . . And, afterwards, there seemed nothing to say. I despaired of ever seeing you."

"Meg, my dear Meg." He rocked me gently. "Were you attended by a physician?"

I nodded.

"Did he say you could not have any more children?"

"No. On the contrary, he assured me my next would probably be normal and healthy."

"Then we shall fill the parsonage with children! You know, we are enjoined to 'redeem the time.' And we shall, with the sound of laughter and the singing of psalms. We must not look back, but press forward. Oh, Meg, my Meg, my cup is flooding over!"

"And your sign? Have you had the sign you desired?"

He paused before answering. "Perhaps, like the Pharisees, I've been blind to proofs all around me. What more do I really need, now that you are here?"

Chapter Twenty-one

Contented, I cantered beside Will. Too soon we reached the curve in the road, bringing us in sight of Tyne. Will halted and I guided Black as close to him as possible.

"Do nothing until Heathton arrives." He leaned over and kissed me.

"Won't they believe us if we told them the truth?"

He shook his head. "They would suspect you are my mistress and hate us. Wait patiently, Meg."

I rode through the deepening gloom towards the lanterns' cheery light at the inn's door. When I entered the yard, I gave the reins to Mr. Wilmot's stable boy. "Has Mr. Heathton arrived?"

"No, ma'am. He no ought to come now dis side o' de dark."

I thanked him, confident whatever Will had in mind could be carried out.

After supper the men went to the taproom, leaving the common room deserted. I was about to go up to my room when Mr. Smythe entered.

"Good evening, Miss Castleton," he said, hanging his cloak by the door.

"Good evening Mr. Smythe."

He looked towards the noisy taproom, then at me and came to sit at my side. "I'm sorry to hear you'll be leaving us soon."

Startled, I made no comment.

"It's a short distance from the manor kitchen to the village," he explained. "I hope it's not because of Mrs. Richards. Few are as violent as her husband."

"Not even the smugglers? I've heard of the bloody Hawkhurst gang."

"True, they were vicious, cruel men. I helped bring them to the king's justice in Chichester before coming here. They're all either dead or in France now."

A gust of chill air interrupted him as the outside door opened and Will entered. "Good evening, ma'am, Smythe."

I murmured a response and looked away quickly to hide my feelings from Mr. Smythe.

"A fine night," Will commented, removing his cloak.

"Clear and pleasant, as long as the fog stands off the beach," agreed Mr. Smythe. "The sort I prefer."

"Too clear for smugglers and other criminals?" Will asked as he hung his wrap on top of Mr. Smythe's.

"Much too clear. There were marks of a landing early this morning. Another reason they'll not be out tonight." He explained to me, "They can't handle more'n one or two landings a week. It's a problem of storage."

Will started to cross to the taproom when Mr. Smythe suggested, "Come sit with us by the fire, Knight. I'm trying to convince Miss Castleton to tarry a while longer in Tyne."

"Oh? Perhaps her plans are already set," he said joining us.

"Surely she can delay a week until Anne and I are wed. It would please her. She's become very fond of you, ma'am. Says you're quite the most pleasant lady she's waited on."

I blushed. "Oh? She's a very sweet girl. I—I should like to see her as your bride."

"Then you'll stay."

I laughed at his easy assumption. "Do you expect to remain in this district?"

"For some time, I imagine. I've no influence to win a better post."

"What if King George repeals the tax?" Will asked lightly.

"That's not to be thought!" Mr. Smythe answered in mock horror. He added with a chuckle, "He's too fancy a court to cut the revenue. He'll be thinking up new taxes."

"Mrs. Cowper confided to me that she worries lest you whisk her daughter away before she can hold her grandchild," Will said lighting his pipe.

Mr. Smythe laughed. "You've yet to perform the ceremony and she's thinking of grandchildren! Well, everything's ready, including our cottage. I'd as soon we were wed now. These last days are too long!"

"Care for a game of chess to speed this evening?" Will suggested. "If you don't mind," he added to me.

"No, no. Would it disturb you if I watched? I often watched my father play."

"We'd be pleased to have your company," Mr. Smythe assured me gallantly.

Will went to the taproom for the chess set. He brought it on a wooden tray with three mugs of ale. As the men set up the game in an efficient manner, I asked, "Do you ever win, Mr. Smythe?"

"Sometimes."

"Sometimes!" Will scoffed. "Half the time. He's fully as good as any I've ever played."

"I do enjoy the game," Mr. Smythe said sitting down. He moved out his white queen's pawn at once.

Will countered immediately with his king's knight.

Shaking his head, Mr. Smythe commented, "Always testing."

They settled to an irregular exchange of moves preceded by much thought and a few sips of ale. Although neither made further comment, we shared a delightful ease of comradeship. I foresaw other similar evenings at the parsonage in coming months.

Once Will raised an eyebrow at Mr. Smythe's careless exposure of his bishop to Will's knight. I thought surely the bishop would be taken, but Will ignored the opportunity, making another move. Pieces were relentlessly removed from the board until each retained only two pawns to protect his king.

"Neither of us can claim this one," Mr. Smythe said leaning back.

"Agreed." Will extended his hand over the board for a handshake.

"I thought you might take my bishop when he happened to be left unprotected," Mr. Smythe said after draining his mug.

"And be checkmated in two moves?"

"You weren't to notice."

"Counting on my greed?"

"And blood-thirstiness. You may not realize it to look at him, Miss Castleton, but Dr. Knight is a dangerous man. It shows on the chessboard."

I laughed. "A country parson dangerous? He is the mildest of men!"

"So he would have us think. But his play reveals a killer's instinct."

"Shall I set them up again?" Will asked.

"No. I'll be walking Anne home shortly."

"Has her father finally accepted you as an inevitable member of the family?" Will asked, putting the men in their box.

"I'm not sure. He seems to hope for some delay. Do you know why?"

"As you know, smugglers abound in this area. He may feel having a representative of the law as a son-in-law is disloyal to his friends or even his family."

"I see. If he's involved, I hope he doesn't continue. It would be embarrassing if I had to arrest my wife's father. Worse!" He shuddered. "Anne would be furious! Her mother would say, 'What's the use having a Preventive Officer in the family if he arrests you?' "

"Would you arrest *him*?" I asked. "Your own father-in-law?"

"I'd have to. I'm sworn to oppose all who set themselves outside the king's law."

My heart sank with his firmness.

"Do you know what I'd like to do?" Mr. Smythe asked, rising. "Before we're wed, I'd like to capture the Red Demon. There's a large price on his head. It would be a nice start."

Will nodded. "That would be quite an accomplishment. You might gain the notice of London and a better post."

"I've felt several times I was close to him, then he'd slip away like a shadow."

"Colonel Snyde wants to catch him too," I observed. "What makes him worth all this attention?"

"He's responsible for most of the crimes around here. I'm certain the men I've caught were members of his gang, although they claimed not."

"Surely you questioned them about him."

"Oh, I did. At length. But torture is illegal. They would have me suspect everyone from the squire to the vicar. Personally, I thought John Richards was the most likely person. But we've had this landing since his death. And two sailors are reported escaped only last Saturday."

"Sailors? What have they to do with this demon?"

"I'm not certain. Quite a number used to be caught in this area because the tides carry them here. Aside from last summer, none of those escaping off shore of late have been captured. It's my theory that the Demon recruits them as members of his gang. Escaped felons are dangerous men."

"Felons!" I exclaimed.

"Naval deserters are felons. They're hung if caught. And any giving them aid. They, too, are guilty of a hanging crime."

"Oh. Poor souls!"

"Poor souls! They'd leave our country defenseless!" stated Mr. Smythe.

"But I thought most sailors were pressed into service against their will."

"True, ma'am. We need them to protect us from France's grand plans. But they're only taken for one year at a time."

"Only a year? Then we should hear about Arthur soon."

"Arthur?"

"Charles Heathton's older brother. He was taken over six months ago at Portsmouth. They've not heard a word."

"Ah, yes, I'd heard of an older brother," Mr. Smythe said slowly.

"Surely you can't suspect *him* of being the Red Demon!" Will objected, abandoning his position of listener.

"Why? Because of his wealth? Wealthy men have been known to dabble in crimes for their amusement."

"But the Demon has been active when Heathton was miles from here."

"True. But he comes and goes at irregular, frequent intervals with an odd assortment of servants. It's a useful way to hide an extra man. He could be part of the gang. Actually, the Red Demon shows more brilliance and imagination than I credit Heathton with."

"The Demon must be one more like yourself, eh, Smythe?"

Mr. Smythe was taken aback. Then he laughed. "Right. Someone more like me. Do you think I might be he?"

Will cocked his head. "Possibly. It would explain why you haven't been able to catch him. And it would be very convenient. By chasing yourself up and down our coast, you'd be certain of employment for some time to come."

"Yes, if I was him, it'd solve many strange things. You're not the first to suggest it. None other than Colonel Snyde has. And he was not laughing at the time."

"Neither am I."

"Ah, you never laugh. But your eyes give you away."

Will went to get his cloak. "I must be going too."

"Seriously, sir," Mr. Smythe said, his hand on the taproom door, "though the night is light, there's sure to be some evil afoot. If you have need of answering a parishioner's call, be sure to wear your sword."

"Mr. Smythe!" I exclaimed, "Do you actually expect a *parson* to wear a sword while carrying out his parish duties?"

"Yes, I do. Thieves are no respecters of persons. It would be a great loss to this area if any ill befell Dr. Knight. I've taught him how to use it and he does quite well. Well enough to discourage most men. Good-night, Miss Castleton, sir."

"Good-night," I murmured, hoping that tomorrow this playacting would be over.

Excited voices roused me not long after dawn. I stretched, wondering at the commotion. It could not yet be Charles. Noon would be the earliest I could expect him. I rolled to my side and revelled in the delights of Will's love. All was well with the world.

As the noise continued, I decided to rise and investigate. Curiosity sped my morning toilet. Later I would be more particular.

Mrs. Wilmot was sweeping and straightening the common room, talking to herself and shaking her head while she worked. She looked up as I descended and promptly set aside her broom. "Good morning, ma'am. Ye'll be wanting chocolate and rolls?"

"Yes." I looked for the people whose voices I'd heard. "What were all the comings and goings about?"

"Oh, ma'am, dis be a larmentaable bad day, it be," she moaned, ringing her hands. "We be allso mucked-up dis morning! And no-body be finding de parson no-one-wheres. First it be Mrs. Richards and now it be Mus Smythe! I swear. I doant know as how things can be worse no-ways de wurreld."

"Mr. Smythe? What's happened?"

"Oh, ma'am, it were in de night. Dat Red Demon, he *killed* him hisself!"

Chapter Twenty-two

I gaped after Mrs. Wilmot as she went out to the kitchen. There must be some mistake. Will would not kill anybody, least of all his friend.

She returned with a mug of steaming chocolate and a plate of rolls. "Mr. Smythe, he be an unaccountable fine man for all he be de Prevention Officer. And Anne! Poor, poor girl. She be abed wud grief. De men, dey in a gurt moil. Why, mayhap he'll murder de squire!"

"I can't believe he's dead. He was here only last night."

"Aye, ma'am. It be terrible, ernful, surelye."

"What happened?"

"He were found on de beach by Old Michael, de shepherd. He seen him from de cliffs. Run clean through wud a sword, he were. I reckon like as not he come on a landing o' moonshine."

"You say they can't find Dr. Knight?"

"No ma'am. He be de one to tell de men what dey ought to do. Dere be nobody nowheres wud a clearer head. And he'll grieve sore. Dey be at one, dey be. Close as two fingers, ma'am."

"Do you suppose he's gone to Docking? Or to call on Goody Hawkson, is it?"

"Dey be looking abroad. Dey find him, be he dere or other-wheres."

"How can you be so sure this Red Demon is the murderer?"

"Dere be nobody that bold, ma'am. And, what do ye know, after killing poor Mus Smythe, he laid him ready to be putt-in! Imagine! Crossing his hands on his breast like dat! Him's one as holds naun holy."

She went about her duties and I lingered over my chocolate, try-ing to take in the news. Whatever the truth, Will needed me. I asked that Black be saddled and went up to dress for riding.

I left Black tied to a tree and approached the cliff above Will's cave. Although the turf was smooth, I detected cuts where the wheatear traps had been returned to their former place and pressed down. Little traps of fear.

For a moment I contemplated the beach below. Possibly Old Michael saw Mr. Smythe there when he came to check on his traps.

Fighting nauseous panic, I held my petticoats close and inched down the scanty trail. Will must be here. Jagged chunks of the chalk cliff pulled at my clothes and once caught my foot, nearly upsetting me. My heart was pounding and my hands shaking when at last my fingertips touched the bush concealing the entrance.

If Will was not here, I should have to go back, alone. I doubted I could. "Please, let him be here," I whispered, pushing aside the branches and the dark hanging cloth.

For a few seconds I stood still inside, rubbing my hands and arms nervously, letting my eyes adjust to the dark. Cool air chilled the sweat on my body and I shivered. Nothing moved! Where could he be? Going up that trail alone was not to be considered. I might die here!

"Why did you seek me out?" Will's voice came from the blackness.

Relief washed over me. Stepping towards his voice, I reached out eagerly.

"Don't touch me! I bear the mark of Cain!"

Immediately I halted, straining to see him. "Will, I had to find you. Mrs. Wilmot said Mr. Smythe—"

"I know!" he interrupted curtly.

"They say that it was the Red Demon. Is that. . . ? Can you tell me what happened?"

"As she told you, the Demon killed him."

"Oh, my dearest!" I went in the direction of his voice.

"Go! Leave this cave. Leave this place. Go back to Oxford! This is a place of blood. You should not have come."

"No! You need me. Please, tell me how it happened."

He shouted in anguish, "I killed a man!" adding in a broken whisper, "and he was a *brother* to me!"

"I cannot believe you *intended* this!"

"Does it matter? He is dead. *Dead!* At *my* hand!"

"He—he found you last night?"

"On the beach below. We'd seen the signal. The poor sailor was in the water, starting to swim toward the boat that'd take him to freedom. Edward rode down upon us. I ran Prince in front of him, and threw myself on him, forcing him out of the saddle. He drew his sword and I drew mine. Would I had none!"

"And you fought."

"I meant to disarm him. But the moon was low and the light deceptive. He became angry that I would not stand but yielded up the beach. Once he tripped."

"You did not hurt him then?"

"He was my friend! Not knowing me, he cursed. Then he said. . . . He said, 'You bastard! I'll run you through!' Suddenly he was all those who called me 'bastard.' I am not! *I* am the rightful earl! Without thinking, I lunged. He shrieked!" His voice dropped to a moan. "I hear him yet!"

Reaching out, I touched him and pulled him into my arms. "Oh, my dear!"

"I held him as his life ebbed away."

His body shook with sobs as he leaned against me. "I am the most evil of men!"

"You have St. Paul for company. Didn't he call himself 'chiefest of sinners'?" His agony recalled mine after hearing Mr. Wesley, and I suffered with him.

"Leave me!" He pulled away roughly. "Leave me here to die. I am cursed! As it is written, 'Cursed is he that smiteth his neighbor secretly.' I will bear the wrath of God in the day of vengeance!"

"And in that same Commination Service, what else do you say?"

He was silent.

"Do you not urge those so cursed to submit themselves to a merciful God? 'If with a perfect and true heart we return unto him,' don't you promise Christ will deliver us from the law's curse, that He is ready to receive us and most willing to pardon us?"

Still he was silent.

"Your people need you, Will. They are looking for you."

"Need *me*? What need have they of a murderer? Better no vicar than one as vile as I." He shoved me towards the opening. "Go!" he shouted, "lest you be contaminated!" His voice vibrated from the walls.

It took all my courage not to run. When I thought I could speak steadily, I said, "I can't. I can't go back up that narrow path alone. You'll have to take me back."

He said nothing.

"That path was a terror to me in coming here. I cannot go back without you. I would fall to the rocks below. I know I would."

For several minutes he made no answer. Then he took my hand. "Come." His voice was almost normal. "I'll take you up. Then I'll see Colonel Snyde, and confess the whole."

"But you must not!" I exclaimed. "He would hang you, and quickly!"

"And so I deserve. A murderer deserves to be hung. I must confess my crime."

"But—but you *have* confessed—to me. God will forgive. Confessing to Colonel Snyde would serve *no* purpose!"

Will made no response.

"If you do that—if you do that, I'll tell him I am your wife and your accomplice."

"No, Meg! You must not do that. You couldn't live in a prison!"

I hesitated a moment, recalling the Borgado and horrible tales I'd heard about its prisoners. "It would not be long. Surely they would hang me with you, and soon, so you wouldn't be able to escape."

"No, Meg. You don't understand." He raised the cloth over the entrance.

"If you tell Colonel Snyde you are the Red Demon, I will tell him I am your wife."

He examined my face, frowning. "Would you do that? Would you really?"

"Yes," I answered firmly.

He led me up the cliff to Black. After assisting me to mount, he took us to a hidden place in the trees where Prince waited.

"Anne Cowper needs you," I said.

He looked at me dully and nodded.

"They're all at a loss without you."

He swung into his saddle. "Yes, I know. There's much to do when someone dies."

At the Curling Horn, my vague explanation of meeting the vicar while out riding was accepted without question. Then I was forced aside while the cares of the village crowded upon Will. As his wife, I should have helped comfort Anne and her family and taken care of the altar candles and other details. But as a visitor, a foreigner in their eyes, I was relegated to the role of observer.

Colonel Snyde and his men bustled in and out, roughly interrogating anyone unfortunate enough to be in their sight. Late in the afternoon I witnessed his meeting with Will in the common room.

The colonel blustered his frustration at not finding the culprit. Among other things he referred to the strange way the body was left.

"I did that, sir," Will explained.

"You! Why?"

"I found him. It was the appropriate thing to do."

"And you did not report finding him?"

"I should have. . ."

"Yes, you should. It was your duty. Your duty as a law-abiding citizen. It was the only thing to do."

"I withdrew for a time."

"Withdrew! Whatever for?"

"Be ye blind, sir?" interjected Mr. Wilmot. "Him be hisn *friend*. Close they be, closer dan most brothers."

Will turned slowly and departed.

A woman said to Mrs. Wilmot, "It wrings me out seeing de parson dat ernful."

I was glad Will's impassive calm was not deceiving his people as to his deep mourning. He needed their sympathetic understanding.

The burial service the following morning was surprisingly well attended. Mr. Smythe had pursued a most unpopular profession in a manner that won grudging admiration by some and a genuine liking by most.

The thud of earth clods on the wood coffin were like tragic exclamation points while Will said, "Forasmuch as it hath pleased Almighty God of His great mercy to take unto himself the soul of our dear brother here departed. . ." His voice thickened. After a brief pause, he continued in his usual manner.

I begged God to give him strength to finish this most painful duty.

When he prayed, "We give Thee hearty thanks, for that it hath pleased Thee to deliver this brother out of the miseries of this sinful world," his voice broke. After a longer pause, he completed the remaining prayers and benediction in husky tones.

The mourners left the churchyard slowly. Weeping, Anne and Mrs. Cowper trailed the others. Will stood alone beside the new grave.

I waited a few steps behind him.

He made no move, staring at the newly turned earth.

Making certain no one was in earshot, I began, "Will—"

"Go away!" he said in a low, tense voice, not looking at me. "Tyne is no place for you. Go away and never come back."

"Will, I love you. I intend to stay."

"You cannot mean that. You cannot love me, a murderer."

"I do love you."

"Go away. Leave me alone!"

"Are you going to Docking today?"

He raised his eyes to the thin sheet of fog diffusing the sunlight. "This is Thursday. Yes. I must not delay longer." His sigh came from the depths of his spirit. "I will return tomorrow. See that you take today's stage. There is no happiness for you here." He pivoted and hurried to the vicarage.

I went down to the crossroads, pondering what I might do to help him. During my sadness, when I sent people away, I really wanted them around me. I actually needed them to bring my thoughts away from myself.

"Beg pardon, ma'am." A timid woman in drab peasant dress, wearing a black shawl thrown over her head, spoke at my side.

Startled, I answered, "Yes?"

"Ye be de lady at de inn?"

"Yes." I recognized her as the widow Bradford.

"Doant ye heed de vicar. He be a good, kind man, surelye. He be a gurt deal hurting for hisn dear friend. He be hisself nexdy, I reckon."

"Thank you, Mrs. Bradford. I'll remember."

Her face brightened at my mention of her name. She dropped a hasty curtsey and scurried down the Docking road.

Needing to be alone to think, I slowly trudged to the ruined abbey. There, I faced northward to survey the serene grandeur of the smooth, curving downs. The sky above stretched in infinity. A western toppling cloud of glistening purity held no promise of the rain Squire Addleby desired. Perhaps I would find peace and ease of soul in this sight of creation unmarred by humans.

Lines from the Psalms surged into my mind accompanied by a jumble of familiar melodies. "I will lift up mine eyes unto the hills, from whence cometh my help. My help cometh from the Lord, which made heaven and earth."

"The heavens declare the glory of God and the firmament sheweth his handywork."

"The earth is the Lord's and the fulness thereof; the world and they that dwell therein."

And again, "O Lord our Lord, how excellent is thy name in all the earth! who hast set thy glory above the heavens. . . . When I consider the heavens, the work of thy fingers, the moon and the stars, which thou hast ordained; what is man, that thou art mindful of him? and the son of man, that thou visitest him?" What, indeed, is puny man, dwarfed by all this?

The psalmist's words continued, "For thou hast made him a little lower than the angels, and hast crowned him with glory and honor. Thou madest him to have dominion over the works of thy hands; thou hast put all things under his feet." No menial position.

And even beyond that, Paul wrote, "God commendeth his love toward us, in that, while we were yet sinners, Christ died for us." Love, great, infinite, giving love.

"The Spirit itself beareth witness with our spirit, that we are the children of God . . . and we know that all things work together for good to them that love God, to them who are the called according to his purpose. . . . What shall we then say to these things? If God be for us, who can be against us? For I am persuaded, that neither death, nor life, nor angels, nor principalities, nor powers, nor things present, nor things to come, nor height, nor depth, nor any other creature, shall be able to separate us from the love of God, which is in Christ Jesus our Lord."

Will loved God deeply. He was called. And so was I. We were God's children—such a special relationship. And nothing in all the universe could separate us from His love. Not even ourselves. My selfish defiance had not thwarted the power of His love to change my life. Neither would Mr. Smythe's death defeat God's love for Will. I must trust that infinite love to use this tragic situation for good.

No longer a puny, shrinking creature, lost in a vast creation, I turned to look on Tyne with a new compassion. They, too, were the objects of God's infinite love. Will tried to demonstrate this in his ministry. And so must I.

The stagecoach jolted past the Curling Horn without a pause, trailing clouds of yellow dust. Will wanted me to be on that. Or so he said. I considered moving into the vicarage. He would not put me out, but the village would be shocked. I must avoid the least appearance of wrong.

Until the shadows of the hills reached up their eastern neighbors' sides, I remained praying for wisdom, guidance, and faithfulness. When I descended to the gloomy vale of Tyne to await Will's return, I possessed no certainty of action. Rather, I trusted God for leading at the proper time.

Shortly after dinner the day following Mr. Smythe's burial, I heard a commotion beneath my window. Leaning out, I could see a coach, but was unable to identify it. Someone ran up the stairs to my door and tapped lightly.

"Come in."

Mrs. Wilmot entered, her face flushed, her bosom heaving. "Ma'am, Mr. Heathton, he be demanding to see you hisself. I doant make no sense of him. He asked ifn ye be here and when I says ye be, he shouted and, and. . . Ma'am, I *never* seen him in such a pucker!"

I went with her promptly.

Mr. Wilmot was serving Charles with a tall tankard and a plate of food. Two or three men stood in the door to the taproom watching. A boy stared from beside the fireplace, his jaw hanging slack. All attention was focused on the elegantly dressed man in the center of the room, stiff with indignation.

He observed my descent through his quizzing glass with an air of disapproval. When I reached the bottom step, he shouted, "Meg, why the devil are you not with your husband?"

I froze with shock and embarrassment. All present seemed to hold their breath.

"Well? Well? Why are you not with him?"

I hurried to him and took his arm. "Please, can't we discuss this quietly?" I whispered. "You must be *foxed* to behave so!" I tried to draw him to a corner away from his avid audience, increased by others crowding in from the road.

Unmoved, Charles looked down as at a stupid child. "Really Meg, someone has to take a hand, the way things aren't going!"

"Please, lower your voice!"

"A woman's place is beside her husband, not in a public inn! Ain't that so, Nancy?" he demanded loudly.

The on-lookers nodded vigorously. Mrs. Wilmot licked her lips, glanced anxiously at her husband and murmured, "Yes, sir. I reckon so, sir."

"Don't mind him, Mrs. Wilmot. He must have been drinking." I tugged at Charles' arm, but he stood firmly in his place.

"Nonsense! Haven't had a drop. You act as if I tippled constantly!"

"And you act as if I was a—a common trollop!"

"Have done with your secrets, girl!" he exclaimed, striking a theatrical pose. "You should be ashamed. . . "

"I am!"

" . . . making as if you're a spinster when all the time you're married to a prince among men!"

"Charles, I must talk with you. You don't understand."

"Do you hate him? Has he been so cruel you cannot abide his house?"

I shook my head, tears trickling down my face.

In a kindly tone he asked, "You love him, don't you, Meg?"

Mr. Wilmot intervened. "Mus Heathton, sir, mayhap ye and Miss Castleton would—"

"She ain't *Miss Castleton*! Hasn't been for years. Can't you understand, man? I'm trying to get her reconciled to her *husband*! Meg, tell him you love him. He'll leap at the chance to have you back. I know it."

I covered my face with my hands, my calm splintering into total confusion.

"I'll get the squire to speak for you, that's what I'll do," Charles said firmly. "You, boy, run to the manor and tell the squire Mr. Heathton desires his attendance here on a matter of great moment."

"Yes, sir!" responded the boy by the fireplace eagerly.

I looked up to see a coin flip through the air to him.

"And there'll be another if you're back in a very short time."

"Yes sir!" He darted out through the crowd at the door, his faded blue shirttail flapping.

Charles put his arm around me. "You'll see, little dove, I'll set all this straight tonight. Bring us your best wine, Nancy. I think she needs encouragement."

At a table, a little apart from the others, I regained my composure while sipping the wine. Charles sat watching me with satisfaction.

"Charles," I whispered, "you don't understand. Have you talked with him? Do you know what's happened here?"

"No. I determined myself to take this course on my way. You see, little dove, I thought my being delayed in Portsmouth would give ample time for you to effect a reconciliation. However, if you and him can't come together on your own, I must bring you together. It ain't right as things are."

"Mr. Smythe was killed day before yesterday. He was buried yesterday."

"Smythe! Good Lord!" He dropped his voice and leaned forward. "How'd it happen?"

"They say—they say the Red Demon did it."

"The Red Demon? Oh, they charge him with *everything*." He regarded me thoughtfully. "Where's Will?"

"In Docking. He went yesterday after the funeral instead of Wednesday. He's taking it very hard."

"He would. Tell me about it."

I repeated the rumors, not certain he was aware of Will's illegal role. As I spoke, Charles' attitude became wary. He asked questions as if weighing each word carefully.

"It's evident some criminal did this," he concluded. "I think Smythe surprised a group of smugglers. You know the locals blame everything to their Red Demon while every man here is a runner or otherwise engaged in the Trade."

"In this instance, they are right. There wasn't a landing."

He stared at me intently, then asked, "You know this for a certainty?"

"I do."

"You've spoken to him?"

"Yes. We were—" Tears spilled again from my eyes.

Charles drummed on the table. He poured us each a glass of wine, and drank half of his quickly. "What does he say about your staying?"

"He—he wants me to go and never come back."

"Hmm." Charles emptied his glass. "He's right, you know. Always is. Under the circumstances this is not the place for you. If they ever find out. . ." He refilled his glass.

"Don't you see, he needs me more than ever." Briefly I sketched in Will's account of the fatal fight.

"A real tragedy. However, I agree. You'd best leave with me. This could get very nasty."

"Charles, I was wrong not to come here in the first place. I'll *not* desert him now. I belong with him and nowhere else. *Nowhere!*"

"Meg, you are so *stubborn!*"

"He must not be left to bear this burden alone."

"As bad as that?"

I nodded. "What were you intending to do today?"

"I thought I'd get the squire to take your side and between us bring it up to Will publicly. You see, I thought he would want it, and . . . I've blundered into something beyond me."

"No, no. This may yet be the best way."

"You're sure, Meg? There's a murder involved."

How could I explain? "I *love* him."

"God, how I envy you both!"

By the time Squire Addleby and Elizabeth arrived in their carriage, most of the village was crowded into the common room. The babble of voices died abruptly when the squire limped through the door.

"Heathton, I understand you needed me here to settle an urgent matter."

Charles glanced at me uncertainly.

"If you don't, I will," I muttered under my breath.

"That's right, sir. It's concerning this woman's husband. Did you know she is married?"

"Yes, of course I did!"

Surprise sped in a ripple over the room.

The Addlebys sat at our table and ordered food and drink. Our audience inched closer.

"Papa is eager to help you, Meg," Elizabeth assured me with a smile and a pat on my arm. "And he will. I understand it all, now."

"Well, sir," Charles cleared his throat. "She's afraid he wants no part of her since she failed to accompany him here from Oxford over a year ago."

The squire's eyes flicked to me quickly and away as he nodded.

All but the dullest surely guessed my husband's identity. The excited whispers around us were hissed silent.

"It's my contention," Charles continued, "that their misunderstanding must end. Now, sir, will you speak to him on her behalf?"

Turning to me, the squire asked seriously, "Miss . . . uh, madam, is this your true desire, to be reunited with your husband?"

"Yes, sir, if he'll have me."

"He will, of course, of course. Under the circumstances, this couldn't be better!" He tipped me a knowing wink. "Seems I recall the vicar himself preaching on forgiveness only last Sunday. We'll ask his judgment on this."

The villagers nodded agreement with his decision and settled to drinking, eating and talking, awaiting Will's arrival from Docking.

Mist droplets sparkled on Will's cloak when he entered. Instead of calling their usual welcome, the people fell silent. He removed his cloak, shook it and hung it by the door, speaking easily with those near him.

Mrs. Wilmot laid a cover for him at a nearby table. As he made his way to it, he nodded a greeting to the squire and Charles, saw me and broke his stride. Recovering himself quickly, he sat down to his supper.

Thoughtful of a man's hunger after a long ride, the squire waited until Will had eaten his fill. When he finished, instead of moving to the fire, Will pulled out his pipe and, leaning on the table, tamped tobacco into the bowl.

Squire Addleby said loudly, "Excuse me for not joining you, Vicar, but my foot's hurting. I have a question about your sermon last Sunday."

The room became quiet.

Will concentrated on lighting his pipe before responding. "I'll be happy to answer if I can."

"Vicar, am I correct in thinking the general theme was forgiveness?"

"Yes. I'm pleased you remember, sir." He sent aloft a floating gray puff and settled back comfortably in his chair. "I used God's forgiveness of our many sins as the basis for us to forgive each other of infinitely lesser offenses."

"Do you mean that *any* wrong one may have done to another is far less than the wrong we have done to God Almighty?"

"Yes, I should think so," he replied in a detached manner. "The greater the one offended, the greater the offense. Our stature in no way compares to God's."

"And you would include lying, cheating, adultery, even murder? All these must be forgiven?"

Will tensed, hesitated, then nodded.

"Even the affront given a man by his wife leaving him?"

Will studied the squire, his right eyebrow raised. "We have an example of such in the Old Testament. Gomer, the prophet Hosea's wife, left him to become a harlot. At God's command, Hosea sought her out, bought her, and returned her to his house, reestablishing her as his wife. Certainly an extreme situation." He leaned forward, cradling his pipe in his right hand. "Are you asking my opinion on an actual matter or one of theory?"

"Actual, Vicar, actual."

"Please give me the particulars. I gather everyone present knows."

"It has come to our ears only this last hour. A woman refused to accompany her husband when his vocation brought him to Tyne. She has since repented and come seeking reconciliation. However, she fears he will not have her. From what you have told us, it is the man's Christian duty to forgive her, if she asks, and restore her to his household. Is that correct?"

Will's gaze remained fastened on the squire, considering his reply. He nodded. "And who are these unhappy people?"

With a dramatic stab of his forefinger, the squire announced, "You, sir, are the man!"

A ripple of subdued excitement ran among the people.

Will's lips tightened. His eyes closed momentarily before he looked at me.

I suppose the longing of my heart was nakedly exposed to public view. For once I did not mind.

Slowly he rose and came to me.

I stood to meet him, my sweaty hands clasped before me.

"Is this your true desire?" he asked, his somber gaze plumbing my soul. Only a light tremor in his voice betrayed his feelings.

Nodding, I whispered, "Yes."

"You are *sure*?"

"Yes, if you will forgive me."

"Of course I. . ." His voice faltered and he extended his hand. I threw my arms around him, and felt his encircle me.

Cheers rose about us and tankards thumped the tables.

"Serve up a round to toast the happy couple!" ordered Squire Addleby.

Will and I stood in the vicarage door waving farewell to our riotous neighbors who had carted my boxes here from the inn.

Frowning, my husband shut the door against the chill night, then methodically secured the oak shutters over the windows. "Meg, I fear you'll regret this. I should not have permitted you to come."

"My place is here," I said, hugging him. "Anyway, how could you deny me before the whole village?"

"By refusing to forgive you. All through my meal, I tried to bring myself to send you away, if necessary to humiliate you. But I could not. Even for your own good, I could not."

"Remember, my love, we are to redeem the time. You said we would fill this home with laughter, the singing of psalms . . . and children."

He shook his head and pulled my arms from about him. "That was before. Everything's changed."

I turned my attention to the whitewashed room with its sturdy oak beams and stone fireplace. Only a large walnut chest was new to me. All else came from St. Thomas', dearly familiar things in a strange arrangement. Silently I vowed we would again share a life of deep joy. "Please show me my new domain."

"Of course." He took a candle and opened a door on the right of the fireplace. "My study."

The room was panelled with new oak boards. His library crammed the bookcase and several crude shelves. On his desk lay a leather-bound ledger. Father's old chair stood beside a low table holding a lamp and a book opened face down.

"This is the room you added?"

"Yes. Being on the southwest side, a great deal of light comes in through the windows much of the day."

"What did the other parsons use?"

"I suppose the north room, which I use for a bedroom. They must have slept upstairs." He pointed to a door in the living-room ceiling beside a ladder attached to the wall. "There's nothing up there now."

We entered the bedroom. Our bed, covered with my blue quilt, the wardrobes and my flowered pitcher and basin greeted me. Here was where I belonged.

"This room never gets any sunshine, a good place for sleeping."

"It—it looks like home," I said softly, my voice sticking in my throat. "Oh, Will, I've longed to be here! I can't *tell* you how much!" In a surge of emotion, I threw my arms around his neck and pulled his head down for a kiss.

Carefully he placed the candle beside the basin and embraced me. I felt his passion sweep away his self-control and engulf me. He spoke huskily in my ear, "And I've dreamed of you being here as a dream beyond hope."

Chapter Twenty-three

Saturday I took up my responsibilities as the vicar's wife. For a time the night before, Will's despondency had vanished, giving me hope for the future. However, it returned to rob our morning devotions of the joy I remembered. While vigorously cleaning the parsonage and the church, I cast about for ways to minister to him.

Charles arrived quite early, anxious to be on his way to Rockivale. I entrusted him with a note addressed to Father, describing my reconciliation to Will. Charles could tell him about us in more detail, but he should read some explanation in my own hand. After much chewing on my quill, I had also begged his pardon for my behavior at our last encounter. Difficult as it was to write, I felt great relief when I gave it to Charles.

He could scarce contain his delight over Will and me. I supposed he was thinking, "And they lived happily ever after."

"Old Knight's taking it pretty hard," Charles observed, watching him walk down the road.

"About the way you'd feel if you unintentionally killed him."

Charles stared at me, shocked. "Of course he would. That's—that's *terrible!*" We watched Will until he turned up a lane and out of sight. "I wish I could do something to help," Charles said. "He needs a change."

"A move might bring him trouble," I answered. "Whoever drove him from St. Thomas' has either forgotten him in this remote place, or thinks it not worth the effort to persecute him further."

Charles brightened. "I know! I'll speak to Father about the preferment at Rockivale. It's far more comfortable than this place and pressure don't matter to us. That'll give him a fresh start."

Knowing what Will once thought about Charles and me, I did not think this a happy solution. "He would never agree to putting another man out of his place."

"Nonsense! Rockivale's sick of old Pettigrew and would gladly arrange another place for him. I know he'll like Knight."

"No, please. Will's worst problem is the wound he carries in his heart. No change in place will help until that heals. It's good of you to think of it, Charles. Maybe later."

"Not good of me, little dove. There's nothing I'd like better than having the old fellow close at hand."

I proudly entered the front pew Sunday morning. Excited, conscious of the villagers' stares, I found it difficult to attend to the service. Afterwards, in the churchyard, many greeted me cordially. Most indicated indirectly they expected my presence in the parsonage would be a comfort to Will for the death of his friend.

We drove in Will's cart to Docking for services. The air was heavy with moisture. Tinkling sheep bells sounded above, as if borne by the circling gulls. Will explained the local people regarded this as a sure sign the dry spell would soon be broken.

The Docking road wound over the downs toward the channel in the general direction of Brighthelmstone. The village perched on the shores of a cove lined with fishing boats. A man delivering fish to the squire's manor the day before was told of my existence. By the time I entered the tiny church, everyone knew about me and came to stare. After they inspected me from a distance, they shyly greeted me and wished us happy. I was pleased to find that here, too, they held their vicar in great affection.

On our way to the squire's for dinner, the skies became covered with a thick layer of dark gray clouds and the wind began rising. I pulled my cardinal tighter about me and asked if we might see Colonel Snyde there.

"Very likely."

"I wonder he has time for sociabilities when he's so energetic in combing the countryside for the Red Demon. How did you come to use that name?"

"It was not of my choosing. The second man I found was wounded in making his escape. I had to build a small fire to see to remove the bullet from his shoulder. On hearing someone come, I threw a handkerchief over my face. The light from the fire must have made it look red. Dick Hanford staggered up, half-drunk as usual. After one look, he took himself off at a run. By morning all the village knew he'd seen a red devil.

"As the vicar, I was called to ease his mind. He stood by his story even when he sobered. So I made a red cloth mask and became hunched and limping. From time to time I was seen, and they called me the 'Red Demon.' Stories built up quickly about this person, crediting him with every crime in the district."

"Without foundation."

"It was an easy way to account for anything unpleasant. Actually all I did was aid the escaped sailors I found. And I used the wild stories to discourage people from roaming about at night. This is a violent district. It's worth your life if you see the smugglers at work."

"Do you think the colonel suspects?"

"No. His arrogance stands in his way. Edward constituted my only real threat, and he. . ." Will paused before continuing bitterly, "and he was blinded by friendship. I pray the colonel's zeal will not bring some innocent person afoul of him."

I had not considered that possibility. Will would never permit anyone to suffer for him.

As we entered the manor, I was more tense than ever. Will, on the contrary, seemed to relax, rising to the challenge before us. At dinner the squire gallantly seated me on his right and Will on his left. Elizabeth graced the other end of the table, dividing her charming conversation between Colonel Snyde on her right and his handsome lieutenant placed between her and myself.

The squire directed his remarks, laden with ponderous wit, to me, and chided me for leading him astray as Abraham's Sarah misled the Pharaoh.

Suddenly the colonel's deep voice caught my attention with, "I'll catch that Demon!" He continued, "If I have to question every man within twenty miles distance, we'll uncover his identity and soon have him swinging from the gallows."

Icy fears froze my fingers into an awkward grip on my fork.

"Surely such severe measures are not needed," Will objected mildly.

I glanced quickly and anxiously towards him as I forced myself to take a bite of I knew not what.

Will's normal, sober expression reassured me, but only briefly.

"That Red Demon is dangerous to the Crown, upsetting the peace of His Majesty's subjects and robbing the royal treasury with every illegal landing he and his men make. We will not rest until we deal finally with him. We will comb the countryside—"

"But you will not find him," Will interjected calmly.

Snyde glared indignantly at him. "Why do you say so, Dr. Knight?"

"Because you are looking in the wrong places, Colonel."

"And where would *you* recommend my looking?" Snyde demanded haughtily.

"Not nearly so far way."

"Are you suggesting one of my own men, Parson?"

"Not at all, Colonel. Look here, in this very room."

Fortunately all attention was focused on Will as I clutched the edge of the table, horrified at what he was saying. Not once did he look at me.

"In this room? Have you taken leave of your senses?"

"No, sir. I am the man you seek."

Those about the table sat in arrested motion. Lieutenant Stevenson's fork was poised in mid air before his open mouth. The squire's wineglass hovered above the table a long moment before he set it down firmly. I wanted to cry out in opposition to Will's confession, but could not force any sound from my parched throat.

Elizabeth's light laugh shattered the spell imposed by shock. "For shame, Dr. Knight! You ought not to tease us so."

Snyde gave a nasty bark of laughter. "*You*, the bloodiest, most illusive criminal along the southern coast? *You*, the leader of countless desperate men engaged in the Trade? Have a care, Parson! Had I believed you, you would have been in great trouble. Such joking is not wise."

"I was not laughing," Will pointed out quietly.

"You never do," Squire Addleby commented drily.

I glanced sidewise at the squire and was further dismayed to meet his narrowed gaze studying my reaction. He knows Will is telling the truth, I thought. A painful constriction in my throat forestalled speech.

"You must think me a fool," Snyde continued with a sneer, still not having seen my telltale reaction. "Anyone who has the slightest acquaintance with you would never believe you capable of such— uh, such reprehensible behavior. No, sir, I'll not be taken in by your wild suggestion."

"No, indeed," agreed the squire, his firm tone mercifully directing any further attention away from me. "It is not to be thought! We must not lose your good offices in Tyne, Knight. No, no. Enough of this idle talk. You are both wrong. The Red Demon has doubtless fled these parts as he did last winter, lest he be caught in our famous mud. I think we might be more successful in discovering him if we looked farther afield, perhaps so far as Chichester."

Lieutenant Stevenson agreed with the squire. Was it only my imagination that the lieutenant lacked conviction in his tone? Might he, too, recognize the truth of Will's claim?

Speculation over the Demon's whereabouts continued and Will's confession seemed forgotten. As the meal progressed, I realized the colonel was unable to give serious consideration to the idea that this unobtrusive, colorless parson could be the lurid outlaw he sought. Will was safe from him unless another was apprehended.

When Elizabeth and I withdrew, leaving the men to their port, she commented lightly, "I never realized your husband had such a romantic imagination."

"How do you mean?" I asked.

"Why, to fancy himself the Red Demon!" She broke into a peal of laughter.

I smiled and shrugged my shoulders.

"He is much too—too calm. Could you imagine *him* engaged in a desperate fight with swords, or master-minding daring escapades as the Demon does?"

Vivid memories of Will's dueling skill flashed across my mind.

"I wonder what caused Dr. Knight to make such a strange suggestion. I suppose he felt the colonel was putting some of our people under undue suspicion. He is ever placing others' welfare above his own, don't you think so?"

I agreed heartily. Our conversation moved into the less threatening areas of my new life as the parson's wife. Here Elizabeth's curiosity took on an intimate, sisterly air.

When the men joined us, Colonel Snyde maintained a frosty correctness with me. Since I was a parson's wife, I had fallen greatly in his esteem and no longer evoked the least interest, much to my relief. Unusually early he decided to depart, a disappointment to both Elizabeth and the lieutenant.

The squire talked at length about the deplorable state of the roads, regretting he had not required the necessary upkeep during the spring. With the rains all but falling, the time had passed for repair. He would not make that mistake next year. If this came to the Duke of Newcastle's notice, the Lord Lieutenant of Sussex, there might be serious trouble over his failing.

Elizabeth chatted excitedly about a trip to Lewes for some new dresses. It was vital they be gone before the roads became impassable. She hoped that once there, she might prevail upon her father to go on to Tunbridge Wells for a short stay. "Even the off season there offers better society and more excitement than Tyne, don't you think, Meg? And it is so miserable here when the roads are aflood."

I murmured assent, thinking any greater excitement than I'd found in Tyne would undo me completely.

Anxiously I shoved Will's sudden confession to the back of my mind, afraid to ask him about it lest he be tempted to repeat it and the next time be believed. I was fairly sure the squire and Lieutenant Stevenson suspected the truth. However, neither gave hint of it in their behavior while in my presence. Before the month was out, the army would move to Portsmouth for the winter, and Colonel Snyde would cease to be a danger.

In the succeeding weeks I came to understand Elizabeth's meaning. The rains varied from steady to storming bluster. Soon the roads were awash, barely passable on horseback or foot. Being confined much of the time to the house, inaction weighed upon Will. Ministering to the needs of others would have provided an escape from his depression.

With the Addlebys on the continent, my contacts were limited to the few village women close at hand. Mrs. Wilmot brought a tasty game pie and stayed for a short visit.

"Dey says us Sussex 'oomen have unaccountable long legs on account of always pulling dem out of de mud. I reckon mine's growed some of late. I dunno as how I'd rather be in dan out dese days."

My sentiments exactly.

When a respite in the weather made it possible, Will rode out to call on the widow Bradford. On his return, I inquired about her circumstances. She and her three children were dependent on parish charity and doing poorly.

Impulsively, I said, "This is a good night for fasting. Let us take her our dinner."

My declaration startled Will. He recovered quickly. I loaded the food into a basket and he permitted me to ride pillion on Prince.

After we returned from delivering the food to the surprised and embarrassingly grateful woman, he said, "I thought you did not care to go hungry on days that were not holy days."

"I don't like going hungry any time," I said putting on the kettle for tea. "But our food will help her. Isn't this the fasting that pleases the Lord?"

"You've changed, Meg. Why?"

"A few weeks before coming here, my heart was very heavy. I wanted desperately to come to you, but, after our—our baby's death, I thought. . . You see, Father had turned his back on me. The manner in which our baby died I took to mean God had turned His back on me too. I expected the same of you. I was desolate.

"Bessie has become a Methodist." Seeing him shake his head in disapproval, I hurried on. "She took me to hear Mr. Wesley preach near St. Clement's. Will, you should have heard him. He speaks with a power not his own!"

"I heard him at St. Mary's."

"I have never been so shaken in my life! Later Mr. Wesley himself called upon me. Under his guidance, I gave my load of guilt and misery to Christ. He forgave *all* I had done. And, miracle of miracles, *He loved me*! I was free!

"For the first time in my life I read the Bible and prayed with real understanding. Morning prayers were no longer burdens. And I now know one may fast joyfully that others might eat."

Will grunted, picked up his cup of tea and withdrew to his study.

On a dull, wintry day, Charles suddenly arrived, bringing me a chestnut mare with a sidesaddle and a bridle of fine workmanship. "We called her 'Checkmate,'" he explained. "She's a full sister to Sultan and Khan."

"Oh, Charles, she's beautiful!" I stroked her face and fed her a bit of sugar.

"She's ideally suited for breeding with Prince Whist."

"Pretty Checkmate, we shall get on famously."

"Yes, well, you must understand she's very spirited. Now, Meg, don't you go riding all over the country without Will. She may take it into her head to bolt."

I laughed at his earnestness. "Please don't read me a lecture, sir. I'm not so foolish as that."

He looked doubtful. "I've known you to do such things. When you take a notion, you can be mighty reckless and *stubborn*!"

With a chuckle I said, "Then Sussex is the place for me. I truly belong. You see, they say our crest is a hog and our motto is 'We wunt be druv.'"

"Oh, Meg!" he shook his head. "Please have a care with her. I was of two minds to bring her."

"I shall be careful," I promised solemnly.

"You look to be happy, little dove."

"I am. I truly am."

"Do you find it hard living here? It appears to be all work and little fun. None of the balls and society you enjoyed."

"I do work hard. But, Charles, all those things I fretted for in Oxford, oh, they'd be nice to have, but I don't really *need* them to be happy. If only Will could be as he was at St. Thomas'! Then all would be perfect."

"He's not back to his old sober self?"

"No. I'm very concerned about him. He's the way I was last spring."

"Where is he?"

"Showing the new Prevention Officer about the parish."

"Oh. Is he a very, well, a very astute man?"

"Not like Mr. Smythe. I doubt he'll give Will any trouble."

As the three of us ate supper, Charles tried various ways to draw Will out of his detached heaviness. None was effective. "And you've no one for me to take out?" Charles asked casually when the men took out their pipes.

"What do you mean?" I asked.

Will frowned and said nothing.

Charles exclaimed, "You mean you haven't told her?"

"I thought the less she knew the safer she would be."

"Well, I guess I set the cat loose. Sorry." Charles turned to me. "From time to time I've taken some of his sailors with me, wearing my livery."

"But, Charles, what if you were caught?"

"I wasn't. It's the closest I can get to being a dashing smuggler." He smiled wrily. "Kept hoping some time you'd turn old Arthur over to me. Well, maybe he escaped and someone else gave him a hand. S'pose it's foolish to think so. He never had much imagination. I don't know's he could do it."

"Are you going to Portsmouth tomorrow?" Will asked.

"Oh, yes, bright and early." He winked at me. "What a shame I've no passengers to take. No one's come ashore of late?"

"A body was washed up last week. The water's cold. I don't think any others will make it until the spring. You'd best continue visiting here, or else the colonel or the new officer might suspect something's amiss."

"Oh, I shall. I shall indeed. I find Portsmouth irresistible."

In Squire Addleby's absence, the parish's problems fell solely on Will's shoulders. Although he maintained a normal facade outwardly, I was acutely aware of his lack of joy. I prayed for him constantly, longing to find some way to release him from his guilt as I had been released.

Finally, one evening, I determined on a bold course. Entering the study, I closed the ledger he was working on, sat on his lap and kissed him. "You must also make time for your wife, Will."

He tried to push me away, but I held my arms around him tightly.

"I have not the plague. You've denied my love too long."

"You cannot wish to sully yourself with me!"

"How is that possible?" I asked, astonished.

"I am evil. A—"

I silenced him with a kiss. "No more evil than I."

"You have not killed your closest friend!"

"Is it possible that you, the greatest scholar in all Tyne, have never read in Jeremiah, 'The heart is deceitful above all things, and desperately wicked: who can know it?' Mercifully God spares us this knowledge, save for rare moments. Then the sight is horrifying. I saw mine above the Cherwell when Mr. Wesley was preaching. There was no good thing in me."

"What *evil* had you done?"

"The worst. I held God responsible for our child's death. I called *Him* a murderer and *cursed* Him in my heart. You know there is no greater sin. Yet He gave me forgiveness and peace."

"I wish I could find peace!"

"He will give it to you if you ask."

Will shook his head. "No. I am not worthy to ask. Go. Go! Let me finish my work!"

"Will—"

"No more, Meg. Please go."

Crushed by his rejection, I despaired of finding a way past his barriers.

While dusting his books, I came across a copy of his thesis on forgiveness. The very thing! I left it on his desk open to his comments about King David.

When Will went into the study to work that evening, I hovered hopefully near the living-room door, watching.

He glanced at the thesis, flipped through the pages, then re-shelved it and opened his parish books.

There seemed no way I could reach him.

The Christmas merrymaking, complete with a mummers' play, seemed at times a mockery. As the psalmist, I pled with God. "Hide not thy face far from me . . . thou hast been my help; leave me not, neither forsake me, O God of my salvation." These gloomy winter weeks it indeed seemed as if God had turned away from us.

"Wait on the Lord," the psalmist advised. "Be of good courage, and he shall strengthen thine heart." For how much longer, I wondered. I had not seen the slightest improvement in my dear husband.

As usual, Will read the morning lesson before setting out on his mid-week trip to Docking in the early darkness. The mellow candle-light and his deep voice repeating the familiar words nearly lulled me to inattention.

Suddenly the passage came alive with special meaning. "If we confess our sins, he is faithful and just to forgive us our sins, and to cleanse us from all unrighteousness."

As he was mounting Prince, I urged him to think about those truths on his way.

"Meg, understand this. I know God in His infinite mercy can forgive, has forgiven me. I am not as great as He. I cannot forgive myself!"

In exasperation I exclaimed, "How can you be so arrogant to deny pardon to a creature upon whom God has already bestowed it? Have you a more select place than Paul who caused the death of St.

Stephan and countless others? Or Peter who denied Christ himself *three* times? Are you more perfect than God that you can demand more than He?"

Will galloped away and I ran inside weeping. We should not have parted with angry words.

"O God, where are You?" I cried out, shaking my clenched fists at the ceiling. "Will You *never* answer the petitions of my heart?"

As I cut suet for oatmeal pudding, I considered how to make amends for my outburst. A loving wife should support her husband, not rail at him. When he returned the next day, I must tell him I was sorry.

Despite the gray clouds scurrying across the dull sky, my restless concern drove me to saddle Checkmate in mid-afternoon. I rode against the raw breath of winter, hoping to intercept Will and accompany him to the Curling Horn for supper.

The thin covering of snow, slushy and dirty with mud from earlier warmth, was crusting again. The landscape varied from white, through several grays to black.

Fresh and playful, eager for a run, Checkmate forced me to keep her reins tight. Several times she shied suddenly at a rising pheasant or the tossing branches of a clump of denuded trees. This was the first time I had broken my promise and ridden her unattended. Charles' warning ran over and over in my mind.

About a mile before descending into Docking, I saw a lone rider approaching in the dusk. Checkmate recognized Prince with a whinny. We waited for Will to come to us, then wheeled and trotted at his side.

"Meg," he chided, "it was foolhardy for you to ride this far alone."

I thought his tone lacked conviction, as if he only scolded because he ought to. "I had to come, to tell you how sorry I am for my sharp words yesterday morning. I shouldn't have spoken like I did."

Will reached over to touch my arm reassuringly. "I disagree. I've been thinking of what you said, and you are right. I know now—"

"Stand and deliver!" shouted a sharp voice from the small grove of trees we were passing. A man rode into the road, blocking our passage.

Both Prince and Checkmate instantly took exception to him by rearing and plunging. Will quickly brought Prince under control, but Checkmate proved more difficult. Of necessity he grabbed her rein and forced her to calm down.

While we struggled with our horses, the masked man held a wavering pistol pointed in our general direction. "Give me your gold!" he ordered.

Will took his pouch from his belt.

"Bring it here, a-foot. And missus, give me de jewels."

"I—I have none," I answered as Will stepped down.

"Wud a fine bit o' horseflesh like dat ye say ye have no jewels! Think ye I be an adle-headed fellow?"

"My husband is the parson. We have very little."

"He be de parson? I should a known! A parson, he have horses like as de gentry."

Will handed the man his pouch. The highwayman weighed it in his hand, then jerked it open. "Dere be unaccountable few! Give me de rest or ye die, surelye."

"That's all I have, besides a bit of bread and cheese."

"Liar! Where be de tithes ye rob from de poor?" The man swung his pistol against the side of Will's head with a sickening crack.

Will dropped. I sprang from Checkmate and ran to kneel on the frozen snow at his side. Blood spread in a widening patch on his hair. "He's hurt!" I cried, ignoring the man's blustering threats.

"Give me as ye have, or I'll shoot him!"

"You have it all!" Pressing on the wound to stop the flow of blood, I murmured, "Oh, my darling!" I took the kerchief from around my neck to bind his head.

"Den I take de horses. Dey be worth a mort o' gold."

I concentrated on Will, paying scant attention as the highwayman approached the horses. Checkmate sidled beyond his reach. Prince stood, his ears flat against his head.

Will moaned. He opened his eyes and blinked.

"He struck you," I explained. "Lie still. He'll be satisfied with our horses, I hope."

Will called out, "Beware. Prince may hurt you!"

"A Prince be he? We'll see!" The man dismounted and swung into Prince's saddle. Suddenly the horse convulsed, somersaulting the man over his head. The gun flew from his hand, discharging when it landed. I dashed to where it lay, determined neither of us would be struck with it again.

Will staggered to the whimpering man. When I gave Will the gun, he looked at it, then down at the man, and threw it hard into the trees.

"Are you hurt?" he asked.

"Goo on. Take me to de gaol. I ain't never done naun right."

Will knelt. "Are you injured?"

"Injured? I be good as dead! Mayhap it's best sen Jennie be."

"Who's Jennie?"

"Me wife. Me poor, poor wife." The man blubbered tears.

"Mind the horses," Will told me, then sat beside the man. He supported his head with one hand as he talked. "Tell me how she died."

"I farmed agin West Grinscombe hither Surrey. De fine and masterful lord enclosed de land and we was left wud naun. Naun at all. Jennie, she took ill. Being as I'd naun for de doctor, she died. Ifn his lordship left de land alone, I could a had de doctor."

"And you turned to being a highwayman?"

"Weren't naun for me to do. And de gentry, dey owed it."

"Would Jennie like you doing this?"

"No, no! We be honest folk. I got purty good heart in de land. I be no good no how at dis. I can't never find naun no place. Nobody cares."

"God loves you, my friend."

"God loves ye," he parrotted sarcastically. "Dat be *parson* talk, surelye. Just talk! Why, dat vicar, he wouldn't let me bury my Jennie in de churchyard on account I owed my tithe for two year!"

"Where did you lay her?"

"Under a tree by de stream. She like gooing dere of a summer evening."

"Would you feel better if I went there with you and said a few words over her grave and prayed?"

The man twisted to look into Will's face. Angrily he said, "Ye be funnin' me! Ain't *naun* dear to you folk?"

Will pressed his hand against my blood-soaked scarf. "If you wish, I will be happy to go with you to your wife's grave."

"It be a long ways and de roads, dey do be unaccountable bad."

"I know."

"I ain't paid no tithes. I be a highwayman. A sinner."

"Aren't we all! God loves you, my man. His own Son, Christ the Lord, died for us, for you and . . . for me. If we but ask, He will forgive us our sins."

"Dat be for de gentry, de fine folk in deir fine houses wud deir silks and satins."

"That's for everyone, whoever, wherever. We all wear rags in God's sight. He wants to dress us properly, as in the story Jesus told of the marriage feast. Do you remember that?"

"No. But I went to de church every holy day and sometimes of a Sunday too. Couldn't never make no sense o' what de vicar say. It be for de gentry. Us common folk, we watched. Dat no be for de likes o' me, surelye."

"It's for everyone, highwayman or—or murderer."

"I ain't done no murder!"

"No matter, God will forgive, if you ask. There was David who had a man killed so he could marry the man's wife. God forgave him and loved him. Think of St. Paul, who helped kill St. Stephen the martyr, and imprisoned countless Christians. God forgave him. All through the Bible are stories of people, sinners, like you and me, whom God forgave. He'll forgive you too, and make your life right." Will's weakening voice broke.

While petting and talking softly to the three horses, I watched him anxiously.

"Lord, I wish it be true!" the man exclaimed. Then, in puzzlement, "Vicar, *ye* be caring about *me* arter I hit ye! Why?"

"I, too, have suffered."

The man stared at Will, absorbing his answer. "Will ye pray for me, Parson?"

"With you. Repeat each phrase after me."

"Here? Will God hear us in de road? Doant we have to goo to de church?"

"He has very good ears. He hears us any place." Will was holding his head with both hands, his face dead white. His voice grew fainter as he prayed slowly, the penitent echoing each phrase.

"Almighty and most merciful Father; We have erred and strayed from Thy ways like lost sheep. We have followed too much the devices and desires of our own hearts. We have offended against Thy holy laws. We have left undone those things which we ought to have done. And we have done those things which we ought not to have done; and there is no health in us. But Thou, O Lord, have mercy upon us, *miserable* offenders. Spare Thou them, us, O God, which confess their, our faults. Restore Thou them, us, that are penitent; according to Thy promises declared unto mankind in Christ Jesus our Lord. And grant, O most merciful Father, for His sake; that we may hereafter live a godly, righteous, and sober life, to the glory of Thy holy name."

Tears flowed down both men's cheeks as they said "Amen."

Will raised his right hand over the bowed man. I saw it waver weakly as he slowly made the sign of the cross and intoned, "Almighty God, our heavenly Father, who of His great mercy hath promised forgiveness of sins to all them that with hearty repentance and true faith turn unto Him; have mercy upon you, pardon and deliver you from all your sins, confirm and strengthen you in all goodness, and bring you to everlasting life, through Jesus Christ our Lord. Amen."

As Will's hand fell limply, the former highwayman remarked in awe, "Dere never be no parson who cared for me more'n me tithes. But to sit in de road wud me and *pray* arter I hit yourn head!"

Will's body sagged. He rolled over on his side. I dropped the reins and ran to him.

"I didn't do naun, ma'am!"

"I know," I answered. Gently I turned Will face up, supporting his bloodied head. Seeing the ashen hue of his cheeks, I felt an aching stab in response. Tears filled my eyes.

Will's eyelids fluttered. His lips curved in a weak smile. "I'll be all right, Meg—heart, soul, and body. *We'll* be all right together. Praise God! He—he's my sign!" As he fainted I heard him murmur faintly, "Praise God!"

THE END